PRAISE FOR VICTOR METHOS

A Killer's Wife

"*A Killer's Wife* is a high-stakes legal thriller loaded with intense courtroom drama, compelling characters, and surprising twists that will keep you turning the pages at breakneck speed."

—T. R. Ragan, *New York Times* bestselling author

"Exquisitely paced and skillfully crafted, *A Killer's Wife* delivers a wicked psychological suspense wrapped around a hypnotic legal thriller. One cleverly designed twist after another kept me saying, 'I did not see that coming.'"

—Steven Konkoly, *Wall Street Journal* bestselling author

"A gripping thriller that doesn't let up for a single page. Surprising twists with a hero you care about. I read the whole book in one sitting!"

—Chad Zunker, bestselling author of *An Equal Justice*

CRIMSON LAKE ROAD

OTHER TITLES BY VICTOR METHOS

Desert Plains Series

A Killer's Wife

Other Titles

The Hallows

The Shotgun Lawyer

A Gambler's Jury

An Invisible Client

Neon Lawyer Series

Mercy

The Neon Lawyer

CRIMSON LAKE ROAD

VICTOR METHOS

This is a work of fiction. Names, characters, organizations, places, events, and incidents are either products of the author's imagination or are used fictitiously. Any resemblance to actual persons, living or dead, or actual events is purely coincidental.

Published by Thomas & Mercer, Seattle

www.apub.com

ISBN-13: 9781542020947
ISBN-10: 1542020948

Cover design by Christopher Lin

Printed in the United States of America

CRIMSON LAKE ROAD

1

FBI special agent Cason Baldwin withdrew his firearm as he leaned against the exterior of the cabin. He took several deep breaths to calm himself, but still the jittery rush of adrenaline coursed through him. He glanced toward the sheriff's deputies silhouetted in the darkness behind him and nodded.

He held up three fingers . . . then two . . . then one.

Heaving a battering ram, Detective Lucas Garrett smashed through the front door, then leapt aside. Everyone else poured into the cabin. The abandoned structure had no electricity, and barely any moonlight shone through the windows. Baldwin lifted his flashlight with his free hand.

Shouts of "Clear!" echoed through the cabin as each room was searched.

"Got something!" a voice shouted from the kitchen. Baldwin made his way over.

She was laid out on the kitchen table, a young uniformed deputy standing beside her. He looked petrified, which Baldwin could understand—it wasn't every day the locals, or even the FBI, came across something as monstrous as this.

Garrett came up behind Baldwin and said, "Rest of the house is empty. No sign of him." That he barely glanced at the body was no surprise—Baldwin had long known Garrett, a former army drill instructor and now a veteran homicide detective with the Clark County Sheriff's Office, to be unresponsive to horrific crime scenes.

"We got any floodlights?" Baldwin asked as he trained his flashlight along the body. The victim wore a black tunic that went from the base of her neck down to just below her upper thighs. Her head was completely wrapped in white bandages, and the bandages were soaked through with blood over the face. She had beautifully detailed tattoos running up and down her arms.

"Got a deputy bringing some up."

It was hard to tell in this light, but Baldwin wondered if she had been beaten before death. The pathologist had suggested that the first victim, Kathy Pharr, had been beaten before dying.

Underneath the bandages on Kathy Pharr, who they'd found four weeks ago, the killer had sliced between her eyebrows with a razor, wide enough to ensure the blood soaked the thick white dressings. The single cut had split open the skin so that it appeared almost like a third eye.

Garrett sighed. "I'm getting sick of this shit, Cason. Been doin' this too long."

Baldwin ran the beam of light over the victim's bare feet. "You and me both, brother."

"Don't tell me you're thinking of taking off? Took you as a Bureau lifer, through and through."

Baldwin glanced toward the door, where some of the deputies had gathered and were talking in hushed but excited tones. Where was the damn floodlight? "Don't know what I'm thinking. But seeing this"—he motioned to the body—"every day for the rest of my life is not how I want to spend my golden years."

Garrett nodded. "Helluva way to go." He bent down near the bandages over the face and said, "Hope you went quick, little gal."

The body violently bucked to life.

It nearly fell off the table as it thrashed and sucked for breath, a muted scream emanating from underneath the bandages. Garrett jumped backward and tripped over a chair, slamming against the wall as he fell. The young deputy lifted his weapon and put his finger on the trigger. Baldwin held out his hand and bellowed, "Lower your weapon, damn it!"

The deputy—eyes wide, hands trembling—lowered the firearm as Garrett got to his feet, uttering a string of profanities.

"I'm going to touch your shoulders now," Baldwin said to the woman. He laid her back down on the table as she fought him, trying to claw at his face. "Hold her arms."

The deputy stood there a second, and Baldwin said, "Deputy, pull it together. I need you to hold her arms."

He holstered his firearm and pinned her arms to the table. Baldwin held out his hand to Garrett and said, "Hand me your knife." Garrett passed over the knife he kept clipped to his belt. As gently as he could, Baldwin slit the bandages up the side. They slipped off a face slick with blood. The woman opened eyes that were wide and frantic as Baldwin said, "It's okay . . . it's okay, you're safe now."

She sobbed uncontrollably, still trying to hit him, as Baldwin shouted, "We need medical. Now!"

2

Reggie's was a local Vegas cop dive owned by two former highway patrolmen. It was always crowded and stank of booze and cigarette smoke, and the food was greasy. Assistant US Attorney Jessica Yardley had been there only once, seen some vice detectives snorting cocaine off a table—no one had even glanced in their direction—and never been back.

An elderly homeless woman stood in front of Reggie's, begging for change. A man with two women, all of them clearly drunk already, even though it was early afternoon, held out a twenty-dollar bill for her. Her face lit up, and her smile was so big it seemed to smooth her wrinkles.

At the last second, before her fingers could touch it, the man pulled back the bill, and the three of them laughed as they went inside. Leaving her staring at them and probably wondering why someone would be so needlessly cruel.

Yardley took out a twenty from her purse and gave it to her.

Baldwin sat in a booth by himself, though the light inside was so dim that Yardley had to scan the place twice before she saw him. He had a steak and beer in front of him. His jacket was off, and his biceps bulged the sleeves of his T-shirt and revealed the wiry blue veins he'd developed the last year since starting to lift weights. He'd had a problem for a while—opioids—and Yardley was glad to see him looking so healthy. Occasionally, a tug of regret would rear its head when she saw him, letting her know that there was something between them that they had missed. Something that should have been but wasn't. She saw that something now as he smiled at her.

She sat down on the opposite side of the booth.

"So it's really happening?" he said. "You're really throwing in the towel?"

A waitress came over, and Yardley ordered a beer and leaned back into the cushions. People erupted at the bar over a play in a basketball game on the televisions. She waited until the noise died down. "I wouldn't describe it that way."

"How would you describe it?"

"I'm just tired, Cason. You can only deal with the insane for so long before it starts seeping into you."

"I just had this exact conversation with a detective." He chewed a piece of steak. "I was thinking, though. You work law enforcement or prosecution too long and you treat everything as black and white, bad guys and good guys. There's some gray areas in the law, too. Maybe you need to transfer and work in those areas more. It might surprise you to find it's not all black and white."

The beer came, and she took a sip. It was warm and frothy.

"I have a trial coming up. A man who killed his stepson because he put a hole in the wall when he was moving a dresser. He hit him with a hammer and crushed his skull. Nothing surprises me anymore except the stupidity of the reasons people kill each other over."

He took a drink of his beer, his eyes never leaving hers. "Two weeks left, right?"

She nodded.

He took out a silver-colored thumb drive and put it on the table in front of her. "Before you leave, would you mind looking at that for me? Your replacement is probably going to be the one working it, so it'd be great if you could go through it with them."

"What is it?"

"A homicide and attempted homicide. We think there was sexual assault, so the Bureau can take it if we want. It's with the Sheriff's Office for now, though. The cases are linked. You'll see why when you go through my narratives."

"There's no point, Cason. I'm leaving no matter what."

"I know. I'm not trying to scam you into staying. I just think this is something you should look at. Who is your replacement, by the way?"

"Kyle Jax. He's coming up from the Wyoming office. Younger prosecutor, twenty-eight, I think. He hasn't worked Special Victims before."

Baldwin took a long pull off his beer, then said, "Well, this is a shit case to get as his first one, then."

Yardley took the long route home to White Sands, Nevada. Two weeks. It was true what she'd told Baldwin—she wasn't having any second thoughts about leaving the US Attorney's Office, or her house, or the area. Too many disturbing things had happened here. But there had also been wonderful things, endearing memories she would carry with her the rest of her life, and she was making an effort to let her last impressions be of those.

Her daughter was one of those wonderful things. Seventeen and a genius. When Yardley got home, Tara went to work: an internship at a robotics company, working on machine learning algorithms. Yardley didn't always understand Tara's explanations about what exactly she did, but she assured her mother it was going to revolutionize the world one day. Yardley believed it, and it was one of the reasons she felt the timing was right for this move: Tara had found her footing in life.

When Yardley was alone, she took a long, hot shower and then got into sweats and poured a glass of white wine. She sat at the computer in her home office and stared at the thumb drive Baldwin had given her, running her fingers over the smooth plastic.

A deep sigh escaped her, and she leaned back in the chair and gazed at the ceiling. She thought about the new home she was buying in a small city called Santa Bonita. A tree outside in the front yard was so massive it prevented sunlight from entering the front of the house. She wondered why the current owners had never cut it down, but it was the first thing she planned to do. She wanted sunlight in her new life, not black and white, not even gray areas.

Two weeks.

She plugged the thumb drive into her computer. She would read the reports, but she wasn't going to do more than that. She had neither the will nor the energy.

The reports were succinct. Two victims: Kathy Pharr, who had died, and Angela River, who was found alive less than a mile from where Kathy Pharr's body was discovered. Both women had been placed in black tunics, their heads wrapped with white bandages. Their attacker had slit open their brows with what the pathologist guessed was a razor, soaking the bandages in blood. The SAFE kits and examinations revealed some evidence of sexual assault: some injuries seen with a colposcope, and semen found inside Kathy Pharr's vaginal canal. Both victims had been beaten.

All Angela River remembered was a blinding pain in her head from something hard slamming into her skull as she came out to her car in a mall parking lot, and then waking up on a table. Unable to breathe and thinking she was blind until Baldwin cut the bandages off. Traces of bleach had been found on both women's skin. Their nails had been clipped and hair trimmed. The killer, or killers, had wanted them pristine before death.

Kathy Pharr had been found sitting in a wooden chair inside an empty cabin. Medical glue, a type they couldn't identify by brand, had been used on her skin to keep the body in place. The autopsy revealed the cause of death as organ failure, though the cause of the organ failure was as yet undetermined. The blood panels had shown nothing but alcohol and prescription medications for depression and anxiety in Kathy Pharr's blood, and nothing in Angela River's.

Both crimes had occurred in an unincorporated area outside of Las Vegas known as Crimson Lake Road.

Yardley opened the folder with the photos and videos the forensic technicians had taken.

The first photo was Kathy Pharr in a chair. Yardley's heart skipped a beat, and she let out a quiet gasp. She moved quickly to the sketches of how Angela River had been posed. After staring at them for what seemed like a long time, she texted Baldwin:

We need to meet right now.

3

The Low Desert Plains Correctional Institute looked like a bunker meant to withstand an atomic blast. Tara Yardley stared at it from the parking lot as she finished a soda and some fries.

She tossed the empty containers into a trash bin on the way into the facility. She liked coming during the last hour of open visitors' hours. The guards were just going through the motions by then and never looked too closely at her ID or asked many questions.

Her mother thought she was at her internship, and she always had a twinge of guilt when she was here because she had to lie. But she was doing this for her mother and knew it was good for both of them long term, even if her mother would be horrified.

After checking in with the front desk staff and being searched, she was allowed through the metal detectors. They held on to her ID—a good fake, stating she was twenty-two—as well as the forged press badge proclaiming her a reporter with the *Las Vegas Sun*. She had, briefly, considered becoming a journalist. The thrill of bouncing around the world investigating stories sounded exciting, but ultimately she knew the job would become irrelevant. None of the old professions would exist in the near future: Machines and machine learning were on the cusp of taking over. More and more, they would overtake all functions in society, and she was glad for it. Machines were indifferent. Machines couldn't choose to be evil.

Death row was rarely quiet, but today it seemed completely subdued. Perhaps it was the weather. She had read weather deeply affected the moods of death row inmates, and she was curious what the weather had been like on the day of their crimes. Dark and gloomy, she guessed.

The room was cold, and the metal stool she sat on was uncomfortable. It didn't matter. Nothing in this facility was comfortable, or meant to be.

Eddie Cal was brought out a few moments later. He sat down across the plastic-covered glass divider. She stared at his graying hair and the pale forearms that had been thicker and more muscular last year. Age was slowly eating away at him. Her father, the loathsome murderer of a dozen people, the Dark Casanova who'd terrorized Las Vegas for over three years, was being humbled by time just like everyone else.

Tara waited until the guard left the room and then took a small device out of a secret pocket in her purse and set it on her lap. Something she had designed herself. It let out a high frequency static sound—nothing any of the guards would hear, but the only thing the audio devices in this room would be recording was a grainy hiss.

"Did you find him?" Cal said.

"Yes. Did you get the food I sent?"

"I did, thank you. The guards eat at least half of everything before it gets to me, but I still enjoy the surprise of seeing what's in the box. I have little surprise in my days anymore."

He smiled at her. Though many people found his gaze unnerving, Tara didn't. She knew exactly why he was staring at her: because in the two years since they'd met, he was amazed how much more she resembled him every day. Something that seemed to thrill him and disgusted her.

Over the past two years, she'd been here eight times, and she didn't enjoy any of the visits, but they were necessary. Cal had something she needed to secure her mother's future so she wouldn't have to worry about money anymore. She figured her father owed them that much at least.

"How's your mother?"

"Fine. She's retiring from the US Attorney's Office."

"What for?"

She shrugged. "Wants something with less blood and horror, I guess. We're supposed to be moving to Santa Bonita, a couple hours from Vegas. It'll be a pain in the ass since I go to UNLV, but we'll make it work, I guess. I'm moving out next year anyway."

"And why do that?"

"I think she's not doing what she wants to do because of me. I want her to find somebody and fall in love, and I don't think she will because she's scared of who she brings around me. She doesn't even have any friends. If I leave, it'll force her to find other people to connect with. And it'll be good to get away from some things."

"Away from me, you mean?"

"Not just you but everything else that came with you. Everything that I've put up with my entire life."

He nodded. "You're scared you're like me, and you think running away, maybe altering your name and appearance, will change that. It won't. Whatever problems you have, they follow you wherever you go. You're like me, and you will have to face that at some point."

"I'm nothing like you."

He blinked slowly, then said, "Are you familiar with Greco-Roman mythology?"

"I don't read fairy tales, sorry."

"Fairy tales are everything, Tara. Every lesson you need in life is found there. Our so-called scientific knowledge is simply a revolution from one set of ideas that will eventually be found incorrect to another set. But fairy tales, fairy tales have been with us since the beginning, and they'll be there with us at the end."

She folded her arms. "I assume there's a point to this, Eddie?"

He grinned. "The gods were having a debate about human nature. Can human nature be changed? Can a person choose who they want to be? Zeus said yes, but Aphrodite said no. To show her she was wrong, Zeus turned a street cat into a princess. The princess was taught manners and etiquette, given elegant clothing and a fancy title. She behaved impeccably and was married to a prince. At the wedding, all the guests were impressed by the charming new bride.

"Zeus said, 'You see, if a cat can be turned into a princess, surely human nature can change.' Aphrodite simply said, 'Watch,' and released a mouse. As soon as the princess saw it scurrying across the floor, she leapt at it, chasing it on all fours. She caught hold of the mouse and tore it apart with her teeth in front of all her guests. Aphrodite was the goddess of lust and beauty, so she understood what was in people's hearts. What was truly in their hearts, not what they pretend is in them."

Tara swallowed as she watched her father. She didn't like seeing herself in him, particularly in the deep blue of their eyes. A unique hue that she could only figure was a genetic mutation, since she had never seen the color in anything else.

"You see, my little princess, the gods were teaching us that we can't change our nature. We can hide it for a short while, but it will always come out. All you need is to see your mouse, and you'll know that we're more alike than you could ever have imagined."

4

“It’s Sarpong,” Yardley said, turning the computer screen toward Baldwin. He had to put a moving box filled with items from her desk on the floor so he could sit.

On the screen was a painting. A figure in black with white bandages wrapped around its head; dark-red blood soaked the bandages where the face should have been. The figure’s arms and legs were human, but something seemed off about the angle of the neck and the shape of the head. Still, the bandages and tunic were unmistakable: it was the same attire Kathy Pharr and Angela River had been found wearing.

“Who’s Sarpong?” he asked.

“A Kenyan painter from the 1960s. He had a series of paintings called *The Night Things*.” Yardley tapped her mouse, and the painting changed. The same figure, the same dress and bandages, this time sitting straight backed in a wooden chair. “This is the first one.” She tapped her mouse again. The same figure, lying on a table. Its arms outstretched, its feet dangling off the edge. “This is the second one.”

It was as if someone had stood over Angela River and painted the scene. Baldwin rose from his chair and came around behind Yardley to get a closer look.

“This is the third,” she said.

The next painting showed the figure inside a home, hung from its neck by something slick. It had been eviscerated, and the entrails were on the floor.

The fourth painting was the worst, a twisted figure with scars over its body, its eyes and mouth sewn shut. Its rib cage spread wide. It barely looked human.

"How did you find these?" he said.

Yardley glanced at him and then back to the screen. "Eddie was obsessed with these paintings for a while. He wouldn't talk about anything else. He actually repainted them himself at his studio and then threw them out when he was done and never brought it up again. He thought the fact that there were four was significant, but he couldn't figure out why. He didn't think Sarpong just stopped at four. There was a reason he chose that number. He also had four wives throughout his life and four children, so Eddie thought that number was important to him."

"Did he figure out why?"

She shook her head. "I don't think so. He was completely fixated on it for a long time, but then he dropped it."

"Why?"

"I don't know."

He got a text just then from Scarlett Chambers, a young woman he'd been dating. She asked why he hadn't returned her calls the past couple of days. A stab of guilt went through him. Scarlett was perfectly pleasant and intelligent and seemed like she was caring, and they spent most of their time together talking about everything from politics to the cosmos . . . but there was that *thing*. There was always that *thing*.

She didn't see what he had seen. She didn't build up a wall around it: gallows humor to save his humanity or sanity or whatever the hell it was people called it now. Scarlett had asked how his day had gone on their third or fourth date, and he described a case he was working: a young mother that poisoned her children. Scarlett had tears in her eyes, and Baldwin couldn't understand why, but he did now: she didn't have that *thing*. That's why so many in law enforcement only dated and married others in law enforcement.

He replied that he would call her later.

Baldwin folded his arms. "This artist still alive?"

She leaned back in her chair. "No. He died of a heroin overdose. This series of paintings is the only work he left behind. It took him six years to paint all four."

Baldwin stared at the third painting, the figure hanging from the ceiling, and realized it was hanging by its own intestines. "What do the paintings mean?"

"They mean," she said, opening a side-by-side view of all the paintings, "that you're going to have two more of these."

5

Baldwin had stayed late talking through the case file with her, but today was Saturday, and Yardley felt like eating out. Tara had gotten home late and been up early, announcing that she wanted to put in some extra hours at her internship, so Yardley decided to have brunch on the Strip.

She went to the Bouchon at the Venetian hotel. They gave her a table overlooking the canal. Tourists occasionally drifted by in gondolas, the operators singing in Italian as the sightseers recorded on their cell phones.

Tara had given her a knowing look when she arrived home and found her mother's head bent with Baldwin's over the case files. He had gentle eyes and always a scent of ambergris cologne that Yardley found appealing. A smell like soft pears. She had dated him briefly and sometimes wondered what a long-term relationship with him would look like.

But her last boyfriend was sitting in a prison cell. Her ex-husband on death row. It wouldn't have completely shocked her if it turned out Baldwin was a serial killer.

It touched Yardley that her daughter held out romantic hope for her. But she and Baldwin had their go once and were better off as friends. She'd lost the friends she and Eddie shared after his crimes came to light, and then the situation had repeated with Wesley. So she'd thrown herself into school and work and raising a daughter. She had no close friends she could call for brunch—but maybe that was a situation she'd rectify in her new life after she moved. For today, it was soothing that so many people were around.

She stirred some Splenda into her coffee with a thin spoon, thinking about Kathy Pharr and Angela River. Kathy Pharr was forty. River even younger at thirty-three. Baldwin had found no overlap in their lives: nothing indicating wherc the women had first caught the attention of what might be a serial murderer. But River wasn't even out of the hospital yet. It would take more time to find any commonality between her and Pharr.

Yardley checked the time on her phone. Visiting hours at Saint Vincent's Hospital started soon. She left cash on the table for her coffee and headed there.

Angela River's hospital room was on the fourth floor. At the open door, Yardley looked in. River was lying in the hospital bed with her hands pressed together as though praying, her eyes closed as she emitted a soft hum. Yardley considered coming back another time, but then she opened her eyes.

"I'm sorry, I didn't mean to disturb you," Yardley said.

"It's fine. I was almost done."

"My name is Jessica Yardley. I'm a prosecutor with the US Attorney's Office. May I come in?"

"Sure."

A nurse came into the room behind her, deposited a fresh pitcher of water, and warned River to press the call button if she felt faint again. It reminded Yardley that they still didn't know what her abductor had used to attempt to kill her.

Meanwhile, Yardley observed her tattoos. Flowers running down her forearms and nature scenes on her legs. A large blue-and-white lotus decorated her right shoulder. Her nose was pierced, and her green eyes shone with youthful energy, making her seem far younger than her years. A cast was on her wrist. Baldwin had stated that he thought she had been transported to Crimson Lake Road in the trunk of a car, and it was likely that her abductor had accidently slammed the trunk on her hand in his haste.

When the nurse left, Yardley sat down next to the hospital bed—but not too close—and said, "I like your tattoos."

"Oh yeah," River said, "little hobby, I guess. Some people collect stamps and I collect these." She pointed to what looked like a chrysanthemum that wrapped around her uninjured wrist. "I got this one in India." She then pointed to an orchid on her thigh. "This one in Japan, this crane on my calf in Shanghai . . . I get one wherever I go. It's like I take a piece of the place with me, ya know? Do you travel much?"

"No, unfortunately. I've never actually been out of the country. What's the lotus?"

"Oh, I just have a bad birthmark on that shoulder. It's huge. Kids always made fun of me for it. So I got the tattoo when I was sixteen, and it was all sleeveless shirts from then on."

"It's beautiful."

River pushed herself up and sat cross-legged. Yardley had been avoiding looking at her brow but glanced now. A thick line ran from one eyebrow to the other where the razor had cut, and Yardley imagined it must have been excruciating when she woke up. She guessed at least ten stitches held the skin together. Her face was heavily bruised, one eye swollen shut and her lower lip split. Yardley thought she looked like she'd been in a bad auto accident.

"You can't really know yourself unless you travel," River said. "You gotta see how you react in places you're not comfortable in. Like how you deal with people. I learned I trust people too quickly when someone in Bangkok stole everything I had."

"That's terrible. What did you do?"

She shrugged. "For a couple days, I just had to figure out how to survive. This really nice widow took pity on me and fed me, and then I had to hitch rides to the American embassy. It was an interesting experience, I guess. Maybe the universe was trying to teach me it wouldn't be so bad to lose everything."

Yardley got a glimpse of another shoulder tattoo as River moved and the hospital gown dipped on that side.

"What's that one on your other shoulder?"

"It's a rune. It means someone who forges their own destiny." She looked sad for a moment and then grinned. "Sorry, you get me talking about travel and tattoos and I could talk forever. You came here for a reason, obviously."

Every trauma victim had a different response. Some turned inward and wouldn't speak for days or weeks—sometimes never again if the trauma was severe enough. Some put on a happy face and pretended nothing had happened. Others fell somewhere in between. Yardley thought that Angela River hadn't yet processed everything that had happened to her, hadn't allowed her mind to absorb and analyze it. Bringing it up might break her right now.

"I just wanted to check up on you," she said. "See if there's anything you need."

"Oh, that's so nice of you. But I'm okay, really. The nurses might think different, though. They're having a hard time with me right now. I had a male nurse and I just kind of . . . I don't know, froze. So I told them I only want female nurses and doctors and there's only two on staff right now."

"Given what you've gone through, that's a reasonable request."

She shrugged and said, "I guess." She took a mala bracelet off her wrist and began rubbing the beads. "So you said you're a prosecutor?"

"Yes."

"That means you work with the police, right?"

"I do. I was asked to take a look at your situation and see if there's anything I can do."

"Situation? You mean my kidnapping and almost being killed?"

Yardley said nothing.

"Sorry," River said. "People always say I'm too blunt. I don't believe in pretending something isn't the way it is. The truth is always better." She looked down at the mala. "I know what happened to me. We can talk about it if you like."

"Are you sure?"

She looked up at Yardley and gave a melancholic smile. "Hey, I survived. From what the cops told me, there was another girl that didn't. I don't think I have the right to feel shitty about it."

"I think you have the right to feel however you want to feel."

River grinned and said, "I'd like to do something with your permission. I'd like to read your aura."

"My aura?"

She nodded. "Yeah. If we're gonna talk, I should know who I'm talking with, right? Here, gimme your hands."

Yardley hesitated, then held out her hands. River faced her and took her hands and then looked slightly to the side, as though watching Yardley on the periphery of her vision.

"Everything has an aura," River said. "Plants, animals, the earth . . . everything. It says so much more than words." She inhaled deeply and closed her eyes. When she opened them, she gazed directly at Yardley for what seemed like a long time.

She spoke quietly as she said, "I'm so sorry."

"For what?"

"You have intense red around your chest. Almost like a blanket of red."

"What does that mean?"

River squeezed her hands tighter. "It means a shattered heart." She loosened her grip and lightly rubbed Yardley's hands with her thumbs, as though comforting her. "There's so much pain. I don't know how you took it all and kept going."

Yardley swallowed and slowly slipped her hands away. "I should let you rest. I've taken up enough of your time already."

"I'm sorry if I offended you."

"You didn't."

"We all break sometimes. But if we know how to put ourselves back together, we'll be stronger in all those places."

Yardley rose. "Better go."

"I'm getting out tomorrow. Do you do yoga? I got a yoga studio. Just a little place where I teach my own brand of joy yoga. You ever tried it?"

"No."

"I think it'll help with your heart. Come by sometime."

Yardley gave a little grin. "It was nice meeting you, Angela."

"Angie. And it was nice meeting you."

When Yardley was on the elevator, she leaned back against the paneled wall and felt a sickening heaviness in the pit of her stomach. River had said a *shattered* heart. Not a broken heart.

Shattered.

It was a word that pierced Yardley because it was so accurate. She had come here thinking she would have to comfort Angela River, and instead she left with River comforting her.

6

The federal building was a massive cube of steel and glass. Yardley parked underground and scanned her ID badge on two different doors before reaching her office. Roy Lieu, the chief prosecutor in the criminal division, nodded hello to her in the hallway. He had just accepted a position as an associate attorney general in Washington. Yardley hadn't even been asked to apply for his job. The ex-wife of a serial murderer on death row would never be put in a position of authority at the most powerful prosecution agency in the world.

She logged into her computer and ignored her forty-seven unread emails in favor of opening the electronic files for the trial she had coming up—the man accused of crushing his twenty-year-old stepson's head with a hammer. A case that was only in federal court because the home it occurred in was on a Native American reservation.

After a few minutes, she realized she had read the same paragraph in the autopsy report three times, and she knew she wouldn't be able to get any more work done. She opened a browser and googled the kidnapping of Angela River.

The *Las Vegas Sun* had a long story on the case, published this morning. The crime reporter, a freelancer named Jude Chance, routinely sold stories to the various newspapers, and his podcast was one of the most popular in Nevada and California. Yardley had used him several times to leak details of cases she needed public, and in exchange, she had given him bits of information he wanted on other cases.

Chance had termed the killer the *Crimson Lake Executioner*, and Yardley knew the name would stick.

Don't know about you folks, but this reporter has seen his share of the Heart of Darkness. As a crime beat reporter for six years, I felt I had a good grip on what people were capable of. "Been there, done that," I would think to myself.

Well, the Crimson Lake Executioner has made me rethink my place in the hierarchy of criminal knowledge. The Executioner takes his time with his victims; he doesn't rush. He cleans them first, a source near the investigation told me. Washes them with soap and scrubs their bodies with bleach. He trims their hair and manicures their nails. Like a young girl with her favorite and most precious dolls. And he does this in only one place: Crimson Lake Road. A place with a sordid history of corruption that collapsed an entire town and left nothing but empty cabins on its shores. A place filled with more ghosts than people. A place the Executioner calls home.

Both women were found less than a mile apart in abandoned cabins. Their owners had left the cabins due to back taxes owed exceeding the value of the cabins themselves. The cabins sat there for years gathering dust and cobwebs, until the Executioner discovered them. And what a discovery he made: a place devoid of people, an hour away from the nearest police station, covered in the darkness of night. When your intrepid reporter went for a visit past the witching hour, I saw only one, just one, light on in a home, but when I knocked to interview this sole occupant, no one answered. The entire town, if you can call it a town, is nothing but shadows and rust.

Chance went on to describe the details of how the two women were found: bandages around the face, cuts along the brow that soaked the bandages with blood, a black tunic covering the torso. No mention was made of the Sarpong paintings.

Yardley opened another window on her computer and brought up the four paintings. The paintings were dark. Not just in theme but in lighting and shadow. Behind each figure, outside the windows, a city burned. The flames nearly reaching up to the sky. The sky itself glowed a bright orange. As if it, too, were on fire.

What does he see when he looks at these?

The FBI recognized four categories of serial murderers: dominance—those who needed power over another for sexual gratification; hallucinatory—those compelled by voices or visions; objective oriented—those on a mission to exterminate a particular class of people like prostitutes or a racial minority group; and lust—those for whom violence and sex were the same things.

No dominance was involved, as the victims had been unconscious during the entire interaction, and dominance killers needed their victims to know they were being dominated. Pharr and River were not from any ethnic, racial, or religious minority groups.

The possibilities were that he was being compelled by hallucinations he believed were instructing him to carry out the killings; that he was a lust killer, though the evidence for sexual assault was sparse; or that this was not serial murder at all but murder for money, for revenge, or for hire, with the allusions to Sarpong thrown in to deceive law enforcement. Or this was an entirely unique type of serial predator as yet unidentified by the FBI's Behavioral Science Unit.

If he was a lust or hallucinatory killer, he wouldn't stop until he was dead or in prison. Until then, all he could do was keep moving forward, which for him meant killing. Like a shark that couldn't stop swimming or else they'd drown.

Yardley went back to Chance's article and read the few paragraphs devoted to Angela River. They were accompanied by a photograph of River with her boyfriend. She was dating a man named Michael Zachary, an emergency room physician she'd recently moved in with. When Baldwin interviewed him, Zachary said he'd fallen asleep early on the night River was kidnapped, and no one would be able to verify he was home. The night Kathy Pharr was abducted, he claimed he'd been out of state at a medical conference.

In the photo, River had sunglasses pushed up into her hair and a broad smile, her arms wrapped around his neck.

A shattered heart.

Yardley sent an email to Roy Lieu, letting him know that there would be federal jurisdiction in what would be called the Executioner case because of the potential sexual assault, and that she would like to screen it and instruct Kyle Jax on how to work similar cases before she left. Then she set up a meeting with Jax.

7

Baldwin had a new ASAC who was giving him more and more white-collar cases and fewer murders. He had a few ideas about resources he could consult to find out more about the connection Yardley had suggested to this painter, Sarpong, but first he had to finish up some paperwork that needed to be time-stamped by the end of the day.

His new boss came into Baldwin's office in the afternoon and stood at the door. Assistant Special Agent in Charge Dana Young looked like what the public likely pictured when they thought of an FBI agent: black suit, white shirt, dark tie. Thick glasses and hair impeccably combed to the side with a part in the perfect place. He was exactly the type of bureaucrat Baldwin disliked: a climber with no regard for the actual victims in his cases.

"So I believe the Executioner case can be resolved fairly quickly," Young said, looking at a scuff on his shoe. Baldwin noticed for the first time that his feet seemed too small for his body. "Which will be nice because it will free up some resources."

"How?"

"Because we'll be shifting those resources away from Behavioral Science. This is just my humble opinion, but BSU has been a waste of assets. One murder is similar to the next and doesn't deserve an entire unit to itself, particularly one practicing witchcraft like criminal profiling. I'm pushing the SAC of the Vegas office to abolish the liaison position and just get us two agents for general use. Once the Executioner case is cleared, we can move forward with that, which will help close all types of cases much more quickly."

Baldwin was used to the Behavioral Science Unit getting trimmed anytime the Bureau was undergoing budget cuts. The BSU focused specifically on liaising with local law enforcement when they needed help with serial murder investigations. The problem was that as of right now, there were only eight special agents assigned to the BSU. And not just for the United States but for the entire world. Eight agents, of which Baldwin was one, to cover dozens of requests for help received every month, and Young seemed to want to reduce it even further.

"Out of curiosity," Baldwin said, "why do you think the Executioner case will resolve quickly?"

Young shrugged. "I've handled a plethora of murder investigations, and witnesses always turn up. Eventually, anyway. He'll brag to someone about one of the killings, and that someone will pick up the phone and call us, and that'll be all she wrote."

Baldwin had the urge to laugh but thought better of it, so instead he just held Young's gaze. "Dana, I've worked with these types of offenders my entire career. You're right, most murders are closed because of witnesses, even serial murders, but not with *this* type of killer. Sometimes, these guys don't even *know* they're doing it. How exactly are they going to brag to someone about killings if they aren't even aware they're doing them?"

A flash of irritation crossed Young's face and then disappeared just as quickly. "Look, I didn't come to argue. I came to inform you that I would like the Executioner case cleared as quickly as possible. Our eyes are on you right now."

"Because it's in the media, right? I'm guessing you wouldn't give much of a shit if nobody knew about it."

Young straightened his tie and said, "I would watch your tone, Agent Baldwin. With BSU getting trimmed, we're going to have to find a new place for you, and where that place will be is up to me." He checked his watch. "Cleared quickly, Agent Baldwin. Do we understand?"

"Yeah, I understand."

When Young had left, Baldwin tossed his pen on the desk and rubbed his face. A friend of his had recently retired from the Bureau and bought a diving shop in Bermuda.

Baldwin pulled up photographs of Bermuda on his desktop and stared at them a long time before getting his jacket and leaving the office for the night. He was the last one there.

8

Yardley ate a quiet lunch at a café near the federal building and watched the crowds. Some kids came in, probably no more than thirteen. Their clothes were dirty, and they asked the hostess for something and then left when the hostess shook her head and said, "Sorry." The youth homeless population had been steadily increasing the past decade in Las Vegas, and vulnerable groups of teens attracted the worst types of predators.

Serial murderers of all types preferred victims that wouldn't fight, and young prostitutes were one group that went willingly with them to secluded locations. Someone like the Executioner, who chose victims who led regular, quiet lives, wasn't as common.

A young blond man parked a giant truck out front. He came into the café and looked around. He spotted her and came over.

"Jessica?"

"Yes."

"I'm Kyle." He sat down across from her without being asked and without shaking hands. He took a sucker out of his pocket and unwrapped it.

Yardley wondered if Lieu had his eye on Jax for a while and was just waiting for her to step down.

She gave him a warm smile, despite his discourtesy. "Nice to meet you."

Jax glanced around the café. "Why'd you want to meet here?"

"Just thought somewhere casual would be nice for a change."

His eyes darted around the room before he put the sucker in his mouth.

"How are you liking Las Vegas so far?"

He shrugged. "Came here a lot before this. I knew what I was getting into."

"I was actually curious about that. Why did you come here?" Yardley asked.

"What d'ya mean?"

"I mean Special Victims is a highly . . . specialized field of prosecution. Most prosecutors view it as a necessary evil. Something you have to put your time into for a few years if you want to move to Homicide or Major Crimes and then become a judge. No one specifically asks to be placed here. But you did. I'm just wondering why."

He shrugged. "Good opportunity, I guess. And I was sick of Wyoming." He stared at her a moment and said, "I thought you'd be a lot older. They told me you were retiring."

"I am. At least from here."

"What're you gonna do?"

"Maybe open a solo practice. Do something calm like wills or contracts." *Something without blood,* she thought.

"I want to show you something," she said.

She took her laptop from her satchel and pulled up the Executioner files.

"This is the case we're going to be working the next two weeks. A reporter in the *Las Vegas Sun* called him the Crimson Lake Executioner and I expect that name will stay." She pointed to a list of files. "You can see the reports are ordered well, but I found a few errors on Clark County's part and one from the FBI. The microscopic findings report from the autopsy was buried with the missing persons report for the second victim, the serological summary was stacked with a supplemental narrative, and a witness statement was embedded in thirty pages of notes from the evidence response team. All things that I fixed fairly easily, but it's imperative to catch mistakes like this in case they turn out to be important.

"You'll find that many detectives bulldoze their cases, and for the majority of murders, where the perpetrator is obvious or there were witnesses, like a drive-by shooting or a convenience store robbery, that can work. But in serial homicides, where the motive is unclear and the perpetrator did his best to avoid detection, everything has to be slow and methodical. I like to start from the ground up, and I suggest you do the same."

Yardley opened a spreadsheet that had twelve cells filled with headings like *Elimination procedures* and *Geographic analysis* and *Forensics (trace, transient & tangible)*.

"These are the primary areas you need to go over yourself. The police and FBI can gather the evidence for you, but they can't organize it in a way that a jury can easily under—"

He took the sucker out of his mouth and interrupted her. "Yeah . . . look, no offense, but that's not how I work these. I did Narcs for a long time and prosecuted a shit ton of homicides. We all got our ways of doing things, and honestly, that just doesn't sound like it would help me much."

"These cases won't be drug deals gone bad, Kyle. These are typically killers of high intelligence. You have to reconstruct their thinking from the evidence you have. It's the only way to work these cases."

Jax leaned forward. "I graduated law school at twenty-one, and ever since it's been a fight to prove I know what I'm doing. I don't wanna get into a pissing contest. You're on your way out, and I totally get the urge to tell the new guy what you think you've learned—"

"What I *think* I've learned?"

He sighed. "Relax, okay. I just mean I have a certain way of doing things that's always worked for me, and filling in spreadsheets ain't it."

He bit his sucker and chewed, then rose and placed the plastic stick on a linen napkin. "I'll look at the files and give you my thoughts."

Jax swaggered out the door; the Rolex on his wrist told Yardley he liked flash.

She could leave now. The new house was waiting for her. Just hand her existing cases over and go. She doubted either Jax or Lieu would mind.

Her fingers hovered over the track pad. She clicked on the personal history Baldwin had included for Angela River.

There wasn't much there. Her place of birth was Santa Monica, California—the same place Yardley had been born. She'd dropped out of Davis Port High School and later earned her GED before attending college. No relatives listed. Zachary was a year older than her and had no criminal history. River had a conviction for resisting arrest. Yardley pulled up the original case file. Officers had tried to arrest River for smoking pot at an outdoor concert, and when they went to cuff her, she mooned them and ran off. It made Yardley grin.

Yardley logged onto Instagram and found River's profile. Photos of her rock climbing, swimming in the ocean, mountain biking, doing yoga, and receiving something around her neck from what looked like a Buddhist guru. The quote under her profile picture was *Be the change you want to see in the world.*

She stared at the profile picture: River in a yoga pose on the edge of a cliff with the sun glowing behind her.

What did he see when he looked at you?

9

Family dinners at least a few nights a week were something Yardley insisted on. Tonight, Tara came home with Stacey, a friend and neighbor she'd been hanging around with the past year. Tara had never found friends easily—due not just to her background as the child of an infamous killer but also to her piercing intelligence. She'd had to change schools more than once after kids found out about her father, and for a while she'd fallen in with a bad crowd.

The girls were laughing about something as they grabbed sodas out of the fridge.

"Smells good," Stacey said.

"It's almost done. Have a seat."

She made up three plates and sat down with the girls.

"How was your day?" Yardley asked.

Tara shoved a forkful of spaghetti in her mouth and said, "The internship is killing me. It's all about putting in hours. Everything takes so much freaking time."

"You can always cut back."

She shook her head. "They're for sure gonna hire me after graduation. I want that job."

"How cool is that?" Stacey said. "She'll be barely twenty when she graduates and making *so* much money."

"I'm very proud of her," Yardley said, looking at her daughter. Tara blushed.

When they were through eating, the girls ran off to a friend's house, and Yardley was left alone. She decided the walls felt like they were closing in on her, and though she had already worked out today, she dressed in shorts and a T-shirt and went to the gym. She ran so fast on the treadmill her legs felt like they would give out, and she had to sit at the juice bar until she had the strength to get to her car.

When Yardley was driving again, she twisted her back from side to side and stretched her neck. Though young, she was feeling the tug of age in her joints and didn't recover as quickly from workouts or illness as she used to. The ache in her back made her think of Angela River's offer to come to the yoga studio.

Yardley debated a few moments and then looked up the address.

The yoga studio was a small space on the outskirts of Las Vegas. Through the glass, she saw about ten people in poses on yoga mats. River ambled around the space, occasionally helping a person with a stretch or speaking to them briefly. Yardley scanned the parking lot, expecting to see a deputy waiting in an unmarked car, but there was no one. River should have been assigned a protective detail for at least a few days: if the Executioner thought she could identify him, he might be back to finish what he started.

She waited until the class was over before going inside. River was speaking with a student when she saw Yardley and waved. She finished her conversation and came over.

"I'm so glad you came. You missed the last class, though."

"I just wanted to check in with you. How are you holding up?"

She shrugged. "It hurts to walk, breathe, and move, and I can only see out of one eye, but other than that I'm fine." She paused and looked down at the floor. "Um, my boyfriend, Zachary, said I was crying in my sleep last night." She forced an awkward smile. "But hey, could be a lot worse, right?"

Yardley glanced at the gash on her forehead. It glistened with some sort of skin cream. She didn't seem as confident as last time they'd met, as full of energy. The trauma was likely beginning to take hold.

"Angela—"

"Angie. My friends call me Angie."

"Angie, I know an excellent trauma therapist. I refer many victims from my office, and she's been able to help them."

"I don't want to think of myself that way. As a victim. Besides, I got yoga and meditation. I'm not sure headshrinking is going to do much more than I can do on my own." She sighed and picked up a yoga mat someone had left behind. "So you want a drink? I have kombucha. Really strong with a nice alcohol kick."

"I'm okay, thank you. I should get back to my daughter. I really did just want to check up on you." Yardley glanced at a large framed photograph of a guru in a robe, an Asian man with a warm smile and a yellow sash over his shoulder. "Did the Sheriff's Office give you a protective detail? You should have a deputy with you for a little while."

"No, no one said anything."

Yardley nodded. "I'll give them a call and get someone with you."

River's eyes widened, and Yardley knew she had misspoken. "You think . . . you think he's going to come after me again?"

"It's just a precaution. Everyone in your situation, when they've survived an attack and the perpetrator hasn't been apprehended, gets a protective detail for a time."

River folded her arms. "Um, Zachary's on shift all night. I kinda . . . I don't feel like being alone right now. Do you wanna maybe go out and get a real drink? Please?"

The *please* was so sincere that there was no way Yardley could say no.

The Black Door, a wine bar, wasn't far from the yoga studio. River gave the owner a hug and spoke softly in her ear. She sat them at a table by the windows.

"She was a student of mine," River said when they were seated. "She lost her husband to a drunk driver, so she's been through some shit herself." She dipped some bread into a small bowl of olive oil on the table.

The owner brought over two glasses of red wine and some cheese with grapes. The wine was smooth with an oak taste, something expensive and rare.

"So are you married?" River asked.

"No."

"Divorced?"

Yardley nodded. "Seventeen years now."

"That's a long time. Any plans on getting remarried?"

She shook her head. "No."

"I've never been. Zachary's actually my second serious relationship. Second guy I've moved in with, too. Honestly, sometimes it just feels like nothing but work." She paused and took a drink. "I'm pretty sure he's cheating on me. I should just leave him, but I don't want to be alone. How weak is that?"

"I don't think it's weak at all."

River fought back tears; her eyes glistened as she glanced away. "I'm sorry, I'm just dumping all this on a stranger."

"It's fine, Angie. I wouldn't be here if I didn't want to hear it."

She shook her head. "Staying with someone like that because you're afraid to be alone . . . I don't know what else to call it but weakness. I just feel so damn stupid." She couldn't hold back the tears anymore. "I'm so embarrassed. You should just go. You don't need to be around a mess like me."

"Angie, it's—"

"No, please just go. I'm a disaster."

Yardley hesitated a moment. "I was married to a serial killer."

River looked at her in silence, the tears still on her cheeks, and then she laughed. Yardley said nothing. She hadn't meant for the words to come out, but somehow they had. It was an odd sensation to say it out loud. She never talked about it with anyone.

River stopped laughing and watched her. The smile slowly fading from her face.

"You're serious?"

Yardley nodded, taking another sip of wine. "If you want to compare whose life is more of a disaster, I think I take the cake."

"Who was it?"

"Eddie Cal. He's sitting on death row right now."

"Wow. I give up, you got me beat."

"Oh, if you think that, then I should tell you who I let move in with me after Eddie. I might win first and second place in a 'whose life is more of a disaster' contest." Yardley watched the way the light reflected off her wineglass. "I've never been good at picking men."

"Join the club. Before Zachary, I was dating a Hells Angel."

"What was that like?"

River shrugged. "Really fun at first. I probably shouldn't say this to a prosecutor, but he took me to a big drug deal once with some Mexican gang. Like a cartel or something. It was like in the movies. Ten guys with guns standing around in the middle of the desert checking suitcases."

"Really?"

She nodded. "I have to admit, I've never been so scared and so excited at the same time." She glanced around and whispered, "I had sex with him on his bike right there when everyone had left."

She chuckled, and Yardley smiled. "On the bike?"

"Yeah. I fell off and thought I'd ruined the mood, but he jumped right on top of me. He was like an animal that way."

"What happened to him?"

"Went to prison, of course," she said with a sigh. "How else could that story have ended?" She held up her wineglass in a toast. "To dating shitty men. Fun while it lasts."

Yardley grinned as they tapped glasses, and River signaled to the owner for more wine.

10

"Missing Persons at the Sheriff's Office got a call from Kathy Pharr's husband. You're not going to believe this."

Baldwin spoke quickly, and Yardley grabbed a pen and pad from the edge of her desk. She could hear traffic in the background like he was on the freeway.

"He hasn't seen his fourteen-year-old daughter in a day. Harmony Pharr. She's not answering her cell. She's never run away and this is definitely not normal for her."

Yardley's heart beat faster. "I'm coming with you."

"Don't think that's a good idea, Jess. Not right now. What if this guy killed his wife and now his daughter, too? If he thinks I don't believe his story, things may go sideways."

"That's unlikely given there's a second victim, and—"

"Absolutely not. I'm not flexible on this."

She sighed. "It's likely she's shaken from her mother's death and is acting out and ran away."

"Could be. But better safe than sorry."

"Either way, call me as soon as you're done talking to him."

Yardley hung up and had started to open the Pharr file to see what there was about Kathy's family—to see if her daughter had a history of running away—when her cell phone vibrated. It was River—Yardley had given out her cell number in case she needed anything. Something she did for victims in every case she prosecuted.

"This is Jessica."

"Hey, it's Angie. Sorry to call your cell. I'm not bugging you at work, am I?"

"Not at all. What's going on?"

"I just remembered something . . . about that day. It was in a dream last night, but when I woke up, I knew it wasn't a dream."

"I'll get Agent Baldwin to—"

"No. I mean, don't get me wrong, he's been perfectly polite, not to mention he's hot, but I don't feel comfortable with . . . I mean, I just feel more comfortable with a woman. The men treat me like I'm crazy or something. Too emotional. Which is really just a way for them to ignore what women have to say."

"I understand." Yardley glanced around her office. She'd been packing up her files, preparing to archive some and hand others over to Jax. There was little room to sit, and it would be better to talk in person. "Can you meet me down on the Strip?"

Midday, the Strip wasn't as packed with tourists, but the streets reflected the intense heat that was barreling down, making Yardley feel like she was being baked in an oven.

"You look nice," River said as they waited to cross an intersection. "Wish I had an excuse to wear a suit."

"I would much prefer leggings and a tank top like you, trust me."

"Yeah, but I bet people just take you more seriously dressed like that. I get obscene comments all the time dressed like this."

Yardley smirked and said, "I get them, too. I don't think the way we dress matters to men like that."

They crossed the street, and a man standing in front of a casino tried to convince them to come inside for free booze. They politely declined, and he followed them for a few steps before turning to someone else.

"I love the sunshine here," River said. "My parents moved us to a little town in Alaska when I was five. Winter lasted ten months there, so anywhere with sunshine and sand is like heaven to me."

"When did you move down here?"

"Seventeen. I ran away and never looked back. Hitchhiked through Canada and ended up in San Francisco living in this tiny apartment with a poet. I worked two jobs as a waitress to pay our bills, and he sat around and wrote really, *really* shitty poetry."

She chuckled, and it made Yardley smile. Then River said, "I looked up your ex. He was an artist, right?"

Yardley had to swallow because her mouth suddenly felt dry. She stared down at the pavement.

"Sorry," River said. "Me and my big mouth."

"No, you're okay. I'm just not used to talking about him. He was an artist, like your poet, but he was quite successful." She watched a young couple hurry by holding hands, the smell of alcohol emanating from them. "I was a photographer when I met him, and he always encouraged me. Told me not to work elsewhere because art needed to consume you to be any good. That you have to sacrifice yourself to it if you want it to be something unique."

"Wow. He sounds deep."

Yardley nodded as they stopped at an intersection near Caesars Palace, the cool mist from the fountains drifting over them. "He had an insight into life I haven't come across again. He understood people and their motivations in a way that the best psychiatrists I've met would be jealous of. That's why he's so terrifying. He knows exactly what we are, he could've been anything he wanted to because of it, and he still chose to be who he is. No horrific childhood, no abuse, no mental illness. He willingly chose to become a monster."

"You really believe that? That he chose it? You don't think we're just born the way we are? I mean, maybe the universe just makes us who it wants us to be?"

Yardley shook her head. "He killed because he enjoyed it, not because his hand was forced by the universe." She looked at a statue of Augustus and said, "I think I'd like to talk about something else if that's all right."

"Sweetie, I didn't mean to pry. Really. I'm sorry."

"It's all right. It just . . . some days are worse than others to speak about it."

She stopped and quietly groaned as she rubbed her head. "Do you mind if we sit somewhere? I get these headaches that come and go."

They sat at a bench near a food court and didn't speak for a while. Finally River said, "Well, different subject—you said you have kids?"

"A daughter. She's seventeen."

"What's she like?"

"She's in the doctoral program at UNLV. She's what they term a savant. A very high-functioning savant." Yardley grinned. "I think she sees it as her job to take care of me."

River was quiet awhile, her eyes down to the pavement. "I'm not sure I'll ever have kids." She glanced at a group of young men driving by in a Cadillac, hollering at pedestrians. "Do you wanna know what the dream was?"

"If you're ready to talk about it."

She nodded. "It was terrifying. When I woke up, my shirt was sticking to me. Just completely drenched with sweat. I've never had that happen before."

"What was the dream?"

"When I was coming out of the mall to the parking lot, I mean, it was, like, ten at night, right? So it was really dark, but I'd parked near one of the light posts in the lot. So I walked up to the car, got to the door, and unlocked it with my key fob, and then I felt, like, this crazy pain on the back of my head, and everything just kinda spun outta control. And then I woke up on a table with bandages around my face. But I've been thinking about that second right before I felt that pain, and I saw it in my dream really clearly."

"What did you see?"

"I looked at my window when I was about to get into my car . . . and I saw a reflection behind me."

Yardley's stomach lurched, but she remained passive and calm on the outside. "Did you see a face?"

She shook her head. "No. It was too fast. Just a flash of a face. When I woke up, I thought it was just a nightmare and I'd dreamed it all, but it's too real. I know it was him."

"What was he wearing?"

"I don't know. I think something black, but I could only see from, like, the chest up."

"Did you catch a glimpse of his hair color? Or his race?"

"No. I saw his arm move, that was it. I didn't see anything that would help me describe him." She thought a moment. "There were other people in the parking lot. He came up to me without even looking at them. He chose me specifically."

Her hands started trembling.

"Shit," she said, folding her arms across her chest.

"It's all right, Angie."

She shook her head. "I teach my students about peace and harmony and using the universe's energy to heal yourself, and I can't even talk about this without shaking."

"It's not up to you. Our brains react how they react. Your brain is still processing the trauma, and whatever you're going through is perfectly normal."

"Sure doesn't feel normal." She exhaled loudly. "What if he was watching me before that? That means he knows who I am, probably knows where I live and work. He's going to come after me again, isn't he?"

Yardley was silent a moment. "I don't know. But I spoke with the Sheriff's Office and a protective detail is being assigned to you today. They were shorthanded and couldn't get someone until now. So you'll have a deputy with you twenty-four hours a day."

"But what do you think? Is he going to try to come after me again?"

Yardley licked her lower lip, which felt dry. "In many cases like this that I've worked . . . no. The unsub, unknown subject, hasn't come back. It's too much of a risk. But there is a type of offender that's . . . I guess you could say detached from reality. They sometimes don't know what they're doing, don't even realize they're doing it. Those types of offenders do occasionally come back for"—Yardley was going to say *victims* but changed her mind—"for witnesses who survived their attacks."

"Is this man that type of person?"

"I don't know. He seems methodical to me one minute and completely disorganized and out of control the next. I just don't know, Angie."

She nodded. "What are you going to do if you find him?"

"I'm only peripherally involved in the investigation. My main job is to make sure it goes smoothly so that he can be prosecuted when we find him. I guess you could say my job doesn't even really start until the arrest."

River smiled. "There's no way your job starts with the arrest. It started the second you cared about what happened to me." She looked out into traffic. "What do I do if he comes back for me? How do I protect myself from someone like this?"

Yardley could have said to get a gun and a dog, an alarm system, or that she would have the protective detail for a while and it would be fine—but that wasn't the truth. The truth was that if someone really wanted to hurt someone else and didn't care about the consequences, there was little that could be done to stop them.

"You can't," Yardley said. "The only way to stop him is to catch him or kill him."

11

Baldwin parked in front of the Pharrs' mobile home. Each house in the park was stacked tightly against the next to cram in as many as possible.

He got out of the car. Several potted plants lined either side of the front door, one of them with cigarette butts sticking out of the soil. He knocked and waited a beat before knocking again.

A man in a sleeveless shirt answered. His face was weathered. Prison tattoos dominated his forearms and biceps.

"You back already?"

"Just some follow-up questions, Mr. Pharr. You got time?"

"You here about Harmony?"

"Yes."

"You find her?"

"I haven't. I only just checked with Detective Reece at the Las Vegas police and read the missing persons report you filed. I was hoping to get some of your time to go over a few things."

"Like what?"

"Well, the first thing we have to do is make sure that she's actually missing. That this isn't something else."

"Something else? You know my wife was just killed, don't ya?"

"Yes, and as you know, I'm working closely with Detective Garrett, who's the lead investigator into your wife's death. I just wonder if it's possible Harmony could be with a friend or at a relative's house?"

"No, no way. She always answers her texts. Always. Especially if I tell her it's an emergency and text me back right now."

"When was the last time you saw her?"

"Two days ago. She said she was going to Oscar's to get some clothes and she didn't come back. I been calling her phone for two days. I called Garrett and told him ain't no way she would just run off somewhere. He thought 'cause'a where we live she must be runnin' with a rough crowd and gettin' high, and I said Harmony's fourteen and she ain't never touched drugs. Coming from where we come, that's something big. She hasn't ever even smoked a joint."

Baldwin thought a moment. Why would Garrett not mention to him that Kathy Pharr's daughter was missing? He thought back to the last time he talked to him and figured he had already spoken to Tucker by then. Why didn't he say something?

"You said she was going to Oscar's. Is that a friend or . . . ?"

"No, store down there on Roosevelt. Thrift store."

Baldwin nodded. "Do you mind if we talk inside?"

Tucker opened the door to let him in and said, "Sorry 'bout the mess."

The floor was littered with clothes and old food wrappers. Several ashtrays cluttered the coffee table, and the heavy scent of cigarette smoke hung in the air. Tucker moved some papers, what looked like past due bills, off a couch.

"Just me and Harmony now." He paused and looked down at his fingers, which he was rubbing together. "Since Kathy passed, ain't no one been around to take care of the house."

"I'm so sorry for your loss," Baldwin said. He glanced around the house as Tucker fished around in his pockets and found a lighter. "So you were released from prison four months ago, is that right?"

He took out a cigarette and lit it. "Yeah, did twelve years up there in Low Desert Plains. Saw my daughter grow up from behind glass. You know what that feels like? It feels like shit. You feel worthless.

Rehabilitation my ass. Everyone I knew inside went in good dudes and came out criminals, and that's the truth."

"You were there for kidnapping a fourteen-year-old girl at knifepoint, is that right?" Baldwin said mildly.

Tucker blew smoke out through his nose and glared at him. "That was bullshit. We was hookin' up, and I wasn't but a young man then myself, and she got into my car that day her damn self. No one said nothin' 'bout kidnapping till her parents found out she was with an older man. And that judge"—he scoffed—"that judge wouldn't hear nothin' at my sentencing. He locked me up and threw away the key like he was handin' out candy. Our justice system ain't got nothin' to do with justice, tell you that much."

Baldwin looked toward a photograph on a side table. Kathy and Harmony smiling widely. The only photograph in the room. "When was this taken?" he said, picking up the photo.

"Guess 'bout a few years ago. Harmony was the cutest damn girl you ever seen. People would tell her mama we should get her into modelin', but I said hell no. Them models is screwed up something fierce."

Baldwin put the photo back. "Are you certain she's never made attempts at running away?"

He shook his head. "Kathy never told me she had. She got straight As in school, too. Not the sorta kid that runs away. Good head on her shoulders. Don't know where she got it from, 'cause it sure as shit ain't from me or her mama. Her mama was inside for a few years, too, for meth."

"Who'd Harmony stay with?"

"Her grandma." He shook his head. "Shit, probably woulda just been better she stayed there insteada comin' home."

"Did you make any enemies in prison? Someone who maybe was released recently and would want some payback?"

"No, can't think of anybody. My time inside weren't so bad, and they kept me outta gen pop since my charges involved a child. People with charges involving kids don't last long in gen pop."

"I've heard."

He sucked in some smoke from his cigarette and then blew it out. "So what you doin' to find who did this?"

"Can't talk about an ongoing investigation, Mr. Pharr. Sorry."

"Yeah, fine. Anything else, then? I gotta get to work soon."

Baldwin glanced around again. "I'll need a current picture of Harmony. And do you mind if I take a look at her room?"

"Nah, it's right there. I'll go find a picture."

Baldwin rose and went to Harmony's room.

A small bed with blue blankets, white sheets poking out from underneath, took up most of the space. The sheets had colorful cartoon ponies on them. Children's sheets. On the mirror over a dresser were photographs of Harmony with friends and several boys. One of the boys, a young redheaded kid, had a heart drawn around his picture with red marker.

Her room was neat and orderly, unlike the rest of the house. Schoolbooks, some of them for advanced placement courses, sat on the dresser, and there was a folding chair in front of a small, dilapidated desk. Baldwin felt a stab of sympathy. Harmony was intelligent and driven and probably had every disadvantage in life already working against her, simply because she'd been born into poverty.

Tucker came in and handed him a school photo of Harmony in a collared shirt.

"She sometimes spends the night at her friends' houses. You checked with them? Garrett said he would."

"Which friends?" Baldwin asked.

"Uma's her best friend. She don't live too far from here."

"I'll need Uma's last name and an address if you have it."

"I don't know the address, but I can take you over there. Ain't far."

"I'd appreciate that."

12

Baldwin drove while Tucker sat in the passenger seat. "I love old Mustangs like this. Used to work on 'em all the time back at my shop."

"Your own shop?"

Tucker shook his head. "Granddaddy's shop. Little place. Not too many customers. Made enough for me, but wouldn't have had enough for a wife 'n' kid workin' there." He looked out the window. "It ain't never enough then, seems like."

Baldwin glanced at him. "So Harmony was two when you went inside, right?"

He nodded. "Wasn't sure she was mine. Truth be told, still ain't sure. Her mama was hookin' up with a neighbor at the time. But I treat her like she was my own, regardless of whatever."

"Must've been hard on Kathy. Single mom with a husband inside."

He shrugged. "Don't know. I guess. Her daddy helped her when he could."

They stopped at a light. "So you grew up in Fruit Heights, right?"

Tucker nodded. "Yeah. You been? Shit little town."

"No, haven't been there. Is that why you left? Not much to do?"

"Something like that." Tucker pointed. "That house right there."

The home was redbrick with a half-dead, yellowed lawn. Baldwin took the porch steps first and knocked. A man in a checkered button-up answered.

"Hey, Chuck," Tucker said. "Harmony over here?"

He stared at Baldwin. "Nah, ain't seen her. Who's this?"

Baldwin said, "I'm Cason Baldwin. I'm with the FBI. When was the last time you saw Harmony?"

He opened the screen door and put one hand on the frame. "Shit. Few days ago, I think. What's goin' on?"

"Is your daughter here?" Baldwin asked. "Can I speak to her?"

"Yeah, hang on. I'll get her."

When he left, Tucker said, "He's good people. Fought over there in Iraq for six years. Didn't come back right, but he's doin' good, considering."

"He live here with just Uma?"

He nodded. "Had a wife. Ran out on him some years back." He took out a package of cigarettes. "You mind?"

"No."

A young teen in a pink shirt came to the door. She didn't have the look of shock or fear that adults had when Baldwin surprised people at their homes. Youth, he thought, always expected the best rather than the worst.

"Uma, hi, I'm Cason. I'm with the FBI. Do you know what the FBI is?"

She glanced at her dad. "Like a cop?"

"Exactly. Like a cop. So I'm trying to help find your friend Harmony. Do you mind if we talk?"

"I guess."

"I was wondering when the last time you saw her was?"

"Like, Wednesday. I think."

"Where at?"

"We sometimes go down to Oscar's. We went there for some new shorts or something."

Baldwin nodded. "So you guys were there Wednesday together?"

"Yeah, and then we walked home."

"Have you heard from her since?"

She shook her head. "I texted her day before yesterday but she didn't text me back."

"Did you see her get all the way home?"

She shook her head again. "My house is on the way. I said bye to her here."

Baldwin glanced at her father. "Uma, did she ever mention a man who'd started talking to her? Maybe he was showing up places, following her around? She might have said this was a really nice man. One who would buy her things and take her places."

She shrugged. "No, I don't think so."

"Did she ever tell you she was scared of anyone? Like a teacher or neighbor? A relative?"

Baldwin suddenly realized his mistake: he should have interviewed her out of earshot of both her father and Tucker.

"No, I don't think so."

"If she decided to run away from home, can you think of anywhere she would go? Anywhere I should be looking?"

Uma thought a moment. "We have a tree house we go to sometimes."

"Where's the tree house?"

"It's in that field behind her house. We didn't build it or nothing, it was already there when we were kids, but sometimes we go there and play around."

Baldwin looked at Tucker, who nodded, letting him know what she said was right. "Okay," he said, turning back to Uma. "If you hear from Harmony, will you call me?" He handed her a card. "Day or night. Okay?"

"Okay."

Baldwin turned to leave, and she said, "Hey. Is she . . . I mean, do you think the man that did that to her mom is . . ."

Baldwin glanced at Tucker, who was smoking and watching them. "I don't know yet, Uma."

"Oh," she said, flicking his card nervously across her palm and staring at her shoes. "Well, I'm sure you'll find her. I bet it's nothing. Right?"

Baldwin was silent a moment and then said, "I hope so."

13

Yardley went home after meeting up with River. Tara was studying at the dining room table with headphones on. Yardley kissed her daughter on the head and went to the fridge. She was too tired to make dinner, so frozen leftovers would have to do.

As she took out the food, she got a text. It was a picture of a bracelet.

Look what I found online, River wrote.

I like it, Yardley replied.

I do too. Should I get it?

You should. That color will look great with your skin.

There was a long pause in the conversation. Yardley put the frozen food in the microwave while she waited.

I know this is crazy and I'm part of your work, and if this is creepy just tell me, but what are you doing tonight?

Why? Yardley replied.

Zachary's out of town and isn't coming back until tomorrow night. I wouldn't mind some company tonight. Want to come over and drink wine and watch trash reality tv?

Yardley's fingers hesitated over the phone. She wasn't used to having friends, and what did she really know about River? Her instincts told her to keep it professional, but something else said that she wanted someone to talk to. That maybe she even needed it.

Why don't you come here? she wrote.

Night had fallen by the time dinner was through. Tara worked equations while they ate and barely spoke.

"How was your day?" Yardley said.

"Fine."

The entire meal had been like that, one-word responses. She understood why; when Tara had a goal in front of her, like solving those equations, everything else dropped away. Yardley had been that way at her age as well. But she couldn't help thinking of the little girl she would take to the movies and push on swings at the park. The little girl who was glued to her mother all day. It was just them against the rest of the world, and Yardley remembered it as both the hardest and happiest time of her life.

"I have a friend coming over," Yardley said.

Tara looked up from her papers. "Who?"

"Her name's Angie. You haven't met her."

Tara grinned. "Where'd you meet her?"

"Work."

"I can go to the coffee shop and study if you want."

Yardley rose and collected the dishes off the table. "No, not at all. I just wanted you to know so you wouldn't be surprised."

"I am surprised. I don't think I've ever met one of your friends. Except that one lady we went to lunch with a few times. Ida. I liked her. What happened to her?"

"She got married and had kids. When you're at different stages in life, it's sometimes hard to maintain friendships."

"So is Angie a prosecutor, too?"

"No."

"Lawyer?"

Yardley took the dishes to the sink and began washing them off. "No . . . she's the victim in a case I have."

"Seriously?"

"It's perfectly fine. There're no rules against having friendships with people you're also helping."

"Yeah, but just seems weird. You're usually so careful about stuff like that."

There was a knock at the door. Tara answered.

"Hi, you must be Tara."

"Yup. And you're Angie? Come in."

"It's so nice to finally meet you. Your mom talks about you all the time."

"Good stuff?"

"Oh, of course."

River had a bottle of wine in one hand and a tub of Ben & Jerry's ice cream in the other.

"Sorry, couldn't decide between wine or ice cream. Not sure which is worse for you."

Yardley said, "Definitely ice cream. But I think we'll be having both."

"Me too," Tara said. Yardley raised her eyebrows, and she said, "Just kidding. I'll be in my room studying if you need me." She hesitated before leaving, her eyes scanning the bruising on River's face and the gash on her forehead before moving to the rune tattoo on River's shoulder. "Nice to meet you, Angie."

"You too." River placed the wine and ice cream on the counter in the kitchen. "I love her. She's adorable."

"She is," Yardley said, getting down two wineglasses from a cupboard. "Fortunately she's calmed some from her early teenage years. I've been helping her get through some issues stemming from her childhood."

"How?"

She poured the wine and said, "Cognitive behavioral therapy. I have training in clinical psychology. Though I never imagined I'd be using it on my own child."

"Life's a crazy trip, isn't it?" They tapped glasses. "But at least we can have fun during the craziness, right?"

—

After a few glasses of wine, half the ice cream, and several episodes of a show about a woman offering to marry whoever did everything she asked—like rolling in a vat filled with snakes or sifting through the sewer for a ring—Yardley and River sat out on the balcony and watched the night sky. They sipped the last of the wine and listened to soft new age music.

"I love it up here," River said. "You can never get silence like this in the city. It's always noisy, even at two or three in the morning. You think that can cause people to be unhappy? Like we're not meant to always have noise?"

"I don't know. The levels of anxiety and depression in society are unprecedented. Maybe that's a factor."

River watched her a second. "It's not there anymore."

"What isn't?"

"You have this small crease between your eyebrows like you're just always concentrating. Like, flexing a muscle or something. It's not there right now. Your face is much more radiant without it."

Yardley blushed and looked away.

"You have to wear a mask, don't you?" River said. "My uncle was a cop. I know what that's like. Those are men's men. Gotta be tough all the time, not show emotions. Are prosecutors like that, too?"

"Some are. There's this belief among some male prosecutors that women are too emotional to be good prosecutors. As if men can set their emotions aside like robots."

"I think a million years of war would discredit that little theory." She took a sip of the wine. "You don't have to tell me, but I've been dying to ask . . . what was he like?"

Yardley knew who she was talking about.

At first, it upset her that River would ask about the most horrific thing she had gone through, especially considering they hadn't known each other long, but then she thought that maybe it was normal. Forming friendships wasn't something Yardley had done much of, or knew how to do well, and maybe this was what friendship was: talking about things you didn't talk about with anyone else.

"To me, he was gentle and sweet. A few times a week, he would leave me notes on the kitchen counter or on the nightstand in the bedroom. Not poems or anything, but just notes letting me know he was thinking about me."

River shook her head. "I can't even imagine what you felt when you found out. What a shit storm. I'm seriously amazed you're even standing, much less helping everyone else."

Yardley leaned her head back against the deck chair and looked at the stars. "Can I ask you something now?"

"Ask away."

"You said I had a shattered heart the first time we met. What did you mean by that?"

River finished her wine with one large gulp, as though it were water. "Clearly it meant something to you if you remember I said it. What do you think it means?"

Yardley stared at her glass and the way the moonlight reflected off it. "I think it applies to someone who can never love someone again. That they're so broken they can never piece their heart together enough to give it to someone else."

River smiled. "Do you know there's a word in Sanskrit for the cracks that plates and cups get over time? It translates to 'unique beauty.' It means instead of fixing them, we should celebrate them, because it's the cracks that make the dish unique. Maybe a shattered heart is something unique to each person, and we need to go through it so we appreciate a healed heart later."

Yardley looked at her. "How are you keeping it together so well? You've just been through a massive trauma, but it seems like you're invincible. That it bounced off of you."

River gave a sad little grin while touching the stitches in her forehead. Then she gazed out over the desert. "I'm not invincible. The opposite. Sometimes it feels like I'm made of glass. This . . . thing that happened to me. I don't let myself think about it. When it pops into my head, I push it out. I've been meditating and doing yoga for fifteen years, so I know how to empty my mind. To not think about anything and just focus on my body." She ran her finger along the lip of her wineglass without looking at it. "I've had to do that every minute of every day since Agent Baldwin found me."

Yardley was silent a long while. "I'm sorry."

River nodded. "I talked to Zachary and . . . something's different. It's not anything we can put into words, I think, but it's something we both feel. I can tell. I don't know what it's going to be like from now on. It'll be different, I know, but how different? Will he look at me the same? Will he be angry with himself that he couldn't protect me?"

"We sometimes forget that loved ones of trauma victims are going through trauma, too. It might be beneficial for both of you to visit with a therapist."

"Why do you keep saying I should go to a therapist? You think I'm going to develop, like, some crazy personality disorder or something?"

"Trauma affects everyone differently."

River inhaled a deep breath and said, "Well, I'll tell you one thing. All this certainly changes my relationship to gauze."

Yardley chuckled. River watched her. "You should laugh more often. I don't think you do it enough."

"Sometimes it doesn't feel like there's much to laugh about."

"There's always things to laugh about, Jess. We're here to have joy, not to pay bills until we end up in a cemetery."

Yardley didn't reply. Eddie Cal had told her almost the identical thing, and the memory sent a cold shiver up her back.

"Um, I think I have a bottle of chardonnay if you'd like to stay a bit longer."

"I'd love to." River hesitated. "I . . . don't really want to be alone right now."

"Me neither."

14

Yardley smelled coffee and bacon when she stirred in bed and wondered if Tara was cooking breakfast. She rose and put on a robe.

River stood behind the stove, frying bacon and making omelets. A stack of pancakes with butter sat on the counter with what looked like homemade whipped cream next to it.

"Hey," she said, noticing Yardley, "you're up. Hope I didn't overstep my bounds, but I figured it's just breakfast."

"Smells good," she said, sitting on a stool at the island in the center of the kitchen. "How was the guest room?"

"*So* nice. That bed is way softer than mine. I seriously love it here. You're so lucky." She glanced at her. "So I found your copy of *Fifty Shades* in the drawer, you naughty girl."

Yardley chuckled. "For research."

"I bet."

Yardley took some bacon and bit into it. "The omelets look amazing. Where'd you learn to cook?"

"It's just necessity. My family wasn't exactly the *Leave It to Beaver* type, so if I wanted to eat, I had to cook it myself."

Tara came out, fully dressed and with her hair still damp from the shower. "Look at you two up all early," she said, going to the plate of pancakes and taking one on a napkin.

"Wanna sit with us for breakfast?" River said.

"Can't. Gotta run," Tara said. "Thanks, though. Mom thinks breakfast is coffee and sweetener." She kissed Yardley on the cheek on her way out. "Staying late at the lab tonight, don't wait up."

River watched her leave and then said, "We chatted for a bit this morning. I don't sleep much, and apparently, she doesn't either. I hope that's okay that we talked."

"What did you talk about?"

"School, mostly. I was in graduate school, too. I mean, not for anything like her, she's a genius, but I was proud I was there. Wish I'd finished."

"What were you studying?"

"Mythology and folklore. The most practical of all degrees, of course."

"Why'd you—"

Yardley's phone vibrated on the counter. She saw from the ID it was Baldwin.

"Excuse me," she said before answering. "Little early, isn't it, Cason?"

"Sorry to bug you."

"It's fine. What's going on?"

"I think you should probably come down to Harmony's house. I found her phone, and some blood nearby, Jess. I think he hit the mother and now he's got the daughter. I certified her case as a kidnapping and we got some deputies here combing the woods—"

"I'm coming right now."

Several cruisers were already in front of the Pharrs' home, as was Baldwin's black Mustang. Uniformed deputies from the Sheriff's Office were going in and out of the house, a few of them photographing the yard and surrounding area.

Inside, the home was cluttered and messy. Tucker Pharr stood against the counter with his hands stuffed into his pockets. Yardley recognized him from the booking photos for his kidnapping charges.

Baldwin stood at the bedroom door, directing a few forensic techs.

"What'd you find?" she said.

He glanced at her and then motioned outside with his head. They stepped onto the porch, and he exhaled loudly. "Found her phone in a tree house out back. Forensics searched the area and found a necklace. I showed it to her dad, and he identified it as Harmony's. Said she doesn't go anywhere without it. The necklace wasn't unclasped—it was broken. Like it had been pulled off her neck."

"And the blood?"

"They found some on the necklace. We'll know soon if it's hers or not, but this isn't looking good, Jess. I think the Executioner grabbed her, and we're going to find her strung up like—"

"Anything on the phone?" she said, interrupting him. She didn't want to think about the third Sarpong painting.

"No texts out of the ordinary. He didn't contact her that way."

"He had to have known about the tree house somehow."

"He could have been following her, like he did Angela River. He saw his opportunity and he took it. I spoke to Garrett and he said he thinks Harmony ran away. That Tucker barely knows her and she's got a file at DCFS showing she's run away twice before. But with the blood and broken necklace, that's really unlikely at this point."

Yardley looked out over the front yard. "We should have had a detail on her, Cason."

"We can 'should have' ourselves into old age. These things are unpredictable. We had no idea this is how it would play out." He placed his hands on his hips and watched a blood pattern analysis technician put his equipment away. "Well, I'm open to ideas."

Yardley glanced around. The mobile park had a playground not far from the Pharrs' home. The equipment was decrepit, rust coating much of it. The grass it'd been built on was yellow, with patches of nothing more than bare dirt.

A truck pulled to a stop, and Kyle Jax stepped out. Baldwin had likely notified him as well, as this would officially be his case soon. He had his sucker tucked against his cheek and a leather jacket on. He nodded to a few of the officers and joined them on the porch.

"Tree house in back?"

Baldwin nodded. "I was just telling Jessica we found a necklace with blood nearby. The girl's dad said she's never without it."

"This place isn't that big. Someone saw something. Keep working the canvass. And let's get the dad in for an interview. I don't like that he's got a kidnapping conviction against a girl his daughter's age."

"I've done this once or twice, you know," Baldwin said.

"No need to get pissy, just making sure we're all doing what we should be doing." Jax took the sucker out of his mouth and said, "Where's the dad?"

"Why?"

"I'd like to speak with him myself first."

Yardley said, "Agent Baldwin has been speaking with him the entire morning. Maybe let's give him a little break."

"I'll be quick. Promise," he said with a wink.

Yardley folded her arms. "Kyle, give the father a little break. He lost his wife and now his daughter."

"He also kidnapped a girl her age. That doesn't seem like too big a coincidence to you?"

Baldwin said, "I'm not ruling anything out, but he has a fifth-grade education. Does he strike you as someone who's intimately familiar with the works of an obscure Kenyan painter?"

"Don't know. Haven't had a face-to-face with him yet. In Narcs, everything is about reading people. I'm going to get a read on him myself. You guys got a problem with that, take it up with Roy." He winked at Yardley. "Don't worry yourself, sweet cheeks. I know what I'm doing."

Once he was inside, Baldwin said, "Me and that guy are not going to have a good time together."

"Well, you better have a come-to-Jesus talk with him because you two will be working closely."

Baldwin looked out at the playground. "You sure about it?"

"About what?"

"Leaving. Don't you have that tingling of excitement right now? That rush when you heard about her phone and necklace? You know exactly what you'll feel when we find out the killer's identity and what happened to Harmony. It's like a shot of adrenaline straight into your heart. I know you've felt it before. You really not going to miss that?"

"I don't feel excitement, Cason. I just feel . . . sad. Sad for her and sad for her family." She inhaled deeply and said, "Call me with any updates. I think I know someone who can help with this."

15

Yardley arrived at the restaurant early to get a table. It was the type of place she hated: glitzy and overpriced. But it was also the sort of restaurant she could see the man she was meeting with liking. Someplace to try to impress others.

She was given a booth, and they brought warm bread and olive oil. She took a few small bites before Jude Chance came in.

He was slim and wore glasses, with a balding head that appeared incongruous for how young he was. He scanned the room until he saw her.

"Looking hot as ever," he said, sitting down.

"Don't make me throw a drink."

He smiled and took some of the bread. "That's what I've always liked about you, J. You got balls. Most people who need something from me, they'd let me say whatever I want, but I have a feeling if I commented on your ass, you would clock me in the jaw."

"Maybe. I have Mace, too."

He chuckled. "Wine or beer?"

"Beer, thank you."

He called over a server and ordered a steak with butter and onions and two beers.

"So what's up?" Chance said with a mouthful of bread.

"I'm guessing you already know about Harmony Pharr."

"Of course. Wouldn't be much of a crime reporter if I wasn't on top of the biggest case this town's had in a decade. I read some idiotic piece on it just before I came here, actually. It was that dickhead Johnny McDermott. He said he thinks there's two of 'em."

"Two?"

"Executioners. That one of them is trying to get caught, and the other isn't. It's moronic and he wrote it just to get clicks, but how crazy would that be? Oh, I haven't even asked, do you like the moniker? The Executioner? I was thinking the Butcher, it brings up more savage imagery, but it didn't really fit since there's not much blood involved. By the way, that was brilliant identifying it as the work of Sarpong. I think that would've taken the FBI and Sheriff's Office months to figure out."

Only a small handful of people knew about the connection to the paintings. So small that Yardley could count them on one hand.

"It never stops amazing me how good your information is, Jude. How do you do it? Everyone who knows about the paintings was warned to keep it to themselves, that lives were at stake, that their supervisors would make heads roll if they leaked it to the public this early, but you still found out."

He shrugged, a smug grin on his face. "Who says it's not the supervisors themselves? You want stuff to stop leaking, pay them more so they don't need my money."

"So I take it that means you won't tell me? Even if I promise it'll stay between us?"

"Not on your life."

The server brought over two glasses of beer. Chance guzzled his and finished it off. Yardley pushed hers toward him and said, "Enjoy."

He began sipping hers.

"So J, you never call me unless you don't have anywhere else to turn. Do you not like me?"

"I like you fine. I just have to be careful. If it ever got out we exchange information, my boss may have an issue with it."

"Why? As long as the prick in the defendant's chair gets convicted, what's he care?"

She shook her head as she folded her arms and leaned them on the table. "Doesn't work like that. Appearances are everything. I sometimes think they'd rather have good public perception about a case than actually get a conviction on it."

He took a big swig of the beer. "Shit, it's like that anywhere. That's what bureaucracy is. Move shit slow and cover your ass. That's why I quit the papers and went out on my own."

"You ever thought of heading back to the legitimate news world?"

He chuckled. "Legitimate? There's no news source that's legitimate. Everyone's got an agenda they're pushing." His phone buzzed with a text, and he quickly typed a response, then said, "Anyway, I haven't talked to you for a bit. What you been up to?"

"I'm retiring, actually."

He put the phone down on the table. "No shit? From law?"

"I don't know from the law, but from prosecution. I'm moving to Santa Bonita. I was thinking of opening a solo practice and just taking simple cases. I would love to do a few wills and adoptions every month."

He glanced toward some young women walking by and said, "Bit of unsolicited advice? That ain't you. Not even close. You'll miss this shit. I've seen it before in some of the detectives and federal agents. I would really think about it before you throw it away." He finished off the beer. "Cops always think they'll be happy retiring and bodyguarding celebrities, but they never are. Some people just need to be part of the chase, you know?"

Yardley leaned back, took a breath, and glanced around the restaurant. "I need what you have on Harmony."

"Yeah?" he said, looking down at the empty glass in his hand. "And how do you know I got anything you don't?"

She shrugged. "I don't, but I know you have sources that won't talk to me."

"What do I get in return?"

"What do you want?"

A sparkle lit his eyes. "You heard about the serial rapist in Bloomington? The one breaking into houses?"

"Yes."

"It's your esteemed colleague Brittney Smith's case. She's always hated me. Won't give me anything. And she went down and talked to the detective sergeant in Sex Crimes and threatened him with prosecution if the evidence they have gets leaked to the press, so he's keeping everything close to the chest. I want you to get it for me."

"That's being handled by the county. I have no jurisdiction to tell them what to do."

"Yeah, but you and Brittney like each other, right? Sisterhood of the Special Victims Traveling Pants or whatever? I don't give a shit how you do it; just get me what they got so I can write a story about it."

"I won't do that on an active case, but I will talk to Brittney for you. I'll tell her you're good people and it's nice to have you owing a favor. She'll give you something."

He thought a moment. "Well, better than nothing. You got a deal."

The server came over with full glasses of beer and removed the empty ones.

"What do you have?" she said.

"The dad. He's got one conviction for kidnapping a girl the same age, which I'm guessing you've seen, right?"

"I have. I also know he has an expunged charge from 2002 for the same thing."

"Huh. Hard even for you guys to see expunged files from that long ago. How'd you learn about that?"

"I have my sources, too," she said with a grin. "You better have something better than that."

"How about this: Did you see how many times Child Services was called to their house on reports of physical or sexual abuse?"

"I did. Eight."

"Yeah, eight. Eight damn times, and that girl still wasn't taken out of that house. Kathy would bring in these pieces'a shit she was dating and some of them would abuse Harmony. There was one boyfriend, though, that was the worst of the bunch. Sent her to the emergency room twice. My source at the PD said Harmony testified against him in one of his trials and put him away for one to fifteen. The DCFS files are protected, but if you get that and get a name, you owe me. 'Cause I bet you another dinner that prick was released and came looking for some payback." He glanced around the restaurant. "I, um, have something else, too."

"What?"

"Well, let's just consider it a little gift. A photograph that I think you're going to be very interested in."

16

Yardley stood behind Baldwin at his desk. They had put in a subpoena with the Department of Child and Family Services for all the files they had on Harmony Pharr and were waiting to hear back. In the meantime, Yardley wanted to dive into Tucker Pharr's background.

"Tucker B. Pharr," Baldwin said. "Born June of sixty-six, eighteen arrests and half a dozen convictions. Most serious one we got is for kidnapping, where he served twelve years in Low Desert Plains and was released four months ago, and we also got that kidnapping arrest in oh two that was dismissed and then expunged. Expunged files from that long ago won't be in the system." He leaned back and looked at her. "He says the one he was convicted for was just a big misunderstanding. What do you think the odds are that would happen twice?"

"Astronomical. I want to see the details of his expunged case. If it turns out he has a predilection for fourteen-year-old girls, our suspect list for Harmony's kidnapping just got really small."

"We gotta go down to the PD and get the actual paper files, then."

"I'll drive."

—

On the drive down, Yardley and Baldwin didn't talk much, but Baldwin glanced at her a few times, and she knew he was about to ask her something. Probably something she didn't want to be asked.

"You know who we should talk to about these paintings and what they mean, right?"

She didn't take her eyes off the road. "You can't be serious."

"I'm just saying. If there was any chance he'd talk to me, I'd go. But I'm right, aren't I? Eddie Cal would know what these paintings mean."

She glanced at him. "I'm not seeing him again, Cason. Honestly, I'm shocked you would even suggest it."

"Jess, we got a fourteen-year-old girl missing, and I don't know how much longer she's going to be breathing. We should at least be willing to discuss all our options."

"Eddie Cal is not an option."

He was silent a moment before responding. "If you say so." He didn't speak for the rest of the drive.

The Fruit Heights Police Department consisted of two police officers: the chief and a patrol officer.

Fruit Heights was built around the trucking industry. Its few restaurants and gas stations were crowded around the two freeway exits, with three motels around them. The single casino boasted about its one-dollar beer during happy hour, and the homes the four thousand residents actually lived in were farther back in the desert. Far enough away not to be noticed.

The police department was in the city administration building, and Yardley parked in back. As she was exiting the car, she got a text from River that Michael Zachary wanted to meet her. That they should have dinner together tonight at her house to repay her for the other night.

"Who was that?" Baldwin asked.

"Why?"

"Your face lit up."

"Jealous?"

"A little. I doubt your face lights up like that when I text you."

"Just a friend." She hesitated. "Angela River."

"Friends with a vic, huh?"

"Yes, Cason, we can actually be friends with people even if they are victims in a criminal case. They don't suddenly have the plague."

"Whoa, easy. That's not what I meant. Just be careful is all I'm saying. I dated a girl once who was part of a case, and it screwed me hard. Turned out she was just pumping me for information about the case to pass along to the defendant, who was her ex-boyfriend. I shoulda waited until the case was over first."

The police department was off to the right. An older woman with poufy red hair greeted them at reception. Baldwin showed his badge and asked to speak with Chief Wilson. A pudgy man with a thick mustache came out of a back office wearing a police uniform with gold stars on the shoulders.

"I'm Billy Wilson."

"Cason Baldwin, FBI, and this is Jessica Yardley with the US Attorney's Office. We were hoping to steal a minute of your time, Chief."

He looked from one of them to the other. "Yeah, sure. Come on back."

The office had seventies shag carpet and no decorations other than a few medals and photos of Wilson with a SWAT team from Las Vegas.

"So just you and your one officer, huh?" Baldwin said. "I can't decide if that'd be a good or bad thing."

"Oh, definitely a good thing. We got almost no crime here, so two of us just about covers everything. The NHP handles the traffic stops; we take care of everything else." He paused and looked at both of them again. "So what's this about? Feds don't usually pop in here to say hello."

"It's an old case of yours that was expunged. We were hoping to get the original reports on it. Tucker Pharr, DOB June twelfth of sixty-six. He was arrested for—"

"Kidnapping. Yeah, I know it."

"You remember it from eighteen years ago?"

Wilson leaned back in his seat, his large belly pulling at his uniform. "I was the responding officer, and we don't get many of those. Fact, I think that's the only one in the twenty-two years since I been with the city."

"Who was the victim?" Yardley asked.

"Poor gal named Sue Ellen Jones. Fourteen years old. She was waiting for the school bus. Stop wasn't more than a hundred feet from her house. We, um, we don't know what happened to her, but we never found a body."

"Why Tucker?" Baldwin asked.

"Witness saw him. Sue Ellen's younger brother, Bobby. He was walking to the bus stop 'cause he was late getting ready." He shook his head. "Just broke Bobby when Sue Ellen was gone. Couldn't talk right or act right. Got kicked outta school and didn't graduate . . . really did a number on him."

"Parents?"

"Just the dad. The mom died of cancer when they were young."

"Dad still around?"

"No, he drank himself to death, the son of a bitch. Died of liver failure just months after Sue Ellen was taken. Bobby was put into foster care. Don't know what happened to him after that."

Yardley asked, "How did he identify Tucker as the one who kidnapped her?"

"Tucker had a truck at the time with a small bull's skull mounted on the grille, and Bobby made the truck and saw Tucker through the windshield. He ran home and told his daddy, who was too damn drunk to do anything, so Bobby ran down to the police station. Family didn't have a phone. By then Tucker was long gone."

"Why no conviction?" Yardley asked.

"Damn defense attorney, that's why. Piece'a shit named Dan Richards. Public defender out here, or was till the bastard died from a coronary."

Baldwin said, "What happened?"

"We brought Bobby with us to ID Tucker. Dan got the judge to agree we were coercive in the ID, and he tossed everything we found in his house and everything he said to us."

"You brought the only witness to ID the suspect in custody without a lineup?" Baldwin said with a tinge of disbelief.

Wilson's face flashed anger, and Yardley quickly said, "Did you find anything of Sue Ellen's in his house?"

Wilson looked away from Baldwin to her and nodded. "Her backpack. Not in the house, though. It was in a dumpster two blocks from Tucker's trailer. Found her schoolbooks in the same dumpster and some of her hair in his truck. What we think was her hair. State crime lab couldn't match it for certain. He said some odd things, too. I don't remember what they were now, but we just knew he was who took Sue Ellen." Wilson breathed out and leaned back in the chair. "Anyway, Tucker walked outta court like nothin' happened. Packed up and moved two weeks later."

Baldwin glanced at Yardley, then said, "I'd like to see the police reports and anything else you got."

Wilson shrugged. "Sure, why not. No relatives left, but if lightning strikes and you find her body, I wouldn't mind at least giving her a proper Christian burial."

17

It was evening when they headed back to Las Vegas. Baldwin drove. Wilson had told them he would have to retrieve the archived files from a storage unit uptown and that he would have his secretary scan and email everything they had on Tucker Pharr.

"It's too easy," Yardley said. "Tucker just happens to have two kidnapping charges for girls the same age as Harmony?"

"He might be trying to stop and is making it easy on us. I've seen that before."

Baldwin remembered one case from years ago: a young father and junior high school teacher. He'd been kidnapping young boys and strangling them in his basement. He would leave little items or notes near the bodies and then cover them as though ashamed. One of the items, a small toy soldier, had been handmade at his local toy store, and he'd signed the notes with his real initials. After his arrest, he had said he wanted to stop but couldn't and hoped they would arrest him.

Why he didn't just walk into a police station and turn himself in, he couldn't say. Just that whatever dark, ugly thing was inside of him wouldn't allow him to do that. The best he said he could do was leave his initials.

"If it is Tucker, why the paintings? They have nothing to do with young girls." She shook her head. "Whoever it is, he's playing with us, and we don't have a choice but to play along. He knows we have to follow every lead just in case. He's distracting us, Cason. I'm nervous he's going to do something big with this third victim and he needs us chasing shadows to do it."

"I get that feeling, too, but you're right—we have to follow everything up. I'll see if I can get someone at the PD or sheriff's to help out with Tucker so we can focus on the vics. He chose them purposely, and if we can figure out that common thread between the two of them, we'll find him."

"Two?"

"I don't think we officially group Harmony in as an Executioner vic quite yet. Tucker said she didn't talk about her mother's death or show that much of a reaction. Seems like a pretty sincere reaction to trauma to me. Something that might cause her to think it'd be better if she just left. I still think she might've run away."

"We both know that's not what happened. Not with leaving her phone and her necklace. And not showing much of a reaction could also mean a lack of sympathy. Her mother let her be abused for years. She might have a lot of anger toward her that won't let her feel for her loss."

"Maybe, but we have to work on all assumptions until we know for certain."

"Until we find her hanging from a ceiling, you mean."

A silence passed between them. Baldwin finally cleared his throat as they stopped at a red light.

"Angela River is our best source right now. It'd be easier for someone she trusts to get anything out of her we might've missed."

Yardley nodded. "I'll talk to her."

Baldwin dropped her off and told her he would email her the reports on Tucker's kidnapping cases so she stayed in the loop.

"I'll have to send them to Kyle Jax, too," Baldwin said.

"I know. It's fine."

"I'll call if there's anything else," he said.

Tara was lying on the couch watching television when Yardley came in. She wore shorts and a T-shirt and didn't look up when she said, "Made dinner. It's in the oven."

"You *made* dinner?"

"Just thought I'd be nice."

Yardley went over and kissed her head. "I appreciate that, sweetheart. We're going out tonight, though."

"Oh yeah? Where?"

"To Angie's house."

Tara stretched and turned off the television as Yardley went to the bedroom to change. She put on jeans and a blouse and had sat on the bed to zip up her boots when Tara came in. She joined her, softly tossing the remote between her hands.

"What is it?" Yardley said.

"What?"

"You can read me, but it works both ways, little miss. What's wrong?"

"I'm worried about Angie."

"Why?"

Tara shrugged. "I read the story in the *Sun* about this case. Just kinda weird that she survived, isn't it? I mean, why wouldn't the Executioner check her pulse and make sure she was dead? It just seems convenient."

"Seems convenient?" Yardley said with a grin. "I think you've been watching too much *CSI*."

Tara tilted her head, as though pondering how to phrase something. "You know that tattoo on her left shoulder? What did she tell you that means?"

"She said it's a rune meaning something along the lines of 'someone who makes their own destiny.'"

"I recognized it, so I researched it a little. That's not the literal translation. The literal translation is 'someone who fights destiny.' Why would that be so important to her she would get it tattooed?"

"Maybe Destiny was some girl she hated in high school?"

"I'm serious, Mom."

Yardley zipped up her boots and faced her. "I am so, *so* grateful that you are always looking out for me, darling, but I can look out for myself, too. I really can. All I want for you is to focus on reaching your full potential. That's why I went through everything I did, Tara. Working two jobs and going to school full-time on no sleep. Going without meals and wearing secondhand clothes with holes in them. I did all that so you would have the best chance of succeeding in life. If you really want to help me, be happy and achieve everything I know you can."

Tara nodded as though she already knew all that. "We've never really talked about what happened with Wesley."

Yardley watched her daughter. The strong facade that held a burning intelligence but also near-crippling insecurity. She didn't know who she was yet or what her place in the world was, and she was traveling a hundred miles an hour into adulthood. Forced there by a monster for a father and a mother who'd been tricked into letting his copycat into their lives.

"We don't need to talk about it. What's done is done. There's no point in rehashing it. But Tara . . . *never* again. I don't want you to even know about my cases, so stop reading the media on them. Focus on school and work."

Tara tossed the remote on the bed behind her. "I know. But . . . you're all I got."

She said it with a sadness that pierced Yardley. She reached out for her daughter, but Tara had already risen and was heading out of the bedroom.

The home was in the center of the city, not far from the Las Vegas Strip. Two stories, a large lawn, and a horseshoe driveway with a Mercedes parked in front.

"Nice," Tara said as they headed to the front door. "If you're gonna make friends, make sure they're rich, right?"

They got to the front porch, and Yardley said, "Best behavior, little miss."

"What, do you think I'm gonna get drunk and punch someone out?"

"Sometimes you amuse yourself by playing with other people. The universe didn't give you that intelligence to toy with others. So please, not here."

"The *universe*? Wow, you really have been spending a lot of time with her, haven't you?"

"Just best behavior. Please."

Yardley rang the doorbell. A man in a white shirt answered. Slim and with curly brown hair, he somehow looked like a conservative politician. Not at all who Yardley would have pictured River dating.

"You must be Jessica," he said, holding out his hand. Yardley shook it. "And Tara, right?"

"Yeah," she said, with her best fake smile.

"Michael Zachary. So nice to meet you both. Come in."

The interior was as exquisite as the exterior. A large atrium, a winding staircase leading up to the second floor, and South Asian art on the walls. A bust of the Buddha sat next to the door on a white pillar, and across the room was another Buddha made of copper.

River came out of the kitchen and said, "Hey!"

She gave Yardley a hug and then hugged Tara.

"I'm so excited you guys came."

Yardley said, "Your house is beautiful, Angie."

"It's technically Zachary's house, but who's keeping track, right?"

"This place kicks ass," Tara said. She looked to her mother, who gave her a disapproving glare. "I mean, you have a lovely home. And car. And I love these paintings, too. Actually, I love this whole place, it's awesome."

"Aren't you sweet. Well, let me show you around."

River led them through the home while Zachary excused himself to catch up on some paperwork in his study. They went to the bedroom, which was massive and taken up by a bed that could easily fit eight people and was bolted to the wall, making it appear like it was hovering in the air. The walk-in closet was the size of a small apartment, and the bathroom was just as large. The toilet was light-blue marble, as was the bidet.

"Two toilets?" Tara said.

"It's a bidet. You've never seen one?"

"Never even heard of it."

River pushed down the handle, and water bubbled up in a stream.

"Oh," Tara said. "Genius."

They made their way to the pool in the backyard. A large white rectangle with deep-blue tile and lights on each wall. The water moved in small waves, reflecting the light beautifully at all angles. Two statues stood by the stairs that led down into the pool from the shallow end.

"I *love* this pool," Tara said.

"Hey, we barely use it. I only uncover it to cool it down. Come over anytime."

"Seriously?"

"Sure. Bring your friends, too."

Yardley said, "You don't have to do that, Angie."

"No, I want to. It'd be nice to hear some kids running around." She cleared her throat and looked back at the house. "Dinner's almost done. Hope you guys are hungry."

Dinner was pleasant, filled with stories of River's travels around the world—interactions with native tribes in the Amazon, surfing at a shoreline infested with great white sharks in South Africa, smoking pot in Amsterdam with police officers at a park. All things Yardley thought sounded . . . magical.

She also learned that River and Zachary had been talking about marriage and agreed that they would take Angela's last name, not the name Zachary. Because, as River said, she'd be damned if she let the patriarchy tell her what to name herself.

Yardley said good night around ten, and River hugged her and said she would text her tomorrow. She gave Tara a hug, too, and repeated that she was free to come over with her friends anytime to use the pool.

Zachary shook hands and then disappeared into the house again. During dinner, he had seemed uncomfortable. Yardley had noticed several obsessive behaviors. His food was arranged symmetrically on his plate, his napkin folded precisely at right angles, fork always on the left, knife on the right. She wondered if it had anything to do with what River had mentioned about Zachary's discomfort with what had happened to her.

When they got home, Yardley stopped the car out front and said, "I have to meet with someone for a minute. Turn on the alarm as soon as you get in."

"I'll probably crash at Stacey's, if that's cool. Her house is closer to the lab, anyway."

"That's fine. Just make sure to—"

"Call you if I go anywhere else. Yeah, I know the drill, Il Duce."

"Tara, that's not funny."

She smiled as she got out of the car. Yardley watched her until she was inside and then watched the alarm app on her phone. She didn't drive until Tara had set the alarm.

As she pulled away, she felt crushing angst. She was about to visit someone who was going to bring up a lot of memories she'd buried deep and didn't want dug up. But the Executioner hadn't given her a choice.

18

The reports weren't long. Baldwin read them on his phone, sitting at a table on the outdoor patio of a burger joint. Night had fallen and the moon was out.

He absently dipped fries in ketchup and chewed much longer than he needed to, fully aware that he didn't even taste them. His mind was elsewhere: inside the Pharrs' home. Trying to picture what life was like between Harmony and Tucker, and if he was actually the man who'd taken Sue Ellen Jones.

Baldwin took out the photograph Tucker had given him of Harmony. She had a wide smile, sapphire eyes, and curly hair. Baldwin had known the second he'd seen her who she reminded him of.

Baldwin had been the youngest person ever to make detective in the San Francisco Police Department, and once there, he cleared case after case to get to where he really wanted to go: Robbery-Homicide. After the death of his mother at the hands of her boyfriend, something the man was never prosecuted for, Baldwin couldn't imagine being anywhere but at the Homicide table.

One of his first cases involved a thirteen-year-old girl, Anne Gordan. The SFPD had their own Child Abuse Unit that handled crimes involving children, but Baldwin had inherited her disappearance as part of the murder investigation of her aunt, who Anne had lived with. After Anne's drunken father murdered her aunt, she ran out into the street and to a nearby public park to get away from him. She was never seen again.

Baldwin had hunted for her like a bloodhound with a scent. During the day, he kept her picture up at his desk, and at night he began to dream about her. He saw her places he went: grocery stores and movie theaters and shopping malls. One time he even grabbed a young girl by the arm, thinking she was her.

The break came seven weeks after her disappearance. A narcs detective had arrested someone who said he had information about "the pretty girl on the milk cartons." Baldwin interviewed him. He said she'd been sold overseas. The first time he said it, Baldwin asked him to repeat it because he thought he had misheard.

"Sold, man. You know, like a car or something. She just merchandise."

Baldwin grabbed him by the back of the head and slammed his face into the desk. The other detective in the room had to pull him off, or he would've done worse.

In exchange for dropping his drug charges, the man gave them the last location he'd seen Anne Gordan. At a storage company that rented units out to pimps and human traffickers who needed somewhere to stash their victims until they could arrange passage to Mexico or the Middle East. Baldwin was the first to open the storage unit, without waiting for a warrant, and was hit with the stench of feces and urine but no Anne. The traffickers had cleared out the unit. Baldwin later learned that he had missed her by two hours. Two measly hours could have saved her a life of torture and slavery.

Two hours, he thought as he stared at Harmony's photo.

He put the photo down. He had to get his mind off the past and focus on the present.

He returned to the reports on Sue Ellen Jones.

The reports were only five pages because they had nothing but circumstantial evidence, and weak circumstantial evidence at that. Sue

Ellen's backpack was found in a dumpster behind a grocery store two and a half blocks away from where Tucker Pharr lived. Some of her clothes were found there as well, but not in the same dumpster. Chief Wilson knew Tucker lived nearby and immediately took Bobby, her brother who had seen the kidnapping, to Tucker's trailer. No request for a warrant, no lineup, no photographic lineup; nothing other than taking him to the house and pointing to Tucker, who was in handcuffs already, and saying, "That him?" A clear violation of the Fourth and Fifth Amendments and about a century of caselaw. The police couldn't just point to someone and say *Is that him?* because the likelihood of a false ID was too high, and any subsequent ID, even if done in a lineup, would be tainted because the witness had already seen who they were supposed to pick out.

The chief was upset with the public defender, but the evidence had been suppressed because of sloppy police work.

When the chief and two detectives from a nearby city searched Tucker's truck, they found one long blond hair on the floor mat. The DNA analysis done could only identify it as human. No certainty on gender or age. But it was the same length of hair Sue Ellen had at the time of her disappearance. No other evidence had been found.

Baldwin read Tucker's statements during the interview after they'd searched his trailer and truck. It was an odd series of "I didn't do it, but if I had, I would've . . ." He seemed to be saying it was possible he would have killed her, but he hadn't, because he'd do it differently if it were him. According to Tucker, he wouldn't kidnap a girl in broad daylight at a bus stop. He would wait until she was out at night sometime and pick her up on some pretense involving her parents. Maybe show her a fake badge.

It was an odd way to say he was innocent, but Baldwin had seen it plenty of times before. Tucker had likely been high at the time. And the scenario he described, patiently waiting for the child to be in a vulnerable position and using a pretense of parents in trouble to get the child into the car, was found in a pamphlet that had been circulating in pedophilia circles. This wasn't a one-off: if Tucker had read the handbook, it meant he was going to the dark net pedophilia forums online, and Baldwin had a feeling the two girls weren't the only victims.

He ran through some possibilities: Either Tucker Pharr was the Executioner and wanted to get caught and thought this was the best way, or he was just too dumb to realize that killing his wife and daughter would put the focus of the investigation entirely on him. Or this mystery man that Harmony's testimony had gotten put away really had been released and decided to come looking for the Pharr family. Though that wouldn't explain why Angela River was mixed up in this.

Baldwin sighed and mumbled, "I'm so sick of you psycho pieces'a shit."

He had turned his phone to airplane mode to concentrate better and changed it back now. It buzzed with a text. From Scarlett.

"Shit," he said. He'd forgotten they'd made plans to have dinner at her house. He hurriedly gathered his trash while he read the text.

Since it seems like you're not going to bother to make it over here, I guess I'll just tell you over text. I'm pregnant.

Baldwin froze, one hand above the trash can. "Shit," he said again.

19

Yardley hadn't been to the Little SoHo neighborhood for years. Named after the bohemian mecca in New York, Little SoHo in Vegas boasted yoga studios, bars, art studios, chic salons, and a couple of sex toy stores.

The art studio was in the same space it had been for twenty years. It moved into the area when this was still a run-down, drug-centered neighborhood where tenants couldn't move out fast enough. The owner of the studio, Jill Perry, had known the area would be revitalized at some point, so she'd bought the building for pennies on the dollar. She'd used it to showcase up-and-coming artists that had caught her eye. The place looked empty now, and Yardley guessed it wouldn't be long before it was sold to a Starbucks or H&M.

The last time Yardley had walked into this building, she was holding Eddie Cal's hand, and they'd kissed before they went inside.

Yardley felt her heart in her throat. She had to swallow and then close her eyes, picturing a calm stream with sunlight coming through trees lining the riverbank, a stick of bamboo drifting lazily by. Once she'd counted to ten, she opened her eyes and went in.

The studio was empty of customers and had closed half an hour ago. The doors were unlocked. The space was open and wide: hardwood floors with white walls. Paintings hung equal distance from each other, interspersed with sculptures. One painting caught Yardley's eye. A young girl reaching for the sun, her face serene. But her other hand had been seized by something coming up from the ground, preventing her from grasping the sun.

"That's an exquisite piece," a female voice said.

Yardley turned to see Perry come out from an office. She folded her hands in front of her as she stood beside Yardley.

"The artist suffered from schizophrenia. She said that this is what she feels like. That she's fully aware how she needs to behave and can identify the behaviors she knows are dangerous and spurred by false beliefs, but that she's helpless to stop them. As if something is holding her back. A prisoner in her own mind."

Yardley turned back to the painting. "It's beautiful . . . and tragic."

"Wouldn't you describe all of life that way?"

Yardley fully faced her now. "You haven't aged much."

"No stress of a husband or children. I'd heard you had a daughter."

"I do. She's seventeen now."

Perry nodded. "It's strange: I'm starting to forget what my father looked like. He's becoming just a hazy face, but I remember perfectly the last time I saw you. Edward had his arm around you, and you told him how proud you were of him. Odd what the mind chooses to remember and what to forget, isn't it?"

Eddie Cal's paintings and sculptures had frequently been featured at Perry's gallery before his arrest. In a review in the *Las Vegas Sun*, she had once called him an unparalleled genius and said that he would go down in history as America's Picasso. Perry and Cal had developed a close relationship, and Yardley had always worried that they might have been having an affair. It seemed almost funny now to think that *that* was the secret she was concerned about with her husband.

"I need your help with something, Jill," Yardley said.

Perry folded her arms. "I'm listening."

"Sarpong. His *The Night Things* series. I need to know about it. And I don't just mean what I can read on Wikipedia and art history blogs. I need to know what it signifies."

"Why?"

"I'm a prosecutor now. I'm helping in the investigation of a case where someone is copying *The Night Things* with real victims."

Perry's eyebrows rose. "Those wouldn't be easy to pull off."

"May we sit down in your office?"

Her office was small and cramped but tasteful. White walls with only one blue painting behind the glass desk. Yardley took out her phone. She opened it to photos of the Kathy Pharr crime scene, and then an artist's rendering of how Angela River's body had been found.

"The second victim survived."

Perry took a long time examining each one. When she was through, she quietly said, "Incredible."

She was impressed, and it sickened Yardley, though she kept her face passive.

"Sarpong was a misogynist," Yardley said. "That much is clear. It could be what the killer's doing, identifying with a kindred spirit by making his art come to life, but I don't think that's the angle he's taking. There's something about these paintings that resonates with him, and I need help figuring out what that is."

Perry glanced through the photos and drawings once more, then leaned into her high-backed leather chair. "Sarpong's a difficult one. He gave no interviews, none of his four wives gave any interviews, none of his mistresses talked, and he had almost no close friends. The only things we know about him are written by his competitors at the time. It's almost as if Sarpong said to history, *No comment.* Everything you've read about him online is pure conjecture. We just don't know enough about his life to say what this work means."

"You have a doctorate in art history and are the most knowledgeable artist I know. You have to have some idea."

Perry grinned and said, "I am not the most knowledgeable artist you know."

Yardley suddenly felt nauseated. A similar feeling to trying to read in a fast-moving car. Vertigo almost.

Perry was right. Eddie Cal had insight into the artistic works of others in a way Yardley had never seen in another person. It was as if paintings were windows into the minds of the artists for him.

"Getting his opinion is out of the question."

Perry exhaled through her nose and watched Yardley a moment. "You look luminous. You have pain inside you, that's clear, but it only adds to your allure. I would love to sculpt you some time."

"Help me catch him and you can sculpt me all you want."

She chuckled. "I'm afraid I can't help you much there. Sarpong's paintings are lost on me. I just see torture and death. None of the scenes seem linked in any way except that the victims are wearing black and have those bloody bandages wrapped around them. If you were asking my expert opinion—say, for a review in a magazine—I would write that the artist conjures images stolen from our nightmares that grip us with both dread and enchanting mystery and yet somehow seem so familiar as to be almost comfortable. It insinuates that the artist is expressing not just his nightmare but our collective nightmare as a species. The fact that many psychotherapists own replicas of these paintings and hang them in their offices testifies to that fact."

"And what about your real opinion?"

"My real opinion is that he was batshit crazy and these paintings are the ravings of a lunatic. They don't mean anything. I'm sorry, but you won't find the man committing these crimes by exposing some hidden theme in these paintings. Whatever theme the man sees in them is written there by himself."

Yardley took back her phone. "I appreciate your time."

Just as she rose and turned to leave, Perry said, "It might be worth it."

Yardley turned to her.

"It might be worth it to visit with him, Jessica."

"I did. Two years ago on something else. And it almost got me killed."

Perry nodded and put her feet up on the desk, white heels clicking against the glass. "You want to ask me if we were having an affair, don't you? I know you wanted to know back then."

"I don't think it matters now."

She smiled. "Doesn't it?"

They were silent awhile.

"We weren't. I wanted to. I tried one night, actually. He said no. That he was faithful to you. Quite rare in a man to be able to deny someone who is so connected to him, heart and soul. Do you know about twin souls? It's a theory that we all have a twin soul, a soul identical to ours that we meet out there in our lives when we're ready. We fall for them because we connect so deeply on a physical, spiritual, and mental level, but the twin soul is not a sexual relationship. Sex is crude. Primitive. The twin soul is far deeper, and the train wrecks of marriages you see are from people trying to make a romantic relationship work with their twin souls, rather than recognizing it's deeper than that. Your soul mate, who you should be in a romantic relationship with, and your twin soul, who you should be in a spiritual relationship with, are not the same thing. But when you meet your twin soul, it's like the rest of the world disappears, and there's nothing you want more than to be with them." She paused and seemed lost in thought a moment. "I was Edward's twin soul. You must have really had a hold on him for him to not even be tempted to make love to me."

"You say he's your twin soul with pride. Do you still admire him?"

Perry raised an eyebrow. "What can I say? I'm a sucker for the disturbed artist. Caravaggio was a murderer. Cellini murdered multiple people and the local villagers let him go unpunished because they were such admirers of his art. Banksy today is greatly admired, and yet he's truly little more than a criminal."

"If you don't see the difference between putting graffiti on a building and slaughtering families, then you've crossed into a place I can't follow."

"I'm simply saying that great art occasionally comes from great insanity. I don't hold what Edward did against him. I doubt he had any more control over it than we do breathing."

She smiled, a smile that Yardley sensed came from a place of enjoying the pain she knew she was causing.

Perry took her feet off the desk. "We were the two people in the world who were closest to Edward. His soul mate and his twin soul. And you and I know the truth: that we knew what he was. Must've been difficult for you to act like the surprised wife after he was caught." She clicked her tongue against her teeth. "Such a shame. He was absolutely drop-dead gorgeous. Do they allow conjugal visits in prison for non-spouses, you think?"

Yardley watched her a moment and grinned. "You know, I used to be jealous of you. Of your confidence and the fact that you had a successful business, and I was just a struggling photographer. Of your intelligence and pedigree. But what I see now when I look around your gallery that no one probably comes to anymore, and the extensive nips and tucks that've made your face appear like plastic over a skull? I see a woman terrified of the world and hiding here to seem like she's not. I envied you when I should have pitied you."

Perry's eyes narrowed to slits.

"Goodbye, Jill. Hope business picks up."

Yardley was out the door when Perry shouted, "If you want to catch your man, you'll have to visit Edward. Tell him hello for me."

Yardley stood still for a second before walking to her car in the dark night.

20

Yardley wasn't able to sleep.

Every ounce of strength felt like it had been sapped from her. Like someone had stuck a spigot into her and extracted the last drop she had.

She checked on Tara and saw her asleep in her room, music still coming from her earbuds. Yardley gently took them out and turned her phone off. As quietly as she could, she bent down and softly kissed her daughter's forehead before leaving the room.

Yardley had grown accustomed to not having anyone in her life other than her daughter. She didn't live with Wesley Paul that long, and before that, she was alone for years after Cal's arrest, and before Eddie Cal, she was alone for almost a decade after the death of her mother when Yardley was eighteen. And she was alone now and thought there was a chance she always would be.

A shattered heart.

Loneliness could be adapted to. It could get so she wouldn't even notice it anymore and being around others would just feel like a special occasion. But these moments, the middle of the night when the rest of the world slept, were the loneliest of the day. The time when she most felt isolated from the world.

She changed into sweatpants and a T-shirt and went to the fridge. Her phone vibrated. It was a text from River asking if she was still up. Yardley said she was, and a moment later her phone rang.

"This is Jessica," Yardley said.

"Do you always answer the phone like that?"

"Like what?"

"Saying your name. You knew it was me, right? Why not just say *Hi, Angie,* or something like that?"

Yardley took out some cream cheese and bread and got down a plate from the cupboard. "Hi, Angie."

She chuckled. "Okay, smart-ass. But seriously, I like to give people the best greeting I can. Like if I know their name, I say, *Hi, Dean,* or whatever. It costs me nothing and perks up their day a little, ya know?"

"I'm not sure I've ever thought about how to greet people."

"You should. It helps to make others happy, even if it's just something small. Gets your mind off your own problems."

Yardley put her bread in the toaster and set the timer.

"What're you making?" River asked.

"Toast and cream cheese, and I'll put some lox on it from yesterday."

"Ugh. There's some gambling. Old fish is scary. When I was, like, twenty, this roommate I lived with made tilapia, and I swear I've never had food poisoning so bad in my life. Had to sleep in the bathtub if you know what I mean."

"Ew, Angie."

"Don't do it, have some Cap'n Crunch."

"I don't have any cereal."

"Pour a glass of wine with me, then. I'm sitting on my porch with pinot grigio. You got any pinot?"

"Let me check . . . I do."

"Pour a glass and sit on your balcony."

Yardley poured the wine and went out onto the balcony. The sky was a deep black, painted with sparkling jewels of stars and planets. She had never seen skies this clear anywhere but the deserts of the Southwest on moonless nights.

"What are you doing now?" River asked.

"Lying on my deck chair staring at the sky."

"You see that really bright one to the west? That's Venus."

"Wait . . . yeah, I think I see it."

"It's the brightest thing in the sky next to the moon. I used to lay around and stare at it and pretend I would make it there one day. That if I could concentrate hard enough, I would just appear there. Zachary, always the scientist of course, reminded me that it's hot enough to melt steel on the surface and everything's orange. He said it's similar to what we think of as hell, or the valley in LA."

Yardley chuckled as she sipped her wine. "That's a creative way to describe it."

"It's a boring way. I pictured oceans of jewels and a bright-purple sky. My version is way better. Why picture hell when you can picture paradise, right?" She sighed. "That's the difference between me and Zachary, I guess. He likes to live in the real world, and I think the real world is boring." Yardley heard River take a drink. "What about you? Where do you fall on the Angela-Zachary spectrum?"

"Between spacey dreamer and scientist?"

"Hey, I'm not spacey. I'm an optimist."

"I'm kidding."

"Oh. It's hard to tell. You can keep a straight face unlike anyone I've ever seen. So where?"

Yardley leaned her head back, watching the sparkling glow of Venus. "I've never given Venus a second thought. I figured I would never see it, so there was no point in conjecture. I only care about things within my control."

River laughed. "Honey, nothing is within our control." She inhaled deeply, and they both sat in silence a moment. Yardley took another sip of wine that warmed her belly.

"Do you miss him sometimes?" River said.

"Who? Eddie?"

"Yes."

"No."

"Jess, it's just us. Do you miss him?"

Yardley hesitated. She wasn't used to opening up, and letting her guard down to do so was not something she was comfortable with. But there was something disarming about River. She was the type of person Yardley *wanted* to open up to, for a reason she couldn't actually name. "Sometimes, maybe. The person he was before I found out who he really was."

"What do you miss about him?"

Yardley curled her legs up. "He could always make me laugh. More than any person I've ever met. No matter where we were, whether it was starving in a two-hundred-dollar-a-month apartment or at one of his five-thousand-dollar-a-plate art functions, he always made me laugh." She looked down at the glass in her hand and the way the starlight reflected off it in a soft pale glow.

"How was he in the sack?"

"Ew, Angie."

River laughed. "I picture you guys having sex with your clothes on. And only missionary and only to procreate. Am I right?"

"Angie, stop," she said, with a flush in her cheeks.

"What? If he's as buttoned down as you, how else would it happen?"

Yardley was silent a moment. "I wasn't always this way. You wouldn't have recognized me before . . . before him."

"Yeah, hey, I'm sorry I brought this up. I was just joking. We can talk about something else."

"No, it's fine. It's just . . . I've never told anyone else these things. Not even my therapist."

"Well, no wonder. Talk about a rip-off. Pay one-fifty an hour and just have someone stare at you and say, *And how did that make you feel?* It's bullshit."

"You've been?"

"It was a long time ago."

"What for?"

"I went through some things as a teenager that I needed to work through. Everyone thought therapy would help. I thought it made it worse. The therapist kept telling me to forgive, forgive and let go. I was like, 'You forgive. Let's see you go through this shit and see how you let go.' It was all bullshit. People giving you advice they would never follow themselves." She blew out a long breath. "Sorry."

"Nothing to apologize for. I've found it to be helpful, though. To have someone that you can say anything to and not have them judge you."

"That's why we have friends." River inhaled deeply, as though clearing her lungs, and said, "So . . . on to something more important: I saw a picture of Eddie online. He was seriously hot. I got a young–Marlon Brando vibe."

"That's how he got the moniker Dark Casanova. Some reporter said he looked like what James Dean would've looked like if he was older."

"Shit, I'll tell ya, for a guy who looks like that, I'd put up with a little serial murder here and there."

A long silence.

"Sorry, bad joke," River said. "I told you, I have a big mouth that works faster than my brain sometimes."

"It's okay. I'm not used to talking about this with anybody, but I'm *certainly* not used to laughing about it."

"You gotta laugh about it, babe. You can laugh about it or have it break you; those are the choices."

Yardley sipped her wine and changed the subject. They spoke of old boyfriends, of what high school was like, of which types of girls bullied them. Then they spent half an hour on Facebook looking up girls they'd disliked in high school and seeing what they were up to and whether they were on their second or third marriages.

By the time Yardley said good night and hung up, the sun was almost up. She hadn't talked to someone on the phone, really talked, since . . . Eddie Cal. It filled her with both excitement and a sense of dread. People she let in had a tendency to hurt her.

21

In the morning, Yardley drank down a cup of coffee and a bottle of water. She had a headache and took ibuprofen and changed into jeans. She didn't feel like driving today, so she called an Uber and waited by the curb.

The sun boiled the city. She checked the temperature on her phone: 110.

The office felt like a cave, and instead of staying, she called another car and went to a public park. They had picnic tables set up near a playground, and she sat and watched children playing, their parents standing around making small talk.

Her phone rang. A Boston number.

"How are you, Daniel?" she answered.

She had put in a request with Dr. Daniel Sarte, a professor of psychiatry at Harvard and consultant with the FBI, for anything he could dig up about *The Night Things*.

"I'm doing well. Have a bit of a cold, so not teaching today. I've been studying your mystery man over there. Fascinating case."

"Unless you're the Pharr or River family."

"Of course. I apologize. I didn't mean to be flippant."

"No, it's fine. I just have a headache right now and didn't sleep much. What did you find out?"

He sighed, and she could hear the cellophane wrapper of what was probably some over-the-counter medication. "I spoke to my colleague here at the art history department who specializes in twentieth-century African art. He actually met Sarpong once. Anyway, apparently Sarpong was a biologist or at least had a biology degree from the University of Khartoum in Sudan. Sarpong was obsessed with human evolution. He believed that humans were inherently good, but that evolution gave us the ability to turn our morality off. Like a switch. This was so that, in survival situations where our self-interest was at stake, we could do what we needed to do. But Sarpong believed that evolution had also done something far more devastating than Freud could have imagined: it hides when our morality is shut off."

She watched one of the children run off from the playground and her mother chase her, stopping her just before she got to the parking lot.

"What does that mean?" Yardley said.

"Sarpong thought that every evil action humans commit is because of this evolutionary adaptation and our inability to recognize that our morality's been turned off. That's why seemingly good people can rape and murder in times of war and not feel guilt, or why prison guards can murder and torture and still believe themselves moral people. Evolution gave us the ability to trick ourselves. *The Night Things* is Sarpong exploring that. All four paintings are victims of someone who has turned their morality off but doesn't know that it's off. They think they're creating art. This colleague believes that whoever is recreating these paintings with living people isn't an artist, which is what I'm guessing law enforcement believes, but is someone obsessed with human evolution. Perhaps an anthropologist or a biologist of some kind. A physician. The paintings are about biology, not art."

"A physician?"

"Yes. Sarpong wanted initially to go into medicine, and who studies the human body and mind more than physicians?"

Yardley considered this a moment. "I'd like to speak with your colleague."

"I'll text you her phone number."

"I appreciate this, Daniel. Thank you."

"Not a problem. I'm also sending the profile to you that Agent Baldwin requested. Please keep me updated on your progress and let me know if there's anything else."

"I will, thank you."

"Oh, and Jessica?"

"Yes?"

"There is one more thing, if I may. My own two cents. I would wager this type of offender is rather proud of their work and wishes for recognition. If you were to rob them of this recognition as a tactic to draw them out, it may get them to do something drastic."

"Drastic?"

"You are the prosecutor on this case, a female prosecutor, and both victims are female. He might see it as some sort of accomplishment to put you into his work. Please, be careful."

An icy chill slid up her back. "I will."

22

The office felt claustrophobic, and Yardley couldn't concentrate. She sat at her desk staring at walls, thinking about what Dr. Sarte had said.

A physician.

One of the custodians for the building walked past the office and then came back around the other way, checking the name on the door.

"Ms. Yardley? I'm here to change the nameplate. I can come back later if it's better."

"No, it's fine. Go ahead."

She watched as he took her name down from the door and put up Jax's name. He brought the nameplate over and handed it to her.

"Sometimes people like to hang on to these."

Yardley took the nameplate and stared at it awhile. Then she put it in the trash and picked up her purse. There was someone she needed to speak with.

—

Redwood Regional Hospital was a small hospital not far from where River lived. Yardley had been here once before, though she couldn't remember now what it was in connection to. Perhaps to see one of the countless victims she had to visit in hospitals. Sometimes she smelled the scent of antiseptic in her dreams.

The emergency room wasn't busy, and the front desk staff sat behind a counter with a police officer behind them.

"Hi, I'd like to speak with Dr. Zachary, please. I'm a friend."

"He went to get something to eat at the cafeteria. Down the hall to the right."

The cafeteria looked out onto a garden that had a walkway connecting the two buildings of the hospital. Several staff and nurses were there with a few doctors. She saw Zachary sitting by himself at a table in the corner.

He looked surprised when he saw her. "Jessica?" He stood up and gave her a hug. "What are you doing here?"

"Some of our victims are brought here," she said. "Not my favorite place to be, as you can guess."

He nodded and looked down at his chicken and mashed potatoes. "Yeah, I see a lot of those. We see the same women over and over, beaten and burned, tied up . . . even when they cooperate with the police, it seems like no one really does anything."

"Mind if I sit?"

"Not at all."

She sat down and crossed her legs, putting on her friendliest grin. "We try to do the best we can, but our budgets are constantly cut. Police departments are the biggest part of the budget for most cities, so when they need to shrink costs, they cut police, and the prosecutor's offices get cut as well. Same on the federal level. When the FBI gets cut, the US Attorney's Office isn't far behind."

He took a bite of food. "I'm not judging, really, I'm not. I just wish I didn't have to see the same victims over and over."

She nodded. "Speaking of, how's Angie doing?"

He chewed a second and wiped his lips with a napkin. "She's tough. Keeps everything bottled up, so it's hard to gauge sometimes."

"How did you two meet, if you don't mind my asking?"

"She came into the hospital for an injury to her hand. She was cutting vegetables, and the knife slipped and dug into her palm." He leaned back in the seat with a grin on his face as he chewed. "Love at first sight, I guess. I think we talked for three hours over dinner the next night. She moved in with me two months later."

"Love at first sight. That's rare these days."

He nodded. "It was strange for me because she's so different from other women I've dated. She's very spiritual. Doesn't have much faith in science."

Yardley watched him take another bite. "That seems to be gaining momentum these days," she said. "Losing faith in science. Evolution seems to be particularly battered."

He shrugged. "I suppose it's been like that since the publication of *On the Origin of Species*. That's why Darwin was initially going to wait to have it published posthumously. He knew how people would react. Anything that challenges the notion that we're the center of the universe rattles people, and they'll fight against it."

"It's funny we're talking about this, because I heard an interesting theory involving evolutionary psychology the other day. That evolution has given us the ability to turn our morality off in situations our brain believes involve self-preservation, but that it's also given us the ability to mask when our morality is off. What do you think about that?"

He put his napkin on his plate before he pushed it away. "An interesting theory. But I wouldn't give evolutionary psychology too much praise just yet. It's still in its infancy." He checked his watch. "It was good seeing you, but I gotta get back."

"Of course. Sorry to keep you."

"Don't be, it was a pleasure. I'll tell Angie you said hello."

She watched as he threw his paper plate in the trash and headed back down the hall to the emergency room. He glanced back to her once before disappearing around a corner.

When Yardley went home that afternoon, she kept running one thing through her mind to the exclusion of all else: cause of death. How was it that the Clark County Office of the Coroner and Medical Examiner, consisting of some of the brightest pathologists in the world, couldn't identify what caused the organ failure that had led to Kathy Pharr's death?

When she arrived home, Tara had just gotten back from her internship. She was sitting at the dining table with textbooks spread in front of her, but she wasn't working on anything. Just staring into space. Yardley had found that her daughter could be lost in thought for hours, and she remembered a story from college that Socrates was once lost in thought in the middle of a battle as a young man—standing perfectly still in contemplation as death raged all around him.

Tara slowly blinked as Yardley came closer.

"Where were you just now?" Yardley asked, kicking off her heels.

"Debating something. How was work?"

Yardley shrugged as she went to the fridge to begin dinner. "Same as always." She paused a moment, then shut the fridge and looked at Tara. At the fierce intelligence that always burned just behind her eyes. Yardley went and sat down next to her. "You have a lot of knowledge of advanced chemistry, don't you?"

Tara shrugged. "Yeah, but only in relation to physical chemistry. I thought it was interesting for a while."

"If I wanted to kill somebody and conceal the cause of death from the medical examiner, what do you think would be the best way to do that?"

Tara grinned. "What an odd question to ask your teenage daughter."

Yardley looked at the title of her textbook. "*Reimann's Hypothesis and Dirichlet L-series Conjectures* . . . I don't think it's a big leap to assume you may have some insight into it."

Tara leaned back in her seat and thought a moment. "Obviously it couldn't be anything that left any type of physical evidence, so the only route is poison. I assume you have a forensic toxicologist who ran assays?"

"A dozen of them."

"So the way it works is you'd have to test for a particular class on the periodic table, and then you'd have to screen for specific molecules of the suspected class, like arsenic or deadly nightshade. But all those are detectable. The only one I can think of where there's no validated assays for detection is ricin."

"Ricin?"

Tara nodded. "The tests you'd need to perform to confirm ricin poisoning are really specific. You can't even test it in fluids. You have to do polymerase chain reactions with DNA to confirm it's there. And it's so rare your toxicologists wouldn't even think to screen for it, and even if they did, they still might not pick it up if enough molecules aren't there."

Yardley had dealt with a couple of poisonings before and had come across a bit of research that suggested if a person wanted to kill using poison, ingestion was not the best method, as traces of the poison would be found in the stomach or intestines. Injection was cleaner and less detectable, and the areas of the body that were best for injection, that had the least chance of being noticed in an autopsy, were the tongue and eyes.

She kissed her daughter, took out her phone, and then hurried to her home office to make some calls.

23

Baldwin got out of the shower and dressed. It was late, but he'd finally made the call he owed to Scarlett. It had gone about as poorly as he expected. He'd tried to explain to her all the reasons he wasn't cut out to be a father—his job, the fact that he hadn't exactly had good role models growing up, his temperament that led him to frequently need solitude. Even as he'd offered to pay for her abortion, convincing himself he was doing the right thing, he'd winced at what a cliché he sounded like. That she'd screamed at him and hung up wasn't a surprise. He wished it could just go back to how it was and then thought how childish it was to wish for things to happen. His mother had once told him, "If wishes were horses, even beggars would ride." He hadn't understood it at the time but now knew she meant if wishes had any power, no one would be destitute.

He looked at himself in the mirror before going out to his living room. The Executioner files were spread out on the table and spilled over onto the floor. He took out the photograph of Harmony and looked at it a moment before going to the kitchen and getting some Scotch Tape. Then he went back to the bathroom and taped it to his mirror, in the upper right corner, where he was sure to see it every time he was in there.

He sighed and wondered what the hell he was doing. Then his phone rang. It was Yardley.

"Hey," he said.

"I think it's ricin, Cason."

"Who is this?"

"Cason—"

"Easy, I'm kidding. What do you think is ricin?"

"I think he used ricin to kill Kathy Pharr and tried to kill Angie with it but didn't succeed for some reason."

Baldwin turned around and leaned against his sink. "The toxicologist spent a week—"

"He wouldn't have tested for ricin. It's a really specific test that takes a long time, and there probably has to be evidence that it was used before they test for it. Call them and ask. And I called the ME and asked if they checked for injection sites in the tongue and eyes."

"You didn't think they did?"

"They did, but not well enough. Use a thin enough gauge of needle, and it's almost impossible to detect in those sites."

Baldwin let out a deep breath, thinking about the stacks of paperwork he was about to commit himself to. "Okay, I'll place some calls and get the labs at Quantico to go over everything themselves."

"Thank you. I appreciate this, Cason."

He hesitated a second. "How you holding up? You're getting close to your last day."

"I'm fine. Just please let me know as soon as you have anything."

"I will."

They hung up. Briefly, he wondered what life would've been like with Yardley. He'd had a chance with her long ago, and looking back on it now, he could see why it hadn't worked out. It had nothing to do with her and everything to do with him and this job. Would the job destroy any relationship he could hope to have with a child, too? He didn't know, but he had always hoped he wouldn't have to find out.

He took a deep breath, then dialed his contact at Quantico and the Trace Evidence Laboratory in Washington.

24

It was nightfall later in the week when Baldwin showed up at Yardley's house. She let him in. Tara was sitting at the table doing homework, and Baldwin said, "What's up, squirt?"

"I'm going to be taller than you soon, Cason. Can I call you squirt?"

"Absolutely not. I'll have to arrest you."

She grinned, not looking up from her equations. "I happen to have a connection at the US Attorney's Office who wouldn't stand for that."

Yardley said, "Out here."

She led Baldwin out to the balcony, where two tiki torches illuminated the table. It was crammed with documents.

"I looked through Kathy's phone records you sent me. There were calls to a number I couldn't place, until I contacted the phone company after sending a subpoena. It was Dr. Zachary's cell number. And take a look at this." She handed him a printout. A phone number was circled with pen. "That's Kathy Pharr's personal cell number on his phone records. They were calling each other."

"You're kidding?"

She shook her head. "April thirteenth is the day she died. Three calls the previous day. He placed at least half a dozen calls to her that month alone. Angie told me she thought he was having an affair, but she didn't say with who. I think Michael Zachary was having an affair with Kathy Pharr."

"Hmm," he said, sitting down at the table.

"That's it?"

He blew out a breath between pressed lips. "Ran a deep background on Tucker. His grandfather owned a property out here that he scooped up when he got back from the Pacific after the war. Tucker lived with him after his father died. Guess the address."

Yardley's heart dropped. "Crimson Lake Road."

He nodded. "Tucker's mom was MIA when he was still a kid. Child Services thinks she OD'd somewhere on the East Coast, and the dad died from a stroke. Tucker was raised by his grandfather from the time he was eight. I looked up the grandfather's history, Marvin Pharr. You name it, he had it on his record. Sexual assaults, aggravated assaults, robbery, burglary, larceny, narcotics . . . it was like a greatest hits of the felony code. And keep in mind we're talking about the sixties and seventies here, when forensic science practically didn't exist. So for every one of those convictions he probably committed another ten crimes he wasn't caught for. Can't imagine what Tucker went through being raised by someone like that."

Yardley bit her thumbnail. "I don't know. I just have a feeling it's not him."

"Have you seen the profile Daniel drew up?"

"He sent it to me; I haven't looked at it yet."

Baldwin brought it up on his phone and handed it to her.

Sarte's profiles were, to his credit, immensely detailed and came with caveats warning the field agents to remember that profiling was an art and not a science and to keep their minds open when pursuing suspects.

He had written that the Crimson Lake Executioner was likely a male in his forties, college educated or at least with above-average intelligence, and married, perhaps even with children. Sarte postulated that he had committed other murders earlier in life but had stopped, possibly due to incarceration for some unrelated offense or because he wished to focus on raising his children. Something that was far more common in serial murderers than most law enforcement realized.

The truly dangerous offenders, the ones that kept Yardley up at night, were the patient ones. The ones who could go ten years without killing and then, when circumstances were more favorable, begin again. It frightened her because it meant that killing wasn't some overpowering need that had to be fulfilled; it was something enjoyable that they chose to do, and they would only strike when the circumstances were perfect. They were the rarest type of killer and the hardest to catch.

The rest of the profile was the standard conjecture Yardley anticipated: Caucasian, early-childhood trauma involving violence, alcoholic. Yardley only skimmed that section.

One thing Sarte had written that stood out to her was what he'd told her previously: that he believed the Executioner had medical training. Either a physician, physician's assistant, or nurse.

"Daniel has this guy as educated, at least a college grad but probably medically educated," Baldwin said as Yardley handed the phone back. "Tucker dropped out in the fifth grade and is nearly illiterate. Not the type of guy who would've studied art history. I guess he could've randomly come across Sarpong's paintings somewhere and become obsessed with them, but I doubt he even has CPR training, much less medical knowledge."

"Where are we on the ricin?"

"Test takes a while, but my guys say that's a good bet."

"The ME said it's too late to look for an injection site on Angela River. Unless they go over that area with an injection sensor within a few hours, it's undetectable."

"What about Pharr? She died, so the puncture wouldn't have healed. Can we exhume the body and look?"

"They said it's too late. She'd be too deteriorated to check for injection sites."

Baldwin shook his head. "No way Tucker is this sophisticated. Zachary makes much more sense."

"Or they could be working together. Zachary would know exactly how much ricin to administer to kill Angie, so that likely wasn't him. If they were working together, that's a mistake someone who's scientifically illiterate, like Tucker, would make."

"Maybe. Seems like an odd pairing."

"Serial murderers that kill in pairs always have a dominant, intelligent leader and a passive, less intelligent follower. Always." She paused. "Jude Chance told me someone conjectured that there might be two of them. Guess it's not quite as ridiculous as I first thought."

"Well, let's assume that they are working together. They first killed Kathy Pharr, which is explainable, I guess. Zachary's having an affair, doesn't want it to come to light because it could ruin his career and relationship, yada yada, so they chose her as the first victim. But then Angela is the second. Zachary's smart enough to know that the boyfriend she lives with would be the first person we'd look at. Particularly since he's a doctor and it's a case where a drug is being administered to cause organ failure in both victims."

"That's why it would be wise to work with someone. He would just have to make sure there was no link between him and Tucker."

Baldwin nodded. "Okay, they off Pharr, and Tucker screws up Angie. A kind of 'you kill my woman, I kill yours' thing. But why Harmony? Tucker's not the brightest bulb, but he would have to know that if his wife and daughter were murdered, he'd be the only person we'd be looking at."

Yardley began pacing. "I need a warrant to search their homes."

"Hey, warrants are your department. Tell me what you need me to do and I'll do it."

"The fact that Zachary called Kathy Pharr three times on the day before her death and the second victim is his girlfriend is good, but maybe not probable cause good, and I want to be certain before we tip our hand. The defense would admit the affair to explain the phone calls and say Tucker is the most likely suspect if he found out about the affair. I need more to get a warrant for Zachary."

He rose. "I'll get on it." He didn't move for a second. "I know you and Angela have gotten buddy-buddy. You know you can't tell her Zachary's under investigation, right?"

"Of course. Just find me more, Cason."

"I'll let you know." He put his hands in his pockets and looked out over the mountains in the distance. "If you need anything, like someone to talk to, you know I'm always here for you, right?"

"I know. Thank you. But I'm fine."

He nodded. "I'll let you know as soon as I got anything. Oh, Child Services responded to our subpoena. The man Harmony helped put away is still inside and won't be released for another two years. Zachary and Tucker are our best bets right now."

After he left, Yardley leaned against her wood railing and looked out over the desert. Darkness was falling quickly, but it seemed to be a starless night.

Anxiety gnawed at her. It gnawed at her because there was one way to dig into Zachary's life without him knowing—and she hated herself for having thought of it.

25

Yardley texted River and asked her if Tara and some friends could come over to swim. She didn't yet know how she was going to use the opportunity to look for evidence against Zachary—maybe she'd get there early to pick Tara up, distract River, and . . . she'd figure something out. It was the first lie she'd told River.

Just past noon, Tara called her and said, "Angie left."

"What?"

"It's what you were waiting for, isn't it? I mean, you asked me to bring my friends swimming, so I figured it was something to do with their house. Unless you have a man over at our house, which I doubt."

Yardley was quiet a moment. When she looked at her daughter, she saw Tara the little girl who would run around their apartment trying to stick toys in the dryer or dishwasher to see what would happen. She forgot sometimes that Tara the young woman had an almost supernatural perception, like a laser beam that could bore into people's minds.

"I'll see you soon, sweetheart," was all Yardley said before hanging up.

Yardley showed up at River's home around one in the afternoon. She heard laughter from the backyard. She walked through the mansion and saw Tara, Stacey, and two other girls in the pool. Music played on hidden speakers, and food and drinks lay on deck chairs.

"Hey, Mom. Hop in, the water's nice."

"I'm fine, baby, thank you. Just wanted to see if you needed anything."

"You mean you wanted to see if we were going to destroy the place or invite over a bunch of boys, right?" Tara teased.

Yardley went back into the house and slid the glass door closed. She checked her watch: River had been gone for forty-five minutes, and Yardley had no clue when she would be back. Yardley closed her eyes a moment as an uneasy pressure tightened her chest. She didn't want to do this, but somehow she knew she would anyway.

She started in the bedroom.

The master bedroom was elegantly decorated and appeared more so now in the daylight. The bed frame was black and the sheets white silk.

She went into the walk-in closet. The clothes were mostly Zachary's. River took up maybe an eighth of the space. Yardley ran her hand over her clothes and spread them to look behind. She did the same with Zachary's clothing, then checked the dresser.

Satisfied that there was nothing in the bedroom, she went to Zachary's study down the hall: fine rugs over hardwood floors, an antique globe in front of a chestnut bookcase that took up an entire wall, and the smell of pine.

She scanned his books and saw nothing but nonfiction titles related to science and medicine, a few reference volumes, and a small collection of books on psychiatry. One of the titles was *The Dealing with Trauma Workbook*. Yardley opened it. About half of it was filled in with pencil, what looked like a woman's handwriting. On one page, the reader was asked to fill in a brief description of what the senses were taking in during the traumatic event they were dealing with:

There was darkness. I remember the darkness most because it was darker than I'd ever experienced before. Like I didn't know if I was awake or asleep it was so dark. I would hear things but I couldn't be sure it wasn't just in my mind. I still wake up thinking of that darkness. I feel like such a damn child, but I have to have a night-light on even now. I can't wake up in darkness because I can't breathe when I do. I guess it's like what someone would feel like waking up at the bottom of the ocean.

Yardley closed the book, heavy guilt descending over her for reading River's most intimate thoughts about the most traumatic event in her life.

River had put on a brave front for her, acting as though the kidnapping didn't affect her, and it saddened Yardley that River didn't think she could trust her with the pain. Maybe one day she would share it with her. Yardley hoped so. But that would never happen if Zachary turned out to be who Yardley thought he was. If he was the Executioner and had used Tucker to kidnap and try to kill her, the impact on River would be wholly and irreparably damaging. Yardley knew what she would feel better than anyone else ever could.

She put the workbook back and searched Zachary's desk.

No locked drawers, and nothing other than office supplies. His computer was password protected. She spun the globe lightly with her fingers before leaving the room.

The bathrooms and guest bedrooms held nothing of interest. As she was about to go to the garage, the sliding glass door leading to the pool opened, and she heard Tara shout, "Mom?"

Yardley went out to meet her daughter. "What is it, darling?"

"What're you doing?"

"Just wandering."

"Huh. Well, I need to use the bathroom."

"It's over there down the hall."

She watched her daughter walk away, leaving wet footprints on the hardwood floors. Yardley took some paper towels and wiped them up. She waited until Tara went back to the pool before leaving the kitchen.

She went to the other side of the house and to the door she guessed led to the garage. She had to try another two doors before she found it.

Inside the garage were a blue Lincoln sedan and a motorcycle. She flipped on the light. The garage was neat and orderly. All the tools put away on the racks in ascending order based on size. No grease stains on the concrete floors. An office was built into the space. It had windows looking out over the cars. Yardley descended the few steps and crossed the garage. A desk wrapped around the entire room, and there was a computer and two printers. Unlike Zachary's study, this office was messy and cluttered.

She flipped through a few documents, mostly bills and some letters about a car Zachary was trying to purchase from Berlin. A rare type of BMW. Yardley saw a door behind her. She tried the knob, but it was locked. She found the garage door controls. The sound of the door gliding up the metal tracks made her anxious, and she pictured Zachary coming home unexpectedly.

No neighbors were outside when Yardley stepped into the sunlight. She went around the garage. She hadn't realized how large it really was until just then. Enough to fit four cars or more.

The outside had only one window, and it was small. She had to stand on tiptoe to look inside.

The room behind the locked door was some sort of workshop—except that there was a recliner and television on one side of the room and a coffee table with empty beer bottles strewed across it in front of the recliner. She ran her eyes over the entire room and settled on some objects covered with black cloth near the workbench.

Yardley went back inside the house. She had noticed a bowl, something Asian and expensive, in the kitchen. It was filled with loose keys. She searched through them. They were clean metal, almost all unused. Spares. She took the bowl and went back to the office in the garage.

It took six separate tries, but one key, a brass one, different from the others, unlocked the door. She waited a few seconds and listened, making sure Tara hadn't come back in the house. Then she opened the door.

The workshop was filled with dust and tools. Despite the window, there was no ventilation, and the door was on a spring hinge and closed on its own. There was a musty scent to the room, like old sweat. She flipped a light switch near the door.

The workbench held scatterings of sawdust, and several woodworking projects were lined up on the shelves near it: incense burners and some bamboo crafted into walking sticks.

Yardley skirted around the bench. The cloth she'd seen through the window was thick, almost like a blanket, and hung over something large and square. She pulled it off.

It was one of Sarpong's paintings.

26

Yardley was lying out on a deck chair watching the girls when River came home. She held two shopping bags and set them down before she kicked off her shoes and lay down.

Yardley thought about the Sarpong painting in the garage as she watched River. It was the second in the series, the one River had nearly died being a part of. Behind that painting were the other three. They were excellent replicas on thick canvas, something that would have to be special ordered.

"I hate the mall during sales," River said. "It's like the jungle for middle-aged housewives. Eat or be eaten."

"Get anything good?"

"Some blouses. Oh, I got you something." She dug into one of the bags and came up with a small blue T-shirt decorated with a rainbow and a puffy bear.

"*The Care Bears*?" Yardley said.

"I guessed you were a fan. Who didn't love *The Care Bears* as a kid?"

Yardley took the shirt and held it up. The bear had a red heart on its chest.

"Tenderheart Bear," River said. "Reminded me of you."

Yardley was grinning like a child who had just received a toy, and then the grin slowly faded as she thought about the paintings in the garage and what she was about to do.

"I love it. Thank you."

River put on her sunglasses, releasing a deep, relaxing breath as she lay back again.

She said, "I love listening to Tara and her friends. It's so . . . I don't know. Just the energy they have is something I've always wanted." She waited a beat. "I can't have children."

Yardley watched her in silence. River glanced at her and then away.

"I didn't know."

"Why would you?"

River watched Tara for a while. "There was just too much damage to my cervix to ever have a viable pregnancy."

"Damage?"

River was silent for a long while. "When I was a young girl . . ."

"You don't have to say it. I'm so sorry, Angie. I don't even know what to say."

"Yeah, well, what can you do? I survived, right? I survived my abuser and I survived the Crimson Lake Executioner. How many people can say that? But I don't know how many of my nine lives I got left." She was quiet a beat before adding, "You think some people can just be cursed, Jess? Like they're just born to suffer and nothing else?"

Yardley took her hand. "No."

She smiled and gripped Yardley's hand tighter. "I hope that's true."

After leaving River's home, Yardley decided to call Baldwin.

She sat in her car outside a burger joint while the phone rang and went to voice mail. She realized that she hadn't eaten today, so she went inside.

The place was set up like a 1950s burger hub, and the menu only had burgers, fries, and milkshakes. Something by Frankie Valli played on the speakers. Yardley ordered and sat down.

Baldwin called halfway through her meal.

"Cason, I have something I need you to do."

"Shoot."

"Do you trust me?"

"Of course," he said in a severe tone. "More than anyone."

"Then do this thing for me and don't ask me about it. Don't ask why I need it done or why I think there'll be something there. Can you do that?"

"Yes."

"Draw up a warrant asking to search the curtilage around River's home, their garbage cans, the garage, and Zachary's car. I'll email you what to put in the affidavit."

"Anything else?"

"No."

"Jess, is this something I need to be worried about?"

"No questions, remember?"

He exhaled. "You got it. I'll get it done right now."

"Thank you."

She hung up and stared at her food, the thought of eating suddenly making her feel nauseated. She pictured River's face as the FBI and local police arrived with a search warrant. The first thing she would ask Yardley was if she knew about it.

She pushed the food away and left.

27

Yardley spent the next day at work reviewing files she was handing off to Jax. He sat in her office part of the day, his feet up on the desk as she gave him summaries of the cases he was about to inherit.

"Do you know I wrote a book?" he said as she looked for a file in one of the boxes stacked in the corner.

"I didn't."

"It's called *Heart of Darkness in the Justice System*. It's about how I went up against the mob and the cartels and a few other gangs. Went on a book tour and everything. You should read it."

"You went up against the mob in Wyoming, huh?"

He smiled. "You're allowed to exaggerate here and there. People expect it."

She faced him. "We should focus on these cases, Kyle. I got the trial I had this week continued, but you're going to have to do it next month."

He shrugged. "I work better under pressure."

"I've spent dozens of hours prepping it. You don't think you could use my insights?"

He shrugged again, looking out the windows. "Not my first rodeo."

She sighed and sat down on the edge of the desk. She folded her arms and glared at him. "You couldn't care less what I think about any of these cases."

"Honestly? No, I don't give a shit what you think about them."

"Why?"

"We just do things differently."

"Bullshit. Be a man and be honest. Have some balls."

He chuckled. "Oh, I got balls, baby."

"Then tell me."

"I just think women prosecute a certain way that I don't agree with."

"And what way is that?"

He leaned back in the seat and took out a sucker, which he unwrapped and put in his mouth. "I'm not getting fired and sued over this."

"Stays between us. You just said you have balls, remember?"

He grinned. "Okay, well, I just think y'all are too emotional. That's all. And when you got the power to have people arrested, you gotta be cool and calm. I just think it's harder for women to act that way a lotta the time."

Yardley's eyes narrowed, but otherwise she didn't allow herself to react.

"I'd like to start movin' my stuff in."

She nodded. "I'll have everything out of here by the end of the day."

He rose, sucking on the sucker as he watched her. "I think maybe we're not ending this well. Why don't we talk about it more over dinner at my place? I can cook a gumbo that would—"

"Try not to scuff the desk with your boots; it's expensive," she said on her way out, disgust coursing through her like a fetid river.

"Where you going? I thought you wanted to go through all these cases?"

"I have a meeting with a judge. We'll finish later."

Baldwin couldn't get the warrant for River's place signed yesterday—no judge was available—and he was busy with another case today, so she'd had him send it to her. She'd made some adjustments and then printed it out this morning.

Judge Thomas Nuhfer was older and near retirement. He was, as far as Yardley had seen, the strictest sentencing judge in the federal system in this part of the country. He routinely gave out ten- and fifteen-year sentences on first offenses and didn't hesitate to impose a life sentence on cases other judges would give twenty years for. He was also the judge most likely to grant a search warrant on thin evidence.

The rumors flew as to why he was the way he was. Some attorneys gossiped that when he was eighteen, his girlfriend had been kidnapped and never found. Others said that his father had been a strict disciplinarian, forcing him to stand on nails and hold books over his head as punishment. And still others said that a defendant he was lenient on went home and killed his entire family, and Nuhfer had never forgiven himself.

Yardley just believed he was a small man who wanted to feel big.

Most defense attorneys quietly accepted Nuhfer's sentences, but she'd seen one who'd found a way out of his web. Dylan Aster, a younger attorney out on his own, had purposely yelled at Nuhfer, calling him every insult he could think of, even mocking his toupee. Aster had been held in contempt and taken into custody for a night, but it created a conflict on all future cases because now it was assumed Nuhfer couldn't be impartial on any of Aster's cases.

Dylan Aster never had to appear in front of Nuhfer again.

None of the other attorneys had understood what he did; they all thought Aster's tantrum was just a childish response to an overbearing judge, but Yardley knew she was right because while being taken into custody, Aster had winked at her.

Nuhfer sat in his chambers with a glass of sparkling water next to his computer. Two packets of Alka-Seltzer were next to the glass. He ate sunflower seeds out of a bag and spit the shells back into the same bag.

"Judge, I think we have an appointment. May I come in?"

He glanced at her, then turned back to his computer screen. "What for?"

"Warrant I need signed."

He sighed like she had just asked him to help her move and said, "Sit down."

She sat across from him, took the warrant out of her satchel, and handed it to him. He put on reading glasses and scanned it, his lips moving as he read.

"It's thin, Ms. Yardley."

"We're not asking to search the home or for a blood draw. Not even to search his place of employment. The garbage cans, the surrounding property, the garage, and his car. I feel that's a minimal intrusion, Judge. Considering that the first victim is his lover and the second his girlfriend, I think probable cause is met."

"Why the garage? Why would you expect to find the evidence there and not inside his home?"

"It's doubtful Mrs. Pharr was ever in Mr. Zachary's home, but she was in his car. And the second victim's presence in the home as an occupant would complicate any evidence found."

Nuhfer thought a moment, staring at the warrant. Yardley felt butterflies in her stomach, and they were beginning to nauseate her.

"Not to be blunt, Judge, but to quote Justice Scalia, nobody knows what probable cause is. I think it just means you view everything in the light most favorable to us and ask if it's at least possible this man committed the offenses he's suspected of. Our profile also suggests the killer works in the medical field, just like Michael Zachary."

Nuhfer signed the warrant and handed it back. "The garbage bins outside the home, the garage, and any cars in the garage or on the property. Nothing else."

"Of course. Thank you."

He turned back to his computer. In the hallway, she leaned against the wall. The only thing she could think about was what River would do when law enforcement showed up at her house and accused the man she loved of being the one who'd tried to kill her.

28

Grove Springs Middle School was a flat building in the midst of a residential neighborhood. The homes were run down, and the school had rust on the handrails and chips in the lime-green paint.

Baldwin came as school was just starting and the kids were roaming around or chatting on the benches or walking to the convenience store up the block. He went in and found the front office. A woman in a beige dress sat at a computer and didn't look up at him as she said, "Can I help you?"

"Yeah, I'm Special Agent Cason Baldwin, I'm with the FBI. I'd like to speak with Principal Reilly, please."

"One second."

He folded his arms and glanced around the office. A bulletin board was up on the wall with announcements for a talent show, basketball games, and *The Taming of the Shrew* put on by the drama club. A young boy sat near him on the bench, his head held low.

"What'd you do?" Baldwin asked.

The boy looked at him. "I put a firework in a potato."

Baldwin whistled. "Blow it up?"

He nodded, a look of terror on his face.

"Well, I wouldn't do it again, but the punishment will pass. Plus, the girls are gonna think you're a rebel," Baldwin said with a wink. It made the boy grin.

A short, pudgy man in a sweater-vest came out of an office. He raised his eyebrows and said, "Ted Reilly."

They shook hands. "Cason Baldwin. I'm with the FBI, looking into Harmony Pharr's disappearance. Could I steal a minute of your time?"

"Of course. Come on back."

Reilly's office was sparse but had a comfortable-looking blue couch against the wall with an incense burner on a table next to it. Both men sat.

"I couldn't believe it when I heard," Reilly said. "First the abuse, then her mother, and now this. I swear the guardian angels must have something against that family. No offense if you're religious."

"I'm not. You're talking about the boyfriends with the abuse, right?"

He nodded. "I called Child Services myself once when Harmony showed up to school with bruises all over her body. I mean these deep-black bruises the size of a baseball. She got put into a foster home for a couple weeks, but then they let her go back to her mother." He shook his head. "She told me she didn't want to go back. That the family that had her was actually nice to her, but her mother wanted her back."

"What about her father?"

"What about him?"

"You know his background?"

He nodded as he folded his hands across his stomach. "I do. You're asking if he did something to her? I don't know. To be honest, my interactions with her were brief and far between. You may want to talk to Margaret. She was Harmony's history teacher. They had a close relationship. She's the one that brought all this to my attention."

Margaret Dimopoulous looked exactly like what Baldwin pictured when he thought of a schoolteacher: petite, with glasses, a skirt, and some marker on her hands. She resembled a teacher he'd had in elementary school who—not unlike Margaret with Harmony—had taken an interest in Baldwin and would bring him lunches when he didn't have any or a coat during the winters, since his mother and her boyfriend wouldn't buy things they considered as trivial as that.

"Ted told me you had a good relationship with Harmony," he said.

"I tried to," she said with a sigh, taking her glasses off. "She was an amazingly sweet girl considering everything she went through. Sometimes when children go through as much as she has, they turn angry and bitter. She was very loving. And smart. If she just had the proper home environment, I know she could accomplish a lot."

"She ever mention anybody to you who might've been following her around or calling her? Anyone she was nervous about?"

She shook her head. "No, not recently."

"Recently?"

"There was a boyfriend of her mother's—this was before her father got out of prison, of course—but he would show up to school sometimes and try to pick her up, and she would refuse to get into his car. I saw him grab her once very hard around the arm and try to drag her into the car. By the time I ran out there, he had already left."

Baldwin took out his phone and opened his note-taking app. "Do you happen to remember his name?"

"I don't, I'm sorry. I brought it up to Harmony once, and she refused to talk about him. But he was kicked out by her mother when her father got released."

"What about her father? She ever mention anything about him?"

"I think she was scared of him. She didn't come right out and say it, probably because she thought it would get back to him, but I could tell." She took out some Tic Tacs and popped them into her mouth. "You have to understand, Agent Baldwin, she hated her parents. She broke down in my office once and said she wished they were dead. That they were the worst people in the world. It would not surprise me one bit if her father had something to do with her disappearance, but it also would not surprise me if she ran away. She tried it twice but didn't get very far. I told her that living on the street would be worse than living at home, and"—Margaret looked down at the table, her eyes suddenly filled with a deep sadness—"and she said nothing could be worse than living at her house." She wiped away a tear and put her glasses back on. "I should have done more. Maybe tried to adopt her myself, I don't know, something."

Baldwin glanced at his phone: a text from Yardley. Probably to say that the warrant for Michael Zachary's property had been signed by a judge and was ready to go. "There's nothing you could've done. You weren't family and had no standing. Calling Child Services and trying to get her out of the home was the best you could do."

She slowly shook her head. "I just made sure I was here for her when she needed me and didn't pry too much. I would probably check with that boyfriend, though. One thing I do remember Harmony saying was that the boyfriend was really upset that her mother was kicking him out because her father was coming home. Maybe if he hurt her mother, he would hurt her, too."

29

The warrant was going to be executed first thing in the morning. Yardley finished up at the office late and went home. Tomorrow was also the official day of her retirement. She'd received paperwork converting her to a 1099 contract employee until the end of the case. Lieu had informed her they didn't have a spare office for her to use but that she could use the conference room when it wasn't occupied.

Instead of going home, Yardley went straight to the gym. She hit a heavy bag for half an hour, then jogged another half hour around the track. An older man who wore his Rolex while lifting weights hit on her and asked her if she had ever been on a Voss yacht.

Tara was sleeping when she got home. Yardley sat on the end of the bed and just watched her. No matter how old Tara got, whenever she slept, she always looked like a little girl. Yardley lightly touched her calf, then rose to shower.

She stayed in the shower until the water went cold, dressed in a robe, took a glass of wine to her bedroom, and turned on the television. She was flipping through streaming channels when her phone buzzed. It was River. Yardley considered not answering but knew she had to.

"Hi, Angie."

She chuckled. "That's a much better greeting."

"What's up?"

"*Thelma and Louise* just came on, and it made me think of you."

Yardley grinned. "I'm nothing like either of them."

"No, you're a mystery wrapped in an enigma."

"No, I'm just a tired middle-aged woman who's going to be officially unemployed tomorrow."

"Seriously?"

"I gave my notice more than six weeks ago, and it still snuck up on me. I'm finishing with this Crimson Lake Road case, and then I'm done prosecuting."

"Well, do you want to retire?"

"Want has nothing to do with it. It's time." Yardley hesitated. "Angie, I want to have breakfast with you tomorrow. There's something really important we need to discuss."

"Huh," she said. It sounded like she'd put some food in her mouth and was chewing. She didn't speak again until Yardley said, "So is that a yes?"

"Oh, sorry, didn't know you were waiting for me. Yes. Yeah, I'll definitely have breakfast with you. Where at?"

"Meet me at Egg and the Bagel at seven."

"Kinda early, ain't it? How about nine?"

"It has to be seven."

"Okay, if you say so. I'll have an extra coffee on the drive over or something." She chewed a bit more. "So what are you gonna do when you retire? And I know all about the 'I'll just relax and pursue what I love' route. The cruel joke is if you can do it all the time, the thing you love turns into the thing you hate."

"No, I won't be doing anything like that. I might just open a small practice taking whatever comes through the door. Like how lawyers in small towns used to work sixty years ago."

"Sounds boring. You get to handle crazy cases right now. See the dark side of people. Why would you want to trade that for, like, taking care of angry people during a divorce?"

"Boring sounds really good right about now."

Yardley heard a crunch and more chewing.

"What are you eating?"

"Jalapeño pork rinds. Don't judge me." More chewing. "Where would you move if you could move anywhere in the world?"

Yardley turned the television low and rested her head against the wall behind her. "I don't know. I haven't been many places. I went to Martha's Vineyard once; I really enjoyed that."

"That is pretty. Really calm during the off-season."

"What about you? Where would you go?"

"Oh, that's easy. There's a place in Belize called San Pedro. It's this little town where nothing happens. The hotel's right on the beach, and there's a bar owned by this guy that serves the best mixed drinks in the world. Pork sandwiches, too, where the pig is roasted right in front of you. And the water's so blue you can't believe it's from this world, and the shore has these, like, emerald rocks that just shine in the sunlight. They're almost blinding . . ." A pause. "You know, I've never told anyone that. Not even Zachary. He has this big retirement plan where we're going to get a condo in Florida or some other hellhole and just fish all day."

"How's everything between you two?"

"Pretty good. Some days I think he's the love of my life and I could never leave him, and then other days I think about him cheating on me and I want nothing to do with him. I don't know, I guess we'll see what happens. I'm thinking of finding out for sure. Maybe hiring a private investigator . . . I don't really wanna talk about it, if that's okay."

"Of course."

"So you got me curious—what's so important you gotta tell me in person?"

"It's not something you tell someone over the phone."

"Oh shit, that sounds intriguing. Now I'm gonna be up all night thinking about what it could be."

Yardley turned her television off, then her lamp, and lay on top of the covers. The moonlight cascaded through the windows and the open doors of a small balcony.

"Do you know I've never been out of the country?" Yardley said. "You talked about travel and how it changes you and the wonders of seeing the world . . . I've never felt wonder at the world. I feel shackled. Maybe it's the city. It feels like it just won't let me go."

"Yeah, Vegas can do that. It feels like a city that brings out the worst in us, doesn't it? Hard to center yourself here. That's why I keep bugging you to come to yoga. You gotta learn to let shit go and not hang on so tightly. I'd love to see you there."

Yardley thought, *You may never want to see me again after tomorrow.*

"I better get some sleep. I'll see you at breakfast," Yardley said.

"Yup. Love ya. Oh, oops, sorry, didn't mean to make it weird. It's just something I throw out there. I'll see you tomorrow."

Yardley hung up and stared at the ceiling until she finally drifted into a dreamless sleep.

30

Yardley woke Tara, who rubbed her eyes and said, "What time is it?"

"Little past six. You've got class."

She closed her eyes again. "It's grad school, Mom, not elementary school. I can be late."

Yardley lightly brushed her daughter's bangs away from her face and kissed her forehead. "I guess that's true. You have to cut your mother some slack. This growing-up thing doesn't come with a manual."

She dressed in a black skirt with a white blouse and turned on the alarm as she left.

Egg and the Bagel was a hip café known for their specialty, the beer omelet. A monstrosity that consisted of an omelet fried in beer. Yardley could smell the burning alcohol as she walked in.

River sat at a small table looking out onto the street, her chin resting on the back of her hand. She stared at the passing traffic and the pedestrians with an air of ambivalence, as though it didn't matter what was going on in the world around her. One scene as good as another.

"Been here before?" Yardley asked as she sat down.

"No. I like it. Feels like someone's kitchen."

"It's owned by three grandmothers."

"Well, they've done a good job. There's been a line since I came in." She took a sip of coffee. "What'd you want to talk to me about that was so important?"

"Angie . . . there's something that's going to happen today that's going to come as a shock to you. It's something that happened to me once, and I didn't have anyone there to help me through it. I was pregnant and alone, without any money or relatives to pitch in. It was the most difficult time of my life. I just want to make sure you don't have the same experience."

River's brow furrowed. "What are you talking about?" she said in a more serious tone than Yardley had ever heard from her.

"In just a few minutes, there's going—"

River's phone rang. Yardley was silent. River stared at the phone a moment before picking it up from the table.

"Zachary?"

Yardley heard Zachary's voice on the other end, frantic and nearly shouting. River's eyes rested on Yardley, and they filled with confusion and then anger.

"I'll be right there," she said, hanging up.

The two of them sat silently a moment, the noise of the café filling the space between them.

"The FBI and Sheriff's Office are searching my house right now. Zachary said he might be arrested. Is that what you brought me here to talk about, Jessica?"

Yardley looked down because she couldn't meet her eyes and nodded.

"You brought me here to occupy me while they arrest my boyfriend?"

"No, that's not why I—"

"Holy shit," she said, slamming her palm down on the table. "This whole thing, the coming over, talking to me, spending time with me . . . were you gathering evidence against him this whole time?"

Yardley shook her head but still couldn't look at her. "That is absolutely *not* what I was doing."

She thrust her finger in Yardley's face. "Then why am I here while the police are at my house? Why didn't you tell me about it last night instead of making sure I was away?"

Yardley reached out to touch her hand, and she pulled away. "Angie, I wanted to spare you. I was just thinking about you."

"Bullshit!" She rose. "I told you things I've never told anyone, and you were just waiting to use them against me, weren't you? What kind of person are you?"

"You're misinterpreting—"

"Go to hell. I never wanna see you again."

31

Yardley had no office anymore, so she went home. She sat on the balcony in a deck chair and nervously checked her phone every few minutes. The scene with River kept playing through her mind. A heavy grayness tightened her throat.

The update came around eleven. Baldwin and Detective Garrett had executed the warrant along with six deputies from the Clark County Sheriff's Office. They found the Sarpong paintings and a roll of white bandages in the garage, along with several vials of pure ricin. Baldwin was having the evidence response team run a match against the bandages found on Kathy Pharr and River.

The Department of Homeland Security had become involved now because of the ricin—another layer of bureaucracy Yardley would have to navigate. The US Attorney's Office had an uneasy relationship with the DHS since the investigations that followed September 11. Many US attorneys had quit over the use of torture by the CIA, DHS, and other agencies, but there had been an uneasy truce since the Obama era.

Baldwin texted her and said, Zachary's been arrested. He's at the station now. Meet me.

Yardley rose and hurried out the door.

Dr. Michael Zachary was being held at a Sheriff's Office community field station. It was a quarter the size of the stations within Las Vegas itself and mostly used when deputies needed to put someone in the drunk tank but didn't want to make a long drive with them in the cruiser. Baldwin had chosen the location carefully, and Yardley was glad for it. Somewhere smaller and quieter, somewhere not so intimidating, where Baldwin could just chat with Zachary as though it were lunch with an old friend.

Somewhere the Department of Homeland Security wouldn't know about for a couple of hours.

The field station was an ugly gray brick building with broad steps leading up to the glass double doors. The Sheriff's Office emblem decorated both doors, the words **Integrity, Fidelity, Compassion** emblazoned below it.

She identified herself at the front desk and was directed to room two.

Baldwin was standing outside the interview room with a detective Yardley recognized: Lucas Garrett. The lead sheriff's detective assigned the Executioner case. He motioned to Yardley with his head, and Baldwin turned to her.

"Did you already speak with him?" she said.

"No," Baldwin said as he glanced at Zachary through the one-way glass. "I've been letting him sweat. Did you talk to Angela?"

"I did. She was less than pleased. She thinks I befriended her to gather evidence against Zachary."

"Did you?"

The question surprised and angered her. She folded her arms and turned toward the glass. Zachary sat at a gray table. He appeared nervous and fidgety, his foot tapping in a manic routine against the linoleum floor.

"Sorry," Baldwin said. "I know you wouldn't do that."

"I'll be watching from out here," she said, ignoring his apology.

Baldwin and Garrett went in. Yardley took a few steps back and leaned against the wall as she watched them.

"What the hell is going on?" Zachary said. "I want to know what's going on this instant. No one has told me anything."

"Sorry about that," Baldwin said. "You like going by Zachary, right? Not Michael?"

Garrett paced the room while Baldwin sat down. He took out a manila folder he'd brought with him and removed some large color photos. They were snapshots of the Sarpong paintings.

"You recognize these?"

"Yeah," Zachary said, glancing at them. "You know damn well I do. You were the one who explained them to me when you told me about Angie."

"Do you know where we found them?"

"How would I know that?"

"Really? You don't recognize your own handiwork, huh?"

"My handiwork? What are you talking about?"

"They're good reproductions. I'm just curious if you did them yourself."

Zachary looked between Baldwin and Garrett. "I have no idea what you're talking about. And why have I been arrested? What is going on?"

"We found these paintings in your garage, Zachary."

"What?" He looked down at the photos. "Are you crazy? I didn't have these in my garage. Why would I keep these paintings? Do you know what it would do to Angie if she saw them?"

Baldwin watched him. "Zachary, listen to me, I'm trying to help you. I don't want this to go past us. I want us to take care of it, just me and you. You tell me everything and be honest, and I'll be honest, too. What I say carries a lot of weight with the US Attorney's Office and the DA. I've seen this a million times, and I'm telling you, the more you work with us now, the more we can work with you down the line."

Garrett chimed in. "One thing Agent Baldwin and I were discussing was keeping this out of federal court and having it stay local. You would much rather stay in state court than federal court. Trust me. Work it right and you could maybe be looking at parole in twenty."

Zachary looked between them again, his eyes suddenly going wide. "Oh shit," he gasped. "You think . . . you think *I* killed that woman?"

Baldwin leaned forward. "You telling us you didn't?"

"Hell no, I didn't."

Baldwin sighed. "Zachary, the roll of bandages we found in your garage came back as a match to the ones found on Angie and the ones found on Kathy Pharr. They all came from the same roll. You hid it well, I'll give you that, but you really should've burned it. And why would you save the vials of ricin? It's easy enough to get more."

"What? Ricin? What the hell are you talking about!"

Baldwin interlaced his fingers on the table. "Zachary, come on. We have a good relationship, me and you. Let's not bullshit each other. You were having an affair with Kathy, and if her husband found out, shit would hit the fan, right? I mean, I get why maybe you had to kill her—but Angie? If you had to, I don't know, make these paintings a reality for whatever reason, seems like you'd pick someone other than the girlfriend you live with, or at least take out an insurance policy on her. But we didn't find one of those. So why do it?"

Zachary's lip began to quiver. The reality of what was happening hit him. Yardley stepped toward the glass, staring at his face, trying to pick up any subtle clue as to what he was actually thinking.

"I didn't kill anyone."

"Zachary—"

"No! Don't 'Zachary' me. I didn't kill anyone, damn it!" Zachary slammed his fists on the table. He rose and shouted, "I didn't kill anyone!"

Garrett went for his weapon, and Baldwin shook his head. Garrett slowly lowered his hand to his side but kept it near the gun.

"Zachary, I'm going to need you to sit down."

"This is bullshit! I didn't do this."

"Then we'll work it out. But first I need you to sit down and stop shouting."

Zachary sat down, shaking his head. "I knew this was a mistake. Helping you. I've seen all those documentaries about how you arrest the wrong man and once it's in your head, you don't let it go. You ruin lives, and you're trying to ruin mine."

"No one is trying to ruin your life. I'm trying to help you."

Zachary leaned forward. "I. Did. Not. Kill. Anyone." He glanced at Garrett before looking back to Baldwin. "I want a lawyer."

"You don't want to do that. It's much easier if we just talk, just you and me."

Yardley opened the door. "Mr. Zachary has asked for a lawyer. This interview is over."

Garrett shook his head but looked at Baldwin to see what to do. Baldwin had a slight curl to his lip but rose and left the room anyway.

Out in the hall, Garrett stared at Yardley and said, "I didn't realize we had a defense attorney at the US Attorney's Office."

"Hey," Baldwin said, "she was right: anything we got after would be thrown out."

Garrett sucked something out of his teeth and said, "I'm going home, Cason. Call me if there's anything."

Yardley leaned back against the wall, watching Zachary through the glass.

"You could've asked to speak with me outside," Baldwin said. "You didn't have to make me look like I didn't know what I was doing in front of Garrett. It was a little insulting."

"I didn't insult you, Cason. This investigation and prosecution have to be done carefully."

He took a deep breath and looked at Zachary, whose foot was now furiously tapping the floor as he rubbed his fingers together. "I guess we should get him his lawyer."

32

"Dylan!"

Dylan Aster felt weight on his chest. It was suffocating him, taking his breath away. He'd had an extraordinarily fat Saint Bernard as a kid that would sit on his chest some mornings; it had felt like a boulder was crushing him, and that was how he felt now.

"Dylan!"

He opened his eyes to see Lily Ricci above him. He was lying on the couch in his office. His tie and suit coat were slung over a chair, but he still wore his slacks and dress socks.

"It's eight," she said.

"Oh shit."

He jumped up and buttoned his shirt. A small sink was behind his desk, the reason why he paid an extra fifty a month for this office, and he rinsed his mouth with Scope, ran a comb through his short brown hair, tried to cover up the scar at the base of his neck with his shirt collar the best he could, and then threw on his shoes as he ran for the door.

"What do you have?" he said as he ran out, Ricci grabbing her satchel before joining him.

"Motion hearing uptown. You need to be in Cook's court now and Prescott's at eight thirty."

He jogged to the elevator, Ricci hurrying behind him, as he took out his phone and pulled up the clients he had this morning. Henry

Smith Miller in Judge Cook's court and Eve Rachel Rodriguez in Prescott's court. Then he had three other clients across town at the municipal court.

The law offices of Aster & Ricci took up two rooms in the Biltmore Building across the street from the Clark County District Court. He nearly got clipped by a cab as he dashed across the street. Ricci shouted after him, "Get our money from Eve!"

"I will."

The Clark County District Court was a square building of multicolored sections that looked like LEGO pieces forced together. Aster hurried up the steps of the courthouse and to the metal detectors.

"Frank, I'm in a huge hurry."

"Can't do it. You know that," the burly bailiff said.

Aster impatiently waited for his turn. Someone started arguing with the bailiff about taking their shoes off, and Aster half wished Frank would tase them to get the line moving.

When he finally rushed through, Frank told him to have a good one, and he shouted the same without turning around as he sprinted for the elevators.

Judge Cook was already on the bench. He started court at eight and expected the lawyers to be there ten minutes early. He stared at Aster as he hurried past the audience and joined the other attorneys in the gallery seats behind the defense and prosecution tables.

Monday morning roll call calendars were the busiest calendars on the criminal court docket. Aster guessed two hundred people were crammed into a room meant for half that. Ten lawyers sat waiting their turn, eyeing each other to see if anyone wasn't paying attention so they could cut in line. Since Aster was last, he took out his phone and browsed his case files.

Miller's case was a straightforward car burglary. He'd been breaking into cars in his neighborhood and stealing whatever valuables he could. Aster saw that his legal bills were paid up, unlike Eve Rodriguez.

"Mr. Aster," Judge Cook said, "thank you for joining us today."

"Um, thank you, Your Honor."

"Since you feel it's your courtroom and you can come in whenever you like, why don't we call your case now."

"Your Honor, everybody here was ahead of me."

"No, no, I insist. You clearly believe you can do what you like in *your* courtroom, so let's just have you run the show, shall we? Who do you have?"

Aster glanced at the other attorneys, who were shooting poison at him from their eyes. He pictured the scene from *Full Metal Jacket* where the trainee was beaten by his fellow recruits because he'd caused all of them to be punished.

"Um, I have Henry Miller, Your Honor."

"Mr. Miller, please come forward."

Aster stood with Henry at the lectern. The judge pulled up his file and said, "What are we doing here today, Mr. Aster?"

"Just setting the matter for a motion to suppress the evidence based on probable cause." Aster figured the judge had made his point and was moving on.

"Yes, of course," Cook said. "Shall I just dismiss the case for you now? It's *your* courtroom; please tell me what you'd like to do."

Aster's discomfort was turning to anger. He'd been a few minutes late, and there was a line of attorneys ahead of him anyway. He hadn't affected the proceedings in any way. Cook was just exercising his power because he could. Few things bothered Aster as much as someone who picked on others because they could.

"Yes, Your Honor, I would like you to dismiss the case now, that would be great, thank you. Also, could we get the prosecution to pay for Mr. Miller's parking? It's expensive as hell down there."

Cook's eyes went wide. He stared with venom at Aster.

Aster didn't budge. A contempt hearing could take half an hour. He was betting Cook wouldn't want to get that behind schedule. He hoped, anyway.

The judge's lip curled as he said, "Four weeks enough time, Mr. Goff?"

The prosecutor stood up and said, "That's fine, Your Honor."

"June twenty-sixth at three p.m. If you're late again, Counselor, I'll have you held in contempt, are we clear?"

"Crystal."

Once they were out of the courtroom, Aster told Henry to call him if he had any questions but that he would reach out to him before the next hearing to go over his testimony. Then Aster sprinted to Judge Prescott's court, fully expecting to go another round with a judge for being late—and he still had three hearings to go today.

33

Yardley saw Jax standing in the hallway of the US Attorney's Office, hitting on one of the paralegals. Her arms were folded, and she had her left hand with her wedding ring on top, making sure Jax saw it.

"Kyle," Yardley interrupted, "can I talk to you?"

He said, "In a minute," without looking at her.

"Now, please. I won't be here long."

He turned his gaze toward her as he grimaced, and she figured it was a tell of his that showed frustration. She didn't bother advising him to correct it, that there were defense attorneys good enough to use it to push him to lose his temper in front of a jury.

"All right," he said, barely able to hide his disdain. She followed him toward her former office. He sat down, putting his feet up on the desk, making a point to bang his cowboy boots against the smooth surface. "So? What'd you want to talk about?"

"When are you going to the grand jury?"

"Tomorrow morning."

"I don't think we should yet."

"Why not? We got him cold."

"It's jurisdictional. I have to figure out a way to keep this in federal court."

"We can take a murder if it happens during a felony sex crime. It's cool. There was semen found inside Kathy Pharr, and there was bruising and tearing."

"The forensic nurse who performed the SAFE kit said the results were inconclusive, and he was having a consensual affair with her. She was also married and Tucker doesn't remember if they had sex that day. I'm just saying let's take a little time with it. Make sure we have good grounds to keep this in federal court before we go headfirst into it. And we don't know how they met; if they met on a dating app, I'd say we have solid grounds to keep it federal because of the commerce clause. Same thing with the ricin. He had to order it from out of state, so we can make an argument there that it should stay federal. But let's take it a little slow and find out for sure. Otherwise we need to give this case to the DA's Office."

Jax scoffed. "Whatever. Grand juries indict on anything. And I'm not handing over the biggest case of my career to some Podunk farmer DA."

"Kyle," she said with a sigh, as though talking to a child, "let me work out jurisdiction first. We can always get the DA to dismiss, and we'll file it up here later."

"We can just amend it later if there's a problem."

"You can't amend an indictment for murder in Nevada. It has to go through the grand jury again. If you go to them now and they decline to charge him, you can't bring the same charges again unless there's new evidence. We could miss our shot if the grand jury declines it."

He shrugged. "I don't know, let the eggheads in Research figure that out. I'm going forward with murder."

She took a breath and sat down across from him. "Kyle, listen to me. I know you want to make your mark out here, and this case is a big one with a lot of attention, but you need to be careful. This isn't some person who stole a television or is dealing marijuana to his friends in the neighborhood. If Michael Zachary killed his lover and tried to kill his girlfriend, he's extremely dangerous. You cannot risk him getting out."

"I appreciate the mentoring, but I told you, I've done a lot of trials. A lot. I came up prosecuting biker gangs rolling through Wyoming. I've had my house broken into twice, gotten my car set on fire, and had some bikers run my mom off the road. And guess what? I'm still here. I don't scare easy. And just because I'm young doesn't mean I don't know what I'm doing. You attack with an asshole like Zachary. Attack, attack, attack, until the defense doesn't know what to do and takes our offer. I've done it a million times."

"Have you ever prosecuted a serial murderer?"

"Murder is murder."

"It's not the same."

He sighed. "Okay, you've said your piece. You done?"

She shook her head. She couldn't hold back anymore. "You're an arrogant little shit, and you're going to get people killed."

Yardley stormed out of his office and went to the restroom to calm down. She closed her eyes and took a few deep breaths, picturing a forest with a stream that sounded like water being poured into a glass. It was rare for her to lose her composure, and she didn't like it. Anger was the most dangerous of all emotions because it overtook every other one. But why this case? Why was the anger bubbling up in this case when it didn't in others? The only answer was Angela River. There was a risk that if Zachary was released, she would be the one paying the penalty for their mistakes.

Yardley left the restroom and went to Lieu's office. He was on the phone and held up a finger. She sat down across from him and waited until he was done.

"Exciting news, isn't it?" he said after hanging up. "You did good work on the Executioner case, Jessica. If you need a recommendation for other employment, wherever you end up, don't hesitate to put me down as a professional reference."

"Roy, you need to take over the prosecution. You can't let Kyle do it."

He watched her quietly a second. "Why not?"

"This shouldn't be his first case here. He's not ready."

Jax said from the door, "Hey, you got something to say to me, say it to my face."

"I think I already did," she said without turning.

"I don't need help, Roy."

Lieu looked to him, then back to Yardley. "We've discussed our strategy going forward. I'm supervising him. You don't need to worry; it'll be handled well."

"You didn't listen to me once on a case like this, Roy, and it very nearly resulted in Wesley being released. At some point, you're going to have to trust me."

"I said that I'm supervising him."

"Then supervise him. Tell him to give the case to the DA until federal jurisdiction is established without any doubt."

"That true?" Lieu said to Jax, who had moved next to his desk. "Do we have jurisdiction issues?"

"It's not going to be a problem. Semen was found in his first victim, along with some bruising and tearing. And I'll bet they met on a dating app. Both of them have profiles; we just need to go through their histories. It's enough for a grand jury to conclude it should stay federal. We need to get the indictment in now to put pressure on whoever is going to be his attorney. We can't wait."

Lieu turned to Yardley with a look that said, *Is that enough for you?*

Yardley rose. "Fine. Do what you want. It's not my problem anymore."

34

Aster finished up all his court appearances by the afternoon. Ricci texted him that she was done as well. They met at a Mexican fast-food place. He loosened his tie as he drank down his soda in large gulps.

"Did you get our money from Eve?" Ricci asked as she ate a tortilla chip.

"Not exactly."

"What does that mean?"

"She had it with her, but I couldn't take it. It was her grocery money."

"Dylan, it's always their grocery money, or their rent money, or their baby formula money. These people say the same thing to their credit card companies, doctors, car insurance people, whatever."

"She's an old lady. I couldn't take it from her. She promised she would pay us everything soon."

Ricci shook her head. "No, she won't."

"It's cool. We're fine. The public defender contracts will be renewed for another six months soon and we're good."

"And then what? I'm sick of relying on these contracts and getting an ulcer every six months not knowing if they'll be renewed."

"Hey, when we left the legal aid office, we both agreed there would be lean times and we couldn't freak out. It takes three years, at least, to break even with your own firm. We read that together, remember?"

She sighed. "I'm just sick of barely scraping by."

"Let me do the worrying. No point in both of us doing it. Besides, you should just marry Jake and get it done with already. He's loaded."

"He's definitely marriage material, but I've already got one adult who acts like a child to take care of. I can't handle two right now."

"Who's the other one?" he asked honestly. When she didn't reply, he said, "Oh." He drank another sip of soda. "Let me worry about the business, Lil. Everything will be cool, I promise."

"This is my business, too, Dylan. I've dreamed about my own law firm since I was on the debate team in high school. If this doesn't work, I don't know what I'm going to do. I don't want to work for anyone else. And even if I did, believe it or not, the good ole boys at the big firms are not in a rush to hire thirty-five-year-old female veterans with criminal histories."

"Hey, that guy deserved the bottle over the head. Not your fault. And you are not going to have to go to any firms. I promise. Just give it time. We're kicking ass and getting a reputation. It takes time for that to spread."

"And that's another thing that pisses me off. You're ten times the defense attorney these jokers are, and they're the ones on TV and getting hundred-grand retainers. You deserve that, not them."

He chuckled. "I grew up cramped in a trailer with my mama and sister. I thank God every morning that I'm where I'm at and making what I make. I got a roof, clothes, enough to eat, and some money at the end of the month. I'm blessed."

"Ugh. You're so nice. Why does it always have to be the assholes who are successful in business?"

Ricci's phone vibrated. She checked the ID and answered. "Hello?"

Aster leaned back in the booth and drank more soda as she spoke. He remembered as a kid going to convenience stores and mixing a little bit of each soda in a concoction he called a Long Island iced tea because he'd heard his mama say that was her favorite drink. At eleven, it was the greatest thing in the world, and he wondered if now at twenty-eight it'd make him gag.

"We'll be right down," Ricci said.

"Who was that?"

"Billy at the jail. You'll never guess who was just brought in."

"Who?"

"The Crimson Lake Executioner."

"What?"

"I know, right? Let's get there before someone scoops him up."

—

As Ricci sped them downtown in her truck, Aster stared out the window. A case with this much media attention was a guarantee of constant local, national, and maybe even some international coverage. That meant interviews for the defense attorneys, articles, speaking engagements, and maybe even book deals afterward. Smaller firms and solo practitioners paid staff at the jails to notify them when someone like the Executioner was brought in.

"You sure we should do it for free?" Ricci said as she raced through a yellow light.

"Yes."

"He might have money. He's a doctor."

"We gotta sign him. I don't care about the money. And slow down. I'd hate to die right before getting rich."

"These cases are a ton of work, Dylan. He could be forgotten after the trial and not bring in any new business."

"Or he could make us famous and 2 Chainz could put us on retainer." He glanced at her. "He's a famous rapper."

"I know who he is, jerk."

"He's not singing about trucks and horses, so I didn't know if you knew."

"Hey, country music is the most popular music in America. You're the weirdo for not listening to it."

The Clark County Detention Center was a modern building of glass and steel and looked more like a trendy office building than a jail. It was meant to defuse the anxiety the surrounding neighborhood would feel with a jail in their midst—any anger would fade over time as people forgot it was a jail since it didn't look anything like one. The interior had white corridors that Aster thought gave it the sterile feel of a hospital.

They paid to park in the lot next door and hurried over. Once inside the jail, they looked over the deputies behind the desk and saw Billy's pudgy, familiar face at the end of the row.

"Billy," Aster said, "anyone been in to see—what's his name, Lil?"

"Michael Zachary."

"Anyone been in to see him?"

"You're the first."

"Sweet."

Billy glanced at the deputy next to him, who was helping a visitor. "Two hundred bucks," he whispered.

"What? I usually give you fifty."

"This guy is huge. We had to almost arrest a bunch of reporters who kept trying to get in to interview him. He's gonna be all over the TV."

Aster tapped the counter, watching him. "One hundred."

"Two hundred." He glanced at the deputy next to him again. "Better hurry. I heard Steven Smith is comin' down to talk to him. That guy's got at least five billboards. Think how many he'll have if he's defending the Crimson Lake Executioner."

"Fine, be a dick. Two hundred. But get me in right now."

After being searched and led through the metal detectors, Ricci and Aster were given visitor badges. They were directed to C Block on the fifth floor. It was for offenders deemed a risk to themselves or others.

They were led back to his cell by a large deputy with a tattoo peeking out over his shirt collar. The cell door creaked as it slid open, the bars gray and dappled with rust near the top and bottom. Michael Zachary sat on his cot.

The last client Aster had visited in C Block was a four-hundred-pound gangster accused of crushing his brother's skull when he found out his brother was sleeping with his wife. Michael Zachary looked like a nerdy accountant whose mom might still be driving him to work. It brought a smile to Aster's face: no way would a jury think this guy was a brutal psychopath.

"You got your attorney here," the deputy said.

"My attorney?"

Ricci said, "Thanks, Deputy, we'll call you when we're done."

Aster stepped inside the cell as Ricci leaned against the bars. He noticed the sink. All of Zachary's personal items were lined up neatly in a row, and his extra set of clothes was folded precisely and positioned at the very end of the cot. Clients with obsessive-compulsive disorder could be difficult to manage since trials were mostly sloppy seat-of-your-pants roller-coaster-type work. Not something that a person with control issues handled well.

"Dr. Zachary, my name is Dylan Aster, and this is Lily Ricci. We're criminal defense attorneys. We're here to defend you."

"I don't understand. I already have an attorney. Charles Duffman."

"Yeah? Where is he? I bet you called him and he said he would make it down when he could, yeah? You seem like the kind of guy who has an attorney on retainer. Probably through some really expensive, bullshit legal insurance scam through the hospital?"

He looked from one of them to the other. "Yes."

"If you got a property dispute with your neighbor and need someone to draw something up, fine, get legal insurance and they probably won't screw it up that bad. Worst that can happen is you have to hire a real law firm to redo the work. But criminal law, Dr. Zachary, is something else entirely. And those guys suck at criminal law. He'll take it for the money and to get interviewed on the news, but he won't know what he's doing. I've never met Mr. Duffman, but I guarantee you he doesn't know anything about this world."

Aster turned fully to him and held Zachary's gaze.

"I know which prosecutors hide evidence and which ones are by the book. I know which cops are dirty, which ones are addicts who use on the job, and which ones try to have sex with suspects when no one's looking. I know which judges fall asleep on the bench and which ones hear every word we say and which ones are only on the bench because they're some politician's nephew. Nevada has the death penalty, you know that, right?"

His eyes went a little wider, and Aster could see that his breath quickened.

"Um, no. No, I didn't."

"Well, you could be looking at the death penalty. I read about your case on the way over. They're accusing you of killing one woman, trying to kill your live-in girlfriend, and potentially kidnapping a fourteen-year-old girl. That's a death penalty case if I've ever seen one. You can't trust Charles Duffman, who's probably got big automobile accident cases to worry about. He's not going to put in the work this needs. He's not following around the lead detective for a week to see if he's having an affair or talking to Kathy Pharr's lawn guys to see if they ever saw anyone hanging around the house. Duffman won't do that, but we will. And we'll do it completely pro bono."

"You're going to do all that for free? And why exactly would you do that?"

"I'm going to be honest with you, because going forward we need complete trust and honesty with each other: I'm doing this for the publicity your case is going to generate. It's going to be all any of the news stations and gossip magazines talk about while the trial is going on. You're going to be famous—well, infamous—and your attorney is going to get a lot of that attention, and hence a lot of new clients."

Zachary chuckled. "So you'll defend me for publicity, huh? Isn't that a bit shallow?"

"Is that a worse reason than why Mr. Duffman would defend you?"

Zachary said nothing.

Aster sat next to him on the cot. "I'm excellent at what I do. And the only way the publicity works for me is if I win and you walk out of that courtroom. If I lose in front of the whole world, I'm not exactly going to have clients lining up out the door. Our incentives are very much aligned."

Ricci chimed in. "Dr. Zachary, Dylan is the best trial attorney I have ever seen. We left the public defender's office together, and do you know what he was known for when we were there? Never losing a trial. And it's not like when prosecutors say they've never lost a trial because they can pick and choose what cases to take to trial and what cases to deal on. Many private defense attorneys will plead out the bad cases or fire their clients if they won't do what they tell them. But public defenders like us had to take all the cases we were assigned, and we had to take most of them to trial because we couldn't fire our clients when they demanded one. We had to take the worst cases, the ones with the worst odds, to trial, and Dylan never lost. Not once."

Aster leaned forward, his elbows on his knees. "I can win this case."

Zachary looked at Ricci, then Aster. He nodded. "Okay . . . okay."

35

Aster had Zachary sign a representation agreement he had Billy print off. Then he told Billy to make sure to put a note in his e-file at the jail that he was represented so no other attorneys could visit him.

Back at the office, Ricci pulled up the court docket, and they saw that Zachary's case was going federal. Federal grand juries convened on Tuesday mornings twice a month—which meant tomorrow.

Federal grand juries were as close to professional juries as existed in the United States. Defense attorneys were not allowed in the room. The government would present evidence that charges should be filed against someone, and they could bring to the grand jury any witness they wanted. No one but the prosecutor was allowed to question them, which was what had led the chief of the New York Court of Appeals, Sol Wachtler, to famously say that grand juries would indict a ham sandwich.

Aster had always wanted to try getting around the rule that defense attorneys were not allowed in the grand jury room, and this presented a perfect opportunity.

Ricci stayed with him for a couple of hours in the office, harassing the FBI and the US Attorney's Office for their evidence. They weren't obligated to hand anything over yet, but sometimes speaking to a receptionist or clerk that you'd been friendly with in the past could get you the police or FBI reports.

When she left, Aster locked up and headed back to the jail.

It was dinnertime when he arrived, but the inmates in C Block had to eat in their cells. Aster was escorted by a deputy, who asked if he wanted an attorney-client room. He declined. He'd found, at least at first, when trust was still being built, that clients opened up to him more if he sat with them in their cells.

He looked down at the tray of food on Zachary's floor: a soggy sandwich, chips, and carrots.

"Sorry to interrupt your supper."

He said *supper* and made a note to say *dinner*. He'd spent the first twelve years of his life in West Virginia, and it seemed like he'd spent the rest of his life controlling the accent and idioms that it had ingrained in him. In court, he had to make a conscious effort to not slip into a West Virginian twang.

"It's fine," Zachary said. "I can't eat this food anyway. You know, I keep seeing you pull up your collar to hide that scar. A good plastic surgeon could get rid of it; it's not terribly deep. What happened, anyway?"

"I met a cop once that wasn't the nicest person. But I'm here to talk about you." Aster sat down next to him. He had a legal pad with him, and he took out a pen from his pocket and said, "You have a grand jury tomorrow. Do you know what that is?"

"Not really."

"There's going to be between sixteen and twenty-three jurors who hear evidence from the prosecution and decide if there's enough of it to bring charges against you. The jurors are trained, they do this for eighteen months whenever they're called, so they know how to get through these things quickly. And they nearly always choose to indict—to bring charges—but not every time."

"Do I have to say anything?"

Aster shook his head. "No, you don't even have to be there, but if you are and you decide to testify, only the prosecutor can question you. No other attorneys are allowed in the room to question anyone. But I'm going to get around that."

"How?"

"Let me worry about that. Anyway, I don't have the reports in this case, but there was a pretty detailed article in the *Las Vegas Sun*. I think they've overreached on this because of the media attention. See, the federal government can't just pick up any murder case it wants. There's requirements for a murder case to be filed in federal court, like the victim is a federal employee or a judge or something like that. There's about a dozen different ways to bring it to federal court, but what they're going forward on here is the sexual assault prong. There was semen found inside Kathy Pharr, along with some vaginal bruising and bruising on her thighs, but the semen was too degraded for a DNA match, so they're asking the grand jury to assume sexual assault took place during the murder and that the semen is yours."

"Assume?"

Aster nodded. "Assumptions are enough for a grand jury. I think what they're doing is hurrying to get the charges filed so they can start tainting the jury pool in the media. They'll hold a press conference and list the dozens of charges you're indicted on. They hope that the jurors that'll eventually be on your jury will see it and that it'll put pressure on me to plead you out early." He clicked his pen. "So before I ask you anything, I need you to listen carefully to me. Don't tell me if you did this. The law doesn't care if you're guilty or innocent, and neither do I. My job is to test the prosecution's case and make sure they're following the constitutional protections you have. My job, Doc, is to save your ass if I can. So if you did it, I don't want to know."

"Because if I told you I did it, you couldn't put me on the stand to say I didn't, could you?" Zachary shook his head. "Our damn justice system. That's what it's come to. Innocent people being railroaded and the guilty going free."

"They found the bandages and ricin in your garage and your alibis don't hold up well, so maybe save the indignation, Doc. I just want to stick to facts. Okay?"

"Yeah, okay."

"So first question is, if they, by some miracle, can retest that semen found inside Kathy Pharr, is it going to be matched to you?"

"Absolutely not."

"You weren't having an affair?"

"No. I would never in a million years cheat on Angie. I love her."

"Most men who cheat on their wives and girlfriends love them, Doc."

Zachary turned fully and looked Aster in the eyes. "I swear to you, I did not know Kathy Pharr."

Aster nodded. "Did your girlfriend know her?"

"No. I mean, I don't think so."

"She owns a yoga studio, yeah? Has she gone back to see if Kathy Pharr was maybe a student of hers at some point?"

"I don't know. I don't think so."

"You said you don't know who Kathy Pharr is, but have you ever met her? I'm not talking about hanging out with her, but have you ever maybe gone to a party she was at, or has she been to your work, or anything like that?"

He shook his head. "No. I have never seen that woman before in my life."

Aster took a few notes. "Ever have any domestic abuse allegations against your girlfriend or anyone from your past?"

"No, never."

"None? Not even a call to the police?"

"Well, I mean, there was a call once. An old girlfriend in college. I'd been drinking and things got out of hand. But I didn't touch her."

"See, this is what I'm talking about when I talk about honesty between us. Now, if I hadn't asked that follow-up question about the call, you wouldn't have told me about it, yeah? If you'd kept that from me, do you know where I woulda heard it the first time? In the courtroom. And it would catch me off guard. I wouldn't have a good explanation for it, and the only person getting hurt from that is you. Do you understand?"

He nodded slowly. "Yeah."

"Okay, good. So let's get to the alibis. Where were you on April thirteenth, the day Kathy Pharr was kidnapped?"

"Out of town. I went to a seminar on advancements in medical glue."

"Medical glue?"

"Yeah. There's a new product coming out that's ten times more effective than stitches or the current glue we have. It'll have some amazing uses for soldiers in battlefields and car accident victims that are bleeding out too fast, things like that."

"Well, to each his own, yeah. Do you have this glue at home?"

"No, it's not even on the market yet. I wouldn't have access to it even if I wanted it."

Aster wrote some notes and said, "Pharr was kidnapped at around midnight, and her body was found by a real estate agent who was getting the home ready for a viewing at nine o'clock the next morning. Where were you exactly during those times?"

"I would have just been at the Airbnb in San Diego where I was staying. I didn't go out or anything. I went to the conference, went to bed, and got on a flight the next day. I have the documentation for the Airbnb I stayed at. Get my phone and I can show you."

"Who can I call who spoke to you out there?"

"Well . . . I mean, no one."

"How long was the conference?"

"Just a day. About six hours."

"How many other people were there?"

"I don't know. A hundred, hundred fifty."

"You were at a conference with a hundred and fifty people for a day, and there's no one I can talk to who saw you there?"

"I didn't know their names," he barked. "If you paraded me in front of them, they'd probably remember me, but I don't know any of them."

Aster nodded as he wrote. "I'll need the title of the conference and a contact I can call over there. I'm going to get the names of the people who were there and pass your picture around. If we can get just a couple people who saw you there on the night Kathy Pharr was taken, that destroys the prosecution's case."

Zachary's face seemed to light up at the thought. "Angie can give you all of that information."

"Speaking of Angie, she told the police she was coming out of a mall after closing when she got struck on the back of the head and woke up in that cabin on Crimson Lake Road. That was . . . May thirteenth. Where were you on May thirteenth around ten?"

"Asleep at home. I'd just finished a twenty-four-hour shift."

"Can anybody verify that?"

"That I was home? I don't think so, no."

"What about Crimson Lake Road? Any connection there?"

"No. None. I didn't even know it was a place until all this."

Aster watched him a moment. "You looked away from me. What aren't you telling me?"

"Nothing."

"Doc, in my line of work, my main skill is reading people. You're holding something back. What is it?"

"Nothing. I'm being honest with you. I have no idea why this is happening to me."

Aster wrote a few more notes.

"I mean, what's the case look like so far?" Zachary asked. "You said you could win. Are you sure?"

"I don't have all the information on what they found at your house to tell you with a hundred percent certainty, but I didn't get into this line of work to lose trials. When I get all the reports, I'll come back and we'll go through them and I can give you a better picture of how this will go down. For now, I need you to sign something." Aster took out a document from his satchel.

"What is it?"

"You just subpoenaed me to court against my will, Doc."

36

Packing was the activity Yardley most needed to do and the one she least wanted to do. Tara was out, and she was too wired for sleep, so now seemed like the perfect time. She grudgingly changed into sweats and turned on some music as she began in her bedroom.

She'd never been a hoarder, and anything that didn't have an immediate use was typically donated within a week or two, so the task of packing wasn't going to be as painful as it could've been. Her bedroom, other than the necessities she needed to leave out, was done in around an hour.

As she was getting ready to start on the kitchen, she walked by Tara's room to go get some boxes out of the garage and stopped outside her door. Nothing had been packed. The room looked exactly like it always had. A twinge of sadness went through her: she wondered if her daughter was holding out hope they wouldn't actually move. Now that she'd found some people she actually liked spending time with and who were kind to her, her mother was ripping her away from them.

Yardley sat on her bed and sighed, staring up at the paintings Tara had in her room. Paintings she had done herself, along with a poster of Albert Einstein sticking out his tongue and one of a woman with the Milky Way galaxy coiled inside her.

She lay back on her daughter's bed with her hands behind her head and stared at the ceiling a few moments, remembering her own bed at that age: a mattress on the floor of her mother's apartment. An apartment Yardley paid all the bills for. All the things Tara was now doing—going shopping for new clothes, attending parties, spending lazy days by a pool—none of them were things Yardley had been able to do. Her entire life from the age of thirteen to eighteen had been school and grueling work with a few hours of sleep in between, all so she could provide for herself and a mother who was slowly drinking herself to death.

Yardley sat up with a deep breath, getting ready to leave the room, when she noticed the open drawer in the night table by the bed. She was about to push it back in but caught a glimpse of something handwritten on a paper inside.

Without Yardley even knowing why, a cold revulsion descended on her. As though an icy wind had just blown through the room.

She pulled the paper out. It was a letter from Eddie Cal to her daughter.

> *Tara,*
>
> *I so look forward to your visits. They add a stroke of color to such dreariness you cannot imagine. Waiting for a certain death is one thing, but waiting in limbo, uncertain of either death or life while my appeals grind through a bureaucracy that treats me as an item instead of a person—as you can imagine—had me in a bit of a depression. Until I realized of course that we all live in exactly this limbo. How many more times will you see a rose in your lifetime? There is some finite number. As there is some finite number to everything. How many times will you kiss a boy? How many sunsets will you see—how many times will you laugh—how many breaths will you take? . . . You have a set number left, and yet it*

all feels endless, doesn't it? As though death won't come knocking on our door one day to collect the debt we owe.

Don't let yourself forget this lesson, the most important lesson in all of life: that it one day ends.

With love,

Your father

Yardley felt like she wanted to vomit. She sifted through the drawer and found at least a dozen letters, dating back almost two years. For two years Tara had been in contact with the one man in the world Yardley most feared her getting to know.

Rage seethed inside her. Not only at her daughter's deception but at her betrayal. The fact that Tara had hidden their correspondence from Yardley showed she knew what it would do to her, and yet she'd done it anyway.

She paced the room a good ten minutes, debating what to do. She chewed so much on her thumbnail that it bled. She went to the bathroom and cleaned it with antiseptic before putting liquid bandage on it.

Then she went back to Tara's room and arranged everything as well as she could to look undisturbed. When she was through, she left her daughter's room.

Tara came through the front door around eleven at night and smiled at her mother when she stepped into the house.

"Hey. What're you doing up?" she said.

"Couldn't sleep. Where were you?"

"At Stacey's studying."

"Is that uncomfortable for her?"

Tara slipped off her shoes and dropped her backpack to the floor. "Why would it be uncomfortable for her?"

"You're studying subjects her *professors* have probably never heard of. It might make her feel insecure to be around you. Don't ever underestimate someone's insecurity. It can cause them to do things they wouldn't normally do."

The two held each other's gaze. Tara's frosty blue eyes fixed on her like she was a hawk analyzing the movements of a mouse in the distance.

"What are we really talking about?"

"What do you mean?"

"Give me some credit, Mom. What are we talking about? Just come out and say it."

Yardley watched her daughter. One of Yardley's greatest attributes, one responsible for so much of her success as a prosecutor, was her ability to read people. To surmise their true motivations quickly and with an accuracy that they themselves didn't have.

There were only three people in her life she had never been able to read correctly. Tara was one of them. The other two wanted her dead. It was not what she wanted to think about when she thought about her daughter.

"It's nothing, sweetheart. I'm just tired."

Tara nodded. "Okay. Well, I'm gonna go to bed. Night."

"Good night."

She watched Tara head to her bedroom, and a sickening dread gave her butterflies: There was more to this than letters. Cal was having her do something for him. He wouldn't correspond with Tara unless it benefited him somehow. And now Yardley would have to follow her own daughter to find out what it was.

37

The United States District Court for the District of Nevada was a much more modern-looking building than any courthouse should be. Yardley had always believed the law was a noble profession, the profession of the founding fathers. When she thought of courthouses, she thought of Corinthian pillars and wooden banisters; old, creaky chairs in windowless rooms.

The grand jury room was on the second floor. A marshal, who acted as bailiff in federal court, stood outside the doors.

"How are we today, Ms. Yardley?"

"Fine, Peter. Thank you for asking."

He held the door open for her as she went inside. No one from the public was allowed to sit in on grand jury proceedings, but everyone knew her here, and she didn't think they'd object to her taking a seat in the audience benches. Most of them probably didn't know she'd quit yet.

She sat at the very back, as far away from everyone as possible.

Eighteen people sat in the jury box. A federal grand jury needed a minimum of sixteen people to hold the proceedings.

All federal felony cases began with grand juries, and they were a completely one-sided proceeding. The rules of evidence didn't apply, and the prosecution could introduce anything they wanted, as long as it was relevant to the case at hand. Most grand jury proceedings didn't even have judges, but for occasional cases, like high-profile murderers or terrorists, a judge would sit in and ensure the process ran smoothly.

Today's judge was an elderly man named McLane, and he nodded at her with a small smile.

Kyle Jax was sitting at the prosecution table. Two other prosecutors sat behind him, waiting their turn. Judge McLane noticed Jax's sucker.

"Mr. Jax, I would appreciate if we didn't partake of any candy in my courtroom."

"Sure," Jax said, tossing his sucker into a wastebasket next to the table.

"What matter may we call for you, Counselor?"

"The government would call the United States versus Michael Jacob Zachary."

"Okay, let's get Mr. Zachary out here, please, Marshal."

Zachary was brought out in a white jumpsuit with shackles. The marshal sat him down at the defendant's table. The door opened then, and the marshal let Angela River in. She exchanged glances with Zachary. It made her stop in her tracks, and it seemed like she would burst into tears right then. He appeared sympathetic to her, his eyes going down to the floor as though unable to look at her. Then he looked up at her and silently mouthed the words, *I didn't do this.*

River noticed Yardley then. She joined her at the back of the courtroom. Neither said anything at first, and given their last encounter, Yardley wasn't sure how River would respond. But instead of anger, she simply sat down next to her and held her hand. Yardley gave it a squeeze back.

"First witness, Mr. Jax."

"The government would call Detective Lucas Garrett to the stand."

The marshal went to get Garrett from the witness waiting room. Garrett was sworn in and took his place in the witness box.

"Detective, tell us how you came into contact with the defendant in this case, Michael Zachary."

Garrett detailed how he'd first learned of Kathy Pharr's death all the way through to what evidence they found and how the FBI came to be involved. He gave a succinct outline of the case and the evidence and then left an opening for Jax to ask the most important question:

"And who is that perpetrator, do you believe, Detective?"

"The defendant, Michael Zachary."

Jax then showed a photo to Garrett and said, "What is this, Detective?"

"That's a photo of Mr. Zachary and Kathy Pharr getting out of a car at a motel together. We obtained it from your office, from an assistant US attorney named Jessica Yardley, who obtained it from a reporter named Jude Chance."

"And how did Mr. Chance have it?"

"He stated he obtained it for a fee from an anonymous source."

"So someone was following around Mr. Zachary and Mrs. Pharr?"

"Possibly, yes. Someone may have hired a private investigator for whatever reason to follow and take photographs. But it's also possible the motel owner or manager took it. Sometimes, the small, seedier motels take photos of couples who arrive and leave quickly, presumably for sex. They attempt to blackmail one or both of the people if they're married, or if someone meets with a prostitute, they'll tell them they'll send the pictures to their employer unless they're paid. It's possible the motel owner or an employee took the photo and then saw Mrs. Pharr in the news and reached out to Mr. Chance to sell the photo."

"So they were having an affair?"

"That is the most likely assumption that we can draw, yes."

Jax then dug into the holes in Zachary's alibis, and it was clear to Yardley that they were going to be a tough burden for the defense to overcome. It just wasn't plausible that no one at a large conference would remember him.

After half an hour describing the kidnapping of Kathy Pharr, Jax glanced toward the jury, then took a step around the lectern, stuffing his hands into his pockets. "The defendant's live-in girlfriend is Angela River, correct?"

"Yes."

"Please tell us what happened to her."

"One month after Mrs. Pharr's death, on May the thirteenth, we received a call of suspicious activity at 612 Crimson Lake Road. Not far from the scene where Mrs. Pharr's body was found. A neighbor saw a car parked outside a home that had been unoccupied for two years. A figure, we assume a male, took someone out of the trunk of a vehicle. The neighbor said they then went into the cabin, the larger figure pulling the smaller figure by the arm in an aggressive manner, and later only one of them walked out. The neighbor had never seen the car before, and he couldn't identify the figure, as it was too dark."

"Could he identify the car?"

"No, other than it was a black or dark-blue sedan. There's minimal street lighting on Crimson Lake Road."

"What does Mr. Zachary drive?"

"A dark-blue Lincoln Continental."

"So what happened after the neighbor contacted 911?"

"Dispatch let us know about the call. Normally, a patrol deputy would be sent out to investigate. But the Federal Bureau of Investigation had taken an interest in Mrs. Pharr's death. Our contact there, Special Agent Cason Baldwin, believed her death to be the work of a serial murderer who had just started a cycle of killing."

"And what is a cycle, Detective?"

"A cycle's a period where the killer engages in fantasy, and then in the actual killing before going into a cooling-off period, and then finding another victim and starting another cycle. So Agent Baldwin had requested he be contacted immediately about any suspicious activity on Crimson Lake Road."

"What happened then?"

"Myself and three other uniformed deputies met Agent Baldwin at the location about an hour later. We found Ms. River on a table, wearing a black tunic and bloody bandages around her head exactly like Mrs. Pharr."

Jax handed photos to the jury of both crime scenes, as well as blood spatter pictures, sketches from the forensic technicians, and a DVD containing video taken at both scenes. He walked Garrett through what had occurred after they discovered River was still alive, how they discovered the ricin, and what the Department of Homeland Security had explained to them afterward. Finally, Jax pulled out photos of the Sarpong paintings and handed them to the jury.

Yardley had to give Garrett credit. His testimony about the paintings and how it was discovered the killer was mimicking them was succinct. He didn't try to impress the jury with legal or investigative terms they might not have understood in order to seem more competent than he was. He got the information across quickly, and the jury didn't seem bored.

The hearing was pushing four hours, and it was apparent to everybody that the jury's attention span was waning, when Jax said, "Thank you, Detective Garrett, that's all I have for now."

Zachary turned toward River with a pleading expression on his face, as though begging her to believe him, until the marshal said, "Eyes forward."

"Next witness, Mr. Jax," the judge said.

"We would call Dr. Mathew Carrey with the Clark County Office of the Coroner and Medical Examiner."

Jax introduced more documents, photographs, and videos of both crime scenes as well as gruesome autopsy photos through Dr. Carrey. He introduced a narrative statement Baldwin had written out instead of having him testify, as it was customary to only have your lead law enforcement officer testify at a grand jury proceeding—in this case, Garrett—and then he rested.

After a quick break, McLane said, "Mr. Zachary, you now have the opportunity to present evidence or witnesses or to testify yourself, if you wish. Please understand, sir, that you are not required to incriminate yourself and do not need to testify. However, if you choose to do so, anything you say here can be used against you in subsequent court proceedings. Do you understand that, sir?"

"I do. Yes."

"With that in mind, do you wish to testify?"

"No, Your Honor."

"Do you have any witnesses or evidence you would like to present?"

"Um, yes, Your Honor. One witness. Mr. Dylan Aster."

One of the prosecutors behind Jax leaned forward, whispering in his ear. No doubt telling him that Dylan Aster was a defense attorney. Jax shot to his feet.

"Your Honor, we would object to Mr. Aster even being allowed into the grand jury room. It's my understanding he is Mr. Zachary's attorney."

"Mr. Zachary, is he your attorney?"

"Yes, Your Honor, but that's not why I'm calling him. I subpoenaed him as a character witness."

Yardley smiled and instantly knew what Aster was about to pull off.

Clever boy, she thought.

Jax chuckled. "Judge, that's ridiculous. There's no way he can testify as to Mr. Zachary's character. The defendant was arrested less than two days ago, so unless they were childhood friends, Mr. Aster knows nothing about the defendant's character."

"Peter, is Mr. Aster here?"

The marshal said, "Yes, Your Honor, he's in the witness waiting room, and he does have a subpoena apparently signed by Mr. Zachary."

"Okay, well, let's bring him in here and see what's going on."

38

Baldwin had no jurisdiction over the Clark County Sheriff's Office. Though popular movies and television shows liked to portray the FBI coming in and taking over a case, the truth was that cases fell within whatever jurisdictions they fell in, and any outside law enforcement agencies that wanted to be involved had to work with the agency that had jurisdiction or go rogue and conduct their own investigations—which more times than not blew up when leads were hoarded and offenders slipped through the cracks.

Detective Kristen Reece was sitting in her cubicle in the Missing Persons Bureau of the LVPD when Baldwin walked in. She looked up from her computer and chuckled.

"I didn't know Brad Pitt was in town. You researching a role? 'Cause tell you what, I'll give you a personal tour of this city like you ain't never seen."

Baldwin grinned as he sat down across from her. He glanced behind her to her marksmanship awards and noticed several more since last time he'd been here.

"Is that an MSRA award?"

"Sure as shit is. First woman ever to win it. Pistol and rifle."

"No shit?"

She leaned back in her seat. "Marines, baby. Deserve somethin' for almost dyin' in that desert over some rich man's oil." She watched him expressionless a moment, and then slowly a smile came to her face. Baldwin got the impression that she, unlike many people who simply said the words, did genuinely miss seeing him. "Forget that shit. It's a beautiful day and I got a handsome man in front of me. What can I do for you, Agent Baldwin?"

"You're the assigned detective on a case I've been looking into on my own."

"Your own?"

He nodded. "My ASAC is trying to get me into white collar and away from Behavioral Science and Violent Crimes. He'd shit a brick if he knew most of my day was spent chasing down leads on this one case."

"Which one?"

"Harmony Pharr. She's attached to the Crimson Lake Executioner."

Reece nodded. "I know the case. Disappeared from her tree house. Thank you for that, by the way. Who the hell knows how long it woulda been before someone found her phone and the other shit back there."

"Don't mention it. I just need to know if . . . everything that can be done is being done."

"You mean you wanna see if I'm screwing up the case at all and if you could do better?"

They both smiled at each other.

"We known each other too long for bullshit, Cason."

"I trust you fully. There's maybe five people I can say that about. But this one has . . . it's gotten under my skin, and I don't know how to get it out. I think you could be Sherlock Holmes and I'd still be sitting in this chair asking you what's going on with the case."

"Oh," she said knowingly, "one of those. I see it a lot with detectives who've never worked juvenile crimes before and they suddenly get a pedophilia ring or human trafficking syndicate thrown in their lap. They don't realize evil like that really exists in the world."

"Evil like what?"

"Like the kind that looks for the most innocent and rips them apart for pleasure. It's some biblical shit, Cason. Sodom and Gomorrah. You never worked a child murder before, right?"

"One case. It didn't sit well with me then either."

She sighed. "My advice? Give me what you got and forget about it. You've already done enough. Because of you we know where she was taken and when. It's a good start. Just let me handle it."

Baldwin nodded, wiping some dust off her desk.

"You ain't going to, though, are you?"

He shook his head. "Nope."

She smiled. "Didn't think so. All right, I'll keep you up to speed on what's going on. I don't have shit now, but as soon as I got anything, I'll hit you up."

He stared at her.

"I promise."

He nodded. "I appreciate it." He took a deep breath and glanced around the cubicles to make sure no one was nearby. "I see her in my dreams. It's only happened a couple of times and just briefly, but it's memorable enough that it doesn't go away in the morning."

"What do you see?"

"Nothing, really, nothing violent. Just her on her back. She looks frozen, almost, just staring up at the sky with these, like . . . blank eyes. A puppet's eyes. And then she fades away."

Reece leaned forward and put her elbows on the desk. "Cason, listen to me—dealing with children is not like dealing with adults. There's no shame in saying it's not for you and just leaving it alone. Especially when your ass is about to be fired by some ASAC dickhead."

He smirked. "He is seriously a dick. Do you know I caught him yelling at one of the cleaning staff because she replaced the bag in his wastebasket with a black bag and he prefers transparent? Not like lecturing or scolding—full-on red-faced yelling so that everyone in the office could hear. Then I hear him telling another agent that he likes to do things like that to make people believe he's unpredictable."

"Wow."

He nodded. "I'm the last one to leave, so every night I take all his pens. Doesn't matter if he's just got one sitting on his desk or a new pack in his drawer—I take them all. Drives him insane."

She chuckled. "Careful, Joan of Arc, you don't want to rebel too hard."

He shrugged. "It's the little things that make life rewarding."

They watched each other a moment with grins on their faces, and Baldwin realized she was actually a good friend of his. Not someone who just waited for their turn to talk and commented on his social media posts but someone who would be there for him if he really needed it. And it made him realize how few of those kinds of people he had in his life.

He inhaled deeply and rose. "I appreciate you being worried about me, but I need to find her, Kristen. If this guy does to her what I think he has planned . . . I don't think I'm going to be able to put this badge on again if I can't stop it."

She looked at him gravely and said, "I'll do whatever I can to help you."

She rose and hugged him, and he pulled away and left without another word.

39

Yardley watched as Aster entered the grand jury room. He was wearing a sleek gray suit with a blue tie. He had boyish good looks and a clean-shaven face.

"Mr. Aster, good to see you again."

"You as well, Your Honor."

"Now, it's my understanding that you are Mr. Zachary's attorney, is that correct?"

"Yes."

"And you are also attempting to testify on his behalf?"

"Yes, Judge. I was subpoenaed not for my capacity as an attorney but as a witness."

Jax shook his head. "That's ridiculous. Attorneys are not allowed in federal grand jury proceedings, Your Honor. That's well established by statute and caselaw. Defendants are usually not even in the courtroom."

McLane said, "Mr. Jax, how about I determine what's ridiculous or not in my courtroom?" He turned back to Aster. "What do you intend to testify about?"

"I'm not entirely sure. I believe Dr. Zachary would like me to talk about his character for the time I've known him."

"And how long is that?"

"Since yesterday."

Jax chortled derisively.

"But," Aster said, "my mama always did say I make friends easy."

The jury chuckled.

"I shouldn't even have to address this, Your Honor," Jax said.

"Judge, I am not advocating as an attorney in any way when I say this, I'm just pointing out a fact, and that is that Dr. Zachary is entitled to subpoena whoever he likes to testify on his behalf. I accepted service of the subpoena and am here to testify. Unless Mr. Jax can point to a statute saying he can bar a defendant's witness from testifying at a grand jury proceeding, I'm not sure what the problem is."

McLane looked over the document the marshal had handed him. "Mr. Jax, this appears to be a valid subpoena. Do you have a specific statute stating a valid witness for the defendant may be barred from testifying at a grand jury proceeding due to a conflict created by representation?"

"Not off the top of my head, Your Honor, but the spirit of this is clearly to get around the barring of defense counsel at these proceedings."

"Well, I'm not here to judge spirits; I'm here to judge the law, Mr. Jax. So unless you can point me to a specific statute, administrative rule, or caselaw that says you may bar this witness from testifying, I'm going to allow it."

Jax turned and started whispering with the two other prosecutors. Aster stood calmly in front of the judge. He noticed Yardley and winked, causing her to grin.

"As long as he's not making legal arguments and sticking to character evidence, I guess that's fine," Jax said with a tinge of anger in his voice.

"All right, then, Mr. Aster, please take the stand and be sworn in."

Once Aster was sitting in the witness box and sworn in, he poured some water into a paper cup and took a sip. He looked to the jury and smiled, his dimples appearing on both cheeks. Some of the jurors smiled back.

The defendant was not allowed to question any witnesses in a grand jury proceeding, so Jax was in the awkward position of having to ask Zachary's attorney questions about his character on his behalf. Jax looked flustered, and he was getting angrier.

"What did you want to say about the defendant's character, Mr. Aster?"

"Oh . . . I don't know. Like I said, I haven't known him that long. I was surprised to even be called here, honestly. If you look at Title 18, starting at section 1111, of the United States Code, which lists all the ways murder can be a federal crime, the way Kathy Pharr was killed isn't listed there. So frankly I was just surprised this was in federal court at all given that there's no jurisdiction—"

"Objection!" Jax shouted. "He's making legal arguments, Your Honor."

"Hey, you asked the question. I'm just answering it."

"Mr. Aster," McLane said, "please just stick to character evidence relevant to this case."

"Of course, Your Honor. And I apologize for mentioning Title 18, section 1111, of the United States Code."

Yardley couldn't help but smile.

Jax put one hand against the prosecution table and stared at Aster, who gave him a shy little grin that only angered Jax more.

"Do you actually have anything relevant to add?" Jax said.

"He seems like a good guy and I believe him. I don't think he killed her."

"That it?"

"I like your cowboy boots, too."

Jax glared at him with obvious disgust.

Aster said, "May I be excused now, Your Honor?"

"You may."

Aster left the room.

McLane then said, "Mr. Zachary, any other witnesses you wish to present?"

"No, Your Honor."

"Mr. Jax, anything else to add before sending this to the grand jury for deliberation on the matter?"

"No, Judge."

"Okay, then we are in recess for deliberations."

River leaned close to Yardley and said, "What does that mean?"

"Grand juries get together after all the evidence is presented, and they decide whether to indict on the charges or not."

"I didn't see anything saying he's innocent. They're going to indict him, aren't they?"

"Maybe not. I'll be right back."

She rose and went out into the hallway. Aster was standing against the wall joking with Peter. Yardley went up to him and took his arm, pulling him along as they casually strolled down the hall.

"That was one of the best things I've seen in there," she said. "Of course, if you'd've tried it with me, I wouldn't have let you get a word out, and then I would have asked for sanctions against you."

He shrugged. "Probably wouldn't have tried it if I knew you were the prosecutor."

They stopped near some windows overlooking a building across the street and the busy road in between.

"Do you know much about the case yet?" Yardley asked.

"Just what I read in the *Sun*. Couldn't get anyone from your office to hand anything over."

"Not my office anymore. I quit yesterday. Well, retired."

"No shit? I hadn't heard. Damn, I'll miss you, Jess. You're the one I always called when I needed to talk to someone reasonable over there."

"I'm sure you'll get by just fine."

The courtroom doors opened, and a marshal came out. He saw the two of them, and Aster said, "Do they have a true bill already?"

"No, no decision yet. They did ask the judge something, though."

"What?"

"If they could have a copy of the United States Code Title 18, starting at section 1111."

40

Yardley went to the soda machine, got two diet Cokes, and brought them into the courtroom. River sat in the same spot. She didn't seem angry or confused . . . just tired. Tired and wanting not to think anymore.

Yardley handed her the can and sat down next to her. She opened hers quietly so the marshal on the other side of the room wouldn't hear and ask them to take the drinks outside. Yardley took a sip, but River just slowly turned the can in her hands.

"How long will this take?"

"Not long," Yardley said. "Grand juries aren't deciding guilt or innocence, so the default is to always indict. They should be getting close by now."

"What's going to happen to Zachary after he's indicted?"

"He'll be arraigned, and then his attorney will get the evidence in the case. You can meet with him and get your questions answered, but it's a little dicey since you're also one of the victims. You may want an attorney to represent you during this process."

"Do I have to testify against him?"

"Yes. You weren't married, so you don't have spousal privilege. There is a way out of it if you can show you'll go through extreme hardship if you testify. But honestly, even if you could get out of it, would you?"

River lifted her eyes and watched as Zachary was brought in and sat at the defendant's table again.

"How can I, Jess? How can I get up there and testify against the man I thought I would marry one day?"

Yardley took her hand. "I didn't know whether to testify against Eddie at his trial either. I had more time to prepare for it than you will, but it ate me up for a long time."

"What'd you do?"

"I thought about my little girl. I had to choose what I wanted her to see. Did I want her to see that I was loyal to her father, even though he was a monster, and that I didn't want to betray family? Or did I want to show her that justice applies to everyone? I chose to testify. It was one of the most painful things I've ever done, but if I hadn't, I know I would regret it now."

River shook her head, tears glistening in her eyes before she closed them and drew in a deep breath. "I can't believe this is happening. I keep thinking I'm going to wake up, but I don't."

"Angie—"

"All rise," one of the marshals said. "United States District Court for the District of Nevada back in session."

McLane sat down. Jax was already seated with the two other prosecutors, but Aster wasn't allowed in the room. Zachary looked terrified. She noticed his hands trembling underneath the table.

"It's my understanding the grand jury has made a decision?"

The foreman rose and said, "We have, Your Honor."

"And what say you?"

"On counts one through fourteen, we do not find sufficient evidence for a true bill. On counts fifteen through twenty-two, we find a true bill. On counts twenty-three and twenty-four, we do not find sufficient evidence for a true bill."

Yardley had no doubt that if there were people other than her and River in the benches, there would be shock and whispering. Counts one through fourteen were the murder, attempted murder, kidnapping, and related charges. The jury had not indicted Zachary on the most serious charges against him and instead indicted him on a handful of lesser charges.

Jax rose and said, "Your Honor, that is a direct result of the manipulation Mr. Aster committed in this proceeding. I would ask to convene another jury and bar Mr. Aster from testifying."

"Counsel, when I asked if you had a statute, administrative rule, or caselaw that said I could bar Mr. Aster from testifying, you told me you knew of none off the top of your head, and you had time during deliberations to find one, but I'm guessing you did not."

"We can find something now, but it doesn't matter, Your Honor, because he tainted this jury. I'd like to question the jury on the reasons why they neglected to find a true bill for those counts."

"The jury deliberations are held outside of our presence for a reason, Mr. Jax, and next to the attorney-client privilege, secrecy in the deliberation process is a hallmark of our judicial system. I will not allow you to question these jurors on their motives for finding the way they found. Now, Marshal, would you please have the foreperson sign the indictment and hand it to my clerk for filing, thank you." He turned to Zachary. "Mr. Zachary, you will be back to see Judge Hardy on July the second for a detention hearing. I am denying bail at this time, but I will make a note that Mr. Aster is your attorney of record, and he will address it with Judge Hardy."

"Thank you."

"Okay, next matter, please."

Jax was on the phone in the hallway, no doubt to Lieu. The media, specifically Jude Chance, with his army of contacts at every courthouse in the state, would quickly know about the jury refusing to indict on the murder and kidnapping charges, and it would be on every local news site within an hour.

Jax hung up and said to her, "I think we need to appeal."

"Appeal what?"

"That was bullshit."

"You can't appeal a grand jury not indicting on some of the charges, Kyle. I warned you this would happen."

"We'll just dismiss and reindict him, then."

"You can't unless you have some new evidence. You've got some felonies on there and can ask for prison. Keep it for now."

"And what?" he growled. "Just let that bastard off for murder?"

"Don't raise your voice at me."

He shook his head and mumbled, "Such bullshit."

Yardley took a step closer to him, ensuring he was looking into her eyes. "It is *not* bullshit. That jury did their jobs. This is your and Roy's fault, not theirs. And by the way, I'm still not convinced there's federal jurisdiction. Aster will get even these charges kicked on those grounds the second he gets in front of a judge."

Aster turned the corner in the hallway, and Jax saw him.

"That is some scummy shit you just pulled in there. Don't think I'm going to forget it. And when this is over, maybe it'll be time to report you to the Bar. And you better damn well believe I'm talking to everyone in our office about it. See if you get any good offers from us anymore."

Aster just grinned and said, "Take a Xanax, Billy the Kid. This much stress isn't good for you." He looked at Yardley. "I'll walk you out."

Once they got to the elevators and away from Jax, Yardley said, "You know the county is just going to pick it up, right?"

He shrugged. "I was planning on it. But county ain't federal. I can work with them on something."

"What are you looking for?"

"Depends how strong their case is, but if it's as solid as the *Sun* made it seem, I'd tell him to take manslaughter."

"Not a chance they'll give you manslaughter."

"Never know."

The thought of Zachary getting manslaughter made her tense. He could be out in as little as five years. What would happen to Angie when he was released? Would he try to finish what he started?

Once outside, Aster put on his sunglasses and said, "Lunch?"

"Can't today. Rain check?"

"Yup. And I was serious about that offer. You wanna jump to the other side, Lily and I would be happy to take you."

"I'll think about it."

She watched as he crossed the street. A wave of irritation gnawed at her about how this had played out. She had told Lieu and Jax exactly what would happen, and they'd refused to listen. If he'd had a lesser defense attorney, Zachary would have been indicted, but Aster had outmaneuvered them. He would likely outmaneuver the county prosecutors as well. On a case this big, with this much media attention, winning for Aster meant his life would change. He would never have to hustle for clients again. So he would pour every ounce of energy he had into this case, and a randomly assigned prosecutor wouldn't be anywhere near as passionate. Sometimes, cases were just about which side wanted the victory more.

Yardley was sitting at home on the couch watching television when Baldwin called.

"Is it true?" he said.

"It is."

"So what are they gonna do?"

"Either the state attorney general's office or the county district attorney will prosecute him. This case is too big to ignore. It's already a PR nightmare for the US Attorney's Office, but if they can get convictions when the federal government couldn't, they'd definitely see that as a nice perk."

He exhaled. "How the hell did this happen?"

"They were sloppy and Zachary's attorney wasn't."

Her line beeped, indicating another call. She didn't recognize the number.

"Give me a minute." She switched lines. "This is Jessica."

"Jessica, this is Brie Johnson."

It took a moment for Yardley to place the name. But then she remembered her as a prosecutor for Clark County she'd worked with on a couple of cases.

"I hope it's okay that I got your number from Roy Lieu. He said you wouldn't mind."

"I don't. What can I do for you?"

"Well, I'm sure you've heard about what happened with the Crimson Lake Executioner case by now."

"I have."

"So Nathan is pissed. I guess the US AG called yelling at Roy, who called the state AG and yelled at him, who called the county and yelled at Nathan . . . I don't know. There was yelling and finger-pointing all day. I guess the failure to indict was on all the cable news shows."

"I imagine it was."

"Well, apparently they're going to dismiss the federal case in its entirety and have us file it down here, and yours truly got the short straw. Anyway, I was wondering if me and Nathan could swing by your house right now? It won't take long."

"What for?"

"Best we talk in person."

She could have asked Yardley to come down to the office, but instead she'd asked to come to her home. A comfortable place. Somewhere Yardley would be more likely to agree to a favor.

Yardley gave her the address and said she would see her soon.

When she hung up, she turned the television off and lay down on the couch, staring at the ceiling. The temperature, last time she checked, was 107. A light sheen of sweat tickled her neck.

She dressed in yoga pants and a tank top and made a fruit smoothie, which she sipped slowly in the kitchen until she heard a knock at the door. When she answered, Brie Johnson and Nathan Salls, the DA for Clark County, stood there. Yardley let them in, and they sat on her couch while she took a spot on the love seat.

Salls had won the district attorney seat only a couple of years ago, when the then DA running for reelection had been indicted on several campaign finance felonies.

A registered independent who spoke plainly and allowed livestock to roam his backyard, Salls had always struck Yardley as someone who should have been working a farm rather than wearing suits and appearing on television talking about justice.

"Love your house," Brie said.

"Thank you. We're moving soon, though. Down to Santa Bonita."

"Roy mentioned that. I was honestly surprised you're retiring. You always struck me as a lifer."

"Just need something new, I guess."

Brie nodded, glancing at the decorations in the home. Yardley refused to have any paintings up, but she had a few oriental prints and decorative incense burners. "So you can probably guess why we're here."

"I have a hunch."

Salls said, "Jessica, I'm going to get to the point 'cause I don't like wasting time. I think it best if you were to come over to our office as a special prosecutor for this case."

Yardley had anticipated the request. It was a win-win for them. If she won the case, the DA's Office would take credit. If she lost, they would say it wasn't their fault if a US attorney botched the trial.

"Why would you think I'd want to do that, Nathan?"

"Because I think you care about the case, and I think Roy didn't let you prosecute it, did he?"

"What makes you say that?"

He leaned forward, his elbows on his knees. "I've known Roy a long time. I know how he thinks."

"Just because I may or may not care about it doesn't mean I want to prosecute it. Brie will do a marvelous job."

"I know she would, but I think you would be even better for this particular case."

Yardley folded her hands in her lap. "What's this really about? Every time we've talked, it's been over the phone, and suddenly you're willing to come to my house at a moment's notice? Why are you pushing for this so hard?"

He shrugged. "I just wanna make sure the good doctor is convicted, and I think you got the best shot at doing that."

"And of course if I lose, you'll be in the news saying I was a federal prosecutor, not a state prosecutor, and I rushed the case and screwed it up, right?"

He exhaled loudly and leaned back into the couch, pressing his tie down against his belly and straightening it. "We talked with Roy and with the AG. He wants someone from the US Attorney's Office on the case, at least tangentially, so it doesn't look like they screwed the pooch quite so hard. If a federal prosecutor, even one who just retired, took part in the prosecution and there was a conviction, they could say they did their jobs and they always get their man or whatever bullshit they wanna spin."

"And what do you get out of it?"

He cleared his throat. "This is a very public case, and a lot of people up on the hill are upset about how it's played out. If there is a conviction, I've been made certain assurances of support when election time comes around."

She chuckled. "The AG said he would support you if you win the case, huh? I figured they would have to give you something better than that. He might support you anyway."

He shook his head. "Maybe, maybe not. The Nevada AG supporting me for DA would be a big win. He's got a lotta pull. It's nothing to take lightly."

"Prosecution isn't about scoring wins for me, Nathan."

"Hey, I could've lied and said Brie is too swamped to take it or some bullshit. I didn't. Besides, we all know you're the best person for the job."

Yardley looked out of the balcony sliding glass doors and considered things. "I'll have to think about it."

"Well, that's better than a no. But don't think too long. I'd like you to be at the press conference when we announce we're filing on him. It's tomorrow."

"I'll let you know by then."

41

When the receptionist at the US Attorney's Office told Aster they didn't have discovery ready for him, he spoke with a paralegal, who told him the same thing. Then he lied and said Kyle Jax said to get him everything as soon as possible. Though he'd have to wait for copies of all the photos, videos, sketches, analyses, and lab reports, he left with the detective and FBI reports, a stack of papers as thick as a novel.

Back at the office, he made copies and put one set on Ricci's desk. Then he sat in his office and read.

On the first read, the case seemed strong. Baldwin and Garrett could write persuasively, and the case they had assembled against Zachary was built on a solid search warrant—it was extremely prudent of them to only search the garage rather than the home—and solid evidence. The ricin, syringes, and roll of bandages alone would be a nearly overwhelming obstacle for the defense to overcome. Not even to mention the replicas of the paintings. The only real error was the filing: the case should have been filed in state court for now, as federal jurisdiction wasn't clear, and he couldn't help but grin at how upset Kyle Jax must be right now.

But on the second read, the major flaws began to appear. Aster took out a marker and highlighted anything even remotely relevant to Zachary's defense. There were only two ways to win a jury trial in a murder case: paint the victim as a monster who deserved it, or point the finger at someone else.

Ricci came in a little later with the stack of reports he'd left for her. She collapsed onto his couch and said, "Interesting reading."

"Baldwin writes good reports. Garrett's not bad, but he skips over too many details. I think he's lazy."

"He misspelled *restaurant* like four times, too. I don't know why, but that bugged the crap out of me."

"It's your English degree. So first impressions?"

"Guilty."

"Seriously?"

She was staring at the ceiling, her head resting on the back of the couch. "You don't agree?"

"I don't know. First off, he's intelligent. He had to have known if he killed his girlfriend and the woman he was cheating with, he's the first person the police would look at."

"Lawyers, doctors, professors—they kill their wives and girlfriends like everyone else, Dylan."

"I know, but he didn't seem impulsive to me. Did you see his sink in the jail cell? His toothbrush, soap, and toothpaste were all lined up straight, and his clothes were neatly folded. He seems OCD to me, and hitting her over the head while she's walking out of a mall is sloppy as shit."

"The ricin isn't sloppy. An injection in the eyes or tongue with a poison that's barely detectible, *after* washing them and clipping their hair and nails? That screams organized doctor to me."

"Or someone wants to make it look like that."

She chuckled. "Dylan, come on. We've done this long enough to know people don't get set up like this."

"Maybe some people do and we've just never had one of these cases before? Or maybe some people get set up so well not even their lawyers believe them when they say they're innocent? I mean, think about it.

The toxicologists from the CDC and Homeland said the Executioner got the dosages wrong and he gave Angela River too little ricin, yeah? Well, if anyone should know that weight makes a difference in administering a toxin like that, it's a doctor. And her boyfriend of all people would know how much she weighed and that he'd have to give her more than he did to Kathy Pharr."

"You said yourself he seems like he has OCD. All the syringes were the same size and held the same volume of fluid. They were all filled to the brim. Maybe he didn't want a bunch of different sizes around?"

"Then use two of them."

"The more he used, the more likely detection would be. The longer investigators don't know what he used, the better his chances of getting away with it."

"I'm just saying the simplest explanation is always best. And here I think the simplest explanation is that a doctor wouldn't make a stupid mistake like this."

She lay down fully on the couch, putting one arm over her forehead. "Okay, let's just pretend you're right and Zachary was set up. This person would have to be close enough to him to know he was having sex with Kathy Pharr, number one. They'd have to know where Kathy Pharr worked and wait there until she had a smoke break to snatch her. Then they would have to know he was also living with Angela River and follow her around and wait for the right time to snatch her. And they'd also have to be able to access a locked room in a garage where only Zachary and Angela know where the key is, *and* they'd have to do all this sneaking around without Zachary or Angela noticing them. And if Harmony didn't run away and this guy got her, he'd also have to stalk and snatch her. I don't buy it. Especially the breaking in and leaving paintings and the rest in the locked room. Someone would've noticed this guy."

"Maybe Angela and Zachary hadn't been in that room for a long time? Maybe there's other ways someone could get in that wouldn't be easily noticed?"

"Okay, again, let's assume you're right. What's the motive?"

"What's the doc's motive for killing Kathy and his girlfriend? He doesn't have life insurance on either of them. If he really wanted to be with Kathy, he would've killed the husband, not her. And he's only been dating Angela a couple of months. Barely enough time to know her. Why kill them at all?"

She shrugged. "I don't know. Maybe he just likes killing."

"That's bullshit."

"They're rare, but psychopaths are actually out there, Dylan. Zachary may have just wanted to see what it was like to kill someone."

"If that's all it was, he wouldn't have picked his lover and his girlfriend. He would have picked a stranger. Someone who couldn't be connected to him."

"So what's your theory then?"

"The husband."

"Tucker Pharr?"

He nodded. "Did you see his conviction for kidnapping and his other prior that was expunged? And he realizes his daughter's missing, and his reaction is basically like, *Oh shit, that sucks*. Garrett wrote in his report he didn't seem overly disturbed in the interview. How many dads you know wouldn't lose their shit if they found out their daughter is missing after their wife has already been murdered? So to buy the government's case, we have to believe the doc killed Kathy, tried to kill his girlfriend, and then kidnapped Tucker's daughter as like, what, revenge against everyone for some reason? It doesn't make sense. They can't give a good explanation to the jury as to why he would do all this."

She said, "But Tucker finds out about the affair, kills his wife, tries to kill Zachary's girlfriend as payback . . . okay, I'm liking this a little more. Why the daughter?"

He shook his head. "That I can't figure out. But whatever the reason, I don't think it's going to end well for her."

42

Tara watched the young engineer attempt to impress her by going through Lorett's theorem on a whiteboard and explaining the application to cold fusion. She observed him rather than eyeing the board—read his face, noticed the way his hands moved, the positioning of his feet, and his posture. Most men in her program and at her internship felt they had to explain things they thought were too complex for her to understand, and she wondered how they thought she had gotten into the program in the first place.

She politely let him finish, and he said, "So you can see the issue we have is with the Dirac equation."

Tara walked up to the board and took the marker from his hand. She wiped away several sections of equations with her fingers and then made the necessary corrections before handing the marker back and saying, "Dirac's not the problem. You are."

She left and got her things out of her locker. She didn't like to be rude, but she had found if she was brash the first time someone attempted to mansplain something basic to her, they wouldn't do it a second time.

She sat in her car a few minutes and watched the sunset. The clouds appeared burned a deep orange.

She could run this lab, run the entire division, better than any man in there—but they wouldn't even let her have the opportunity to prove that she could. She hadn't realized until recently that it was on purpose. They didn't want a woman to best them, even if it meant the company would jump ahead of its competitors by years, maybe decades.

Only now did she appreciate the amount of patience and hard work it must've taken for her mother to reach the position she had in her profession.

Their loss, she thought.

She looked at the time on the car's dash. Her meeting was in twenty minutes.

He had asked to meet somewhere secluded—a warehouse on Fremont Boulevard.

She parked up the street to ensure no one would see her license plate or what type of car she drove. She smoothed her hair down and put on a tight wig before adding on a baseball cap. She'd bought a fake tattoo kit, the best she could find, and she took a few minutes to place a tattoo of an Asian tiger at the base of her neck and Arabic writing on each wrist. She popped in green contacts, then looked at herself in her side mirror before heading into the warehouse.

The building was dark and smelled of grease and wet cardboard. She scanned from one end to the other, noting the number of people inside and where the exits were. A few men glanced at her, but she could tell it was more out of lust than any type of curiosity about why a stranger was in their midst.

A man in a blue suit with a thick black beard stepped out of a room and motioned with his head. She went over to him. He stood by the door as she looked inside. A bald man in a silk shirt whose pattern looked like vomit or soggy cereal sat at a desk snorting cocaine. Tara glanced at the guard and then went inside.

"You gonna sit or what?" the man at the desk said.

Tara sat down in one of the chairs in front of the desk. Garos Vasili took one more line of coke and then put the straw and mirror in his breast pocket before wiping his nose and leaning back in his chair.

"How old are you?" he said.

"What does that matter?"

He shrugged. "Just making small talk." He exhaled loudly. "So you work for someone who works for someone, huh? And why would they hire a little girl for something like this?"

"If I get arrested, I get a slap on the wrist."

"And that's okay with you?"

"For what they pay me it is."

He smirked. "Smart girl. I'm worth millions. You know how much time I've done? Four years. Now you tell me, is it worth four years of your life to be rich for the rest of it? That's what those people driving to jobs they hate every morning don't understand. Everything's a trade of your time, and most people don't know it. That's what it's all about. Evaluating the trade."

"Thanks for the lecture, but do you have the money or not? I'd like to get the hell out of here."

He chuckled. "You got balls for a little girl."

"Yes or no? I don't have time for this."

"Why? You gotta be back at the playground?"

She rose to leave, and he held out a hand. "Sit down." They stared at each other a moment, and he said calmly, "Don't worry so much. Sit down."

Tara sat. Her heart was pounding, and she had to make a conscious effort to calm it down. She couldn't allow him to see any fear. This wasn't the type of man who would show compassion; he was watching for any weakness in her.

Vasili motioned to the guard by the door, and a moment later the guard came in with a gym bag. Vasili unzipped it, revealing hundred-dollar bills tightly packed with rubber bands.

"Two million, assuming of course that my expert can verify the paintings are actually his."

"They are," Tara said, unable to take her eyes off the cash in front of her. More cash than her mother would earn in a lifetime busting her ass in a courtroom.

"My appraiser will be here in a couple of weeks. Bring the paintings then, and you'll get your money." He paused as he looked down at his nails. "I would really like to know who you work for. I want to know who I'm in bed with."

Tara shook her head. "They don't work that way." She rose. "Text me when the appraiser's here."

"Little girl," he said as she turned to leave, "I don't know you, and you don't know me, but I need you to know, if you try to—"

"Save your threats. I don't scare easy. And if I wanted to screw you, I would've done it already. You took the nameplate on the door down—I can see the outline where the wood is faded—and those shoes in the corner are probably an eight or nine. The shoes on your feet are an eleven or twelve. This isn't your office. Which means you don't work here and don't want me to know where you really work out of. So that bag of money is not going to be left in this warehouse. If I were more devious, I would just wait outside until you left and shoot you both in the back of the head and take the money. Easy as pie. But I may need to do business with you in the future, so best we both treat each other well. Agreed?"

His eyes narrowed a little before he burst out laughing. He pointed a finger at her. "I like you. You make me happy. Keep it that way, and we won't have any problems."

Tara nodded and turned to leave. At the door, she glanced at the guard, noticing the handgun tucked in a holster underneath his left arm. Looking into his eyes, she could see nothing there. No emotion. She had no doubt if Vasili told him to kill her, he wouldn't hesitate for a second.

She glanced back once before leaving. Vasili smiled at her and winked.

43

Yardley had dinner prepared before Tara got home. When she finally came in, she dropped her backpack by the door and went immediately to the fridge. She opened a bottle of apple juice and chugged half.

"You would not believe this professor," Tara said, wiping her lips with the back of her hand.

"I made dinner, don't eat anything. What'd they do?"

"He was, like, totally hitting on me, and Jared, one of the other grad students, was in there, and he was like, 'Um, Mike, this is a little uncomfortable,' and the professor's like, 'I'm just kidding.' But it was such bullshit because I totally caught him checking me out. Guy gives me the creeps. I would drop his class, but I figure you can't get away from it, right? I could end up with someone worse."

"Maybe. But sounds like I'll be going down to have a talk with him."

"No, don't. I took care of it. Once you call guys like that out, they run the other way."

She went up to her mother and put her head on her shoulder. Yardley leaned her head against her daughter's and closed her eyes. Tara still smelled the same as when she was a child, or perhaps it was just in Yardley's mind. If it was, she wondered if Tara would always smell like that to her.

"You doin' okay, Mom?"

"I'm fine."

"You seem sad."

"Not sad. Nostalgic, maybe. There was a time in life when everything seemed simpler, and I've just been thinking about whether it's ever possible to go back to that."

"Is that why we're moving? You think it'll be simpler?"

Someone knocked on the door. Tara put her juice on the counter and went to answer it. Yardley heard a woman's voice, and a few seconds later River stood in the kitchen.

"Hey," she said. "Sorry to just pop in. Can we talk?"

"Of course. Tara, stir this every few minutes, would you?"

Yardley led River out to the balcony. River didn't sit. Instead, she went to the railing overlooking the desert. Stars were beginning to come out. A heavy wind blew, and the sand could rise high enough to whip someone's face if they were standing at the railing, though Yardley occasionally found the sensation pleasant.

"I visited him at the jail," River said.

"Why?"

"Honestly . . . I don't know. Just to hear him deny it, I guess. To see if I believe him."

"And?"

River shrugged. "I don't know. I don't know what I felt. I don't know if he was telling the truth or lying to me . . . I don't know anything anymore." She took a deep breath, her gaze unwavering from the sand and red rocks spread out in front of her. "He looked terrible. Pale and tired. He had these really dark circles under his eyes. He said he didn't sleep at all last night."

"The shock of it will wear off. Jail isn't prison; it's not as violent. He'll be all right."

She gave a heavy sigh. "I don't know if I believe him, Jess."

"The evidence certainly points his way."

"Do you believe it? That he killed her and tried to kill me?"

"For me, cases are about probabilities. What is the probability that he had those Sarpong paintings, multiplied by the probability that he had the exact roll of gauze used in the murder, multiplied by the syringes full of ricin, multiplied by the fact that he was romantically involved with both victims, multiplied by the probability that he happens to have no solid alibi for either night?"

A long pause.

"What about that girl?" River asked.

"I called the Missing Persons detective again today, and she said they don't have anything. Their best guess is that Zachary took her and . . ."

River turned. "And killed her?"

Yardley nodded. "I also think Zachary was working with the girl's father, Tucker Pharr. That's the most likely explanation. It's just proving it that's going to be the problem."

River turned back toward the desert. "Is he getting out?"

Yardley hesitated. It wouldn't be fair to lie to her. "Possibly. His attorney is one of the best, and he's extremely motivated to win. But the evidence is solid, so he'll have to find someone else to blame for the murder and your kidnapping. The most obvious choice is Tucker Pharr. He has a conviction for kidnapping, and he has the motive to kill you and his wife."

"Will that work?"

"It could be enough to put reasonable doubt into the minds of the jurors, sure. But even if he only gets one, it will be a hung jury, and we'll have to try this case again. Get a couple of those, and the DA will offer an extremely lenient deal to get it out of the press quickly. So yes, he could get out again."

River's head lowered, and she spoke quietly. "What if he tries to kill me again?"

Yardley moved to stand next to her. "I won't let him."

44

The press conference was a zoo. Roy Lieu, the state attorney general, the chief of police for the LVPD, and the county sheriff were all there, flanking Nathan Salls on a podium as he read a prepared statement in front of a microphone. Kyle Jax stood nearby and puffed up his chest for the cameras.

Yardley had accepted Salls's offer. River was at risk, a young girl was missing, and it didn't seem like anyone but she and Baldwin cared. Salls had asked her to join the press conference, but Yardley took a spot in the corner and remained seated, out of view of the cameras.

When the question-and-answer period came around, the first reporter with their hand up was Jude Chance.

"Do you have any information on the whereabouts of Harmony Pharr, and if not, are you willing to cut a deal with Dr. Zachary in exchange for that information?"

"I cannot comment about ongoing discussions with the defendant in this case," Salls said. "You'll have to speak to him and his attorney about that."

"But prosecutors at your own department have said they believe Harmony's father is just as viable a suspect as the defendant in her disappearance."

"Which prosecutors said that?"

"You know I can't tell you that, Nathan. But I'm just relaying what the front-line prosecutors in your office are saying."

"Look, I get people's apprehension about this and why they believe Mr. Pharr to be a suspect, but that's all he was—a suspect. The evidence we have in this case was found in Dr. Zachary's possession, and no one else had access to it, save his girlfriend, who is herself a victim. More details will come out during the preliminary hearing, if there is one, and your question as to why Mr. Pharr isn't a viable suspect any longer will be answered then."

Yardley didn't know if anyone else on the floor recognized the lie. Tucker Pharr *was* a viable suspect. But Yardley believed them to have worked together, and in the coming weeks, she would have to piece it all together for the jury until she found enough evidence to charge Tucker as well.

Salls had started to call on someone else when Chance added, "Are you even actively searching for Harmony Pharr anymore, or do you assume she's dead at this point?"

"It's an ongoing investigation currently being handled by the Missing Persons Bureau of the—"

"Cut the political bullshit, Nathan—is the girl alive or not?"

Salls's face turned a light pink, and he had to clear his throat and take a sip of water, probably so he wouldn't immediately explode in a storm of profanity at Chance.

"We don't know if Harmony Pharr is alive or not. Mr. Zachary has not spoken to us since he retained an attorney. I think that's all for—"

"Whose fault was it that this case wasn't indicted at the federal level? Someone on the grand jury informed me that the government wasn't well prepared and attempted to move forward on a case they hadn't researched thoroughly. Seems like on a serial homicide, you'd want to put in the work first, doesn't it? Can we expect the same treatment of this case from the DA's Office?"

Salls gritted his teeth, causing striations in his jaw muscles. Roy Lieu stepped forward and said, "I can probably best answer that. Sometimes things slip through the cracks due to misunderstandings by the grand jury. This isn't exactly a science—we're dealing with people, and when you deal with people, you're bound to deal with mistakes."

Chance said, "So you're saying it was the grand jury's mistake, not yours, that resulted in no indictments for the murder and kidnappings?"

Salls chimed in. "Right now our main focus is to ensure that this man is behind bars the rest of his life and cannot hurt another person. That's all the questions we're taking at this time. Thank you for coming."

A few reporters shouted questions, but the group was already leaving the podium. Yardley waited until everyone had left and then went up to Chance. "I don't think he's going to invite you to the DA's Christmas party this year."

He chuckled. "Shit, they wouldn't cross the street to spit on me if I was on fire. I noticed you didn't talk much. Off the record, you really think Zachary is the guy?"

"Yes. At least one of them."

"Huh. And I'm guessing you think the other is Tucker Pharr? I'd love to hear your theories, especially considering we made fun of old Johnny for speculating there were two of them early on. Guess I owe that prick a beer."

"Anything I say will be off the record. Zachary's defense counsel is going to blame everything on Tucker Pharr, and the last thing we need is me making a statement that I think Tucker had something to do with all this."

"Well, regardless, you're gonna wanna say your prayers and take your vitamins, 'cause I think this case is going to kick your ass."

45

It felt strange to leave the house in the morning and drive to the Clark County District Attorney's Office. The building was modern looking: glass and steel, lined with palm trees. Yardley checked in with a security guard.

The DA's Office on the third floor was a cacophony of sound. Phones ringing, people talking, laughing, and a television somewhere turned to a news show. It seemed the opposite of the somber US Attorney's Office.

"Hi," Yardley said to the receptionist. "Jessica Yardley. Brie is expecting me."

"One sec."

Brie came out a minute later. They shook hands, and Brie led her back through the employee entrance that didn't have a metal detector. The entire floor was a large space with offices on the outer edge and cubicles pushed together in the center.

"We have the next floor up, too," Brie said as they walked. "That's mostly the appellate team and civil guys. You won't see them much. Nathan's office is up there, but he's never around. If you need anything, you can talk to Wendy—she's the office manager—or just ask me. Yours is right here."

She gestured inside a small office with large windows looking out onto the street. The desk was L shaped and massive, with a computer and monitor set up. Other than the chair and some shelves above the desk, there was nothing in the room. Yardley noticed holes in the walls where the previous occupant had hung things.

"I'll have someone get you all the files, and you'll be set up with passwords for our server. Have you met the defense attorney before? Dylan Aster?"

"I have."

"He's smart. Be careful. He's got that cute charm that disarms you, but I've seen him slit prosecutors' throats when they let their guards down."

"I'll be careful."

Brie grinned, but Yardley could tell it was forced. "I'm so glad you're here. We need more women in the office."

With that, she left. Yardley placed her satchel on the desk and sat down. She took out the only things she had brought with her: her laptop and a photo of Tara, which she placed next to the computer.

She rose and went to the windows. As she stared down at the traffic below, it hit her suddenly that, as a county prosecutor, she no longer had access to federal agencies like the FBI. If she needed specific evidence gathered, she would have to use the Sheriff's Office, the LVPD, or in-house investigators, very few of whom she actually knew. It had taken years for her to learn which federal agents worked hard and were efficient and which ones cut corners. Which ones could be trusted and which couldn't. She didn't have time to learn all that with local law enforcement, and it made her anxious that she wouldn't know who she was dealing with.

When the files were brought to her, she sat down again, the chair creaking, and began to read.

The DA's files had some good information, particularly Detective Garrett's supplemental narrative, which she hadn't had in the federal file, but it didn't contain much she hadn't already seen. There was a note that the police had executed another search warrant at Zachary and River's home but found nothing else relevant to the case. She hoped River hadn't been there to watch the police tearing apart her house.

When she got through the files, she stacked them neatly on the shelves above her computer and left the office.

—

It'd been a long time since Yardley had seen the inside of a state district court. The atmosphere felt frantic. In federal court, she typically had only her case slotted for a particular time, but in state court, the entire court calendar was packed into the morning or afternoon session, and the gallery overflowed with people. Attorneys at the lectern quickly told the judge what they needed, and a lot of the time the judges set dates or said yes or no without looking up from whatever documents they were signing.

Yardley took her place on the bench behind the prosecution table, where two prosecutors sat with files spread out in front of them. A man was at the lectern with his attorney, pleading guilty to carjacking and fleeing from a law enforcement officer. The plea took less than four minutes, and then the next case was called.

Yardley saw Aster hurry in a few minutes late, still putting on his suit coat. He came over and crouched in front of her.

"He's innocent."

"They're all innocent, Dylan. Didn't you know?"

"Yeah, but I think he's *really* innocent."

"I disagree."

"Jess, none of this makes any sense. He kills his lover and tries to kill his girlfriend and then keeps all the evidence in his garage? Maybe if he's got a fifty IQ, but not a freaking doctor who would've planned this for weeks or even months."

"Maybe he wanted to get caught."

"Jess, come on."

"If it helps ease your conscience, I don't think he acted alone."

He grimaced. "What's the motive? There's no life insurance; there's no indication they were having relationship issues or that the guy is violent or anything. Why do it?"

"Ask him."

"Come on, don't be like that. Really, what's the motive?"

"What was Ted Bundy's motive, Dylan? What was BTK's motive? They killed strangers and no money was involved. They did it because they enjoyed it."

"You're comparing him to Ted Bundy? Good luck saying that with a straight face to the jury."

"So I take it he's not interested in a plea deal?"

"I don't know. Maybe manslaughter."

"I'll pass, but murder two with life and the possibility of parole in thirty years might be an option."

"Pass."

"Well, we'll see if you stick to that as the trial gets closer."

The clerk called out, "The matter of the State of Nevada versus Michael Jacob Zachary, case number 14923A."

Aster went up to the lectern, and Zachary was brought out of the holding cells in back by a bailiff. He wore a white jumpsuit and had thick cuffs around his wrists. Yardley stood and went to the jury box, leaning against it as the judge opened the file. Her phone buzzed, and she sent it to voice mail.

"Dylan Aster for Mr. Zachary."

"Jessica Yardley for the State."

"What are we doing here, Counselors?" the judge said without looking up from the file.

Aster said, "Waive reading and ask for a preliminary hearing date, Your Honor."

"Next Monday work for everyone?"

"Should be fine."

Yardley glanced at Zachary, who was staring at her. "That works, thank you."

Aster whispered something to Zachary before he was led away by the bailiff. As Zachary passed by Yardley, he said, "I didn't do this, Jessica. You know I didn't."

The bailiff barked at him to not speak. Yardley left the courtroom, and Aster followed her.

"I don't think he had help," Aster said as they headed to the elevators. "I think someone else did all this and put those things in his garage."

"Who?"

"Tucker Pharr, who you guys almost arrested for this anyway."

"I agree. If Zachary wanted help getting rid of his girlfriend and his lover, who better than the husband of his lover, who also wants to get rid of her? And if Tucker was the one who tried to kill Angela, it would make perfect sense that he might get the dose of ricin wrong. Where we differ is that I think they were working together."

"You think they each agreed to kill for each other? That's stretching, Jess. No jury is going to buy that. And why pose them and go through all that nonsense? Just shoot 'em in the middle of the night and leave them in the street."

Yardley stepped onto the elevator. "I disagree, Dylan. Show me more and I'll hear you out, but as of right now I'm going forward."

She stared at her reflection in the chrome as the elevator doors closed. The possibility that she was wrong, that Zachary had nothing to do with this, weighed on her. Sometimes, when she was prosecuting someone who could potentially be innocent, she would get physically ill. As though her immune system were weakened along with her resolve. She didn't feel that here, though. She felt justified going forward, even if a feeling in the pit of her stomach told her to keep digging.

Her phone buzzed, telling her that she had a voice mail she hadn't checked. It was River. Yardley listened to it, and a shot of adrenaline coursed through her.

When the elevator stopped, she rushed to her car.

46

Yardley came to a quick stop in front of Angela River's home. She hopped out and hurried to the front door. It was unlocked.

Inside, the home was still and quiet. The air conditioner wasn't on, and the air was muggy. Sunlight poured through the floor-to-ceiling windows.

"Angie?"

A faint voice replied, "I'm in the bedroom."

Yardley hurried toward her.

River lay on the massive bed. Several amber bottles of medication were scattered on the duvet, and an empty bottle of red wine sat on the nightstand. Yardley read the labels on the medicines. Antianxiety meds, tranquilizers, and an antidepressant. The only one that worried her was the tranquilizer.

"Did you mix this with alcohol?"

River's eyes were red and puffy. Used tissues were wadded up on the nightstand.

"I only took a few."

"How many?"

"Just a few."

"Get up. We're going to the ER."

River gently took her wrist. "No, it really was just a few. I can take six of those in a day, and I only took a few. I drank most of the wine last night."

Yardley watched her a second and then sat down. "Your message said you didn't know how much more you could take. I thought you were going to do something stupid, Angie."

"I thought about it, but I called you instead. Maybe I'm just a coward, I don't know. I'm sorry I bugged you."

"Don't be sorry."

River closed her eyes and shook her head. "Life seems like it's just one shit storm after another. It never lets up."

Yardley put her hand over River's, and they sat in silence a long while.

"Well, at least I can keep all the old records we have when Zachary's in prison. Guess he won't be needing *Hall & Oates Live*."

Yardley grinned. "No, he won't."

She sniffed and took another tissue before sitting up in bed and pulling back her hair. "I bet I look like shit warmed over right now."

"Well, I didn't want to say anything, but Animal from *The Muppets* came to mind when I saw your hair."

River chuckled. She rose and looked in the mirror above the dresser. "Think maybe I should start playing the drums?"

"Never too late to change careers."

River turned to face her, letting out a deep breath. "Thank you for coming here. I, um, don't have any other friends."

Yardley picked up an empty bottle of medication off the floor and put it on the nightstand. "Neither do I."

Five days later the preliminary hearing got underway. Many attorneys thought of preliminary hearings as minitrials, with evidence presented and testimony given, but a growing trend had been for prosecutors to submit what were called 1102 statements in lieu of testimony, robbing the defense of the chance to cross-examine witnesses before trial.

Yardley had brought 1102 statements from Baldwin, Detective Garrett, the assistant medical examiner, Angela River, a forensic toxicologist with the Centers for Disease Control, an investigator with the Department of Homeland Security discussing the ricin, the neighbor who had made the initial call on River's case, and the real estate agent who had found Kathy Pharr's body. Several statements from people tangentially involved were included in case the judge had any specific questions the other statements didn't address.

Yardley sat at the prosecution table until the judge came out. The courtroom still held the scent of lemon disinfectant from last night's cleaning.

Judge Harvey W. Weston was an older judge close to retirement. Yardley had asked around at the DA's Office about him, and the consensus seemed to be that he didn't have a pleasant demeanor but didn't have an unpleasant one either. Many prosecutors said he tended to rule randomly, one day favoring the defense and the next favoring the prosecution without much regard to the actual arguments.

Judge Weston groaned as he lowered himself into his chair and said, "Please be seated." He booted up his computer. "Who's first?"

The clerk, a young man Yardley had never seen before, said, "State of Nevada versus Michael Jacob Zachary, case 14923A. Set today for preliminary hearing."

The attorneys introduced themselves for the record, and then the judge said, "Ms. Yardley, go ahead."

"May I approach, Your Honor?"

"Certainly."

She went to the clerk and handed him a stack of documents, a stack she had scanned and emailed to Aster days ago.

"The State would like to introduce the following 1102 statements marked as prosecution exhibits one through eighteen in place of live testimony."

"Mr. Aster, what say you?"

"I would certainly object, Your Honor."

"Of course you would," he said.

"I'm sorry?"

"I said, 'Of course you would.' Go on, though, tell me what you're dying to tell me."

Aster glanced at Yardley, then said, "This is an obvious attempt by the State to get around the *Kimball* ruling that gives the defense a meaningful opportunity to challenge the State's assertion of probable cause. I can understand one or two . . . I'm sorry, did you just roll your eyes, Your Honor?"

"No, keep going. Let's just get through this."

Aster hesitated, gazing at Weston as Weston gazed back.

"As I was saying, the Ninth Circuit in *Kimball* looked at the issue of whether 1102 statements provided an adequate opportunity for the defense to fully challenge probable cause in a criminal proceeding. What they found was that while 1102s are perfectly acceptable for instances . . . Your Honor, that time was definitely an eye roll."

"It wasn't. Now, do you want a ruling or not?"

"Well, yes, but I'd like a proper ruling based on what the Ninth Circuit—"

"Ninth Circuit's a bunch of pot-smokin' hippies. Don't know how the hell we didn't end up in the Tenth. You tell me that, Mr. Aster. How exactly is Nevada so similar to Hawaii and California that we should be grouped with their jurisprudence rather than Utah and Colorado? Can you answer me that?"

Aster looked at Yardley, who gave a little shrug.

"No, Your Honor, I couldn't say. But I would like to talk about the matter at hand."

The judge grumbled something and said, "Ms. Yardley. Your take on *Kimball*."

"In *Kimball*, the Court stated that it was a unique circumstance applicable only very rarely. Essentially, they didn't know if the confrontation clause had been violated because the State couldn't be certain they had the right person, namely because the defendant had an identical twin. Whereas here, Mr. Zachary was caught, to put it mildly, with his hand in the cookie jar and has no twin. The confrontation clause is not an issue here based on prevailing caselaw dealing with 1102s, and there is no doubt probable cause will be found."

"Frankly, Judge, that's not up to her to say. That's for you to decide."

"It is, and I find these statements to be sufficiently reliable and trustworthy in lieu of live testimony. I will admit all—"

"Your Honor, that's ridiculous. You haven't even read them yet; how can you possibly know they're sufficiently reliable and trustworthy?"

The judge's face went stern. "I have known Detective Garrett since you were in grade school, Mr. Aster, and Cason Baldwin appears to be an instructor at the FBI Academy in addition to a nearly fifteen-year field agent. If I can't credit their sworn affidavits as reliable and trustworthy, then whose can I? Now, please don't interrupt me again."

The two of them stared at each other in silence. The anger Aster was holding back was evident in his face, but he said nothing.

Weston said, "I'm admitting all eighteen statements and will take an hour break to read them and determine if they constitute sufficient probable cause to bind the defendant over for trial. Unless you have anything you'd like to present to the Court, Mr. Aster."

"No, Your Honor."

"Then we're adjourned for an hour."

Yardley watched as Zachary was taken back to the holding cells. He kept looking at the gallery, but Yardley knew River wasn't there. She wouldn't be coming to any more of his hearings.

"Cheap shot, taking away my prelim," Aster said.

Yardley lifted her satchel. "Why? Because you don't get to look at my cards before we bet?"

"Hey, don't hate the player, hate the game. Our system gives me prelims for a reason. And it's not so he can speed-read through affidavits and then just agree with you. If he even reads them at all. I'll bet you he just watches YouTube back there for an hour."

"Do you have any doubt that I would've won the prelim?"

"No."

"Then what are you complaining about?"

"That's not the point. The process has to be respected, Jess."

"I know it does. No one in this courtroom is more aware of that than me. But the courts have given me the ability to get this nonsense out of the way so we can get to a trial. That's what you want anyway, isn't it? To get in front of a jury?"

"I'm just saying," Aster said, "you play fair and I'll play fair. You're one of my favorite prosecutors, and you've got a good rep, but you start pulling shit like this, and maybe I gotta not play fair."

"You do whatever you have to do to defend your client, Dylan. I promise I won't take it personally. But don't think I won't use every avenue the law gives me to make sure he doesn't get out and get a second chance at Angie."

They stared at each other a moment, and then Aster grinned, as though he'd just come to understand something he'd been puzzling over.

"I saw you two in court at the grand jury. That wasn't just prosecutor/victim, was it? You held her hand through the entire thing."

"She was frightened."

"They're all frightened. Is that why you're fighting so hard on this, Jess? You're buddies with the girlfriend, so you'll do anything to make sure he gets a life sentence? Whether he's guilty or not?"

Yardley stepped close to him so they were nearly face to face. "I like you, Dylan. But if you ever question my integrity again, I will make sure you regret it."

He chuckled. "That might be worth it just to see what you'd do." He took a few steps back to leave and said, "We'll still take manslaughter whenever you're ready to offer it."

"Ms. Yardley?" the clerk said from behind her.

"Yes?"

"Sorry, I forgot to ask. Do you know how many pretrial motions you and Mr. Aster are anticipating? I'd like to give you a special setting before the calendar fills. If the judge binds over, of course."

"Nothing from me, but I have a feeling you better set aside as much time as you can." She looked at Aster. "I don't think Mr. Aster is going to let this case move forward without a battle on every issue."

Weston came back an hour later and declared that there was enough evidence to bind the case over for trial. Michael Zachary was officially arraigned and entered not guilty pleas. Aster requested the case be set for a motion hearing challenging the search warrant that led to the evidence in the garage, saying it was deceptive and should not have been granted. The hearing was set for eight days from today. Yardley objected and asked for more time.

"I have to respond to whatever motion Mr. Aster files, and he has five days to do it, leaving me three to draft a response and prepare my arguments."

"What can I say?" Weston said. "Life kicks you in the nuts, and then you die. Next matter."

Aster leaned over to her and whispered, "Don't feel so nice when the idiocy gun is pointed at you, does it?"

She said nothing as she took her satchel and left the courtroom.

47

Aster and Ricci parked in the strip mall parking lot and got out of the truck. Customers from a marijuana dispensary took up most of the spaces, but at the end of the first row were a couple of spots reserved for a retail space that didn't have any signage up.

Anyone at the door had to be buzzed in. Aster knocked on the glass. A tall man with a smooth bald head and a suit came to the door.

"Sweet Mary," he said as he opened the door. "You buying your suits at the grocery store now?"

"Comfort first," Aster said.

"Well, get your comfortable ass in here before my neighbors see that ugly thing."

Aster sat on a couch across from a massive oak desk, and Ricci sat next to him. Brody Hanks groaned as he sat in his executive chair and said, "Damn knees. Hate getting older. Anyway, you ain't here to listen to me complain." He took a thumb drive out of a drawer in his desk and tossed it to Aster. "Agent Baldwin seems clean. Found a few too many OxyContin prescriptions going back a few years, but you didn't hear that from me. Could lose my license for knowing that. The HIPAA people live for that shit."

"Illegal scripts?"

He shook his head. "All doctor prescribed. And nothing recent. Other than that he's clean. But you're gonna wanna see what I got on Lucas Garrett."

"What?"

"First, I got reports on about twenty cases in there where he didn't do shit. Lazy as hell. But his disciplinary record is clean, so I had to dig a little harder." He smiled.

"What are we, on a game show? Just tell me."

"See, now that little comment just added a hundred bucks to your bill."

"Sorry, oh wise Brody. Please tell me what you found, pretty please. With sugar on top."

"Tell me I'm the best first."

"You're the best."

"That wasn't very sincere."

"Brody, for shit's sake—"

He laughed. "All right, man, don't piss yourself. So get this: Garrett used to be married, right. Few years ago they had all sortsa problems, mostly I'm guessing because of his drinking. Talked to an old neighbor of his who said the wife told him Garrett was a high-functioning alcoholic. Anyway, the missus, she goes out and finds another man, right. A bodybuilder. So Garrett is going insane 'cause he doesn't want a divorce. I included some transcripts of the divorce hearings, and you gotta hear the shit he says. He lost his damn mind. And then one day, outta the blue, the police show up at the wife's new condo. This is before the divorce went through. They went there on a call of a stabbing. Some gangbanger up the road was stabbed the previous night, and they received a tip that the bodybuilder was the one who did it. So they asked to search the house."

"And I'm guessing they found something."

He nodded. "The knife. They arrest the dude, only he's got a solid alibi; he was in Canada at the time."

"You're kidding me."

"Nope. So they think maybe it's the wife, which would be weird as shit for a soccer mom to go out and stab a gangbanger fresh outta the can, but all right, whatever. But she's got a good alibi, too. The condo only has one entrance, and she's got a doorbell camera. The camera recorded her and her kid going into the condo at around nine and not coming out again until seven the next morning to take the kid to school. The stabbing was around midnight."

"They find anything else in the condo?"

He nodded. "A shirt with some blood on it. No signs of a break-in."

Ricci said, "What about the door cam? Was Garrett on it?"

"Wasn't in the reports, but I'll bet my ass he is."

Aster shook his head. "He planted it. He planted the knife and the shirt. How'd you even find this out?"

"Hey, man, you want dirt on cops, you hire an ex-cop. We got the connections."

"They ever bring charges against him?"

"No. And all this was buried. Buried deep. I'm talkin' the reports were purged from the system."

"Someone wanted it gone that bad, huh?"

"I've seen it buried like this a few times, but it's always for higher ranks when they don't want to embarrass the department with a drug or prostitution charge. Never seen it for just a low-level detective. He's got connections somewhere."

Aster looked at Ricci. "Thoughts?"

She glanced between the two men. "Get his ex on the stand and tear Detective Garrett a new one."

48

Yardley was loading the dishwasher when Tara told her she was going out. Yardley checked the clock on the oven: it was past eight.

"Where to?" she said casually, not looking up from the dishes.

"Just some stuff I gotta finish up at the lab before tomorrow. Be back soon."

Yardley waited until Tara was out of the house before she threw on her shoes and left. She hated having to do it, but she opened an app that she had gotten installed by the US Attorney's Office IT division when she bought her and Tara's phones. It allowed her to track Tara's phone from anywhere in the world, even if it was off and its location services disabled.

She got into her car and gave Tara a few minutes' head start, then pulled out into the street and followed the map. Tara got onto the freeway, and Yardley followed. Anxiety gnawed at her. What if Tara really was going to the labs? It was entirely possible she was corresponding with her father because she felt she had never had one, and maybe she wanted to get to know him before she didn't have the chance anymore. Though his appeals were stalled, they wouldn't be forever, and eventually the State of Nevada was going to kill Eddie Cal. Maybe Tara just wanted some conversations with him first? The problem was that Tara didn't know Cal like she did.

Cal would never do anything out of some sentimentality, even for his own daughter. If he was taking the time to correspond and meet with her, he was using her for something. And he had an ability to put people under a spell. A combination of superficial charm, intellect, and stunning good looks. It disarmed people in the way the beauty of a spider's web might disarm a fly.

Tara got off the freeway and drove to an industrial section of Vegas consisting of cheap office space and warehouses. Several storage unit businesses were in the area, and the train tracks cut right through here.

The road wasn't busy, and Yardley was worried Tara would spot her, so she stayed far enough back that her headlights wouldn't be visible. The map showed Tara's phone as a blue dot on the surface streets, and Yardley would glance at it every half a minute or so.

The area became even more industrial the farther she drove, with factories overtaking most of the office buildings. The factories were all pushed up against the red rock mountains, giving the place an otherworldly feel. Like a colony on some distant planet.

Tara pulled in front of a small office building.

Yardley turned her lights off and parked on the street. She watched Tara hurry up a set of stairs to the second floor, and the blue dot stopped on the map. No one was around, and the area had an abandoned feel to it.

Yardley got out and made her way over to the stairs and went up. There were two offices on each floor, and the light was on in the second office. The blinds were drawn, and she couldn't see inside, but she put her ear to the door and could hear movement inside. She went back down the stairs and around the corner and waited.

A few minutes later, Tara came down the stairs carrying something. They were large boxes but must've been filled with something light enough for a lithe seventeen-year-old girl to carry. She put them in the trunk of her car and then got in and pulled away. Yardley lifted her phone and sent out a text.

It was a good forty minutes before the sedan pulled up to the office building. Yardley had been sitting in her car, trying to distract herself by listening to music. Her stomach was in knots, and horrific scenario after horrific scenario kept running through her mind of what Eddie Cal had gotten her little girl to do for him.

An Asian woman in sweats hopped out of the sedan and came over as Yardley got out of her SUV.

"So do I even want to know?" the woman said.

"I would really appreciate if we just kept it between us, Ella."

"Hey, snitches get stitches, right?"

Yardley led her to the office. Ella was an in-house investigator at the US Attorney's Office who had worked closely with Yardley over the years. They were both in male-dominated professions ruled by a machismo culture. It had created a bond between them, a sense that they had to look out for each other. So when Ella said she wouldn't tell anyone what she saw, Yardley knew she meant it.

Ella pulled out the universal lock pick, and within seconds the lock was opened. Yardley was about to open the door when Ella said, "Stop!"

She pointed to the top of the door and the sensor that was attached. Ella had brought a small leather case with her. She took out what looked like a tuning fork and held it up to the sensor. It made a soft humming noise, and after a few seconds Ella put it away.

"All yours," Ella said. "Better I don't see what's in there."

"I really appreciate this."

"Good, because you're taking me out to an expensive dinner for it. And if you do something that ends up on the news, I'm denying I was ever here." She grinned and hesitated a moment. "Good luck, Jess. I'm going to miss you at the office."

They hugged, and Yardley waited until she left before opening the door.

49

Baldwin couldn't sleep. He lay on his silk sheets staring up at the ceiling, thinking about meeting Scarlett at her house for dinner earlier, her words running around his head, haunting him.

"I'm keeping it. I'd like you to be a part of the life of your child, but if you don't want anything to do with us, then fine, we'll do it without you."

"You have no idea what's out there in the world, Scarlett. No idea what people are capable of."

"It's not your choice, Cason."

She went to get up, and he held her wrist.

"Having a child would be like being held over a cliff every second of every day, wondering what was happening to him. If he was alive or dead or tied up in some freak's basement."

"Let go of me," she said, pulling away.

He'd always thought he'd feel some elation at becoming a father, some sense of immortality that a part of him would live on after he was gone, but he felt neither of those things. The only thing he felt was a sickening dread.

He rose and went to the bathroom to splash some water on his face and take some CBD oil, something he'd been using to help him sleep, when he noticed the picture of Harmony he had taped up. He stared at it a long time. The thought of what she might be seeing right now, of what she might be going through, wouldn't leave him. Like some poison that was seeping into his skin and going deeper and deeper into him. He looked at himself in the mirror a moment and then got dressed.

Detective Reece had been right about one thing: Child crimes investigators were not like other investigators. The child crimes detectives and federal agents he had known, the great ones, had a stomach for it. They could place their feelings aside and work the case. He wasn't sure he could do that.

The apartment complex he drove to looked like a place that was near being condemned by the health department for unsanitary living conditions. The dumpster overflowed with trash, garbage was scattered on the sidewalk, and the parking lot was full of broken-down cars that probably hadn't moved in weeks or months. The complex itself was outside of the city, a place that wasn't near any schools, churches, shopping malls, or anywhere else children might gather. The majority of residents here weren't allowed anywhere kids might congregate.

There were different tracks for sex offenders depending on what they'd been convicted for and how severe a threat their parole officers deemed them to be to the public. Track C allowed them to live at home and be around children, a track reserved for people who'd committed crimes against adults and had no proclivities toward children. Track B was for those with proclivities toward children but who were deemed not to be a severe threat, like those who had undergone chemical castration. Track A was little used and reserved only for those who had served their prison time but were still deemed a severe threat to the public. They couldn't live anywhere near children, but they had to live somewhere. So places like Green Leaves Apartments were funded by the Bureau of Prisons to house them until they could prove themselves capable of moving to track B.

Baldwin had been here a couple of times years ago, and the place hadn't changed at all. Music blared from somewhere, loud metal, and empty beer cans littered the halls. A garbage can against the wall flowed over like the dumpster, mostly with bottles of booze, packages of cigarettes, and the cream-colored boxes with no outer markings the marijuana companies used when they delivered the drug.

Baldwin knocked on the door of the apartment. A thin man with glasses and a short mohawk answered. He had large brown eyes and was missing one hand. He swallowed when he saw Baldwin and said, in his soft voice, "What do you want?"

"I need to talk to you, Orson."

"I haven't done anything. I've been straight and narrow."

"I'm sure you have. I'm not here about you."

"Who then?"

"Can we talk inside?"

Orson hesitated, then opened the door for him to come in. Baldwin entered the apartment. It was clean to the point of obsession; the carpet even had the freshly vacuumed wave patterns, and the air had the scent of bleach.

Baldwin had used Orson in the past for information on cases unrelated to child crimes, and he had proved reliable.

He pulled out the photo of Harmony Pharr. "I'm looking for this girl. She was taken from behind her home on—"

"The Executioner, right? Yeah, I've been reading about it."

He took the photo in his good hand and looked at it for a few moments. His other hand had been taken in a car accident and replaced with a thick plastic replica that looked like a mannequin hand. Baldwin didn't like him holding the photo and felt itchy till he'd handed it back.

"Sorry, can't help you. I'm not connected to that world at all anymore."

"I'm not your parole officer. I just want to find her. And I know you're connected to all the right forums on the dark net. I was hoping you could see if anyone has posted anything about her."

"Of course they have. She's beautiful."

A stab of anger coursed through him, and he had to swallow it down. "I mean maybe if someone posted something about taking her, or someone who maybe knows something about it that isn't in the news."

"You work child crimes now?"

Baldwin put the photo away. "Can you help or not?"

"I can look around. What's in it for me?"

"Hey, I saved your ass when—"

"And I paid that back. That info I gave you on the guy who was stabbing cab drivers led right to him, and I sure as shit didn't see my name in the news. Didn't get any credit, and my parole officer didn't believe me when I told him."

Baldwin took a deep breath. "Fine. Find me something, and we'll say that I owe you a favor. And as long as the favor is within reason, I'll do everything I can to make it happen."

Orson nodded. "I've got a job now and a steady girlfriend. I'm on good meds. I gotta move out of this shithole, Cason. I want a house and a dog and all that normal shit. So you come testify at my hearing that you think I'm ready for track B, and I'll see what I can find out."

Baldwin watched him a moment. He bit his lower lip and then released it. Taking out a card from his wallet, he said, "This better not come back to bite me in the ass, Orson." He laid the card on the coffee table. "Find me anything you can. I don't know how much time she's got left."

50

Yardley flipped on the light. The office Tara had entered was large, with two additional rooms and a long hallway that led down to a bathroom. But it was completely bare. Nothing on the walls, the carpets clean—when she glanced into the first office, she didn't even see the pressed-down markings on the carpet indicating a desk had been there. She continued down the hall to the second office, next to the bathroom. She opened the door and quietly gasped.

Paintings were lined up against the wall. At least six of them. She would recognize the style anywhere. Sharp slashes of paint, human figures so accurate they could pass for a photograph, the sky always in the middle of a chaotic storm of black or gray. Never blue and sunny.

The angled signatures in the lower right corner just confirmed what she'd known the second she saw them: they were Eddie Cal's paintings. Ones she'd never seen before. Ones he'd hidden from her.

Yardley slid down against the wall and sat there, staring at them. To an objective observer, the paintings would appear expert and beautiful. The beauty would be almost stunning—until one stared at them long enough. After a certain time, a quiet unease would grow. At gallery showings, Yardley had watched people stare at Cal's paintings with wonder but then quickly move on and not look at the rest. Some couldn't help but stare for a long time, and those were the ones who purchased them. The ones who Cal's work spoke to on a spiritual level.

Was her daughter one of those people?

The box she'd carried out of there must have contained some of his paintings, but why? What possible use—

It struck Yardley just then in a flash. In one powerful moment she saw the entire relationship between Tara and her father and why she was leaving with his paintings.

Yardley inhaled deeply and then exhaled slowly, trying to release her growing panic with the breath. Then she rose and left the office, locking the front door behind her.

51

The trial seemed to come much too quickly. The days had gone by in a flash, with Yardley working from sunup to sundown at the DA's Office, only taking breaks to go on walks and eat lunch at her desk.

She found herself so exhausted in the mornings she'd taken to drinking three cups of coffee right on waking up and another three at lunch and dinner. To sleep at night, she had to take pills, which would make her even groggier the next day.

She had won on all five of Aster's arguments in his motion. Weston and Aster kept getting into it again in court, but each time Ricci took over and calmed down the tension. Yardley offered life with the possibility of parole again, which Aster turned down.

She and River met for lunch frequently, with a trip to a wine bar late one Saturday thrown in at the last minute. River insisted they go, arguing that Yardley needed to take a break from work, and they only went because River came to the house and dragged her out.

Yardley told her about what she had found Tara doing.

"So she's selling them?" River said.

Yardley nodded, staring down at her wineglass. "He needs money for his appeals, and he's using her. I don't know what her motivation is, but he's got something planned for her."

"So you haven't talked to her about it?"

"I don't think she'd tell me the truth right now. I need to find out what he has planned first." She finished the wine and put the glass down. "I hate dancing around it when we talk. It feels like I'm betraying her somehow."

"Sounds like you're protecting her."

Yardley stared down at her empty glass for a few seconds. "I'm not sure I can anymore."

Another night, they spoke on the phone for an hour about anything other than the trial, even having a few laughs over the idiotic things they had done when younger to get the attention of boys. Then there was a long silence in the conversation before River said, "I'm scared, Jess."

"I know."

"Part of me wants to make plans in case Zachary gets out. Just to disappear. But part of me is still convinced he didn't do this." She paused. "I'm going to see him tomorrow."

"I'm not sure that's a great idea."

"I don't care. I need to see him. I miss him."

Yardley didn't argue with her. She wondered if River would resent her if Zachary was convicted. If she would picture the future she should have had with him and think Yardley had taken that away from her. It didn't matter. At least she would be alive to resent her.

On the day of the trial, Yardley dressed in a black suit and stared at herself in the mirror. Dark circles had appeared under her eyes, and she looked pale. The coffee had suppressed her appetite, and she barely ate, causing her to lose too much weight on her already lithe frame.

She arrived in court early and was let through the metal detectors without getting searched. Aster was already there, along with Ricci, at the defense table. He'd replaced his suits with simple slacks and a sports coat, to give the jury an underdog impression. Yardley took her place at the prosecution table and sent out a reminder text to Detective Garrett to make sure he was near the courthouse today. She then took her files and papers out of her satchel and arranged them neatly on the table. A witness list was placed on the far end, and she glanced it over quickly.

"All rise," the bailiff said. "Eighth Judicial District Court is now in session, the Honorable Harvey Weston presiding."

"Please be seated," the judge said as he sat down as well. "Parties ready to go?" he asked.

"We are, Your Honor," Aster said.

"Yes, Judge."

"Then let's bring out the defendant and then the jury pool."

Zachary was brought out in a crisp black suit and gold watch. He sat between Ricci and Aster before another bailiff brought in the jury pool. Fifty men and women from Clark County. They had filled out questionnaires through the mail, and Yardley picked up her copy from one of the neat piles, along with a sheet of notes she had made.

The questionnaire was broad: *What magazines do you subscribe to? Do you vote? Have you ever been convicted of a crime? Have you ever sat on a jury?*

There were ninety questions in all, and Yardley didn't think any of them were terribly relevant. Few of those with serious crimes in their backgrounds, mental disorders that affected reasoning abilities, or bias against police or people of different races or religions would be honest, due to the embarrassment they might feel. Yardley, instead of focusing on the answers, liked to focus on their body language as they were asked questions.

After a roll call to verify all the potential jurors requested had shown up, Weston instructed them that this was a serious matter involving various charges ranging from homicide to assault with bodily injury and gave the floor to Yardley for voir dire.

Yardley worked through the questions involving the history of the potential jurors' interactions with the criminal justice system, then their family members' interactions, and finally their friends'. She then moved on to potential bias, mental or physical ailments that could interfere with reasoning abilities, and then general questions meant to make the jurors a bit uncomfortable so she could see how they responded. Primarily, she watched for fidgeting, glances away from her, shifting in their seats, and folding of the arms across the chest. Indications of untruthfulness or hostility.

When she was through, it was six in the evening, and the defense began their voir dire in the morning. Ricci was the one who rose and began questioning the panel. She didn't cover the same areas Yardley had and instead engaged in light banter with the group, discussing various aspects of the case. It was subtle, to avoid an objection, but she was slowly feeding them their theory of the case.

Could you acquit someone if you believed someone else had committed the crime but there wasn't a lot of evidence to back up your belief? Would you find someone guilty if you thought they were innocent but other members of the jury did not? How would you feel if you knew the real perpetrator of the crime was going to get away with it?

Yardley didn't object, though there were quite a few times Ricci crossed the line. She didn't want to create a combative impression with the jury just yet.

Yardley was surprised how quickly they went through voir dire, considering this was a homicide trial. Since she wasn't asking for the death penalty, the jury didn't have to be death qualified, which could have taken as long as two or three months.

Aster asked for only three jurors to be brought back in chambers and questioned, and Yardley only had one. Mostly questions about bias given something in their backgrounds. On the third day of jury selection, when they were through questioning the panel, they sat in the judge's chambers and went through the list.

"I would ask to have juror number four stricken for cause," Aster said.

"Denied," Weston said, making a note on the sheet of juror numbers and names.

"Judge, her dad was a cop."

"So what? She isn't a cop. Denied."

"That's nonsense," Aster said. "We can't have the daughter of a cop on the jury."

"We can have whoever I say we can have on this jury, Mr. Aster. And I would watch your tone."

He shook his head and said, "Fine, I'll use one of my peremptory challenges and strike them. I would ask then that juror number twelve be stricken for cause."

"Denied."

"His father died from a drunk driver, Judge, and the man was acquitted. He's got a chip on his shoulder. There's no way he's going to be objective."

"Denied. Next."

Aster was quiet a second, and the two men stared at each other. "Juror number sixteen needs to be stricken for cause."

"Denied."

"You're kidding."

"Do I look like I'm kidding?"

"He was a prison guard. Those guys are looking to hang anybody even accused of a crime."

"He said he could be objective when you questioned him."

"Of course he said that. What's he gonna say? *No, I'm an emotional jerkoff and can't control myself?*"

"Your motion is denied. Next."

"This is bullshit," Aster said, his voice raised.

Ricci put her hand on his forearm and said, "Dylan—"

"What the hell are you doing, Harvey?" he almost shouted. "Are you drunk again?"

"Hey! Don't you dare yell in here. I will not tolerate yelling!" he bellowed. "This is my courtroom, and I can do whatever the hell I deem necessary to—"

"Now you're yelling," Aster said.

"I'm a judge, damn it! The whole reason we become judges is so we can yell at people. Now, this better not be the tone you're setting for the next five days, or you are going to have a seriously miserable time."

Ricci said, "It's fine, Judge. Let's just move on."

Yardley asked to strike two people for cause, and she was denied as well but didn't object. Weston seemed in a particularly bad mood, and she guessed he wanted to get this trial over with as quickly as possible. Maybe he thought he was molding a jury that would come to a verdict quickly rather than taking days of deliberations?

By late afternoon, they had argued and compromised their way to twelve jurors and four alternates. Weston said they would break for the day and then start with opening statements in the morning.

52

Yardley couldn't eat breakfast and instead sat at a café across the street from the courthouse and read through Detective Garrett's reports again. He would be the first witness after opening statements. She got a text from Tara that said, Good luck! It made her grin but also gave her a twinge of sadness. For the next eight days, she would hardly see her daughter. Worse, she wouldn't be able to keep tabs on her.

She went to court early and sat at the prosecution table. She watched as the bailiff set up the large portrait of Kathy Pharr she had asked to be put on an easel near the jury. Kathy with Harmony and Tucker at a water park. It was the only photo she could find where all three were smiling.

When the jury and attorneys were all seated, Weston came out. He cleared his throat, then told the jury that what the attorneys said during the trial was not evidence but only their opinions of the evidence, and the jury could give the statements whatever weight they deemed appropriate.

"Ms. Yardley, go ahead."

Yardley rose. The fatigue came in waves, and she felt sluggish but hoped the adrenaline of the trial would energize her.

She glanced toward Zachary and then approached the jury, careful not to stand too close or too far away.

"I remember before I became an attorney, there was a news story on one night about a man who had robbed a convenience store. There were two witnesses who saw him stick a gun in the cashier's face and snatch the cash out of the register before sprinting out of the store. There was also a video of him doing it. The news anchor said his case was set for trial, and I remember thinking, *Who could acquit him? The evidence is overwhelming.*

"Two months later, I happened to catch a follow-up story. The man had been found not guilty. Someone on the program I was watching, some cable news show, said that our justice system was a farce. This was just a few years after the O. J. Simpson verdict, and so everyone was on edge, thinking that our system didn't work. I've always believed in our system, and I remember having to defend it to people, but I kept hearing that word: *farce*. Our system was a farce. And that word just wouldn't leave me."

She put her hands together in front of her and glanced over the jury.

"I thought of that word as I was preparing for this trial. The evidence here is overwhelming. Like it was in the case of the man who robbed that store. You're going to hear from several police officers, forensic scientists, detectives, and federal agents about the details of this case. And the details are horrific."

She turned and looked at Zachary before walking to the portrait of Kathy Pharr.

"The defendant, Michael Zachary, killed this beautiful woman, Kathy Pharr, in a cabin on Crimson Lake Road not two hours from here. A woman with a husband, a daughter, and an entire life still ahead of her. The defendant was having an affair with Kathy. We don't know how or why the affair began—people rarely do—but it did. And somewhere along the way, it went bad. So bad that the defendant decided Kathy Pharr needed to die. Maybe it was because she wanted to tell his live-in girlfriend, Angela River, or maybe she wanted to call off the affair and he didn't . . ." She paused. "Or maybe he simply felt like killing her." She inhaled and put her hands behind her back. "The fact is we may never know why he killed her. In the end, it doesn't matter. As I've sometimes heard homicide detectives say, dead is still dead."

Yardley removed the portrait of Kathy Pharr and replaced it with another. It was the first of Sarpong's paintings. Then she turned around a whiteboard that had photos of Kathy Pharr's crime scene neatly arranged over its surface.

"This is a painting made in 1964 by a painter named Sarpong. You can see that the painting and Kathy Pharr's scene of death are identical. Kathy Pharr's body was posed to mimic this painting. She was kidnapped from her work while on a smoke break, injected with ricin, strapped to a table, cut along the brow to get the blood flowing down the face, and then wrapped in bandages and a black tunic like the one in the painting. Then she was sat in a chair, and an industrial-strength medical glue was used to give her the appearance of life. Her arms, thighs, and back were all glued to the chair, and she died there. Alone and afraid, in complete darkness.

"A month later, a neighbor reported suspicious activity at a different cabin on Crimson Lake Road. The Clark County Sheriff's Office and an FBI agent rushed to the scene." She paused. "What they found shocked them.

"Mr. Zachary's girlfriend, Angela River, was laid down on a table." Yardley went to the easel and took down the Sarpong painting, replacing it with the second painting in the series and, next to that, a blown-up sketch of what River looked like when Baldwin found her.

"The second painting, brought to life again with a real human being, Angela River. This time, however, Mr. Zachary made a mistake. Angela survived. She was ill and near death from the ricin injected into her, but Mr. Zachary had miscalculated the dose, and she was able to fight and survive.

"A warrant was executed on Mr. Zachary's property. What the officers and agents found was this." She picked up several transparent bags from the prosecution table. She then went through the evidence one item at a time, explaining its significance and making sure the jury had a chance to examine it up close. She described Zachary's lack of alibis and how he'd had the perfect opportunities to commit both crimes. Several times, she glanced to Zachary and saw him staring at her with hatred in his eyes.

She approached the jury after an hour of going through the evidence and looked each member in the eyes.

"The defense is going to make this trial about anything they possibly can other than the evidence. They will make it about Kathy Pharr's husband, Tucker Pharr. He has a previous conviction for kidnapping, something the defense will no doubt bring up several times. He has many tattoos; he works a blue-collar job and doesn't have an education. The defense will tell you he *looks* like a killer.

"They will try to make it about Kathy Pharr's infidelity, about bias in the prosecution or police . . . they will make this case about everything except for one thing: the evidence. They will tell you that Mr. Zachary is a successful doctor. He's from the upper strata of society, from the wealthy and elite, and the wealthy and elite don't commit crimes like this." She stepped closer to the jury. "Never mind that all the evidence was found inside Mr. Zachary's garage. Never mind that his alibi doesn't hold up for either night. Never mind that Sarpong paintings were found in his possession. The defense will tell you never mind all that because someone else *looks* more like a killer than Michael Zachary does."

One of the jurors slightly shook his head, as though in disbelief.

Yardley put her hands behind her back.

"I was thinking about the man who robbed that store this morning. My daughter occasionally asks me about my job and about the justice system, and I pictured her asking me, *Did you ever see the system fail?*

And I would say, *I had a case where all the evidence was found in the defendant's possession, where he didn't have one witness who could verify his alibi, where he was in possession of paintings that were identical to the scenes of the crimes, and the victims were his mistress and his girlfriend . . . but the jury acquitted him because someone else* looked *more like a killer than the defendant. The system failed those two victims that day.* If that happens, ladies and gentlemen, then those people on the cable news show were right. Our system is a farce. Don't let that be the case. Don't let the defense make this about anything but the evidence. Michael Zachary killed Kathy Pharr and tried to kill Angela River. Don't let him get away with it."

Yardley sat down. A few jurors kept their eyes on her and then looked away. Weston said, "Mr. Aster."

53

Aster rose and stood in front of the jury. He looked them over a moment and said, "Ms. Yardley's right." He picked up the bags of evidence from the prosecution table. "All this stuff was found in Michael Zachary's garage. He was at a conference on the night of the murder of Mrs. Pharr, and no one seems to remember seeing him there. He was asleep at home when his girlfriend was kidnapped, and no one can verify that. So why even bother with a trial? Let's just read the police reports and stick him in prison. Why bother bringing in a jury and wasting everyone's time? When they don't have a decent alibi, let's just not bother with all this," he said, waving his arm around the courtroom. "I know a lot of cops that think that way, and hell, maybe they're right? When the evidence is obvious, let's just lock 'em up."

He looked each juror in the eyes.

"Why don't we do that? Because sometimes, appearances are deceiving. Sometimes, *sometimes*, everything looks like it points one way, when in fact it goes another. Yes, those things were found in his garage, but he will tell you he has no idea how they got there. Ridiculous, right? Just like Ms. Yardley said. Well, ask yourself: Why would he be stupid enough to keep those things in his garage, knowing his girlfriend could stumble onto them? Dr. Zachary's a respected emergency room physician who went to Stanford Medical School. Would he really be so stupid as to not know that Angela River, who outweighs Kathy Pharr by almost one-third of her body weight, would need more ricin than Kathy Pharr did to cause death? Would he be so stupid as to kill his lover and then kill his girlfriend a month later? Did he not know that he would be the police's top suspect? Would he really be so dumb as to not establish better alibis?"

Aster took a step to the side, resting his hand on the defense table close to Zachary.

"And let's chat about motive. What exactly is Dr. Zachary's motive? Did you hear the prosecution even address that? All they said was, 'Hey, we'll never know.' Well, that's not good enough. Our system is set up precisely for this reason: to tell the government that before you can take a man's life away, you have to prove what he did. *Prove it.* You don't get to shrug your shoulders and say, *Well, we can't know, so convict him anyway.* What's the motive? The fact is there is none. The prosecution will not present a single shred of evidence to tell you why Dr. Zachary would do any of this."

Aster paced in front of the table. "Ms. Yardley's daughter could get another answer to her question. She could hear, *Yes, I'll tell you when the system failed. When the jury didn't even consider what* beyond a reasonable doubt *means, didn't consider any contradictory evidence, didn't question motive, and didn't believe an innocent man. The system failed that day and took away a man's life because the prosecution told them to do it.*"

Aster stared at the jurors in silence a moment.

"But it doesn't have to be that way. I mean, you could go back in that room and say, *It's good enough.* We've got the evidence in his garage, good enough. Sure, it doesn't make sense and there's no motive, but the stuff was in the garage. Good enough. You could do that.

"Or you could go back there and really consider what *beyond a reasonable doubt* means, really take seriously that oath you gave to place your emotions aside and consider the evidence fairly. Really think about why our founding fathers gave us the Constitution—not to protect us from ourselves but to protect us from our government. But if you go back there and just say, *Hell, good enough, lock him up and throw away the key,* well, then Ms. Yardley is right . . . the system is a farce."

Aster sat down. Weston leaned back in his chair and said, "First witness, Ms. Yardley."

54

Yardley had Detective Garrett sworn in. He wore a freshly pressed suit, and his gun was in a holster on his hip, his badge around his neck on a lanyard. Yardley gave him a moment after swearing in to drink some water out of a paper cup.

"How are you, Detective?"

"I'm fine, thank you."

"Good. Well, I'd like to go through some of your qualifications first, if we may. Please spell your name for the record and tell us a little bit about your background."

Garrett did as she asked and looked at the jury while doing so. The mark of a witness who had spent a lot of time in court. He told them about his time in the army, his civilian police work, and his promotion to detective in the homicide division of the Sheriff's Office. He recapped the trainings he'd provided to other detectives and the trainings he'd received from the DEA and FBI. Yardley also asked about what he liked to do in his spare time to relax so the jury got to know him. She limited the introductory questions to fifteen minutes to make sure she still had their full attention.

"Tell us about the case at hand, Detective."

He described the initial call about Kathy Pharr, how he was sent to the scene and what he found. He then described what had happened with Angela River. Yardley glanced back once to see if River was in the courtroom, but she wasn't.

"Detective, did you find any evidence linking these crimes to any other person besides Michael Zachary?"

"No, we did not."

"Did you have another person of interest?"

"We did. Mr. Tucker Pharr was briefly a person of interest. In addition to his wife, his daughter—"

"Objection," Aster said, rising. "May we approach?"

"Yes."

Yardley leaned against the judge's bench as Aster did the same. The judge hit a button that sent static through the courtroom speakers, and Aster said, "Your Honor, I would object to any mention of Mr. Pharr's daughter as missing. It's clearly more prejudicial than probative and has nothing to do with this case."

"That's nonsense," Yardley said. "It's clear that whoever killed Mrs. Pharr took Harmony Pharr as well. The jury should hear that."

"What evidence will you be presenting that that's the case?" Aster said.

"We'll be presenting Tucker Pharr's testimony, as well as Agent Baldwin's, about the tree house she was abducted from and what they found."

"In other words, nothing, Judge. She could have run away, and they have no evidence to present that would contradict that, other than she left her phone behind. This is just an attempt to inflame the jury. The jury would be prejudiced against my client just by the fact that a child is involved, and that's exactly what Ms. Yardley is counting on."

Weston considered it a moment. "Smells like bullshit, Ms. Yardley."

"Judge, the disappearance is part of this case. There is no way she happened to disappear shortly after her mother was murdered. The probative value for the jury is that they can get a complete picture of the series of events."

"Or she ran away," Aster said, "and it has nothing to do with any of this."

Weston shook his head. "I don't like it. I don't think it adds anything to the question of whether the defendant killed Mrs. Pharr and tried to kill Ms. River. I'm excluding any mention of Harmony Pharr or her kidnapping under Rule 403."

"Your Honor—"

"That's my ruling. Step back."

Yardley avoided showing any reaction and went back to the lectern. "Detective Garrett, you were the one who actually found the evidence in this case, correct?"

"When we executed the search warrant on Michael Zachary's premises, it was Special Agent Baldwin and myself who did the primary search, yes. I found the items taped underneath the chair in a room to the side of the garage."

Yardley introduced photographs of the space as he spoke: the chair, the paintings, and the box the evidence was found in.

"When you and Agent Baldwin arrested him, what was the defendant's response to the situation?"

"He was belligerent. He kept arguing with us, and at one point, he tried to slip away from me by pushing against me, and I had to pin him against the wall to double-lock the cuffs on his wrists. We then transported him to a nearby station for interview, but he wasn't responsive. He was extremely nervous, kept fidgeting and looking around. His foot kept tapping against the floor in the obsessive manner of someone that was really anxious. Agent Baldwin exchanged a few words with him, which I'm sure he'll discuss. The interview was the end of my involvement in this case."

"Thank you, Detective, nothing further."

Aster got up and leaned on the lectern. He watched Garrett a moment and then said, "You said my client was nervous, right?"

"Yes, he was very nervous."

"You ever met him before this case, Detective?"

"No, I had not."

"You ever talked to him on the phone?"

"No."

"Ever seen a video of him before this case?"

"No, I had not."

"So you couldn't say what Dr. Zachary's general level of nervousness or anxiety is at any point in the day, could you?"

"I don't know what you mean."

"He could've been acting perfectly normal at the time you said he was nervous, but you wouldn't know, would you?"

"Well, I can tell when someone is nervous. We're trained to detect deception, and nervousness is one of the clues we look for."

"People differ in levels of anxiety and nervousness, don't they?"

He thought a moment. "Yes, they do."

"And again, you don't know Dr. Zachary's general level of nervousness on any given day, do you?"

"I suppose not."

"So you could not say whether he was feeling his normal level of nervousness on that particular day or not, correct?"

He glanced at Yardley. "I suppose not, but—"

"Thank you, Detective. I would appreciate if you answered honestly in front of the jury instead of attempting to be evasive."

"I wasn't—"

"You said he was combative, correct?"

Garrett glanced at Yardley again as though expecting her to do something about Aster interrupting him. "Yes."

"You'd just arrested him for murder and kidnapping, yeah?"

"Yes, I had."

"You ever been arrested for murder?"

"Of course not."

"Would you agree it's probably pretty traumatizing?"

"I wouldn't know."

"Again, don't be evasive, please, Detective. Would being arrested for murder be traumatizing? Would it shock someone?"

He glanced at the jury. Yardley thought it would be idiotic if Garrett denied this. He could lose credibility. He seemed to be taking too long to answer, so she stood up.

"Objection, Your Honor. This isn't relevant to the case at hand."

"Overruled."

"Detective," Aster said, "traumatizing, yeah? To be pulled out of work, have the cops tearing apart your house, and then be arrested for murder when Nevada carries the death penalty. Traumatizing, yes or no?"

Garrett glanced at the jury again. "Yes, it would be."

"When people are traumatized, they don't act perfectly rational, do they?"

"No, I wouldn't think so."

"They act nervous and anxious, yeah?"

"I suppose."

"And if an innocent man is arrested for murder, which would be even *more* traumatizing, you wouldn't expect him to act rational and calm, would you?"

"I don't know."

"If an innocent man were arrested for a murder he didn't commit, you'd expect him to be nervous, yeah? Even extremely nervous?"

"I couldn't say. Like I said, I've never been arrested for murder."

"Huh. Yeah, well, we'll get back to that."

Yardley watched Aster a moment before turning back to Garrett. Aster was purposely trying to throw him off balance, but that murder remark gave her pause. It wasn't customary for prosecutors to do background checks on the law enforcement officers they were putting up as witnesses, but just in case, she had run Garrett's background and found his record was clean.

"Now let's chat about this evidence you found under the chair. You were the one who actually found it, yeah?"

"Correct."

"And you were searching the entire garage with Agent Baldwin and, I believe, three other deputies, correct?"

"Correct."

"But you were the one who pulled off the tape and took the box out from under the chair?"

"I did."

"And you showed it to Agent Baldwin."

"I did. Yes."

"Before you found it, Agent Baldwin and the other deputies didn't know about it, correct?"

"Correct."

"They didn't see it until you had it in your hands?"

"Correct, I was the first one to locate it."

"Detective, you ever fabricated evidence before in a case?"

"Of course not. That's a stupid question, Counsel."

Weston said, "Why don't you let me be the judge of that, Detective."

"Sorry, Your Honor. It's just—sometimes you get sick of these defense attorneys attacking good cops so they can get their scumbag clients off."

Aster ignored his statement and said, "So you've never fabricated evidence?"

"No, I have not, Counsel."

"Ever stabbed anybody?"

Yardley nearly laughed at how ridiculous the question was. Sometimes defense attorneys made up nonsense questions to put an image in the mind of the jurors, like, *Have you ever done heroin?* The attorney might not have any basis that the officer had ever done heroin, but the jury would wonder why the attorney had asked the question.

Garrett should have laughed, too, or become furious. He did neither. He flushed and gave Aster a hard stare. Something passed between the two of them that she wasn't privy to. She rose quickly and said, "Objection. This entire line of questioning is irrelevant and inflammatory. I would ask the Court to instruct Mr. Aster to move on to questions about this case."

"Whether the detective has ever tried to murder someone and fabricate evidence is extremely relevant, Your Honor, considering he was the one who allegedly found the primary pieces of evidence against Dr. Zachary."

"Do you have a basis for asking these questions, Counsel?"

"I do. Just need a little bit of leeway."

"A little bit, Mr. Aster. No more."

He nodded and turned back to Garrett. "Ever stabbed anyone, Detective?"

"No," he said sternly, his gaze never leaving Aster.

"Ever been accused of stabbing someone and trying to cast blame on someone else for the crime?"

"No," he said with fury in his eyes.

Aster watched him a moment, and Yardley could tell he was debating something.

"No further questions right now, Your Honor."

"Very well. Ms. Yardley, any redirect?"

"None."

"Then you may be excused, Detective Garrett."

Aster said, "Your Honor, we would ask to call a rebuttal witness."

"Who?"

"Mrs. Kimberly Alley is her name now. She was at one time Mrs. Kimberly Garrett."

Yardley rose. "Sidebar."

Weston nodded, and the two of them went up. Yardley said, "I would object to this witness unless she has something material to add to this case."

Weston said, "I don't like fishing expeditions, Mr. Aster."

"I'm not fishing, Judge. Detective Garrett got up there and said he has never been accused of stabbing anyone and never been accused of fabricating evidence. Neither of which is true."

"That's ridiculous," Yardley said.

"Then you got nothing to lose by agreeing to let her testify."

Yardley held his gaze a second and decided he wasn't bluffing. Something was there. "I want to interview her first before she takes the stand."

"That's not how impeachment witnesses work, Your Honor. The evidentiary rules are clear that if someone lies on the stand, the opposing party can call a rebuttal witness with no notice to opposing counsel. The presumption is that the opposing party should have known their own witness was going to lie and shouldn't need time to prepare."

Weston sighed. "This better not be bullshit, Counselor. I need a cigarette and don't want to sit here through bullshit feeling jittery."

"It's not."

"Then I'll allow her to testify, but if I feel it's bullshit at any point, I'm shutting you down."

Yardley said, "Your Honor, I deserve to have a brief recess to interview this witness. We filed a reverse discovery request, and Mr. Aster never mentioned a word about a Mrs. Kimberly Alley. Unless he just found out about her a moment ago, I should have been given some notice that she was a potential impeachment witness. Even if it was right before Detective Garrett's testimony."

Aster said, "I'd like Ms. Yardley to point me to one statute or evidentiary rule that says I have to give any notice for an impeachment witness. It's a bullshit argument because she didn't dig deep enough into the detective's background and now—"

"The reverse discovery specifically asked for any potential impeachment witnesses. You purposely withheld this from me so you could—"

"Calm down, both of you." Weston blew out a long breath as he thought. "No, let's just get this over with. Request denied, Ms. Yardley. If he's lying, you should've known it."

"Your Honor—"

"Request denied. Don't make me put you on my shit list like Mr. Aster here."

Aster said, "I'm hurt, Judge. I thought we were friends."

Weston grimaced and said, "Just put her on so we can break."

Yardley went back to the prosecution table. She motioned for Garrett to sit behind her on the bench reserved for other prosecutors. He did so, and she leaned back so they could whisper.

"What's she going to say, Lucas?"

"Nothing good. But it's all bullshit. I was cleared of everything. They didn't even file a formal IAD notice."

"Cleared of what?"

"Her boyfriend stabbed some gangster in their neighborhood and then hid the knife. They made up some horseshit about it being me and that I broke into their condo and planted it. It was all a big show so she could get full custody."

Yardley stared at him. Just as he had received training on detecting clues of deception, so had she, albeit hers was in graduate school in behavioral science clinics. He appeared calm and relaxed and gave lengthy answers to her questions. A sign of honesty. But he'd also had rage when Aster brought it up. Anger was a normal reaction to a false accusation; rage was not. And the fact that divorce and custody of his child had been in play complicated everything. It was too difficult to get a read on him.

"Did you have anything to do with it, Lucas? If you did, now's the time to tell me because once it's on the court record, it's going to be public information."

He looked over to Aster, and a sneer came to his lips. "Little prick bastard. I swear if we weren't in a courtroom, I would—"

"Hey, let me worry about him. You worry about yourself. Tell me everything she's going to say."

The courtroom doors opened, and a bailiff brought in an attractive woman in a red dress. Garrett's eyes went wide as he saw her, and his gaze followed her through the courtroom to the witness stand, where she was sworn in.

"Your Honor," Yardley said as she rose to her feet, "I would request a brief recess to confer with Detective Garrett."

"Denied."

"Then I would ask for a five-minute bathroom break."

"Denied. I'm not stupid, Ms. Yardley."

"Some of the jurors might need to use the bathroom before we get into this."

Weston turned to the jury. "Any of you need to use the bathroom?"

Yardley hoped someone would raise their hand, but no one did.

"Recess is denied," Weston said. "Go ahead, Mr. Aster."

Aster stepped toward the witness but stood near the jury, so when Kimberly Alley was looking at him, she appeared to be facing the jury and speaking to them directly.

"State and spell your name for the record, please."

"Um, Kimberly—that's just the normal spelling—Michelle Alley. A-L-L-E-Y."

"Mrs. Alley, do you know Detective Lucas Garrett?"

"I do, yes."

"How do you know him?"

"We were married."

"When?"

"Um, we got married in 2011, and we divorced about four years ago."

"What happened to split you two up?"

Yardley said, "Objection, Your Honor."

"Sustained. Facts only pertinent to this case, Mr. Aster."

He put his hands in his pockets and watched Kimberly Alley. "Do you know what this case is about, Mrs. Alley?"

"Yes."

"And I know you weren't in the courtroom, but your husband just testified that he has never stabbed anyone and never been investigated for stabbing someone."

"I'm sure he did say that."

"Is it true?"

"No, it's not."

Murmurs went up from a few people in the courtroom. Yardley glanced behind her. At least half a dozen people were there, all in plain clothes without press tags. Most of them, she was sure, were reporters and bloggers attempting to get around Weston's bar of any media in the courtroom. She was surprised not to see Jude Chance.

"Please tell us what you mean," Aster said after allowing a good ten seconds to go by so the jury could soak in what was just said.

"Lucas and I had a . . . troubled relationship. It was really good in the early years, but he started drinking a lot after he became a detective. It was—"

"Objection," Yardley said. "Your Honor, none of this is relevant."

"Overruled."

Aster nodded to Kimberly. "Go ahead, Mrs. Alley."

"I was just gonna say that he started drinking heavily after he became a detective." She glanced at Garrett, then turned her gaze back to Aster. "Some cops just aren't cut out for it. A lotta cops don't like the detectives because they get all the glory and their faces in the papers and interviewed for documentaries and stuff, and a lotta the detectives don't like the uniformed officers because they get regular schedules and get to clock in and out at regular times. They're two different worlds. And so when Lucas became a detective, he had to live and breathe those cases, and he lost all his friends. Didn't hang out with them anymore. It caused a lot of stress. Anyway, I think that's what started the drinking, and um, after about a year it got outta control."

"Out of control how?"

She tucked her lower lip underneath her upper lip as she gazed out the windows of the courtroom. Yardley thought her eyes began to glisten with tears.

"He, um, beat me up one night."

Yardley shot to her feet. "Sidebar."

"Denied."

"Your Honor, I requested a sidebar."

"And I said denied." He looked at Kimberly. "Go ahead, Mrs. Alley. Continue."

Yardley sat back down. She glanced at Aster, who winked at her.

"What do you mean, he beat you up?" Aster said. He proceeded to gently question her, eliciting the details of a fight during which a drunk Garrett had shoved her into the shower, then punched her repeatedly in the face. He asked her questions about what she did after and the ride to the hospital. How their son had to go to the emergency room with her and lie to the doctor so his dad wouldn't be arrested and lose his job, their only source of income.

Yardley could see the sympathy in the jury's faces. Garrett leaned forward and whispered to her, "That's bullshit. Object to it."

"I tried," she whispered back. "What else aren't you telling me?"

"Nothing. It's all made up. Put me back on that stand after so I can explain everything."

"We'll cross that bridge when we get there."

Kimberly had started crying. Aster took a lot of time letting her compose herself and then said, "Was that the only time he hit you?"

She shook her head. "I never called the cops or anything. They weren't going to do anything when it was my word against his, so I let it go. I loved him, too, and we have a son together. I figured he would change once the stress in his job was reduced or he cut back his drinking . . . I don't know. You don't know what to think in that situation. You love him and hate him at the same time."

Yardley felt an intense revulsion: How many times had she lain awake in bed and thought that same thing?

"Did he change?"

"No," Kimberly said. "It became . . . not a routine thing, but it happened enough that I knew he needed help. When I tried to get it for him, he said he would die before going into a treatment program with a bunch of junkies. So I decided right then to leave him."

"When was this?"

"Four years ago. April something. I remember it was a Saturday. He'd gone fishing with some friends, and I packed up a few things and me and my son left."

"What happened then?"

"He was angry. There was a lot of screaming. He came to my work one Monday morning. Broke things, screamed, pushed around my boss, who was trying to protect me. He was so drunk I could smell the alcohol from ten feet away."

She glanced at Garrett, then quickly looked away.

"Did this continue past that Monday?" Aster asked.

"Yes. It got worse and worse. I was going to take out a, what do you call it, a restraining order, but my lawyer said it wasn't a good idea until the divorce was finalized. That it would complicate things since we had to talk about custody and how to split everything."

"What else happened at this time, Mrs. Alley?"

She inhaled deeply, exhaled slowly. "It was just my income now. I was working full-time at a low-paying job while I went back to college to finish my degree, so we didn't live in the best area. Some teenagers sold drugs on the corner. There was a little convenience store, and you could see them hanging out there. People would give them money, and then they would give them something. It was more unsettling than anything scary, but sometimes there'd be a fight. So one day—this was in June, I want to say June tenth of that year—the police come to my door. I'd just gotten home from work, and I'm exhausted and was about to tell them I didn't know anything because I was sure they were there to ask about some fight, but then they told me that my boyfriend at the time, my husband now, Nathan Alley, had maybe stabbed someone. One of the boys on the corner selling drugs."

"Did he?"

"Absolutely not. He was away on business in Montreal when it happened. He owns a nutrition supplement store and was at an expo. I showed the cops his Instagram, where he posted tons of pictures of him there, but they didn't care. They said they were searching the condo, and there was nothing I could do about it."

"What happened when they searched?"

"They found a knife. Like a military knife. One of those ones that folds. They found it wrapped in a T-shirt that had blood on it."

"Your knife?"

"No. I'd never seen it before."

"Nathan's?"

"No. The cops said that Nathan stabbed that boy, and they arrested him until their sergeant or whatever talked to several people that were in Montreal with him. Then they thought it was me until they watched the video of my condo. I had one of those video recorders on my front door where it starts recording if there's movement nearby. On the night of the stabbing, it recorded me and my son coming home and not leaving until the morning. But it did capture something else the next day."

"What?"

"Objection, hearsay. We need to see this video if she's going to discuss it."

Aster laid a DVD on the prosecutor's table and said, "May I approach the clerk, Your Honor?"

"You may."

He handed the clerk a DVD. A projection screen came down across from the jury near the wall while a bailiff turned down the lights. The clerk inserted the DVD, and an image flickered to life on the screen.

The entire courtroom watched, rapt, as the video showed Kimberly and a little chubby boy leave the condo. The screen went blank. When the camera activated again, it was brighter, midday, and Lucas Garrett was on the porch. He hurried to the door, glancing around a few times. He had something in his hands, and he fiddled with the lock for a while before the door opened, and he went inside.

"What did we just watch?" Aster asked.

"That was Lucas breaking into my condo. The camera is hidden really good. He didn't know it was there."

"I'm going to fast-forward now fifteen minutes."

The screen went blank, and Aster fast-forwarded about fourteen and a half minutes, and the image came back. Garrett came out of the condo and rushed over to his car and drove away.

"Did you show this video to the police?"

"I did."

"What happened?"

"They immediately dropped the investigation against me and Nathan and said they wouldn't be bothering us anymore." She looked at Garrett now. "They said they were going to bring Lucas in for questions. I never heard anything from them again."

"Do you think Lucas stabbed that boy and planted the knife in your condo to get your boyfriend arrested and make you look bad during a custody fight?"

"Objection, speculation."

"Sustained."

Aster said, "Thank you, Mrs. Alley, that's all."

Yardley stayed seated and watched her. She appeared fragile and, still after all these years, frightened. A tough cross-examination could alienate the jury. And Yardley hadn't become a sex crimes and domestic violence prosecutor to tear apart victims on the stand. She turned to Garrett, who was staring at Kimberly, and whispered, "Is it true?"

"No. Hell no, it isn't true."

"You're lying to me."

He grimaced and shook his head. "You know what, I don't need this shit from either of you. Convict that asshole by yourself."

He rose and stormed out of the courtroom. Yardley gave no reaction other than a flex of her jaw muscles from her teeth grinding together. She stood up.

"No questions for this witness, Your Honor."

55

The sky was a deep gray. Baldwin lay on the hood of his car and listened to the birds in the nearby trees and the buzz of the occasional fly that zipped by. There was a case he remembered from years ago, a young mother murdered in this park while pushing a stroller. It seemed like if you were in this job long enough, everywhere would hold ghosts for you.

Detective Kristen Reece pulled up a few minutes later in her blue Chevy. She got out wearing black pants with a red shirt, her gun in a sleek black shoulder holster. She put on her suit jacket and said, "You sleepin' on the job again?"

"Gotta get it where you can." Baldwin sat up and stretched his neck. "So who is this guy?"

"Just said his name's Leonard and he's got information on Harmony Pharr. I called you right after I spoke to him."

"I know, and I really appreciate that. A lotta cops wouldn't have."

"Hell, that's just you men with your 'who's got the biggest dick' contests. That's why only women should be police chiefs and sheriffs. We just want to get the job done."

"Who would make all the coffee and get the donuts if you guys were running things?"

She punched his arm. "Don't make me shoot your ass."

He chuckled as he got off the car. "I miss hanging out with you."

"Me too. Where the hell you been anyway?"

They walked across the parking lot into a grove near a large playground. A cement path had been cleared through the trees.

"The ASAC I told you about. He's got me running down people passing off fake checks and other bullshit like that twelve hours a day now. Takes all my time."

"For real?"

"For real. I'm actually here off the clock."

"Shit. Well, that sucks."

He shrugged. "Yeah, well, what can you do. It's probably getting time for me to move on anyway. I've always wanted to run a bar. You think I'd be good at that?"

"I think you'd make a lotta tips with those looks."

He grinned and put his hands in his pockets as they strolled through the park.

"So you don't know anything about this guy, huh?" he said.

"Nope."

"Seems weird to just rush out here instead of inviting him in first and getting some more info."

"You seen the file in this case? We got nothin'. When it first hit the media, we got calls from cranks and Good Samaritans leaving tips, but even those stopped after a few days. No one cares anymore. She was news for an afternoon, and now it's done. If I don't find somethin' in the next few weeks, this'll be transferred to open-unsolved, and Harmony Pharr can kiss her ass goodbye, 'cause ain't no cop ever gonna look at it again."

He nodded. It was nearly the same protocol at the Bureau. Once the case went cold for a certain length of time, the file was closed and buried and never thought about again. Except by the family members left behind.

He said, "I made contact with a CI that I used to use in the sex offender community. Made him a deal to testify at a track hearing for him if he got me any info on Harmony."

"He find anything?"

"No. He said he looked everywhere and there was just nothing out there. Not a peep. Just the same nutjobs making disgusting comments on the dark net, but nothing that people can't learn from the news. Whoever took her is probably not a part of that community, and they're doing a good job keeping their head down."

She stopped at a clearing. The park bathrooms were ahead with another playground to the right and a full-length soccer field on the other side. Covered pavilions with benches and tables were behind them.

"Said he'd meet us here."

They sat down on a bench near the playground.

"You ever get sick of this shit?" Baldwin said.

"Mm-hmm. What cop doesn't?"

"Then why don't you leave? You got other options, don't you?"

She shrugged. "My daddy has a good business. Sells rec vehicles, like boats and four-wheelers. Could go work for him. But I just can't see myself in another job. Maybe I just don't wanna see pictures of missin' kids on Instagram and think maybe I could've done somethin', but instead I'm selling Jet Skis to rich douchebags."

He grinned. "Some days I would gladly take a pay cut just to stand in a store and sell Jet Skis to douchebags."

"Some days," she said, looking at him, "but not every day, I bet." She took nicotine gum out of her pocket and chewed on a piece. "How come they got you on white collar now? You're a homicide investigator through and through."

"The ASAC, Dana Young, thinks it's all bullshit. That Behavioral Science never should've been given the attention it's gotten and we just should've had a general homicide division. He doesn't see the difference between a gang slaying and a sexual predator. Murder's murder."

"Shit. Have him come out and do my job for a week. Find kids stuffed in sewage pipes with nooses around their necks and then tell me a drive-by is the same thing."

He nodded and watched the trees sway with a breeze. "I'm not kidding, Kristen. I think I'm done. After this, I think that's it for me."

"Well," she said, taking his arm in hers, "whatever happens, you'll land on your feet. You always do."

A man approached through the playground. He wore a long white-sleeved shirt, and his acid-washed jeans were faded and torn. His face was sunburned, and he was nervous, constantly looking behind him as though he were waiting for someone to attack him.

He came up with his hands in his pockets and stood in front of them. "You Detective Reece?"

"I am."

"Who's this? I said to come alone."

"Cut the shit and just tell us what you know. Gonna rain soon, and I don't wanna be out here."

Baldwin noticed the man's hands trembling as he pulled them out of his pockets and the jitteriness of his movements. His pupils were large, and he was unhealthily skinny. If Baldwin had to guess, he would say this man was addicted to speed. Probably snorting it, since his teeth didn't have the black stains addicts got from smoking out of pipes.

"So I want two hundred. Up front."

"Two hundred what? Dollars?"

He nodded.

"Get the hell outta here," she said. "You didn't say nothin' about paying you."

"What's the girl's life worth to you? Two hundred seems small."

Baldwin said, "What do you know about her disappearance?"

"I know where she is."

Baldwin and Reece exchanged a quick glance before Baldwin said, "She's alive?"

He nodded. "I ain't go talk to her or nothin'. I just seen someone bring her to this place I know. I seen her picture. I know it's her, I got a good look at her."

Reece said, "We could just arrest you and charge you with obstruction. Then you can sit in a cell until you're ready to talk to us."

"No," Baldwin said, taking out his wallet. "I got a hundred seventeen. This pans out, I give you my word I'll get you the rest."

The man mumbled under his breath. "Yeah, all right, gimme the money."

Baldwin handed it over and then took out his phone and opened the audio recording app. He turned it on and put it next to his leg on the bench.

"No recordings," the man said.

"I might forget things I need to go back to."

He shook his head. "No, no recordings. Write it down if you want, but I ain't givin' you my last name, and I ain't bein' recorded."

Reece said, "Hey, listen here, shithead—"

"No, it's fine, Kristen." Baldwin turned the recorder off and pulled up his note-taking app and showed it to the man. "No recording. Just taking notes on this."

He nodded and nervously glanced around again.

Reece said, "So? Start talkin'."

"I was at this bar called Henry's. You know where it is?"

"No," Baldwin said.

"It's on Forty-Two and Main. I was there the day after that girl's story about her missing and all came out. I seen someone with her in the parking lot. They don't serve under twenty-one, so he went in and got some food from the grill and came out and they left."

"Where was she when he went inside?" Reece asked.

"In the car. It was, like, a red car. Little tiny car. She was in the passenger seat and waited, and he went inside."

"Was anybody else around?"

He nodded. "Least five people were smoking outside. She even came outta the car and walked around talking on the phone."

Reece folded her arms and said what Baldwin was thinking. "She had a phone, huh?"

"Yeah. She walked around the lot just talking to somebody, and then the dude came out with two Styrofoam boxes and got in the car, and they left."

Baldwin said, "You recognize the guy?"

He shook his head. "Never seen him before. White dude, my height, wore a Padres hat."

Reece said, "Give this man's money back before I arrest you."

"What? Why?"

"She didn't have no phone. We found her phone."

"Then it wasn't hers, 'cause I'm telling you she was on the phone. And she didn't look like she been kidnapped or nothing. She coulda yelled for help, and ten people woulda come running. She didn't do none of that. She was there 'cause she wanted to be there."

"Mm-hmm," Reece said, eyeing him up and down.

Baldwin took a few notes and said, "What kind of car? Sedan, hatchback, four-door, two-door?"

"Red two-door. Hatchback, I guess."

"If I showed you pictures of different cars, could you recognize it?"

He lit a cigarette as he nodded.

"What was she wearing?"

"Just like a striped shirt and shorts. I was close, too. When she was out on the phone, she walked right past me. I was standing against the wall, and she came as far from me as I am to you now. It was her. I seen her picture the night before."

"Did you hear anything she was saying on the phone?"

He shook his head. "She was laughing, though. She didn't look like she was in trouble."

"Why'd you wait so long to call?"

"I didn't. I left a message a while ago, and no one called me back."

Baldwin glanced at Reece but let it go. "I'm going to need your phone number, and I'll need you to get with a police sketch artist to get us a rendering of the man you saw."

"No, no way. I keep my head down and stay outta other people's business, and that's how I get by."

"How am I supposed to get you your hundred bucks if I can't reach you?"

The man thought about this a moment and said, "All right. But I don't want to come down to no police station. You can meet me at a Del Taco or McDonald's or whatever."

"That's fair."

"My name's Leonard."

"I'm Cason."

Leonard rattled off his phone number and then left the park the way he'd come.

Reece said, "That was some bullshit. I can't believe you paid the man."

"He's a hardcore addict. How many addicts you know willingly call the cops to report a crime?"

"He did it for money."

"Yeah, but he still did it. Two hundred bucks wouldn't even make his bail if we arrested him for something. And he gave us his name and phone number. I'm not saying he's the pope, but let's at least follow up on what he's saying."

"You sure you got time? Shouldn't you be chasing someone embezzling money from Goldman Sachs?"

"I think Goldman Sachs can survive without me. Harmony might not. Also, he could be the one who took her."

She nodded, looking off in the direction Leonard had walked. "I'll follow him for now and get surveillance on him. Maybe it's our lucky day."

56

Kimberly Alley's testimony had been bad, but Yardley figured she would put Garrett up on the stand again before closing and let him explain himself, then argue that suspicious behavior during a nasty divorce didn't mean he'd framed an innocent man for no reason. She had no choice but to move on.

Yardley called the pathologist to the stand next. Dr. Mathew Carrey was bright and calm, and she had found him to be a convincing witness. He did as well as he had with the grand jury when Jax had put him up.

Yardley only got a couple of hours of testimony in before Weston called a dinner break. She lifted her satchel after the jury had gone, and when she turned around to leave, she saw River sitting in the back of the courtroom.

"Let's get dinner," Yardley said, noticing the makeup that had washed down her cheeks with tears and then been wiped away.

River nodded. "Yeah, okay."

The courthouse had its own cafeteria. It was run by a single man in a chef's uniform. Yardley and River ordered salads and soup and sat at a table next to a window looking out onto the street. Only a handful of people were there, mostly attorneys and judges.

"Are you holding up okay?" Yardley asked.

"No."

Yardley swallowed and waited a beat. "Angie, a detective followed up with everyone they could find at the conference and with the airlines. Zachary was on the flight out to San Diego and the flight back, but he never signed the attendance sheet, and he didn't pick up the packets they handed out at the conference. They couldn't find a single organizer or attendee who could say he was there. I think he flew out and then rented a car and drove it back to throw off suspicion." She paused. "You knew he didn't go, didn't you?"

River had a napkin between her fingers, and she slowly tore at the edges. "He didn't do this."

"Angie—"

"I know that man. He did *not* do this."

Yardley sighed. "Then who, Angie? Who would go to all this effort to get him convicted for something he didn't do?"

"I don't know. If you thought he was innocent, what would you do next to prove it?"

"What I would do next is try to find someone who would benefit from Zachary being convicted of this."

River nodded. "Then do that. I know I have no right to ask, but please, for me . . . will you do that?" She reached out and took Yardley's hand. "I don't want to lose him. If he didn't do this . . . I mean, I can't even think of something more tragic than if he's convicted."

Yardley looked down at River's hand. "I'll look into it. But if there's nothing there, if I don't find anything—"

"I know . . . I know."

57

Yardley didn't sleep much the next couple of nights, and she sipped double espressos before court started. Aster and Ricci were joking with each other at the defense table. Yardley glanced behind her but didn't see River there. She hadn't come yesterday either.

When Weston came out and the jury was seated, he covered a yawn with his hand and then said, "Next witness, Ms. Yardley."

"The State would call Special Agent Cason Baldwin to the stand."

Baldwin wore a black suit and had some scruff from not shaving for a few days. He was sworn in and sat down in the witness box, giving a shy grin to the jury. Yardley asked for his name and occupation and ran through his qualifications, slowing down only briefly to discuss his law enforcement history with the navy and the San Francisco Police Department. When she finished, she said, "What do you recall about this case?"

They'd worked together enough that they had a rhythm. Yardley would ask broad, open-ended questions, and Baldwin would tell stories to the jury, creating a closer bond with them.

"Well, I first heard about this case from a colleague at the Sheriff's Office. He mentioned the particular pose and the ritualistic way in which Mrs. Pharr was killed. It struck me initially as an occult killing."

"How so?"

"With occult killings—for example, satanic murders—there's a lot of ritual involved. It's not just about the killing but about killing in a certain manner. So we'll find symbols painted on the walls and floors or on the victims themselves. Many times cut into their flesh with sharp instruments. We also see things like burned-out candles or dolls or scraps of paper from some document they think is sacred. The ritual requires symbolism, and there'll be a lot of evidence of that. Most of the time, there's no effort at cleaning up. The scene itself is the message they want to send. So I thought initially, from the way it was described to me, that Kathy Pharr's murder was an occult murder, and occult murders don't just stop at one."

"Why not?"

"Because they believe they're fulfilling some higher purpose. They're fanatics, and death or incarceration are the only means, in my twenty years' experience in law enforcement, by which a fanatic can be stopped."

"So what did you do after you learned the details of Kathy Pharr's murder?"

"I called the assigned detective, Lucas Garrett, and asked if he would fill me in on any calls involving suspicious activity on Crimson Lake Road. The cabin chosen for Mrs. Pharr's murder was abandoned, and that area has many such cabins and homes. It's out of the way and doesn't have its own police force, so it takes a while for the nearby police to reach it. Detective Garrett and I both agreed that the killer or killers might come back to deposit the next victim because the chance for detection was so low. So we thought it best to have it monitored a bit more closely. That's when we got the call about Angela River about a month after Mrs. Pharr was found."

"What happened with Ms. River?"

Baldwin described the call from the neighbor who'd seen a car pull up and a man dragging another person inside one of the cabins. "I quickly drove over to meet Detective Garrett, who had three deputies with him, and the five of us went down to the cabin. We didn't see a car, but we did see fresh boot prints in the dirt leading to and from the back door. We were worried about another potential victim inside the cabin, so we didn't have time to wait for a warrant. Detective Garrett had a small battering ram in the trunk of his vehicle, and he brought it out."

Yardley placed a blown-up photo of the kitchen near the jury and had him describe finding River there, still alive, as well as his initial interview with her at the hospital.

"When did you first meet the defendant in this case, Michael Zachary?"

"It was the next night at their home."

"What was your impression of him?"

"Objection," Aster said, "he's not a psychologist."

Yardley turned to Judge Weston. "He's a veteran law enforcement officer, Your Honor. I think he's earned the right to tell us his general impressions."

"Overruled. Go ahead and answer."

Baldwin said, "He seemed extraordinarily nervous. Some of his answers didn't make sense, and he seemed to have a difficult time answering our questions without stuttering or looking around. Fidgeting and shifting in his seat. He asked to go to the bathroom twice when he was stumbling over his answers. In my experience, those are signs of deception."

"Why do you think he was trying to deceive you?"

"I've been in these types of situations before, where a wife or girlfriend is attacked and I have to go speak with the husband or boyfriend. In my experience, the husband or boyfriend usually bombards us with questions about what we're doing to catch the perpetrator. They know their wives or girlfriends won't feel safe while the perpetrator is still out there unidentified, so they want to know what's being done to apprehend them. There was none of that with Mr. Zachary. He asked almost no questions. In my opinion, I think he knew we were looking at him as a suspect. He also fit the profile that our expert and I later worked up."

"What is that?"

"Well, it's my understanding that Dr. Daniel Sarte, a professor of psychiatry at Harvard Medical School who works with the Bureau on special cases like this, will be testifying more thoroughly about profiling and the profile we created, but in essence profiling is where we determine a set of characteristics the offender we're after might have, extrapolated from the crime scenes and victims. In this case, we postulated we were looking for a white male Mr. Zachary's age who had medical training. As Dr. Carrey testified, the eyes and tongue are the sections of the body that are most difficult to detect as an injection site during an autopsy, something that's not generally known, and so our perpetrator having some medical training was a good assumption since we never found an injection site. We also determined that he would have some compulsive disorders and be prone to being overly neat and in control. I noted in my report that the first time I visited Mr. Zachary, his home was spotless, everything arranged perfectly. In fact, I moved a coaster on the coffee table to place my recorder down, and Mr. Zachary moved it back as we were speaking."

"And you noticed all this right away?"

He nodded. "I did. In cases where a female is a victim, unfortunately, seven or eight times out of ten, the husband or boyfriend is the perpetrator. So I observed Mr. Zachary carefully in that first meeting and wrote my report that night while my memory was fresh."

Yardley glanced at the jury and noticed they were all paying attention. With Baldwin's smooth voice and good looks, he held their attention well.

"Tell us about the search warrant and what you found in the garage, Agent Baldwin."

Baldwin went into detail about why the warrant was necessary and how the search had been conducted. Yardley was able to get him to say that he and other officers had been in close proximity to Garrett when he'd found the gauze and the syringes, something she hoped would persuade the jury that Aster's earlier insinuations were unfounded.

"Anything you want to add, Agent Baldwin?"

It was a question they had worked out in advance through the years: if Yardley missed anything Baldwin wanted the jury to hear, he didn't interrupt her but instead added it at the end.

He hesitated for a moment, and she guessed he was wrestling with whether to say something about Harmony Pharr. Yardley had already warned him that Weston had excluded any mention of her. It was good evidence that should've been allowed in, and he shared her frustration.

"No," he finally said. "Nothing to add."

"Thank you. Nothing further for this witness, Your Honor."

"Mr. Aster, the floor is yours."

Aster didn't go to the lectern and had no notes with him. He just went to the center of the courtroom, halfway between Baldwin and the jury. He kept quiet, his eyes on Baldwin a long time before he finally said, "You said you had a profile in this case, right, Agent Baldwin?"

"We did, yes."

"What is a profile?"

"As I said, it's a system of analysis where we try to determine various behavioral characteristics of offenders based on aspects of the crime scenes they've left behind."

"So you take a guess at what an offender is like based on the crime itself?"

"It's more complex than that. We go through different intricate stages before writing up the profile, like the crime assessment stage, the motivation, crime scene dynamics, victimological traits . . . but in general, I suppose you could describe it as trying to determine what an offender is like based on the crime itself, yes."

Aster took a set of papers off the defense table and handed them to Baldwin. "Could you read the profile the FBI had for the murderer of Mrs. Pharr and the attempted murderer of Ms. River, please?"

"I believe Dr. Sarte—" Baldwin started.

"I'm sure Dr. Sarte can explain his involvement in the creation of the profile. Right now, I'm interested in your involvement and who you thought did this."

"Well, it's not who I thought did it; it's just probabilities of certain characteristics the offender may have."

"Sure, just read that portion. Please, Agent Baldwin."

Baldwin flipped through some of the fourteen pages and began reading.

"It's believed the offender would be a male, Caucasian, between thirty-five and forty years old. He would likely be highly educated and in fact would have some medical training as a nurse or physician. He is likely unmarried and has a difficult time maintaining steady relationships.

"Based on the orderliness observed at both scenes, he would have an affinity toward compulsive behaviors. A diagnosis of obsessive-compulsive disorder along with concurrent personality disorders would not be surprising. He would likely have a history of abandonment beginning with his parents, which would lead him to a life of unstable relationships. His self-image, from this fear of abandonment, would constantly be shifting to protect his conscious mind from his deep-seated belief of inferiority. He would also display a history of self-destructive behaviors, but rarely to the point of law enforcement involvement. Though he would possibly have an explosive temper due to the deep insecurity, his intelligence would give him enough self-control to avoid contact with law enforcement." Baldwin stopped and flipped the page. "That was the section I wrote. Dr. Sarte then goes into more detail on the psychological aspects of the crimes that led to each conjecture."

"No need to read that, thank you." Aster went to the lectern and leaned on it with one arm. "That was damn detailed, Agent Baldwin. My hat off to you."

"Thank you," he managed to say without a hint of annoyance.

"Now I'd like you to read something else."

He took some documents off the defense table and laid a copy down on the prosecution table before approaching Baldwin. Yardley lifted it. It was a profile from a previous case Baldwin had worked.

"What did I just hand you, Agent Baldwin?"

"It looks to be a profile I made in a previous case."

"Yes, and I would like to start with the top page there. It says *Leo Ester Nolan*. Who is he, sir?"

Baldwin hesitated. "He was a suspect in a murder out of Henderson, Nevada, who we apprehended three years ago."

"Please read the profile starting from the highlighted passage."

Baldwin was quiet a moment, his eyes locked to Aster's, and then he began to read. "A forty-three-year-old African American woman was found at 2:31 a.m. in her single-story home where she lived alone on Maurice Drive. She had been beaten and shot once in the head with a .38 caliber pistol. Her engagement ring was missing and presumed taken by the offender. Her wrists had been bound with duct tape from a roll owned by the victim that the offender left behind. There were multiple postmortem wounds, including lacerations and bite marks."

Baldwin stopped reading and said, "I then go into the six stages of profiling generation and the medical examiner's report, along with a profile of the victim and her whereabouts and actions on the date of her death."

"No need to read that, let's just get to the heart of it. Read the profile you wrote."

Baldwin flipped another page. "For the offense to occur in a high-risk area that could lead to detection of a stranger, the offender must've been in an area known to him. He quite possibly lives in the neighborhood or on the same street. Since the offense occurred midday during the workweek, he likely either works part-time or is unemployed. A physical description of the male in question would be African American, the same race as the victim, and aged forty to forty-five, in the same general age range as the victim. He would be of average intelligence, and if he did work, it would be in unskilled labor. Narcotics and alcohol likely didn't play a role since the murder took place before noon.

"The offender would be sexually inexperienced and—though his hatred of women is clearly present in the scene—shy with women. He would have an extensive pornography collection, particularly violent pornography. The fact that all the wounds were inflicted postmortem suggests an inability to interact with live human beings. The offender will have a history of mental illness, as the sudden nature of the attack suggests disorganization and easy confusion. Interviewing should begin with all African American males who live in the neighborhood, the surrounding neighborhoods, or have relatives that live in the neighborhood or surrounding neighborhoods."

"Great, thank you, Agent Baldwin. Please now read about the apprehension of Mr. Nolan in the addendum."

Baldwin glanced at Yardley. She rose and said, "Objection, Your Honor. This isn't relevant to anything in this case."

"It'll become clear why it's relevant in my next question, Your Honor."

"Overruled. Go ahead, Agent Baldwin."

Baldwin read, "Nine days after the death of the victim, a suspect was identified. He lived in a home four houses north from the victim and was found to be a psychiatric patient with a history of severe mental illness, living with his parents. He is African American, forty-one years of age, and works as a janitor at a local high school. He is unmarried and has a history of unstable relationships of short duration. His IQ is estimated to be ninety. He has a history of suicide attempts, and an extensive pornography collection was found on his electronic devices."

"Let me stop you there, Agent Baldwin. So Nolan meets your profile perfectly, doesn't he?"

He exhaled loudly, his face stern. "Yes, he does."

"And you garnered a confession from him?"

"I did."

"And he was later convicted of first-degree murder and given life in prison?"

"He was."

"Where is he now?"

Baldwin's gaze never wavered from Aster's. "Last I heard he was living in Rosetta Park, working as a custodian again."

"He was let *out*?" Aster said, faking surprise.

"He was."

"In fact, he was let out because the Rocky Mountain Innocence Center did a DNA analysis independently of the FBI laboratories and found twelve different flaws in the analysis that had matched semen to Mr. Nolan."

"It was one lab technician's error, but yes."

"A lab technician who screwed up how many cases?"

"We're uncertain."

"A hundred? Two hundred?"

"Probably not that high. Her mistakes were identified quickly, and she was fired after approximately two months of employment."

"And someone else was eventually convicted for the murder, weren't they?"

Baldwin hesitated. "Yes."

"A Mr. Bruce Hooper, the man the victim was engaged to, correct?"

"Correct."

"Mr. Hooper had a degree in sociology, yeah?"

"He did."

"He was white?"

"Yes."

"He had no known psychiatric disorders and functioned very well at full-time employment in a city government position, correct?"

"Correct."

"And he was caught because he bragged about killing the victim to a friend, and the friend contacted the police, yeah?"

"Yes."

"So Hooper eventually confessed, yeah?"

"He did."

"And Nolan was let free?"

"Yes."

"Nolan was innocent?"

"He was. Yes."

Aster approached Baldwin, close enough that he almost touched the witness box. It was apparent that this was a sensitive subject for Baldwin, and Aster seemed to be deliberately trying to upset him. "You sent an innocent man away to prison for life."

"That's not what—"

"In that case, you had a confession. Did Michael Zachary ever confess to this crime?"

Baldwin glanced at Yardley. "No. He did not."

"You had the killer's bite marks. Are there bite marks in this case?"

"No."

"You had DNA. Was Dr. Zachary's DNA at either crime scene?"

"No, we did not find his DNA at either scene."

"But he fits the profile?"

"Yes."

"Nolan fit the profile, too, right?"

Baldwin hesitated. "Yes, he did."

"Agent Baldwin, you have less compelling evidence in this case against Dr. Zachary than you did against Nolan, correct?"

Baldwin ran his tongue along his cheek. "I suppose you could say that."

"Then he may be innocent, and you would have no idea, would you? Because he fits the profile?"

"That's not how profiling works. You're making it seem like—"

"Could an innocent man be sitting right there, Agent Baldwin?" Aster said forcefully, pointing to Zachary. "Could he be innocent, and you wouldn't know it because he fits your profile?"

"No, that's not—"

"Were you convinced of Nolan's guilt when you testified against him?"

Baldwin let out a breath. "Yes."

"Hundred percent convinced?"

"Yes."

"How convinced are you, then, that Dr. Zachary committed these crimes, considering all you got are some syringes and a roll of bandages found by a detective who's planted evidence before?"

"Objection," Yardley said.

"Withdrawn." Aster stepped away from Baldwin and leaned on the lectern. Yardley couldn't tell from looking at the jury how successful he'd been at painting a picture of a federal agent relying too much on pseudoscience and a detective who, for whatever reason, set Michael Zachary up.

"Agent Baldwin, you were a hundred percent certain Nolan was guilty of murder. If you had to put a percentage on it, how certain are you Dr. Zachary is guilty?"

"I couldn't put a number on it."

"Sure you can. Try. Ninety? Eighty? Five?"

The two men glared at each other. Baldwin took a breath and said, "I'm a hundred percent certain he committed these crimes."

"A hundred! Wow. The exact certainty as when you got an innocent man convicted. Well, I hope for the public's sake we can go up to a hundred and ten percent at some point before you destroy more innocent people's lives."

"Objection."

"Withdrawn. No further questions."

—

Weston called it a day in the late afternoon, citing personal reasons, and said they would continue in the morning. Aster came over to Yardley's table and said, "We'll still take manslaughter."

"I don't see much has changed, Dylan."

"You kidding me? That jury thinks your detective is an evidence-planting machine, and Baldwin's profile might as well have described Bugs Bunny. And just wait until I get Tucker Pharr up there and go into how he kidnapped and tried to rape a fourteen-year-old girl."

"It's not that clear cut."

"That's not the question. The question is, Is it clear cut enough to get to reasonable doubt? You sure you wanna risk that? They could just let Zachary go."

Yardley slung the strap of her satchel over her shoulder. "I'll think about it."

58

Yardley left the courthouse, but she didn't want to be at the office. Everyone there had been friendly enough, but it was apparent that she was an outsider. There for one case and gone. She was never invited out to lunches or told about poker games or outings, and sometimes she would turn a corner and hear the conversations stop.

When she got home, she made a quick dinner of quiche and fried potatoes and set the table. Tara got home a little past seven and stripped off her backpack and let it hit the floor. "OMG, I am so freaking exhausted."

Yardley watched her, wondering how to bring up her father and what she'd done with the paintings. Instead, she said, "Rough day at the office?"

Tara grabbed a piece of fried potato and tossed it into her mouth before sitting down at the table. "We're working on this algorithm to help with diagnosis of medical conditions, right? But Jared is like, people will hate this because they don't want a machine to diagnose them."

"You're working on something that complex?"

"Well, I'm helping with the back end. Just, like, grunt work. But it's a lot of grunt work because none of the freaking bosses know what they want. Some of them are trying to disrupt the medical field, and some of them just want to copy other products and make money."

Yardley watched her daughter, the way her eyes sparkled and her skin flushed. She wondered if that enthusiasm was something only the young felt. Was there a time she'd felt it, too, when she was a budding photographer, or maybe even when she first started prosecuting? She wondered if moving, starting over, would help her feel that way again.

In the end, she said nothing about Eddie Cal. They ate together, talking about things other than work, and Yardley lay on the couch after dinner and read while Tara took a shower. Baldwin had texted asking if he could come over to talk, and he showed up a little later still wearing a suit. He had two bottles of foreign beer in his hands and gave her one.

"For interrupting dinner."

They went out to the balcony.

"You all right?" she said. "You look exhausted."

They sat down on the deck chairs. Baldwin opened his beer and took a sip. "Haven't been sleeping much. That testimony didn't go well, did it?"

"It went fine."

"The Nolan case . . . it was just a perfect storm of shit. The lab screwed it, I screwed it, the odontologist and prosecutors screwed it, and he happened to fit the profile just right." He shook his head. "It's worked as a good tool so many times, but you pull out just one bad case and it makes it all look like witchcraft."

"Don't worry about it too much. On redirect, I'll get in a dozen times when it's helped apprehend the offender, and you can talk to the jury about it as long as you like. Just be prepared."

He let out a sigh. "My ASAC thinks it's bullshit, too. He's got me running down some cases that're nothing but going through boxes of documents. Takes my whole day. In comparison, getting the shit kicked out of you in court for an hour isn't so bad."

"You might change your mind if this gets a hung jury and you have to do it a second time."

"Yeah, maybe."

"What did you want to talk about, Cason? Anything trivial could've been handled over the phone."

"It's not trivial. There's some things about Harmony's disappearance you should know."

"What?"

"Kristen Reece got a call from a man who says he's seen Harmony Pharr. That he recognized her from the picture in the media. So she set up a meeting and gave me a call. We met, and the guy said he saw her at a bar in the passenger seat of someone's car. He said she got out and talked on her phone and was laughing. Didn't look in trouble at all."

"Is he credible?"

Baldwin took a long swig and shook his head. "He's a tweaker. You could almost smell the meth on him. Probably cooks it himself, too, poor bastard. Reece got a surveillance team on him. He lives in a halfway house near Florence Boulevard. He got out of prison eight months ago on a drug beef. But here's the part you need to know: he says he saw her the day after Harmony officially disappeared, around lunchtime. Michael Zachary was at the hospital and Tucker Pharr was at work. There's people that can verify that for both of them. So if this guy's right, neither one of them took her. So they're either working with someone else, or the disappearance is completely unrelated to Kathy and Angela's cases."

"Why did he come forward?"

"He wanted two hundred bucks. You shoulda seen Reece's face when he told her that. I thought she was going to Taser him in the balls right in front of me."

"He didn't mention he wanted money on the phone?"

Baldwin shook his head and took a sip of beer. "Blood on the necklace came back a match for Harmony, by the way. Totally possible she ran away and just nicked herself or something, but we got blood on a necklace she never takes off and a phone left in a tree house. How many teenagers you know can live without their phone? And Tucker didn't think any clothes or shoes were missing, so she didn't grab anything before taking off either. I don't believe it. I don't think this guy's being straight with us. She didn't run away."

Yardley looked out over the dark desert and watched as the moon began to appear as a slit in the sky. "What are the odds that she happened to be kidnapped in the middle of all this by some random stranger?"

"Unlikely."

"I'd say virtually impossible. If she really didn't run away and was taken, it has to be the same person. We have to assume whoever killed her mother and tried to kill Angie took her."

"So what do you wanna do?"

She rubbed her temple, attempting to alleviate the headache she could feel working its way up from the base of her skull. "I thought you weren't working this anymore?"

He waved her off. "I had the entire day off for court. It's my free time—screw Young."

"Well, I appreciate it. Lucas Garrett won't return my calls, so I don't think he'll be much help anymore."

"Why won't he call you back?"

"Long story," she said, opening her bottle of beer and taking a sip. "I want to talk with the man who saw Harmony."

"He's under surveillance. Let's see what plays out first."

She ran her thumb along the smooth label of the bottle. "If I'm wrong, Cason, and Zachary is not the man I think he is, then I won't be able to live with myself if he gets convicted. And if he didn't do this, then every day he spends in jail is because of me. I can't wait and see how things play out. I need to meet with him."

He thought a moment as he watched her and then shrugged. "Was supposed to have a late dinner with Scarlett. Lemme text her and tell her I'll take a rain check."

59

Later that night, Tara dressed in jeans and a baggy hoodie along with a baseball cap. She took the tattoo kit from her closet and went to the bathroom, where she slowly applied the dyes to her skin. Her eidetic memory recalled with complete accuracy the shapes and locations of the previous tattoos.

Garos Vasili was a big-time art dealer her father had told her about. She'd done some digging, and in addition to art, he had a reputation for selling narcotics. There had been an arrest by the DEA for trafficking, but the case was dismissed because they couldn't figure out how he smuggled his drugs into the country. Tara knew almost instantly: his art. Likely tucked behind the paintings.

When she'd asked Eddie Cal how they knew each other, he'd just grinned and said it wasn't important.

Tara looked at herself in the mirror. It would be difficult for even someone who knew her to recognize her like this. It felt odd, like a stranger was looking back at her. Her heart was racing, and she couldn't tell if it was from excitement or fear.

The meeting was going to be held in a secluded apartment near what was called the Old Strip, a seedier section of Las Vegas now made up of run-down bars, strip clubs, and tattoo parlors that catered to the drunken tourists that rushed into getting something permanent to remember the night.

The complex was three buildings and poorly lit. Tara parked two blocks away and walked there. The night air was warm. A car filled with younger men honked and yelled something obscene, though she doubted they could even tell what gender she was, much less what she looked like. Harassment just to harass.

She stood in front of the complex for a few minutes. There was a black SUV parked at the third building, but no one was around. She stuffed her hands into her pockets and kept her head down, strolling as casually as she could force herself to. In a doorway were two men smoking, and they stopped speaking when they saw her. She glanced at them and then away as she continued to the third building.

She took the set of stairs to the third floor. The first apartment was unoccupied, but the one behind it had a light on.

The guard from earlier answered her knock. He towered over her and was as wide as the doorway. He smirked as he stepped to the side. Tara went into the apartment.

The entire living room and kitchen held only two things: a desk and chair. Vasili sat in the chair, smoking some kind of black cigarette. He placed it down on the desktop without looking at her and put on his glasses. Scanning her up and down, he leaned back in the chair and said, "Did you bring them?"

"No."

"How exactly is my appraiser supposed to appraise without the paintings?"

"I'll take him to them, and he can spend as much time as he needs with them."

He sighed and watched her a moment. "They're in that car you parked two blocks north, aren't they?"

Tara didn't reply.

Vasili chuckled. "Little girl, I've been doing this since before you were born. You really are in a world you don't understand. How did you even know how to reach me in the first place?"

She didn't say anything.

"Hmm. I suppose it doesn't matter." He picked up the cigarette again. "Here's what's going to happen . . ."

Two other men came out of the bedroom, both large, one of them with tattoos going up and down his forearms. A spiderweb on his elbow. Tara watched them as she heard the door shut behind her. The guard had locked them inside.

Vasili inhaled a puff of smoke and let it out through his nose. "Well, I should warn you, you're not going to like this part."

60

The halfway house was a nondescript brick building by a park used as a campground for the homeless. Dim shapes of tents were haphazardly spread across the grass in the darkness.

"I don't remember this many tents here," Yardley said.

"Been an uptick of homeless the past couple years," Baldwin said as he parked. "Don't know why they come to Vegas. Hot as shit and we have terrible services."

The building had a statue out front, a male in the classical Greek style. His nose was missing, and the rest of him was covered in graffiti.

There was no key-code entry, so they just went inside. The hallways smelled of mildew and were dimly lit. Dirty floors with a thin red carpet.

At apartment A8, Baldwin knocked. Yardley folded her arms as she leaned against the opposite wall. He knocked again, this time louder. She heard the sound of a lock slipping out of place, and the door opened. A thin, sickly-looking man appeared at the door. When he saw Baldwin, his eyes went wide.

"What the hell you doin' here?"

"Easy, Leonard. Just want to talk."

"I don't wanna talk. I said I wanted to be kept out of it, damn it. So you can just go to hell."

Baldwin put his foot in front of the door as Leonard tried to shut it. Then he took out five twenties from his wallet. Leonard looked at the money and then to Baldwin. He took the cash and let them inside.

The apartment was sparse and had only wicker furniture. A desk was pushed up against a wall, but there were no books or papers. Just some marijuana spread out on the desktop with a scale and pipes surrounding it.

"So?" Leonard said. "What the hell you want?"

"Leonard, my name is Jessica Yardley. I'm with the District Attorney's Office. I'm helping with the disappearance of Harmony Pharr."

He glanced around nervously and shifted from foot to foot. He wouldn't look her in the eyes. "I already told this one here everything I know. You want more, you talk to him."

She put on her best warm smile. "Agent Baldwin, would you mind if he and I spoke in private?"

"Yeah, I mind," Baldwin said, surprised. "I'm not leaving you alone with him."

"It's okay," she said. "Leonard's not a threat. I can tell. Please."

Baldwin glanced between the two of them. "I'll be in the hall."

Once the door was shut, Yardley took a casual stroll around the living room, looking at what few decorations there were. One poster of Iggy Pop caught her attention, the image taken live at a concert.

"I wanted him to leave because he's law enforcement. He's a cop. I'm not a cop."

"What does that have to do with anything?"

"Agent Baldwin told me about your meeting."

"Yeah, so?"

"It seemed strange to me that you called and asked the detective to meet you, but you never said anything about money up front."

He shrugged. "Thought they'd say yes if I asked them in person."

"But the thing is, you didn't know if they'd have money with them, did you? Or that they wouldn't just arrest you? Why chance it? Every time a confidential informant has called into my office, the first thing they ask about is the money because they know we pay for good information. They work that out completely in detail before they offer anything." She took a step toward him. "It's odd that you didn't care."

"So what?"

She took another step forward, dipping her head to catch his gaze and then straightening up so they were face to face. "I think someone told you to make that call, didn't they?"

"No."

"Leonard, this is not the kind of attention you want. Trust me. I don't have to tell you all the things I could do to you if you don't help me. I think you're smart enough to know that we will be watching you for weeks, if not months. Everything you do, every purchase you make, every outing you go on, every time you go into or out of work, someone will be there watching you. Any little infraction on your part, and we'll swoop in and violate your parole and you can serve out the rest of that twenty-year sentence you received for dealing."

He swallowed and shifted from foot to foot again. "I want you to leave now."

"No, but I do have a suggestion for what comes next. I have a hundred dollars with me. I'm going to give you that hundred dollars, and you're going to tell me who it was that told you to call in with that story and why. Or you're going to ask me to leave again. In which case I'm going to go out into that hall and tell Agent Baldwin that I think you kidnapped Harmony Pharr."

"What! That's bullshit. I ain't done nothing."

"Then prove it. Who told you to make that call?"

She waited a beat, and silence passed between them. He wouldn't look her in the eyes, but suddenly his posture changed. His shoulders slumped forward, and his chest didn't puff out quite as much.

"It was, um, just some guy."

"Who?"

"I don't know who it was," he mumbled. "He came into the bar one night. Henry's. Asked if I wanted to make five hundred bucks."

"Doing what?"

"He said I needed to call a cop and tell them I seen a guy with some missing girl. I told him I didn't want any part of that." He glanced at her and then sat down on the wicker couch and stared at the floor. "So then he said he'd make it a thousand."

"What did you do?"

"I just went out on my phone and left a message for the detective. He said I had to do it again until she answered. So he came back another day. He knew where I lived. I don't know how. But he knocked and he made me call. When she said she wanted to meet, I said no, but he told me I had to do it." He swallowed. "He'd been friendly up till then, but he didn't seem friendly no more. I think he coulda hurt me." He took a deep breath. "So I called, and then I went down and told 'em what he told me to say. The two hundred was just to, I dunno, get a little something extra."

Yardley considered what to do next. If she showed him pictures of their suspects, the identification could be tainted because it wasn't done in a lineup. But she also couldn't wait. Harmony Pharr was still out there somewhere, and Yardley had no idea how long the Executioner would keep her alive.

She took out her phone and pulled up a picture of Michael Zachary. "Ever seen him before?"

"No."

She pulled up a photo of Tucker Pharr. "Was it him you spoke with?"

"No."

"You're sure?"

"Positive. He was a white guy, but that wasn't him."

Yardley thought a moment. "Did you see what he drove?"

"No. Told me his name was Don, that's it."

"Did he say anything else to you?"

"No."

"And you didn't ask?"

He folded his arms. "I figured the less I knew, the better. Thousand bucks is two months' rent for me."

She nodded, her eyes narrowing on him a little. "That girl is fourteen years old, and she's been missing for weeks."

"I didn't know that."

"You mean you didn't want to know." Yardley glanced at the poster again. "Stay here. I'm going to get a sketch artist out tonight."

She went into the hall and told Baldwin what had happened.

"Shit," he said. "So either Zachary is working with someone we don't know, or he's telling the truth and he had nothing to do with all this." He shook his head. "What a shitshow they've turned this into. If Jax and Lieu had just let us work this from the beginning without getting involved—"

"We might still be right where we are. We don't know." She bit her thumbnail as she paced the hallway. "It's Sarpong. Those paintings weren't chosen randomly; they mean something, and we don't know what. If we can figure it out, we'll find him."

"Maybe. Or maybe he chose them precisely because he knew we'd think they meant something."

She kept pacing. "You're supposed to testify again tomorrow. I can't let you up there."

"Sure you can. You just gotta disclose this to the defense."

She shook her head. "Aster'll tear us apart, and if Zachary is one of the people involved, he'll walk. I need to delay the trial."

"How?"

"I'll worry about that. Can you get a sketch artist out here?"

"Might take a few hours to find one, but yeah, I think we can drum one up."

"I'll let you know about court as soon as I find out," she said, turning to leave.

"You don't have your car."

"I'll call an Uber."

As she was heading out of the building, her phone rang. It was Jude Chance.

"Hey," she said. "Little busy right now. Can I call you back?"

"You owe me an update, J."

"Haven't you been following the trial? There's been plenty of journalists in court acting like they're not journalists."

"No, I can't do that. Weston knows my face too well. That's why I need an update. I'm selling a piece to the *Tribune* in two days."

She let out a long breath as she stood on the sidewalk. "Off the record for now?"

"Okay . . . for now."

"There might be a witness. That's all I can say right now."

"Witness that saw the Executioner?"

"That's all I'm saying. I promise you, as soon as I have more, you'll be the first to hear it."

"Huh. That's crazy. Well, all right, I'll trust you. Don't screw me on this, J."

"I won't."

"And hey—gimme a call anytime. I'm a night owl."

Yardley got an Uber to take her home so she could get her own car, then called Dylan Aster.

"Hello?"

"Hey, it's Jessica. We need to talk."

61

The four men stood motionless while staring at her. Tara could feel their eyes on her. She glanced from one to the other and was acutely aware that the one behind her had taken a step closer. Her hands slowly went into her pockets, and she didn't move.

"Hand your keys over," Vasili said.

"Is the money here?"

He glanced to the guard behind her. "I don't think you understand what's going on here. Give me the keys and maybe we let you go. Or maybe I let my boys here pass you around and then put a bullet in your head. I haven't decided yet. How cooperative you are right now is going to make that decision for me."

Tara's gaze didn't waver from his. "You keep scratching your arm. Are you itchy?"

"What?"

"Your arm. You've scratched it four times since I've been here. One of your men keeps scratching his neck and the other one his fingers. I'll bet the one behind me is scratching somewhere, too. Probably right now."

Vasili said nothing, his eyes narrowing on her.

"Have you ever heard of batrachotoxin? It's an amazing poison. It comes from one species of frog, *Phyllobates terribilis*. Some of the native tribes in western Colombia put the frogs near a fire to make them sweat and then scrape the poison onto their arrows. It kills their prey almost instantly. Poisons have a numeric value on what's called the lethal dose scale. It has one of the smallest LD values in the world. Just two micrograms can kill an adult human. About two grains of table salt."

The man behind her took a step forward, and Tara quickly moved out of the way. She continued speaking as she backed up near the wall.

"What's really interesting about batrachotoxin is that you can make it into a spray form and spray it onto surfaces. It has a half-life of dozens of hours. So if anyone were to spray it on, say, a bunch of doorknobs and the arms to an office chair, just touching them even for a moment would get the skin to absorb the toxin. First it causes itching as the sodium ion channels in your muscles and nerves can't close. After the itching come the convulsions, and then paralysis. It's really slow, actually. It starts in your feet and works its way up, and you just have to sit there and wait while you feel it crawling up your body."

Vasili's eyes were wide now, as were the other men's. They were watching him, trying to figure out what to do. One of the men scratched his arm and the other his neck. The large bodyguard took a step forward to grab her, and Tara quickly said, "I have an antidote."

The men froze.

"I want the money. You can have the paintings and the antidote, and we'll each go on our merry way."

"You're lying."

"It's possible. It's also possible I'm telling the truth and you have"—she took out her phone and looked at the clock—"about an hour to live. Breathing should already be getting more difficult, and twenty minutes from now you'll break out into violent convulsions. Then the paralysis will start with your feet and work its way up. When it gets to your lungs, you'll suffocate to death. By then there's nothing you can do. You need the antidote within the first few hours of exposure, or it's useless."

The men looked at each other. She saw something she had been waiting for just then: the first hint of true fear. It wasn't from Vasili or the bodyguard but from one of the other two men. He was sweating, and he kept swallowing, as though testing whether he still could.

He was slowly becoming crippled by fear, and panic wouldn't be far behind.

"Where's the money?" she said.

"You're not getting a cent."

"Then you're all going to die."

Vasili took out a handgun he had tucked in his waistband and put it on the desk. "If we die, you die with us."

He gestured with his head to the guard, who moved toward Tara to grab her. She reached underneath her hoodie and withdrew a silver canister and held it low, waiting for the guard to get a little closer.

Someone knocked on the door, and they all froze.

62

Aster lived in a plain one-story house on the outskirts of the city, in a small town Yardley had only driven through. She noticed toys out on the front lawn but didn't remember him having children. The front door was open but the screen door locked. He was sitting on a couch and came and opened it for her.

"Find it okay?"

"Took a few wrong turns. It's not on Google Maps."

"It's unincorporated territory, so they don't come out here. Want something to drink?"

"I'm fine, thank you."

The home was small and clean. She saw a few drawings up on the mantel, one of them a child's handprint in paint on a white plate.

"I didn't know you had kids."

"I don't. It's my little sister's. I live here with her and my mama."

She glanced at a photograph on the side table of Aster with a young girl and an older woman. "I wouldn't have expected all this. You seem like a big-city person to me."

He sat down where he'd been on the couch, and she sat on a love seat. The magazines on the coffee table were all legal journals.

"My mama's really ill. Has been for a long time, so I asked her and Markie to move in with me so I could look after them." He turned the television off. "It's late, Jess. What did you need to talk about?"

She took a quick breath as though building up her courage to jump off a cliff. "I need to postpone the trial."

"Postpone? We're almost through."

"I need to take a recess. A few days, maybe."

"What? I'm in the middle of crossing your primary LEO. No way."

She leaned forward, placing her elbows on her knees. "The girl, Harmony Pharr, we have a lead on her. It's the closest we've come to finding out where she is, and if I don't move fast with all this, we'll lose it."

"What lead?"

"A man claimed to have seen her. When Agent Baldwin and myself confronted this man, he admitted that someone had paid him to call into the police and say that. We believe whoever paid him, if he's telling the truth, is the man who kidnapped Harmony Pharr and now wants us to believe she ran away willingly."

Aster leaned forward now, excitement clearly written on his face. "And he's the one who killed Kathy Pharr and tried to kill Angela River."

"I don't know. Maybe they worked together, maybe it's a coincidence, or maybe Michael Zachary isn't to blame. I don't know. But what I do know is that I won't have an answer until I follow this through."

He thought a moment, then lifted a beer and took a swig. "Three days?"

"I think that'll be enough."

"Let the doc out while you're investigating."

"You know I can't do that."

"How about this, then: I'll stipulate to continue the trial three days, but if it goes past that, you have to stipulate to bail. Take it or leave it. If you don't agree, the first thing I'm going to do tomorrow is cross Baldwin on the kidnapping of Harmony Pharr, and then I'm subpoenaing your man to tell the jury what you just told me."

She nodded. "Okay, I agree. Three days."

At the door, she turned and said, "By the way, you're one hell of a trial attorney."

"You too. I'm not wishing you good luck, though."

She grinned. "Same."

She texted Tara that she'd be home soon as she walked to her car. She hadn't even gone inside her house when the Uber dropped her off earlier.

But when she pulled into the driveway, she was surprised to see that all the lights were off.

She picked up her phone, but Tara hadn't replied. Yardley opened the tracking app, expecting to see that she was at Stacey's house. But the blinking blue dot showed her phone in the Old Strip. Once the cultural hub of Las Vegas, it was the place where celebrities had come to make appearances at the casinos and be seen eating at the various restaurants that were paying them in either cash or drugs to do so. It was glitz and glamour and money—everything Hollywood was—but with a little bit of a darker underbelly. Just a little more permissiveness than elsewhere. So it had come as a shock to all the residents when the area died off, slowly bleeding all its business to the corporations that moved into what would become the new Strip.

Like all things in life, Yardley thought, it was cyclical. The Old Strip was now regaining its reputation as being the place where the true partiers went. Those who wanted to do whatever they felt like while the police left them alone.

She zoomed in on the map and caught her breath when she recognized the apartment complex. The Red Rock Downs. It was the type of place where the police were called several times a week and knew most of the residents on a first-name basis. She guessed she'd probably prosecuted twenty cases out of this complex.

Tara had absolutely no good reason to be down there.

She backed out of the driveway and sped down the street.

63

Tara kept her eyes on the door as the men did the same. If there were more men, she knew she would be in real trouble. The gun on the desk was maybe ten feet away. If she rushed for it and Vasili was distracted, she might be able to get it before he did. Might. Otherwise, he would just put a bullet into her. Though she could tell from the faces of the other men that they weren't going to kill her until they knew for sure whether she was bluffing or not.

Another knock.

No one moved. Finally, Vasili nodded to the tall guard, and he unlocked the door. He opened it only a crack, but it was enough for Tara to see out. Her mother stood there in the dim illumination of the exterior light next to the apartment door.

Damn it, no, she thought.

Yardley's eyes rested on her, and though there was no reaction that most people would have picked up on, Tara could tell her breath quickened.

"That's my daughter. Move asidc."

The bodyguard didn't know what to do until Vasili said, "Let her in."

The bodyguard opened the door and stepped to the side. Yardley walked in and looked at Tara. "Are you all right?" she asked.

"I'm fine," Tara replied, glancing to Vasili.

Yardley stood in the middle of the room, and then there was a sound Tara didn't recognize at first because it was so inappropriate to the situation. Laughter.

Vasili had tilted his head back and was laughing so hard he'd put his hand on his belly as though in a cartoon. When he stopped, he crossed one leg over the other and rested his hands across his stomach.

"I should have seen the resemblance," he said, staring at Tara. He turned back to her mother and said, "You look beautiful as ever, Jessica. I think the last time I saw you, you were at my gallery with Eddie, who was trying to convince me to buy a painting he had made of Yosemite."

"I remember that painting," she said calmly. "I hated it."

"Me too. It was too dark. The sky was gray, the river was almost black, the trees looked twisted and menacing . . ." He picked up his cigarette and took another puff. "He never saw that part of his paintings. Isn't it odd what an artist sees in his own work and what the rest of the world sees? He put his entire being into each painting but was completely blind to it."

Yardley glanced at Tara. "Whatever her father's gotten her into, it ends now. I'm taking my daughter and leaving."

Vasili turned to Tara and ran his eyes over her body. "Eddie's daughter . . . amazing. I'm assuming he's the one who told you where all these paintings were?"

Tara said nothing.

He sighed and turned back toward her mother. "Here's the problem, Jessica. Your daughter has apparently poisoned us."

Yardley looked at her. "She what?"

Vasili shrugged. "She says she sprayed some . . . what did you call it? I don't know, some toxin on the doorknobs and my desk. To be honest, I'm feeling it on my skin. She says it's going to start paralyzing us soon but that she has an antidote."

Yardley faced her daughter. "Is that true?"

The look of shock and horror on her mother's face pierced Tara. She had never seen her look so disappointed. Tara swallowed and looked down.

"Tara . . . is it true?"

"No."

"Did you do anything to them?"

She nodded. "I came earlier and sprayed everywhere with a liquid form of *Mucuna pruriens*."

"What's that?"

"It's . . . it's a type of legume that causes severe itching."

Vasili burst out laughing again. "Itching powder? You tried to swindle me out of two million dollars using itching powder?" He laughed again.

Yardley looked at Vasili and said, "I'm taking her and we're leaving. This never happened as far as I'm concerned."

Vasili watched her through the thin gray haze of smoke, and his eyes narrowed. "I still want the paintings."

"I don't care. I'm not some undergrad photographer anymore, Vasili. I'm a prosecutor at the District Attorney's Office. If you try to stop me, I'll have you arrested. Is that clear?"

He watched her a moment, then nodded. Yardley said, "Let's go, Tara."

They walked out of the apartment, and her mother appeared calm and unconcerned, but Tara noticed that she wouldn't turn her back to the men until they were outside. Once they got down the stairs, her mother hurriedly walked to her car, and Tara followed.

"What the hell were you thinking?" Yardley nearly shouted. As far back as Tara could remember, her mother had never raised her voice at her.

Tara kept her eyes low and said nothing.

"I can't believe you would be so stupid." Yardley exhaled loudly and looked back at the apartment complex. "Aren't you going to say anything? Don't you have some sarcastic remark for me?"

"No," she said quietly.

"Get in the damn car."

"I drove my car. It's down the street."

"Then get it right now and go straight home. Straight. Home."

She nodded. "Okay."

Tara walked toward her car. She saw her mom start her car and pull into the street and wait for her. Tara got into the car and pulled away from the curb. Her mother sped up toward an intersection, and Tara followed her about a block and then let other cars in between them. When she was certain it was difficult for her mother to see her, she turned right on a side street and then went back to the Red Rock Downs.

She parked in front of the building and went up to the third floor. She opened the door. All the men were still there. They were scratching at their skin and speaking in agitated tones. They watched her as she slipped a few small vials out of the pockets of her hoodie. She tossed them on the carpeted floor near the men, who stood there in silence.

"It's not itching powder," she said coolly. "Drink up, and try not to die."

She turned and hurried back to her car.

64

Yardley was sitting on her front porch when Tara pulled into the driveway and parked. Her daughter came over to her and sat down. They were silent a long while. Tara had her hands stuffed into the pockets of her hoodie, and it made her look so much younger. It reminded Yardley that she was still a child.

"How long have you been corresponding with him?"

Tara was silent for a while. "About a year and a half. But I only sold the first painting like six months ago. I put the money in an account. I haven't touched it."

"How many have there been?"

"Just a couple, and not for much money. But he said this guy, Vasili, was a major art dealer and would pay a lot for his work. He offered me two million dollars for three of his paintings."

Yardley shook her head. "Why on earth would you think this was a good idea, Tara?"

She swallowed and looked away. "I did it for you."

"For me?"

She nodded. "I don't think you're happy, Mom. That's why we're moving and you're quitting. You think you're quitting because you're sick of what you do, but you're just not happy and you don't know why. You think going somewhere else will make it better, but it won't.

I thought if you at least didn't have to worry about money anymore, it might help you."

Yardley reached out and put her hand on her daughter's knee. "Tara, what makes me happy is you. What if something happened to you? Did you think of that? You want to protect me, well, what would've happened to me if I'd lost you? Especially in that way. Shot in some dirty apartment because of your father."

"He told me it would be easy and nothing would happen."

The anger that rose in Yardley seemed to almost burn through her skin, and she had to close her eyes a moment and just breathe.

"Tara, look at me . . . whatever that man tells you is a lie. Whatever you think he's doing to help you, or to help me, only helps himself. If for nothing else, he'll just use us to amuse himself. You can't trust him any more than you could trust a snake. Do you understand?"

She nodded. "I do now," she said sternly. Yardley got the impression that her daughter was holding something back, something she didn't want to tell her, but she wasn't going to press the issue now.

Tara said, "So you've got some tracker on my phone, huh? I figured you would."

"I'm sorry. It was just for your own protection."

She shrugged. "I don't think I'm in a spot right now to be pissed, am I?"

Yardley sighed and looked out at the moon bathing the street in a pale glow. She took her daughter's hand and rose. "Come on."

"Where we going?"

"To have a bonfire."

The tinder encircled the paintings. They were far out in the desert behind their house, and Yardley looked around to make sure she didn't see any cars, not that anyone would stop out here anyway. A breeze was blowing, and it put the flame of the lighter out a few times. When it stuck, she pressed it to the wet portions of the paintings that had been soaked in lighter fluid. The entire cluster lit and smoldered briefly before bursting into flame.

Yardley stood away from the fire, feeling its heat on her face and hands as she stared unblinkingly at the flames. Tara stood next to her and said, "Do you know what the proudest moment of my life was?"

Yardley looked at her but said nothing.

"It was when I got a full ride to UNLV with a stipend. One of the youngest people ever admitted to a mathematics doctoral program. Of course I wanted to share it with you, but . . . what I kept thinking was, *I wish my father could see it.* I just kept thinking I wished he was there when I opened that letter." She looked at her mother. "The greatest moment of my life, and all I could think about was that I wished the person in the world that would care the least was there. Why do you think I did that?"

Yardley took her daughter's hand. She didn't have an answer for her. So they both turned back to the fire and watched as it consumed Eddie Cal's surviving paintings.

Your work is dead, Yardley thought, *and I hope to hell you soon follow.*

65

Yardley texted Baldwin after Tara had gone to bed. He replied that he was having a difficult time finding a sketch artist and it might be tomorrow morning until they sent someone out to talk to Leonard.

Yardley lay in bed and drank a glass of merlot to help her sleep.

It was just past five in the morning when her vibrating phone woke her. She didn't remember falling asleep but knew she had dreamed, though she couldn't remember her dream. She was still fully dressed.

"Yes?" she said, sleep still in her voice.

"Jess," Baldwin said quietly, "I'm going to text you an address, and I'd like you to come down here."

"What is it?"

"It's Leonard. I left to find a sketch artist, and by the time I got back, he was gone. But we found him now by pinging his cell phone."

"Where is he?"

"In a cabin on Crimson Lake Road."

66

Yardley stood in the middle of the street, staring at the cabin. The spinning blues and reds of the patrol cars flickered in the dawn. The medical examiner's people had just arrived, and the forensic technicians were scurrying around the cabin. Every once in a while, she would see the bright flare of a flash camera.

Baldwin ducked under the yellow barrier tape and approached her. He turned toward the cabin, too, without a word, and they both stood in silence for what seemed like a long time.

"Exactly?" she finally said.

He nodded. "Yeah. He copied the third painting perfectly. Do you want to go in before they take him away?"

"No." She watched some forensic technicians go into the cabin carrying what looked like fishing tackle boxes. "Cason, I only told two people about our meeting with Leonard."

"Who?"

"Dylan Aster and Jude Chance. But Chance called me as I was leaving the halfway house and asked for an update on the case. He called *right* as I was leaving. Like he was watching."

Baldwin's eyes never left the cabin. "I'll pay him a visit."

Only when her eyes watered did she realize she'd been gazing at the cabin without blinking. "I'm going home, Cason."

"Jess—"

"I'm fine. Dylan already stipulated to a continuance of the trial. I'm going to take the three days." She watched as the ME's people went in with a stretcher. "Maybe more."

—

As she drove home, Yardley felt a pain she hadn't felt in a long time. Something between loss and physical illness. Something that made her body feel like it could fall over and not have the strength to lift itself up again.

That man was dead because of her. Because she'd talked to him.

The headache had turned into a migraine and wouldn't leave her alone. She stopped at a twenty-four-hour pharmacy and got some ibuprofen and juice, then took four of the pills while sitting in her car. The image of the third painting kept forcing its way into her mind. She pictured Leonard in place of the black figure, his organs slick with blood as he hung from the ceiling.

She'd made a mess of this case and hadn't helped anyone. There was no reason she should have prosecuted this. She wished she'd retired at the time she had planned.

Michael Zachary would likely be released, and it wasn't even certain yet who he was working with or why, or if he truly was innocent in all this. Whichever prosecutor inherited the case would have to play catch-up with any new suspects, but Zachary's case would be over. Double jeopardy attached the second the jury was sworn in, and he couldn't be prosecuted again for the same crimes. If he was the Crimson Lake Executioner, or one of them, he'd just gotten away with it.

Yardley had to pull over to the side of the road. She massaged her temples. The migraine felt like it could crack her skull open. A tall billboard near her advertised an upscale vodka, and it read, **MAY THE NIGHT NEVER END, BABY.**

She took a few deep breaths and pulled into traffic again.

67

When she arrived home, she saw a black Mercedes parked at the curb in front of her house. She pulled into the driveway and got out. River was sitting on her porch steps. Yardley sat next to her.

"Sorry for just dropping by this early. I wanted to catch you before court."

"It's all right."

Yardley looked up to the sky, which was now filled with gray-black clouds. Farther off over the desert, she could see rain falling. "I got the trial postponed."

"Why?"

"I found a man who claimed to have seen Harmony Pharr and then later told us he fabricated it. Someone paid him to call it in to make it seem like she ran away. The police wouldn't look too closely anymore if they really believed she ran away." She paused. "That man was just found dead in a cabin on Crimson Lake Road. Hung from the ceiling."

A long silence.

"I'm so sorry, Jess."

Yardley nodded. She had been wondering what River would say. If she would be elated that Zachary likely wasn't who'd tried to kill her. Instead, she had attempted to comfort Yardley.

"They'll probably end up dismissing the case against Zachary," Yardley said. "It's not certain he wasn't working with someone, but I don't see how they can go forward after this goes public."

"They?"

"I'm not prosecuting this anymore."

River nodded but didn't say anything awhile. "What are you gonna do?" she finally asked.

"I don't know, but I'm not going back. I'm done with this damn profession."

"You blame yourself for that man and the girl?"

"This was my case from the beginning."

"No, it wasn't. It was *his*. Whoever killed Harmony and her mother, and whoever tried to kill me. It was always his case. He was in control, not you."

Yardley shook her head. "I could've done something different."

"What?"

"I don't know," she snapped, looking at River. She turned away again, staring out into the street. "I don't know."

"If you don't know, that means you did everything you could. What more could you have given that damn job? You have to do everything you can, and then the rest is just up to the universe."

Yardley felt an icy chill hit her heart. It was so pronounced it took her breath away. The realization overtook every other thought: she hadn't done everything she could.

There was one thing she had resisted doing, one thing she had refused to even consider. After she did it, then she could tell herself she'd done everything she could, but not before.

"I have to go," Yardley said. "Will you do me a favor? Will you stay here with Tara until I get back? I'm sure she's sleeping, but I'd feel better if you were here."

"Of course. Where you going?"

"To see someone I really don't want to see."

68

Yardley called Warden Sofie Gledhill. She explained what she needed, and the warden agreed, but only after telling her, "You sure? You remember last time what it felt like? You told me being in the room with him felt like being stuck in a coffin."

"I know, but I have to."

Yardley sat in the Low Desert Plains Correctional Institute's parking lot until she received a text from Gledhill that a room was ready.

The deputy at the reception desk had been waiting for her, though she still had to sign the log-in sheet and go through the metal detectors. After that, she was let through a set of steel doors and then a sliding door made of iron bars. A guard, a short man with a buzz cut, led her through the hallways to death row.

The room they had set up for her was an attorney-client room. The last time she had been in this particular room, she'd watched Tara meet her father for the first time.

"I'll bring him in."

"Thank you."

Yardley sat down on a metal stool and waited patiently. A clock was in the corner, and the only sound in the room was the ticking of the second hand. It was discomforting that it was so quiet; prisons were always loud. Filled with shouting, laughter—and occasionally screams.

The steel door across the thick glass barrier opened, and Eddie Cal was brought in. Yardley had to force herself not to shiver, though her body felt like it had frozen in place, and she couldn't move if she wanted to.

He sat down and looked at her with his deep-blue eyes that looked so much like Tara's she had to look away and prepare herself before looking back.

"I didn't expect to see you again," he said softly.

Yardley looked at the guard. "Can you give us a moment?"

"Sure thing. Holler if you need me."

Yardley waited until the guard had left and then looked at Cal. He appeared the same as he had two years ago, maybe more gray in his scruff and on his temples.

She wanted to scream at him, to throw things, to call the guard back and tell him to hurt him in some way . . . but she couldn't. She needed his help, and whatever he had done to Tara would have to wait until later.

Yardley swallowed down her anger and forced her face to remain passive. "I suppose congratulations are in order for staying your execution indefinitely."

He gave a small shrug. "There's lawsuits by various bleeding-heart groups pending, and the new governor is opposed to the death penalty, but it's just delaying the inevitable. You look beautiful."

The comment revolted her, but she showed no reaction.

"What are you doing here, Jessica? I don't think I have any more fans living in your home, do I?"

She interlaced her fingers and placed them on her knee, appearing as calm as possible, though the comment filled her with terror and disgust in a way she hadn't been prepared for. She inhaled deeply to relax herself and said, "I need your help."

A smile crept to his lips. He blinked slowly, taking her in.

"You must be desperate to see me."

"I am."

"And what do you have to offer me for my help?"

"Nothing. Other than I'll put some money on your commissary account."

He chuckled. "Doesn't sound like much."

"You'll either help me or you won't, Eddie. I'm not going to beg you."

He inhaled deeply and shifted on the stool. His chains jangled and made her think of a rattlesnake.

"I would say no if it were anybody else, but it's stimulating to see you. I have drawings of you up in my cell. Would you like to come back and see them?"

"No."

He watched her in silence. "How is our daughter?"

Yardley had to swallow, just to have some sort of movement, but didn't avert her gaze or snap at him. He was testing her to see how much she knew. "She's studying robotics at UNLV. She's working with a company right now that has plans to hire her after graduation. She'll be their youngest engineer."

His head tilted slightly. "Has she exhibited any behaviors that have disturbed you?"

"What do you mean?"

"By now, if what I have is perhaps genetic, she should have exhibited traits you recognize in me."

"She is nothing like you, Eddie. And no, she's fine. Perfectly happy. Or at least as happy as someone can be considering the life you put her through."

"If I recall, you agreed to marry me. Aren't we both at fault for her suffering? You maybe a little more for not seeing who I was?"

He grinned, and his grin was awful.

"What do you need?" he said.

"Do you remember Sarpong? *The Night Things* paintings?"

"I do."

"You were obsessed with them for a long time. You wouldn't talk about anything else. You never told me why."

"They struck a nerve in me. It was rare for someone else's art to do that, but it happened occasionally. I had the same reaction to a few of Caravaggio's works."

She nodded. "I remember that. But it wasn't like with Sarpong."

"No, it wasn't." He leaned forward slightly. "This is about the murder on Crimson Lake Road, isn't it? I read a fascinating article on the whole thing in the *Sun*."

"I know the journalist who wrote that piece. It was accurate."

"Yes, I'm sure it was. He's a good writer. Detailed. He had some illuminating insights on the motivations of the killer."

"He's always written like that."

"I'm sure . . . there's a certain something in your voice when you talk about him. Are you sleeping with him?"

"You don't have the right to ask me questions like that."

"But you have the right to come here whenever you like and ask for my help?"

She was silent as they watched each other. "This was a mistake." She rose.

"You want to know why your killer is inspired by the Sarpong paintings, don't you?"

She watched him a moment, then sat back down. "Yes."

"What do you think they mean? Why did Sarpong paint them?"

"I spoke to a psychiatry professor I trust, who consulted an expert in twentieth-century art. The expert said they're about morality and our consciousness. About how evolution has given us the ability to turn off our morality when it suits us, and we're not even aware when it happens. Sarpong was a biologist by profession, so it would make sense that the themes of his paintings would reflect evolutionary ideas."

He grinned. "How poetic. Utter bullshit, but poetic."

"What do you think they mean?"

"They're not about evolutionary psychology. It's much simpler than that. Much more primitive. What do you feel when you look at the victims in his paintings?"

"I feel . . . pity for them."

"Why?"

"They suffered before their deaths."

"And what type of person would make them suffer?"

"A sadist."

He shook his head. "There's no evidence Sarpong was a sadist or into any type of deviant sexuality. Who would want to make someone suffer before they killed them yet isn't a sadist?"

Her brow furrowed as she ran through the possibilities. "I don't know. A person filled with rage?"

"And why would rage lead them to that?"

"Because they're unstable, and they don't have insight into themselves to know when they're rageful."

"No, Sarpong knew exactly what he was doing. Those paintings took more than six years to complete. What kind of rage would a person have to feel to take six years to paint an expression of that rage? What type of anger could sustain itself that long?"

Yardley suddenly lost her breath, almost like a gasp, and she shivered. "Revenge . . ."

Cal was silent, watching her unblinkingly.

Yardley's heart raced. "He's taking revenge on them, and it has something to do with Crimson Lake Road."

Cal leaned forward more, as though trying to smell her. A grin perked his lips as his eyes gazed into hers.

She wanted to leave, to run out without another word, but she forced herself to say, "Who was Sarpong taking revenge on?"

"Four wives, four divorces, four paintings. In life, he was a cowardly man who was dominated in his relationships by stronger women, but in his paintings he was God over those women. He could do whatever he wanted to them."

Yardley looked into his icy blue eyes, and she thought they suddenly looked dead. The eyes of a corpse. "Thank you for your help, Eddie."

"You don't have to thank me. Seeing you is reward enough," he said with a smile.

She ignored his comment and said, "I'll put some money on your account."

"I appreciate it. You wouldn't believe how expensive donuts are in here."

She rose, and as she turned away, she suddenly stopped and looked at him again. "If they're about vengeance, why were you obsessed with them? Who were you taking revenge on?"

He gave a quiet grin, then said, "I'll see you in your dreams, Jess."

69

Aster and Ricci sat on the couch in Weston's chambers and Yardley in one of the plush leather chairs. Weston was running late.

Yardley felt jittery, anxious. It felt like the smell of death row—old concrete, sweat, and dust—was still on her and wouldn't come off.

"Thought any about manslaughter?" Aster said.

"I might be doing better than that," Yardley said.

"Why? What's going on?"

"There was another killing on Crimson Lake Road last night. Once I confirm a few things, I'll be dismissing the case against Zachary, unless I find more evidence of his involvement."

The door opened, and Weston hurried in. "Sorry, sorry, it's this damn IBS. Kicks my ass in the mornings." He went to a rack that held his robe. He slipped it on and sat down behind his desk, before taking out some antacid from a drawer and a bottle of water from a minifridge underneath the desk.

"So I received your motion, Ms. Yardley, and frankly I'm not inclined to grant it."

"It's necessary, Your Honor. And it's only three days. We'll start the trial again right where we left off on Friday, or I'll be dismissing the case, depending on what I find in the next few days."

"That's not fair to that jury to sequester them for three days because you didn't do a thorough enough investigation before filing this case."

"I'm not asking for them to be sequestered. I don't want to impose any more hardship on anyone because of this, but it's something I need to do."

Weston looked at Aster. "And you're on board with this?"

Aster shrugged. "Gotta go with the flow."

Weston let out a long breath. "Fine. Three days. Trial starts again Friday morning at eight, or I'll expect a motion to dismiss on my desk at that time. Not one hour more, Ms. Yardley."

"I understand. Thank you."

Aster said, "We should grab lunch and talk."

"I can't; I've got a drive ahead of me."

"To where?"

The drive to Fruit Heights didn't take as long as she remembered, but the temperature sat at 110. By the time she pulled into town, her blouse had stuck to her with sweat. She went into a diner bathroom to clean up before ordering ice water and taking a few minutes to think. Baldwin was meeting her down here later in the afternoon after he finished testifying in another case. He had tried contacting Jude Chance and couldn't find him. Yardley had told Chance they had a witness, and hours later the witness was dead. That thought kept running through her mind, over and over. The idea of him doing it himself was preposterous, but was it possible he had let *someone* know that they were close? Did he know who the Executioner was? The possibility sat on her chest like a heavy weight. The truth was she liked Chance and didn't want to believe it about him.

Chief Wilson was at his desk eating a tuna sandwich with coffee when Yardley got to the station house. When he saw her, he took another bite, then set the sandwich down.

"You're late," he said with a mouthful of food.

"Sorry, just needed a minute."

He took a manila folder out and tossed it onto the desk. "Names of all the neighbors and friends of the Jones family that we had at the time. I could've faxed it to you."

She took the folder and opened it. It held only seven names. "I need to visit with them today if they're still here."

"Those are the ones that aren't dead and haven't moved. They're still around. The first three are at work—I wrote down the addresses there. The others are retired."

Yardley looked through the file. What she really wanted were photos of Bobby Jones, Sue Ellen's brother. The boy who saw Tucker Pharr kidnap his sister and get away with it. If anyone had the motivation for vengeance against Tucker Pharr and his family, it was Bobby Jones.

"Did you find any photos of Bobby Jones?"

He shook his head. "Probably all got tossed when their father died and he went into foster care."

"Any idea where he could be? I would really like to talk to him."

"Couldn't say. I placed a couple calls after talking to you, and DCFS completely lost track of him after he ran away from his third foster family. No criminal convictions or credit cards in his name, nothin' like that. I don't think he wants to be found, if he's even still alive. Why you so desperate to talk to him anyway?"

She rose. "I really appreciate this, Chief. Thank you."

He shrugged as he sipped some coffee. "Hell, no skin off my nose."

The first on the list was a man named Reginald Perez. He had been a friend of Sue Ellen Jones's father. Chief Wilson's note said they had served in the army together. He worked at a trucking warehouse. Two men were in the main office when Yardley walked in, one in dirty coveralls and the other in a collared shirt and jeans. They stopped speaking and stared at her.

"I'm looking for Reginald Perez."

The man in the coveralls said, “You found him.”

“My name is Jessica Yardley. I’m an attorney with the Clark County District Attorney’s Office. Mind if we speak in private?”

The other man said something about finishing up tomorrow and then left the office. Yardley strolled to the counter. Behind them on the wall was a calendar of nude women, a tall blonde displayed for the month. Oily fingerprints had stained the photo over her breasts.

“I’m here about Sue Ellen Jones.”

He looked surprised for a second but then sat down behind the counter. “That’s a name I haven’t heard in a bit,” he said. He took some chewing tobacco out of a tin in his pocket and put a pinch between his cheek and gums. “What about her?”

“I’m following up on some things in a current case that relates to her. I was told you were close to the family.”

He nodded. “Yeah. Her daddy was a good friend of mine from way back. We’d play poker at their house every Friday. Sue Ellen would get us food and drinks and we’d give her a quarter here and there. Her daddy said she never spent the money. She was a good kid.”

“Tucker Pharr was never convicted for her disappearance. Do you believe he was the one responsible?”

“Hell yeah, I believe it. I know it. Everyone knows it. Sue Ellen’s brother, Bobby, saw the whole damn thing. Everyone knew it was Tucker and no one could do a damn thing about it.” He spit into a cup on the counter. “I hope he’s dead.”

“No, no, he’s not dead. But his daughter’s missing. She’s the same age Sue Ellen was.”

He nodded. “Well, that sucks for her, but I hope it gives him a worlda hurt.” He spit again. “What you here for really? This shit is from a long time ago.”

“I’m looking for Bobby Jones. Chief Wilson had no photographs of him and assumed that all the family photos were thrown away when his father died. Bobby went into the foster care system, and the last thing we know about him is that he ran away at the age of sixteen."

"Yeah, I feel for the boy. First his mama dies of cancer, then he loses his sister, and then two months later his daddy drops dead. He was just a kid, he didn't deserve a life like that." Perez was lost in thought a moment. "Wish I coulda helped him. I just didn't have room. I had five kids in the house back then. I just couldn't do it."

"I was given this list," Yardley said, pulling out the folder that Wilson had given her, "and told that these people might know something about Bobby. Can you think of anyone else I should talk to?"

He shook his head. "No, ain't many people left that knew them. I'd talk to her, though," he said, pointing to one of the names. "Gail. She would watch Bobby and Sue Ellen most days when their daddy was at work."

"And she's still in town?"

He nodded. "She's old, don't go out none. That's her right address."

"Do you have any photographs of Bobby?"

He shook his head. "No. I wouldn't keep that shit if I did. Bad memories."

"If you saw a picture of Bobby today, you think you'd recognize him?"

"Who the hell knows? Been a long time, and that's a part of my life I wanna forget."

Gail Rhodes's home was a light-blue house with red shutters and brown shingles on the roof, making the entire structure look like a patchwork thrown together randomly. The chain-link fence was rusted, and the gate hung by only one hinge.

A light rain had started. The speed with which desert storms came and went was something Yardley thought she could never get used to.

They would sweep in, occasionally cause deaths with flooding or mudslides, and then disappear just as quickly.

Nature sometimes likes to show us who's in charge.

Eddie Cal had once said that to her.

She knocked, and it took a long time for someone to answer. The woman wore a muumuu with a flower-print pattern and had an oxygen tank on wheels behind her. Transparent tubes led from the tank to two inserts in her nostrils. Her eyes were deeply bloodshot.

"Gail?"

"Yes."

"My name is Jessica Yardley. I'm an attorney for the District Attorney's Office. I'm, um, well, this is going to sound a bit strange, but I'm looking for information about Sue Ellen Jones and her disappearance. Do you remember her and her brother, Bobby?"

Gail watched her a second and then said, "Come inside."

The home was cluttered to the point that Yardley had to step over stacks of old magazines and overflowing cardboard boxes; plates had been piled high on the floor rather than taken to the kitchen. The home smelled of muscle balm and cigarette smoke.

Gail muted the television, which was turned to some old variety show, and slowly sat down on the couch. Yardley could see the multiple elongated scars on both knees from surgery. She sat at the other end of the couch.

"Why you looking into that now?"

"I'm trying to find Bobby."

"Why?"

"I'm looking for someone who's been committing crimes up north in a place called Crimson Lake Road. I think Bobby might have information about it."

"You talked to Tucker?"

"Yes, I have."

"Hmm," she said, giving a dismissive shake of her head. "Never liked that man. He had a cold feeling to him. Just seemed off."

"You knew him well?"

"Not well, but I knew him. He lived but across the street."

"Across the street?"

"Uh-huh. And the Joneses lived on the corner down there. We all knew each other."

"I was told by Chief Wilson that they thought Sue Ellen was taken while waiting for the school bus. It was on this street?"

"Yeah, but the stop's long gone. School's gone, too."

"Did you know Bobby and Sue Ellen well?"

She nodded. "I was their babysitter during the day. Good kids. Especially her. Bobby was a bully, but weren't his fault. Their daddy was a real bad drunk and Bobby got the worst of it."

Yardley placed her arm on the back of the couch. "Gail, I'd really like to speak with Bobby. Do you have any idea how I could find him? Child Services lists the last foster couple he stayed with as deceased, so there's no one else I can talk to."

"What's going on exactly?"

"There's a young girl missing, Tucker's daughter. She's fourteen. Sue Ellen's age when she disappeared. Tucker's wife was killed in April. Some other people were hurt who have some sort of connection to Tucker that's unknown. I need to speak with Bobby about it."

Gail took a deep breath. It was a raspy inhalation, like there was fluid in her lungs. "I wish I could help. But Bobby went into the care of the state, and I don't know what happened after that." She inhaled a few more times. "Last time I even thought 'bout 'em was years and years ago when a reporter came by asking 'bout 'em."

Yardley's stomach dropped as if she were on a roller coaster. She pulled up a photo of Jude Chance on her phone. "Was this the reporter?"

Gail lifted some eyeglasses off the coffee table and looked at the photo. "Maybe. My memory ain't what it used to be."

Yardley felt the sting of frustration. She was so close but just kept missing. "Well, I won't waste any more of your time, then. I appreciate you talking to me."

"Of course."

Yardley rose and helped Gail off the couch; she insisted on walking Yardley out. At the door, Yardley said, "Do you happen to have a photograph of Bobby? The chief didn't have one."

"Yeah, yeah, I got one of them both at Halloween. Hang on and I'll get it."

She disappeared for a moment. Behind Yardley the rain pattered softly against the pavement.

"Here it is," Gail said, returning.

Yardley took the photograph. Two children in Halloween costumes, arm in arm. A boy and girl. They were smiling widely, but the boy had deep bruises on his neck and arms.

She had looked at it for only a second before she heard nothing but the pounding of her pulse, and the picture nearly slipped out of her fingers. Her knees felt like they would buckle if she didn't consciously brace herself.

"Can I keep this?" she nearly whispered.

"I suppose so."

Yardley ran through the rain to her car, her phone glued to her ear as she called Baldwin.

She was opening the door when an immense pain popped on the back of her skull, and then something wrapped around her mouth and nose so tightly she couldn't breathe.

Yardley fought, trying to reach into her purse for her Mace with one hand while clawing over her head to reach her attacker's eyes or face with the other.

Her attacker brutally slammed her into the car, and her purse dropped to the ground.

The chemicals burned her nostrils and throat, and then the world went dark.

70

Baldwin arrived in Fruit Heights a little before one in the afternoon. He parked at a convenience store and waited in his car for the appointed time he and Yardley were supposed to meet. He rubbed his eyes and suddenly felt fatigue in his muscles he hadn't noticed before. He hadn't slept much last night. He'd woken up at two and then sat on his porch and drunk coffee until the sun came up, something he hadn't done in years.

He called the police station in Fruit Heights, and a receptionist answered and told him Chief Wilson was out on a call. Baldwin left his name and number and said he'd like a return call. Then he leaned his seat back and closed his eyes and fell asleep to the patter of rain against his windshield.

The vibration of his phone woke Baldwin. It startled him at first, and when he looked around, he didn't recognize where he was. Then, when everything came back to him, he answered and opened his window to get some air.

"This is Cason."

"Agent Baldwin? This is Billy Wilson."

"Yeah. Thanks for the call back, Chief."

"It's all right. I'm glad you reached out, actually. We got a call from a Gail Rhodes. She said an attorney came and visited her earlier today and asked about Bobby Jones. When she came out a bit ago, no one was in the car and her purse was on the ground. I gave Gail's address to Ms. Yardley earlier today to visit with. It's her car and her purse."

Baldwin felt his heart in his throat. "What's the address?"

The home appeared odd, the coloring not like the surrounding homes. Chief Wilson was talking on the phone when Baldwin parked and got out. It was definitely Yardley's SUV. He went to open the door and then stopped. The chief had a box of latex gloves on the trunk of his police cruiser, and Baldwin took out a pair and snapped them on. He opened the driver's side door and began searching.

When Wilson was done on the phone, he said, "It's been here at least three hours. Doesn't look like anything is missing from her purse. The wallet, cash, and two credit cards are there."

"Did Gail see anything?"

"No. She said goodbye at the door and then came out a little later to get her mail. That's when she saw the car and the purse. She said she showed Ms. Yardley an old photo of Bobby Jones, and she asked if she could keep it and then left in a hurry."

Baldwin ran his hands underneath the seats. "We need to get some men out here to canvass the neighborhood and see if anyone saw anything."

"It's only me and my officer."

"I'll call the LVPD and ask for some officers. Can you make a call to the Sheriff's Office?"

"Sure thing." Wilson wiped some rainwater off his face. "She could just be walking around," he said hopefully. "I gave her a list of addresses of people that knew the Joneses. The addresses aren't far from each other."

Baldwin looked back at him. "And she left her purse on the pavement and walked in the rain?"

Wilson looked down to the ground. "I'll, uh, make those calls."

Baldwin finished searching the SUV, then stood back and stared at it. He put his hands on his hips and looked around the neighborhood.

Where the hell are you, Jess?

71

Her entire face felt like it was on fire.

She tried to open her eyes, but the eyelids wouldn't respond. Then the pain began, slow and throbbing. It started in the back of her skull and emanated in every direction. The headache pounded hard enough to fully wake her, and she finally managed to open her eyes.

She squinted until her eyes adjusted to the dim light. The skin on her face burned from where the chemical-laden rag had pressed against her mouth and nose. She rubbed it with her fingers instinctively before realizing that whatever was on her face would rub off on her fingers.

She noticed the exposed insulation in the ceiling and the wooden beams that ran from one wall to the other. The vents were bare as well. She was in a basement.

A sound caught her attention. A muffled word. She briefly thought she might be gagged and that she had tried to speak and heard her own voice, but when she opened her mouth, there was no resistance. She turned her head and saw a man strapped to a metal gurney next to her.

Tucker Pharr was nude. Thick leather straps bound his arms and thighs to the gurney, and his head had duct tape wrapped around it several times, covering his mouth entirely. His eyes were wide as he stared at her. He tried to say something as he struggled against the restraints.

"I'm glad you're up," a voice said. "I wanted you to see this."

Jude Chance stepped out from the corner of the room, where he had been sitting in a chair. He went next to the gurney and placed his hand on it, watching Tucker. He wore a sweat suit and over that a butcher's apron.

"Don't do this," Yardley said.

"Oh, it's done. Everything's here and ready, ain't that right, Tuck?"

Tucker screamed, but the duct tape only allowed out stifled moans. Chance put his hand on Tucker's shoulder as though comforting him and then stabbed into the muscle with a scalpel. Causing him to scream and fight against the restraints.

"It's all right, buddy. I know you're excited to start, and we'll get going soon, don't worry."

Yardley sat up. She was on a cot. Her head spun as she went upright, and she had to put her hand on the wall to support herself so she wouldn't fall over. She had to close her eyes and take a few moments before she could open them again.

"It won't help, Jude. Whatever reason you're doing this for, it won't make up for it."

Chance watched her a second and then grinned. "I still think you and I would've been great together. It'd be pretty fun to get to know you, I imagine." He let out a long breath. "I'm not a monster. Not like your ex-husband."

"Is Harmony dead?"

He gave Tucker a hard stare. "I don't know, Tuck, what do you think? Maybe I want to make you watch her die? It'll be quick, though, and she'll be unconscious. Much more mercy than you gave Sue Ellen and the others, ain't that right?"

"Jude, this isn't the way. Whatever you think he's done to you, it won't bring you peace."

"Peace? Is that some sort of joke? You think he gave that family peace?" he nearly shouted. He looked down at Tucker. "Bobby Jones watched his sister taken from right in front of him, screaming his name, and then he watched his father drink himself to death, because of this human turd."

He slapped Tucker hard across the face, and Tucker fought again.

"You found him, didn't you?"

Chance looked back at her. "Yeah, I did. Thought this story would make a good piece and then a good book, so I tracked Bobby down. I found him in a flophouse in San Francisco. So strung out he could barely remember his name. I spent a few weeks with him, getting to know him, hearing his story, and right when I really thought I could help him, he killed himself. Left a note saying goodbye to me." Chance shook his head. "You know what this piece of shit did to young girls? Do you want to know what they went through before they died, J?"

"This isn't the way. Let me get the FBI down here. He'll pay."

"How? With what? What evidence do you have that he's hurt anyone?"

Yardley quickly scanned the room for her purse, which held her Mace, but didn't see it. Her head pounded again, and vomit rose in her throat. She had to lean forward and put her head in her hands. Her eyes felt so heavy she wasn't sure she could keep them open. Like she was fighting against sleeping pills.

"Why would you do this? If you could find Bobby, surely you could find evidence—"

"Tried. This jerkoff, believe it or not, did a pretty good job cleaning up after himself. My best guess is that he dumped the bodies in Crimson Lake and weighed them down, or maybe fried them in acid first. Nobody's doing a dive down there, and even if they did, it's too big to search the entire thing. Maybe we'll get lucky and bring up a bone or two, but how you gonna connect that to him, hmm? You can't. If I didn't do something, he would've kept doing it."

"It's not your place to kill because of him."

He chuckled. "At some point, J, you gotta make a choice. What he put those families through . . . I kept hearing story after story. Seeing families that could barely hold it together while they stared at pictures of their dead children . . . and I just decided I couldn't sit on the sidelines anymore. I had to do something."

"So you killed his wife? How is that justice? What did she ever do to deserve that?"

"Plenty. Trust me."

"And what did Zachary do to deserve almost going to prison for the rest of his life?"

Chance checked his watch. "I'm afraid I'm in a little bit of a rush, J, otherwise I promise I'd try to get you to understand. I really think you'd see my side in all this."

Chance went across the basement to a wooden door and opened it. He reached in and pulled out a painting on a large canvas. He brought it out and placed it on a stand and then gently adjusted it to make sure Tucker could see it clearly. Then he brought out a toolbox and placed several sharp knives, cleavers, and a bone saw on the ground next to the gurney. When Tucker saw the bone saw, he fought again, and urine dripped off the gurney like raindrops.

"Ha! He pissed himself." Chance grabbed Tucker by the hair and bent over him. "Did Sue Ellen piss herself with fear, too?"

Tucker started to cry.

Chance put his hands on Tucker's chest and then rested his chin on the back of his hands. He grinned as he watched the man cry and struggle. "Do you have any idea how long I've waited for this, Tuck? How often I've fantasized about this very moment? How many families will be overjoyed when I send them a picture of your corpse and let them know their little girls can finally rest?"

"Is Harmony alive, Jude?"

"Maybe," he said without looking at her.

"She's innocent in all this. You need to let her go."

"She isn't innocent," he said without looking away from Tucker.

"She is. She's as much a victim of his as Sue Ellen was. You're going to do to her what he did to those girls. How are you better?"

Chance leapt at her, a knife in his hand. He thrust it in front of her face, and she instinctively jumped back, pushing herself against the wall. The tip of the blade touched the skin of her throat. He pressed it in just a little, enough that she felt a warm trickle of blood.

"I am *nothing* like him," he growled. "Nothing."

She swallowed. "You're scaring me, Jude. Put the knife down." He didn't move. "Jude, put the knife down," she said calmly.

He lowered the knife and took a few steps away from her. "I had a sister, too. Ivy," he said, his eyes glazing over as he retreated into a memory. "She disappeared one day walking to school. Just like that. Poof. As if the earth swallowed her alive." He pointed to Tucker with his knife. "A piece of shit like him ended her life. Where's the justice in that? My parents are dead. She never got the chance to have kids. After I'm gone, will anyone remember her? Is anyone going to cry for her, J?" He got a look of hard resolve on his face, his jaw muscles flexing as he stared at Tucker. "I can't do anything for Ivy, but I can for all the girls he's taken from their parents."

"Jude," she said calmly, "please let Harmony go. She hasn't done anything to deserve what you're going to do to her."

He smiled as though he hadn't heard anything she'd said. "I'm glad you're here to see this. I really am. I thought I would be the only one to get to enjoy this, but having you here really just makes it." He exhaled loudly while staring at Tucker. "All right, dipshit, we ready to get started or what?"

Yardley looked at the fourth painting, the most violent of the series. No tunic or bandages on this one. Just a nude figure lying on their back, scars from their removed organs dotting their body like mountains on a topographical map. The figure's eyes and mouth were sewn shut with thick leather or string. Both hands had been removed and the wounds stitched closed.

Chance glanced around the basement. "Forgot the garbage bags. Got all excited. BRB, don't go anywhere."

He left the basement through a wide wooden door, and Yardley heard a lock snapping into place. She immediately rose and then almost fell over. She closed her eyes, swallowed—though her throat felt like it had been scrubbed raw with sandpaper—and then pushed herself up using the wall behind her. When she was on her feet, another wave of dizziness hit her, and she put her hand against the wall to steady herself. Tucker was struggling again, staring at her with wide, wet eyes, eyes that were begging her not to leave him.

She made her way over to a window on the far wall. It was small but wide enough for her to fit through. She went over to the chair Chance had been sitting in, brought it over to the window, and climbed onto it. She opened the window all the way. As she was about to pull herself through, she heard footfalls coming downstairs.

Quickly, she jumped off the chair and ran to the door Chance had gotten the painting from. It was a closet. She stepped inside and quietly shut the door.

The main door to the basement opened. She heard Chance say something and stop midsentence. Then he chuckled.

"There's not many places to hide, if you haven't noticed, J."

His boots sounded against the bare pavement, and she could tell he was over by the window.

"Shit!"

She heard him run to the basement door again and then dash upstairs. She opened the closet door and hurried over to where Tucker was. There was no time to cut him loose. She grabbed a knife from the tools Chance had laid out and rushed to the stairs.

72

Baldwin waited on Gail Rhodes's porch only long enough for the forensics team he'd called down from Vegas to pull up. He stepped off the porch and directed them to the SUV. Down the street, several LVPD uniformed officers were going door to door. Chief Wilson was inside Gail's home, helping her search for a photograph. Whoever the Executioner was, Yardley had come closer to finding him than he felt comfortable with. He must've followed her and known she would recognize him, which meant it could be someone Baldwin would recognize, too.

He had officers stationed outside Jude Chance's home and an APB out on him and his car, and the same for Tucker Pharr. All he had on Chance was a coincidence—Leonard happened to die after Yardley told Chance they had a witness—but a coincidence was more than nothing.

The chief came out of the house. Baldwin met him on the porch. "Anything?"

"She only had the one photograph and it's gone. You're not thinking it's him, are you? Bobby Jones?"

He shook his head. "Found a death certificate for him in San Francisco. Suicide."

"Then who?"

Baldwin put his hands on the porch railing and watched the forensic people dust around the door handles of the SUV. "I don't know, but it's not an outsider. The man who took her has been involved in this case since the beginning."

He couldn't wait any longer. He told Chief Wilson he was going to check somewhere else. If the Executioner saw Yardley as part of this now, there was only one place Baldwin thought he would take her.

Traffic wasn't bad, and Baldwin got to Crimson Lake Road as the sun was setting. By his estimation, there were at least a hundred cabins and houses surrounding the lake. It would take days to search every one.

He drove slowly through the neighborhoods, uncertain what exactly he was looking for. The Executioner could cross the street right in front of him, and Baldwin would have no idea. Still, it was better than sitting on his ass and doing nothing, hoping something turned up.

He pulled the car over to think and tapped his finger against the steering wheel while he did so. Though searching every home here in time would be impossible, he could start with the ones the Executioner was likeliest to know. The cabins Kathy Pharr and Angela River were found in were two, and Tucker Pharr's grandfather's old house was another.

Baldwin put the first address into his GPS and began to drive.

73

Yardley gripped the knife tightly. Her feet were bare, so her steps were quiet. The stairs were carpeted, and they looped around to the left. She stopped halfway and peered onto the higher floor.

The house was empty. No furniture, no decorations. Just carpet, walls, and cobwebs. She had no doubt she was in a home on Crimson Lake Road.

When she got to the top of the stairs, she paused and listened. She couldn't hear anything but the water churning outside. This cabin was on the shore of the lake.

A sliding glass door led outside from the kitchen. It was dark now, and she wondered how many hours it had been since she'd been in Fruit Heights. Outside the glass was a thicket of trees, and past that she could see water.

Yardley made her way across the linoleum, stopping and listening again when she got to the sliding glass door. She hadn't heard a car start, which meant Chance was looking for her on foot. Could she outrun him if she saw him? She didn't know. And most of the cabins and homes were abandoned. There might be no one nearby who she could run to and ask to use their phone.

As slowly as possible, she unlocked the latch on the door and slid it open, an inch at a time to avoid making noise. It got stuck on something. She saw a stick of wood the width of a finger pressed between the door and the wall to keep it from opening all the way. She bent down and removed the wood and laid it on the floor. Then she slid the door open.

There was no rain here, and the night air was warm. Yardley stepped out onto the back patio and looked down the street. Only two homes had lights on, both near the end of the street. She made a run for the road. Her bare feet hurt as they pounded against the street, which was speckled with pebbles and had large cracks in the pavement.

She heard noises behind her. Glancing back, she saw Chance run out from between two cabins. He looked up the street and spotted her.

She pumped her arms, and her legs burned as though battery acid flowed through them. She was in a full sprint now. Chance was shouting something. Yardley didn't try to figure out what.

She held the lights of the homes up the street in her field of vision and nothing else. They took up her entire focus, like she was lost at sea in the dark and the lights of a ship had just appeared in front of her.

Chance was nearly to her.

She ran to the first cabin and tried the door, but it was locked. She turned to run to the next. Chance was coming up behind her.

Yardley jumped off the right side of the porch and dashed to the back of the cabin. There was no fence, and she raced across the backyard, which was nothing but dirt. Looping around, she was back out onto the street. She could hear Chance's breathing.

She couldn't run forever, and she had no idea if people were anywhere near here. She sprinted up the road, hoping she might spot a car headed their direction.

Her legs were tiring, and it felt like her chest was charred by fire. Chance was panting behind her, too, and she didn't know which of them would give up first.

Then she thought of Tara. Of Tara growing up in a world where people like Eddie Cal and Wesley Paul and Jude Chance were alive but her mother was not. Yardley had no doubt that if she died here, Tara would turn to Eddie Cal for solace. Despite everything else he was, he was still her father. She couldn't let that happen. She had to live for Tara.

Yardley stopped running and turned to face Chance underneath one of only a few streetlights on the road. Winded, sweat rolling down her face and neck, her chest heaving, she raised the knife. Chance smirked as he sprinted right for her. Yardley gripped the knife tighter and braced herself.

A car engine roared past the corner, tires screeching.

Baldwin's black Mustang clipped Chance at the hip. Chance went flying, spinning through the air, then crashing onto the pavement. Baldwin leapt out of the car with his weapon drawn.

"Lemme see your hands. Now!"

Chance struggled to get up. He groaned as he got to his knees and spit a glob of blood onto the ground. Blood ran down his cheeks and forehead. He sat back and breathed heavily, watching Baldwin before turning his eyes to Yardley.

"Tucker needs to die," Chance said, out of breath.

Yardley didn't respond.

"You know he needs to die. Let me do it. Let me do it and you can do whatever you want with me after. I don't care. Full confession. But he has to die."

Baldwin said, "Sorry, Jude, but that's not happening today."

Chance took several deep breaths before leaning forward on his hands. "Do you got a sister, Agent Baldwin? I did. What if he did to your sister what he did to Sue Ellen or what some sick piece of shit did to my sister? What would you do to them?"

Baldwin shook his head. "Whatever I would've done to him, it wouldn't have involved his daughter. Now make your choice—you wanna live or not? If you wanna live, get down on the ground and lay flat with your hands out."

They watched each other a moment, and then Chance lay down.

"Look left, Jude."

He did as he was told. Baldwin thrust his knee into Chance's back and pulled his arms behind him. He holstered his weapon and then slapped cuffs on him.

"He has to die, Jessica," Chance shouted. "He has to die! Don't let him get away with it. You can't! He'll keep doing it. You know I'm right. He has to die!"

74

Yardley was checked by the paramedics but refused to go to the hospital, though her lungs burned with every breath. She guessed Chance had used chloroform on her, but a paramedic told her that chlorine could have the same effect, except it also burned the lungs, and she would need breathing treatment for it.

Baldwin came up to her. "We're getting you to the hospital."

"I'm fine. I just want to go home."

"Yeah, well, sorry, you're going to the hospital. Even if I have to arrest you to do it."

She looked at the police cruiser that held Jude Chance. He was staring at them, motionless. An officer got into the driver's side, and the car pulled away. Tucker had already been taken by ambulance to a nearby hospital. Baldwin said some deputies were heading down there to get his statement.

"The cabin used to belong to Tucker's grandfather."

Yardley nodded. "I thought it would."

"Why do you think here? Crimson Lake Road and Tucker's grandfather's house?"

Yardley had to take a moment to just breathe, as talking made it more difficult to get air. "Tucker used this house as a prison for the girls and dumped the bodies into the lake."

Baldwin took a deep breath. "Poetic to kill him here then, I guess. Gotta say, I can't blame Chance. I checked out what he said, and it's true. Ivy Chance disappeared when she was twelve and was never found. Someone does something like that to your sister . . . I don't know. You don't know what you'll do until it happens, but anyone would be looking for some payback. Even if it wasn't against the guy who did the actual deed." He sat down next to her on the bumper of the ambulance. "He's right about one thing—it's not fair. It's not fair that Kathy and Sue Ellen Jones died, but Tucker gets to live. Guess that's just life, though, isn't it? Has nothing to do with what's fair."

Yardley stared at the cabin. "No, it doesn't." She looked at him. "I need to go."

"Where?"

"Can I borrow your car?"

"What? What are you talking about? We're going to the hospital."

She held his gaze and said softly, "There's someone I need to see first, Cason. Please."

"Who?"

She held out her hand. "Please."

He didn't move for a few seconds, then mumbled, "Shit," and dropped the keys in her hand. "I'll get a ride back to my place with one of the deputies. You gotta tell me where you're going, though."

"No, but I'll call you when I'm done."

Yardley parked the car up the street from River's home. She still felt a tinge of light-headedness, but not enough to impair her ability to drive. The skin around her mouth had burned and become light pink. A cough had developed that wouldn't go away. She would have to go to the hospital, but not yet.

Yardley went to the front of the house. No lights were on. She looked through a window of the garage and only saw one car, Zachary's.

She tried the front door and several windows before she discovered that a window by the back door had been left open. She lifted it up, and no alarm went off. It was wide enough that she could easily make it through.

The house was quiet and still.

Yardley checked the living room and then went to the bedroom. Clothes were scattered over the floor and bed. Someone had packed in a hurry.

She closed her eyes and leaned against the doorframe. Then she took out her phone and dialed Baldwin.

"I was just about to call you," he said.

She rubbed the back of her neck, attempting to alleviate the pain radiating out from the base of her skull. "Have you interviewed Chance yet?"

"Letting him cook a little first. Where are you?"

She ignored his question. "I'll be at my house. If you want to pick up your car, you can, or I can swing it by to you tomorrow."

"Are you really not going to tell me where you are right now?"

She looked over at River's bed. "There's nothing to tell. I just wanted to check something. I'm going home now, Cason. Tell the detectives they can get a witness statement from me in the morning."

"Yeah," he said, confused. "I'll swing by. Look, um, you okay, Jess? I mean, this is a big—"

"I'm fine. I just need some rest. Thank you again."

"Yeah, well, I'm gonna come by in a few hours and we're going to the hospital."

"Good night."

She hung up and found she didn't have the strength to stand. She sat down against the door, brought her knees up to her chest, and wrapped her arms around her legs. The closet door was open, and several pieces of luggage were out on the floor. Some of River's bracelets were on the nightstand. A watch had fallen near the bed.

After a few minutes, Yardley rose and left the house.

75

Her house was dark when she got home. Tara was asleep.

Yardley decided she wouldn't be telling Tara everything. She would find out enough on her own, but there would be details left out online, and those wouldn't be filled in by Yardley. Tara didn't need an image in her head of her mother unconscious in a dark basement.

Eddie Cal would hear about it as well. She thought back to her conversation with him and how he had praised Jude Chance's article.

He knows his subject well.

She wondered if it was just a little praise for a graphically violent article that excited him, or if he had somehow pieced together that Chance was responsible.

Yardley stood under the shower, letting her head rest against the tile in front of her. Her eyes closed, and she felt like she could drift off to sleep right there. When she got out, she put on a robe and then rubbed aloe vera on her face, but it did nothing to alleviate the sting. The steam had fogged the mirror, and she swiped her hand across it, revealing a blurred image of herself. Placing both hands on the sink, she stood there and enjoyed the heat from the steam that permeated the skin on her face.

When she came out of the bathroom, she jumped and gasped.

Tara yelped with shock and dropped the bottle of water in her hand.

"Holy shit! You gave me a freaking heart attack, Mom."

Yardley put her hand to her chest, as though physically trying to calm her heart, and took a few deep breaths. "Sorry, sweetheart."

"Why were you out so late?"

She let out a long breath. "I'll tell you all about it tomorrow. Tonight, I'm going to sit on our balcony and drink wine until I'm drunk."

"Can I join you?"

"No, you may certainly not. Get to bed."

"I just gotta pee."

Yardley slipped past her as she went into the bathroom. She turned while in the hallway and said, "Tara?"

"Yeah?"

"I love you."

She smiled. "Yeah, I know, Mom. I love you, too."

Yardley pulled out a bottle of wine from the pantry and got a chilled glass from the fridge. She sat out on the balcony and leaned back into her deck chair. The cushions were soft but, she decided, not soft enough. She would be getting softer ones. She would order them from . . .

Stop.

Her mind was filling the blank spaces between her thoughts so she wouldn't have to think about what she already knew to be true about the reasons why Angela River had suddenly left town.

She debated her options for a while. She took a deep breath and knew the only decision she could come to was that she couldn't come to a decision. So instead, she went inside and got a quarter out of a drawer and then went back to the balcony. Sitting on the deck chair, watching the sand dunes and canyons behind her home, she tossed the quarter into the air and caught it. She opened her hand. Heads.

She tossed it again, and it was heads again. Letting out a heavy sigh, she placed the quarter on the side table next to her.

Yardley picked up her phone and dialed the number for the extradition division at the US Attorney's Office so she could leave a voice mail.

76

Baldwin went with Lucas Garrett to the hospital to interview Jude Chance after he'd been cleared medically to have visitors. It wasn't Baldwin's case—it was Garrett's—and he'd have to cover his ass with Young, but he figured the Bureau being seen as involved in the apprehension of the Crimson Lake Executioner would more than make up for any blowback.

Kyle Jax was standing outside the hospital with a sucker in his mouth.

"Come to pick the bones clean, Kyle?"

He smirked. "Just want to make sure the interview goes well. I'm gonna nail this guy and can't have one of you making some rook mistake like not Mirandizing him properly."

"Don't worry, we'll let you know when we're done so you can get the credit."

They went inside and left Jax out front.

On the elevator up, Baldwin hit the emergency stop button. A loud beeping started. Garrett said, "What the hell you doing?"

"Is it true?"

"Is what true?"

Baldwin folded his arms and leaned back against the wall of the elevator. "Don't bullshit me, Lucas. We've known each other too long. Did you stab that poor son of a bitch and try to pin it on her husband?"

Garrett's face flushed red. "No, I didn't. She and that prick made that up to make sure I didn't get custody of my boy."

"They stabbed some gangbanger and kept the knife and T-shirt just to frame you, huh?"

Garrett faced him squarely, his jaw muscles flexing. "I don't know what the hell they did or why, but I know I didn't stab anybody."

"Why'd you break into her condo?"

"I was checking him out. Some guy moves in with your son, you wanna know about him. I had no idea who that bitch brought into that house. I did all the background, but you know that only gets so much. So I checked out what they had there."

Baldwin stepped close to him so that their faces were only inches apart. "I swear to you, Lucas, if I find out you're lying, I'm going to bring you in myself."

"Back the hell off me. And don't you think for a second you can threaten me, boy. I was wearing a badge while you were still popping zits in gym class."

Baldwin held his gaze a little longer and then hit the emergency button, allowing the elevator to move again.

The elevator doors opened, and he stepped off. "Let's get this over with."

Garrett nodded to the officer stationed outside Chance's room and then opened the door.

Jude Chance lay in a hospital bed holding a cigarette. He hadn't lit it. Instead, he tapped it against his thigh, his wrists and ankles cuffed to the metal railing of the bed. He stared at a spot on the wall, and his eyes didn't waver.

Baldwin followed Garrett into the room. Chance watched them, and a slow smile crept to his lips. He held up his cigarette and said, "Got a light?"

"Do you even smoke?" Garrett said.

"No, not really. Figure I'll probably start since I'll just be sitting in a cell most of my days now."

Baldwin said, "So you know you're going away?"

"Of course I know. You got everything you need for a conviction. At least for Leonard's death, if nothing else. That was stupid. I rushed into it too quick. But hey, we had a gentleman's agreement and he bit me in the ass. And I didn't know how much he knew about me. Might've seen my car driving away. Couldn't have that."

"Why'd you have him call in?"

"You tell me," he said with a grin.

"You wanted us thinking Harmony ran away, but why? If she's dead, what does it matter?"

He put the cigarette in his mouth. "Shit, you really are clueless, aren't you?"

"Is she still alive somewhere, Jude? If she is, tell me where and I swear to you we'll make it worth your while. I'll get the US Attorney's Office and the DA on the phone right now to get a deal in writing. Let you avoid the death penalty. But only if we find her alive."

He lay back and stared at the ceiling. "I'm not getting the death penalty, Agent Baldwin. Not when all the shit comes out about what Tucker's gotten away with. They'll give me life, maybe even life with parole, just to get all this out of the media."

Baldwin and Garrett exchanged a glance before Baldwin said, "Why this case, Jude? You must've investigated other disappearances on your beat. What was it about Sue Ellen that got you to cross the line? It couldn't be just your sister."

He lost his smile. "I found out what he does to them. He's a sexual sadist. He's gotta have the pain with it, so he puts those girls through agony like you and I can't even imagine. I just kept seeing my sister there . . . I knew I had to do something because you guys sure as hell weren't."

"Did you ever find out what happened to Sue Ellen?"

He nodded, staring off into space. "He kept her for a few months at his grandfather's cabin on Crimson Lake. Tucker usually only kept them for a few weeks, so there was something about her he . . . liked, more than the others."

Garrett said, "Did you find out how she died?"

"What the hell does it matter how? Dead is dead. Too bad I can't say that about Angela, too, right?"

"What happened there?"

"Ya know, you just don't think about some of the details when your heart is pounding and you're in the moment. Those syringes were completely full. Enough to take a linebacker down. Who would've known Angela River could've survived? I guess we metabolize things differently. Would've been nice to see her dead, too, though."

"Why? What did she ever do to you?"

"It wasn't about her, it was about Michael Zachary. Making him hurt. Guess who Tucker's neighbors on Crimson Lake were? Felix and Ana Zachary. Michael Zachary was seventeen, and he saw Sue Ellen there, knew she was being held in that house, and did shit about it. He's lying through his teeth. He knows exactly who Tucker Pharr is. They were friends and he covered for him for years. The good doctor deserved what he was going to get. He was supposed to be the third painting, but hell, I figured getting him life in prison was good enough. And you guys would stop looking for me once you got that conviction." He shook his head. "But shit happens, right?"

"How do you know Zachary knew she was there?"

"There was a girl who survived Tucker. She never came forward, but I found her. She said she made one escape attempt before she finally got away, and Zachary was out in the yard on the first one. She begged him for help and he took her inside his house and said he was going to call the cops, but instead he called Tucker."

"Bullshit."

"Believe it or don't, man. I don't care. I'm just telling you what she said, and she was credible. That dickhead knew exactly what was happening." He looked up to the television, which wasn't on. "He took part in it somehow. I could never verify that, but I'd bet my ass he did. That's who Jessica is going to release back into society, Agent Baldwin. Him and Tucker out partying while all those girls are in the grave and I'm in a cell. You really think that's justice?"

Garrett shook his head in disbelief. "You throwing a damn pity party right now? Do you feel bad at all for all this shit? Harmony was fourteen."

"That girl died unconscious without a hint of pain. I guarantee you Tucker's been abusing and torturing her since he got out of prison. It was a mercy, what I did. Do you know Child Services was called on Kathy Pharr eight times? She dated dope fiends and let them move into her house. Eight times, and you guys never tried to get Harmony out of that house. Shit, what I did lasted a minute. You guys let her go through torture for years."

"She wasn't having an affair, though, was she? Kathy Pharr," Baldwin said.

Chance tapped the cigarette against his leg. "Nah. I made that photo. I did that hoping Tucker'd kill Zachary, but he was too much of a chickenshit. And how about faking calls from Zachary's phone to Kathy's? Company in Canada can do it for five hundred bucks. Easy enough. Especially when you and Jess are too stupid to actually verify if it's real before using it as evidence."

"It's not stupidity, it's trust. Jessica trusted you."

"Yeah, well, that'll teach her, I guess, right?"

Baldwin shook his head. He had one last question. "Why Sarpong?"

"Your mother told me during pillow talk she likes him, that's why. And I'm done talking. Get me a lawyer."

77

Tucker Pharr watched as the nurse checked the stitches in his shoulder. It stung, and he ran his finger over it and thought it felt like a zipper. The scalpel that psycho had stabbed him with had been so sharp that the doctor said he was lucky it didn't go all the way through.

He complained of the pain several times, so they said they would give him a Demerol drip.

"I'll be back to check on you later," the nurse said.

When she'd left, he rested his head fully onto the pillow and picked up the remote to turn on the television.

Kathy and Harmony, he thought.

Shit.

Well, two less mouths to feed. Kathy was just a marriage that had to happen because she was pregnant and he had nowhere else to go. There hadn't been a ceremony, and he was told they were only legally married because they'd lived together so long, and she'd filed something for disability benefits and listed them as husband and wife.

Harmony . . . he would miss Harmony. She hadn't come to visit him in prison, and Tucker smiled when he thought of the look on her face when he'd gotten home.

"Forgot about me for twelve years, but you ain't gonna forget about me now," he had told her through the door when she locked herself in the bathroom that first night.

Shame about her. But she was getting too old anyway. There was that girl that Harmony hung out with sometimes . . . what was her name . . . Uma. Tucker had watched her playing with the hose in his backyard in a swimsuit with Harmony. She had freckles on her shoulders but nowhere else on her body.

The door opened, and another nurse came in. He could see the tattoos on her arms, and he stared at them as she said, "Looks like someone ordered some pain meds."

"Sure did."

"Arm," she said, as she took out a syringe and a small bottle.

"They said it was gonna be a drip."

"That takes a minute to set up. Guessed you'd want to get going now."

He chuckled. "You guessed right." He let out a long breath. "Helluva shit day, I'll tell ya that."

"Oh yeah? What happened?"

"You ain't heard?"

She shook her head. "Shift just started."

"Well, ya gonna hear about it. I was a hostage of some sick peckerwood."

"Seriously?"

"Yeah. Got out of it by kicking his ass. He's lucky I didn't kill him. Ow!"

"Sorry. Your veins are hard to find."

Tucker felt the warmth of the oily fluid in his arm, and it slowly rose up into his shoulder. He felt dizzy but didn't feel the instant floating sensation he liked with pain meds.

"You sure you gave me enough?"

"What's the matter, not feeling it?"

"Don't feel the same."

The nurse pulled up a stool and sat next to the bed. "It's an interesting drug. You're going to feel everything, be wide awake, but none of your muscles are going to respond to you."

"What?"

She inhaled deeply and looked into his pupils. "Do I look familiar, Tucker? Do you remember me?"

"Should I?"

"What if I was fourteen and wearing a pink-and-white-striped shirt? Would you recognize me then?"

"Um, hey, I'm feelin' kinda weird. Maybe we should get the doctor."

She rose. "They're going to be busy awhile."

He opened his mouth and realized no words came.

"Oh yeah, you're not going to be able to talk. Probably for the best. I should do all the talking, don't you think?"

The nurse took out a phone and opened a picture. It was a painting. The same painting the man had set up in that basement.

Tucker tried to fight, to grab her, to jump out of bed, to scream . . . but his body did nothing.

"You kept me in that basement for months. Did you keep any other girls that long? I wondered every day if you did. I knew you'd kill me eventually, and I think that was maybe the worst part. You'd come back and I would think, *Today's the day. Today I'm going to die.*" She exhaled and went to the sink and took out some instruments from the pockets of her scrubs: scalpels, strands of leather, and a needle the size of a pocketknife.

"I'm going to take out your organs, Tucker. One by one. You'll live through the entire thing because I'm not taking out your heart until last. I'm going to sew your mouth shut, but I'm going to leave your eyes. I want you to see it. To watch me do it. Then, before I take your heart, I'm going to sew your eyes shut. But once I take out your heart, your brain will survive for six minutes. For six minutes, I'm going to put you through as much pain and terror as you put all those girls through. And you'll be unable to scream or move while I do it. I can't imagine a worse way to die, can you?"

He tried to scream again, but nothing happened. His eyes burned because he couldn't blink, and the only movement was the rise and fall of his chest as he breathed and the motion of the blood in his veins. He had never noticed his body like this. Never noticed how loud his heart could be.

The nurse lifted a scalpel. "Ready? Okeydokey, let's get started."

78

Baldwin got the call around five in the morning from Young. He called Garrett, who told him what had happened.

"It's bad, Cason," he said on the phone. "I've never seen anything like it."

He threw on slacks and a sports coat. The hospital was an hour from his house.

Several uniformed deputies milled around the entrance to the emergency room. Garrett was out in the lobby. Without a word, he led Baldwin to the room.

The forensic technicians were already there, and he watched one of them come out with a camera. The tech looked pale and was sweating, like he might vomit any second. Baldwin stepped past him and into the room and froze.

Blood was everywhere. The floors, the walls, even the ceiling. Tucker Pharr's body lay on the bed, a grotesque caricature of what had once been a human being. His organs had been placed neatly on the counter by the sink. Thick leather strands had sewn his eyes and mouth shut. Much of his skin had been removed, and the torso was open, the ribs spread wide.

The fourth painting.

"Looks like he finished his series," Garrett said. "I'm goin' down to sweat Chance and find out who he was working with."

Baldwin couldn't speak or take his eyes off the body. It didn't look real, more like something in a Halloween haunted house. Plastic, rubber, and paint.

"You don't need to. I think I know who did this."

"Who?"

Baldwin thought back to his last conversation with Yardley and her refusal to tell him where she was going and why she had to be there in such a hurry. She'd been hoping to catch River before she left.

He shook his head. "Doesn't matter now," he said, his eyes still on the body. "She's gone."

Baldwin sat at the park near the federal building in his car and held Harmony's photo. She was smiling, and several times he had wondered what she was thinking about. If the smile was real or if she had to fake it because she knew she had to go home to Tucker later and couldn't bring herself to give a real one.

He saw ASAC Young running by on the sidewalk that looped around the park, and he set the photo down on his passenger seat and got out. Young didn't notice him at first, then glanced at him and did a double take. He stopped jogging. The blue sweat suit he wore was soaked with dark rings around the neck and underarms, and he puffed heavily as he put his hands on his hips.

"Something happen?" Young said.

Baldwin put his hands in his pockets, looking out over a distant playground and a few children playing on the equipment. "I want to be in Child Crimes."

"What?"

"I'll let you transfer me out of Behavioral Science. But no more bullshit assignments. I want Child Crimes."

Young watched him a moment. "What the hell you want that for? Nobody *wants* to be there; they have to be there. It's like putting in your time at a shit job before getting a promotion."

"Yeah, well, I got my reasons."

Young spit onto the sidewalk. "You sure you can handle it? It's not what you think. It takes a piece of you."

Baldwin looked down to the ground and then back to the children off in the distance. "It already has."

Young took a couple of breaths and said, "If you're sure, you got it."

"No more white collar?"

He shook his head. "No, but remember you asked for this, Agent Baldwin. Like they say, careful what you wish for."

It was afternoon when Baldwin got to the house. He knocked and waited, knowing she was home. Her car was in the driveway, and she had left it unlocked, something he had begged her not to do several times. Some lessons people needed to learn the hard way.

He got a text just then from Kristen Reece. All it said was, Case is over. Wanna grab a beer or . . . maybe dinner?

Baldwin grinned but heard the lock on the door slide open before he could answer.

The door opened, and Scarlett stood there. Neither of them said anything.

After a long while, Baldwin said, "Hi."

She hesitated. "Hi."

He reached out slowly and put his hand on her stomach. He ran his fingers across her belly and pictured the child inside . . . his child.

"I don't know what kind of father I'm going to be, and I don't know if we're meant to do this together or not . . . but I wanna try. I wanna try to be there for my kid."

Scarlett watched him a moment and then held the door open for him. He went inside, and she closed it behind them.

79

Tara wore a dress for the first time in her life. She'd never been to any fancy restaurants or upscale social functions and had never had a reason to put one on. The dress felt as alien to her as a Halloween costume and just as uncomfortable.

She stared at herself in her rearview mirror and was shocked how much older she could make herself look. Or did she just look that way permanently now? She wondered if stress could age a person as fast as time.

She wiped at a bit of lipstick on the corner of her mouth with a napkin, then got out of the car.

The prison was quiet today. Only one person waited in the visitors' lobby, and the guard at the desk knew Tara by now. He let her sign in without checking ID and asked her how she was today. He was younger than most of the other guards, and handsome, with jet-black hair. *Ethan*, read his name tag. He told her about a new movie that he was excited about and suggested they see it together. She told him she'd think about it.

The metal stool was warm today, and she wondered if someone else had been sitting there before she came in. She hadn't seen anybody leave.

Her father was brought in and sat down. The guard left the room. The glass-and-plastic barrier was freshly cleaned, and she could see her father clearly: the hue of his eyes, the wrinkles by his mouth, and the shine of his hair. His jawline was angular, as though drawn by an artist with extraordinary precision. When he smiled at her, his cheeks didn't bunch up like other people's but seemed to move at angles: every section perfectly proportionate to the rest.

He blinked slowly, and his lids lowered just a little over his eyes. "How was my dear friend Vasili?"

"Actually, he didn't look very healthy. When his temper flared a little, his face grew too flushed. I think he has abnormally high blood pressure."

"He has a stressful career."

She nodded and watched him quietly. "Did you know for certain he would try to kill me, or did you just guess that's what would happen?"

"Why would I send you there if I knew that?"

She exhaled through her nose. "He was my mouse, the one I was supposed to tear apart. You wanted me to kill him to show me we're the same."

"Did you?"

"No." She folded her arms. "He had three other men there and they didn't seem friendly. What if he'd killed me instead?"

"I knew he wouldn't."

"You couldn't know that."

He grinned. "I knew."

She watched him in silence and wondered what her mother saw when she looked at him. Did she see his beauty, or was he the twisted mess Tara saw in front of her now? A weed that had disguised itself as a flower, but the flower had withered and died.

"I thought you wanted the money," she said. "That you needed it for lawyers, and that's why you were splitting it with me. But you never cared about the money at all. It was always about me killing him. Is death the only thing you think about?"

"Death and love. What else is there?"

"Love," she scoffed. "What do you know about love?"

"A lot more than you could ever imagine, my little princess."

There was a single window in the room on her side of the barrier. A perfect square. It let in the sunlight, but only in a stream that didn't seem to reach her father's side. As though it was just darker wherever he was.

"I realized something when I was standing there and I knew they were going to try to kill me. It was one of those things where you realize it, and then you can't believe you didn't realize it sooner. Like it's something you should've known the whole time. Something so obvious that it was hidden from you."

He leaned back and tilted his head slightly to the side, like an animal watching something bizarre. "And what did you realize?"

She stared into his eyes. They were cold and empty. "You're going to get out of here one day. I don't know how or when, but it's going to happen . . . and you *know* it's going to happen. You're inhumanly patient, and once the opportunity presents itself, you're going to attack it with everything you have, and you're going to succeed. And then you're going to try to kill my mother."

The grin came back to his lips, but he said nothing.

"So I wanted you to know, Dad, that I'm inhumanly patient, too. I'll be waiting for you on the outside . . . and I'm going to kill you first."

Cal leapt forward, his chains clanking against the metal stool and floor. A snarl came to his lips, and he bared his teeth like a predator about to tear into his prey.

He got within an inch of the barrier, just a foot away from Tara's face. She didn't move, didn't gasp, didn't even flinch, and she knew that if anyone had taken her pulse, they would have seen that it didn't speed up. She wasn't afraid of him anymore.

When he saw her calm, it made him laugh.

"I have no doubt, my little princess, that you're going to try. But trying is not doing."

Now she was the one who grinned. "Guess we'll find out, won't we?"

He leaned back again, the casual smile returning to him. "I suppose we will."

Tara rose and left the room.

On the way out of the prison, she stopped at the front desk and wrote her name and phone number, her real name and phone number, on a slip of paper and slid it over to Ethan, whose smile revealed dimples that she thought were adorable.

"Pick me up at seven on Saturday," she said. "And don't be late. It's not polite to keep a girl waiting."

She lightly touched his hand and then left the prison. Knowing she wouldn't see the inside of this place again—one way or the other.

80

The small beach led out into a sapphire ocean. The sand was golden and smooth, the type of sand your foot sank into and felt like it had slipped into a bed of silk. The water rolled in softly, crackling on the shore and foaming around the ankles of several children playing near where the surf broke.

Yardley stood in a sundress with a wide straw hat and watched them. Some of them were locals and others the children of tourists. A dog, a black Labrador, bolted in and out of the water and chased the children until they dived into the waves. It was the most serene beach Yardley had ever seen.

Someday, she would have to bring Tara to Belize.

The bar was right on the beach. Stools were set up in the sand, and the bar was made out of bamboo and had a thatched roof. Yardley scanned the few people seated there. A large bartender, darkly tan and with a thick mustache, mixed drinks in a blender.

A strong breeze lifted the brim of Yardley's hat. She took it off and strolled to the bar. A woman was sitting on a stool in a red bathing suit with a black see-through wrap around her waist, a large purse at her feet. Her skin was now darkly tan, and the tattoos were even more vibrant somehow. A teenage girl stood next to her in a bathing suit and sunglasses.

Yardley sat on the stool next to the woman and took the photograph out. She placed it on the bar between them.

Sue Ellen Jones looked at the photograph of her and her brother in their Halloween costumes. She was a fairy and he a ghost. The fairy costume had no sleeves, revealing a massive dark-purple mark on the girl's right shoulder.

"Was it my birthmark?" she said.

"Yes. Though I probably would've known it was you even without it. Your face hasn't changed much since then."

Sue Ellen looked at her. "How long have you been here?"

"Not long. There's only one hotel right on the beach in San Pedro. The extradition division at the US Attorney's asked to be notified of any single women with American passports checking in. They flew me out a couple of days ago. I told them you would've changed your appearance, and I'm one of the only people who could identify you."

The bartender placed a fruity red drink in a tall glass in front of her. "Gracias," Sue Ellen said. The bartender raised his eyebrows to Yardley, who said, "The same, please."

"Harmony," Sue Ellen said, "why don't you go back to the hotel room and pack our things."

The young girl looked at Yardley. "I can stay."

"No, baby, you go get our things ready. Okay? I'll be fine, don't worry. Just go on back."

She didn't say anything a moment, glaring at Yardley, before she said, "Okay."

Yardley watched the girl walk away. "She's beautiful."

"She is."

"Is she all right?"

Sue Ellen shrugged. "You have no idea what her father put her through. She wanted to be there when he died, but I wouldn't let her. She didn't need that in her head."

"What about her mother?"

"Kathy was just as bad. She walked in on one of her boyfriends attacking Harmony once. Harmony cried for help, and Kathy turned around and shut the door." She shook her head as she took a drink. "That girl has been abused by everyone that was supposed to care about her. I wasn't going to add to that. But when she found out what we were going to do to Tucker, she said something I'll never forget."

"What?"

"'Let me help.'" She glanced back at Harmony walking away. She picked up her drink, sipped it, then set it down. "I didn't know if you'd remember this place."

"I remember because I closed my eyes that night and tried to picture it. The way the water looked like blue crystals and the emerald rocks that you said lined the shores." Yardley looked at the waves. "I still didn't picture it as striking as this."

Sue Ellen watched her now. "I'm sorry I lied to you."

"Is that the only thing you're sorry about?"

"Yes."

"An innocent man is dead because of you. Leonard had nothing to do with this."

She lifted the straw from her drink, staring as it glistened in the sunlight. "Tucker likes to tie you down and cut you. From your legs up to your neck. Harmony has scars all over her back and thighs. She asked me why he cut her so much, and I told her that he likes to hear the screams." She smiled. "Well, he *liked* to hear the screams, anyway." She glanced at Yardley and then turned back to the drink. "I'm so sorry Jude tried to hurt you. If I'd known—"

"Don't. You knew exactly what would happen to me if I got close to discovering him."

"No, never. I would *never* have let him hurt you. I swear it."

The drink came, and Yardley took a sip. It was so cold and sweet it hurt her teeth. "Tucker held you in his grandfather's house on Crimson Lake Road, didn't he?"

Sue Ellen's face changed, and she stared off at nothing. "The grandfather was so drunk all the time he had no idea what was happening, or if he did, he never stopped it. Tucker had a place set up, that basement you were in. The first day he took me there, he carried me in. I was fighting him and trying to get away, and then I saw, like, scratch marks on the walls near the door. From other girls he had carried in who tried to grab at anything."

"How many were there?"

She shrugged but didn't move her gaze. "I don't know."

"How'd you get away?"

"After three months, he began trusting me. He would let me out into the backyard sometimes. One day, he trusted me enough to go to the store and get a few things for him. I ran away. All the way home. But it wasn't my home anymore. I asked for my father, and the man who answered the door told me my father was dead and that Bobby had been taken away. I didn't want to go to the police, I just thought Tucker would find me again, so I ran. I ran until I couldn't run anymore. I don't even remember how I got to Vegas. I think this family picked me up and dropped me off at a shelter there. I gave them a fake name. They didn't have anything that could prove otherwise, so I stuck with it. I thought it would protect me if Tucker came looking for me. Angela River. My mother's name was Angela."

"When did Jude find you?"

"He found Bobby first. Jude had a young sister who disappeared, Ivy. I'm guessing you know that. He was obsessed with her for a long time. That's why he became a crime reporter. He thought maybe if he could develop enough contacts, find enough places to dig up information, there was a chance he would find out what happened to her one day. When he came across my case, he became obsessed with it, too. He saw a picture of me, and I look a lot like Ivy." She paused. "Bobby didn't really kill himself. I mean, it was drugs, and other things, too, but . . . it was *really* Tucker that did it. Tucker killed him more than the drugs.

He had grown close to Jude, and after his death Jude wanted to prove what Tucker had done. Instead, he found me."

"How?"

"I was looking for Bobby and we crossed paths. I called him asking a bunch of questions. I don't even remember who I said I was, but we met and . . . I don't know. There was something I trusted about him and something he trusted about me. We fell in love and didn't leave each other's side. Until now, anyway."

Sue Ellen was silent a long time, lost in her memories. "I don't think we talked about Tucker much. Not until one day when Jude came home and said he'd found him. That he was in prison and wouldn't be getting out for a while. He asked if I wanted to come forward and try to have him prosecuted . . . but I said no. That there was no amount of time he could spend in prison that would make up for what he did. And so he said that we should kill him. That's how much he loved me. He thought it would bring me some closure, so he was willing to kill someone for me."

She paused and put her elbows on the bar, her gaze drifting until it landed on her hands. She straightened her fingers and then curled them again.

"You have no idea what he did to me, Jessica. You can't understand unless you've been through it. He would use me and then put me away like a toy. Like something that wasn't human. By the end, I didn't believe I was human. It took me *so* long to know I was a person again. I don't know. Maybe I still don't."

"Jude said Michael Zachary's parents had a home next to Tucker's grandfather. We looked into it, and it was a lie. Did he have anything to do with this?"

She shook her head. "No. Zachary was just convenient. Jude convinced me that we needed someone for you guys to blame, otherwise we'd be caught. He knows how your offices work since he reports on you. He said if it got out that you had arrested someone, the pressure would be so great to get a conviction you wouldn't bother looking for anyone else."

She took another drink.

"I feel for him. Zachary isn't a bad person. I figured eventually you would sort it out and his charges would be dropped. It was a necessary evil. I needed to know what was going on in the investigation, how close you were to finding us, so making it seem like the Executioner was my boyfriend and I was the one that got away was perfect. All the pieces just fell into place."

Yardley watched the Labrador run out of the water and shake himself off near the bar. She felt a few droplets land on her bare legs.

"How long did you know you would use the paintings?"

"I don't even know. It was almost like they were always there. Remember when I told you I was in graduate school? We studied those paintings in a mythology class. I remember a professor telling us nobody knew what the paintings meant, but I knew right away. Vengeance. And they haunted me for weeks after I saw them. I couldn't get them out of my head. I kept seeing Tucker in each one of them, and the more I could picture him there, the happier I became. It was like the pain went away only when I thought about killing him. That's when I knew it wasn't just me and Jude fantasizing. We were actually going to do it one day. And it felt good to wait. I knew somehow that the anticipation of it was better than the act, and it would definitely be better than the memory. I wanted the anticipation of it to last as long as possible." She looked at Yardley. "I'm not a bad person."

Yardley watched her but didn't say anything.

She nodded and looked away. "Leonard. I know. But that was Jude, not me. He didn't want you to keep looking into Harmony's kidnapping, so he paid Leonard to make up that story. I told him there was no way Leonard could ID him and to leave it alone, but no one ever tells Jude what to do. Always the tough guy. He's not a monster, though. He thought he was doing it for me—for us. And the life we were going to build together after this was all over."

She paused a moment and looked out over the water. "I didn't want anyone else to get hurt."

"What about you? You could've died from the ricin. Was this worth dying for?"

"Yes, it was. And I knew I wouldn't die. We diluted it well. The only reason they thought it was the same amount as Kathy Pharr is because Jude left identical empty syringes at both houses. I researched it a long time and found out the labs can't test for exact amounts in the body unless they excise a piece of your liver, and I certainly wasn't going to let them do that to me."

She let out a deep breath, and they sat in silence as the waves lapped the shore.

Yardley took a sip of her drink and, without looking at her, asked, "Is that story about the Hells Angel and the drug deal in the desert true? Are you really not able to have children? Is anything you told me true?"

She didn't respond for a long time. "That day you came over to my house, when you thought I was going to kill myself, I really did think about it. I drank that wine and took those pills because I just couldn't take it anymore, Jess. What he did to me happened almost two decades ago, and when I close my eyes, it's like I'm still there in his basement. It feels like I'm untangling wreckage that just won't be untangled. I thought it might be better if I just did it and got it over with. So I called you hoping . . . I don't know, maybe that you'd talk me out of it. You're the only person in my life who cares about me other than Jude. The tears were real, the pain was real, and you helped me through it . . . our relationship was real."

Silence passed between them, enough to hear several waves.

"Are the police here?" Sue Ellen asked.

"They're waiting for my text identifying you for them. The FBI has an extradition order for you."

"You can't let them take me, Jess. I won't live in a cage. Tucker put me in a cage, and I will *never* go back."

"What am I supposed to do? What choice have you given me?"

"I won't do it. I have a gun. I'll try to shoot my way out."

"You won't last five seconds. What would be the point of surviving Tucker if you just die out here on some beach?"

Sue Ellen looked out over the water and didn't say anything for a long time. "I don't think you should retire. It won't help you to run to that small town. I ran for a long time, but you can't run from anything, Jess. It all just follows you."

Yardley watched her, the way her hair whipped her face when the breeze grew. Her bright eyes and the colorful tattoos that seemed to dance in the sunlight. "I canceled the sale of my house. I took the DA's offer to be a special victims prosecutor for the county. They'll let me choose which cases to take without anyone looking over my shoulder."

She nodded. "That's good. I'm happy you're not running. I really am." She closed her eyes and took another drink before setting the glass down. "You have to let me go."

"I can't," Yardley said desperately.

Sue Ellen looked at her and said softly, "Jessica, you have to let me go."

"Please don't ask me to do that."

"Do you want to hear about what he did to me? About what it felt like to hear his footsteps come back every night and know what was about to happen to me? To beg him, 'Please, please not again, please' . . . and to have him laugh? He laughed when I would beg him." Tears streamed down her cheeks, but a smile came to her lips. "He wasn't laughing at the end."

"I can't just let you go. You have to leave the gun and come with me. They will kill you if they see a gun."

"It's not happening. You have to choose. I'm going to stand up and walk away, and you're going to either let me go or tell them to come. And if they come, I'm going to die."

"No, don't do this. Don't die here. Please."

She rose.

"I wish, Jessica, that you and I would've met in different circumstances. It's not every day you meet your soul mate, is it?"

"Don't—"

Sue Ellen took Yardley's face in her hands and gently kissed her lips. "Beautiful girl. You're so much stronger than you know. You'll heal that shattered heart one day."

She pulled away, and Yardley let her hand slip from hers.

"Not soul mates," Yardley said. Sue Ellen turned and looked at her. "Not soul mates . . . twin souls."

Sue Ellen smiled and then turned around.

Yardley watched as she left the beach and strolled into a crowd on the street. She glanced back only once. Then she was gone.

Yardley felt emotion choke her, and she had to swallow it down. She closed her eyes and inhaled deeply, absorbing the salty scent of the ocean.

She took out her phone and sent a text message: She's not here. We'll try again tonight.

Then she watched the children playing in the water again, a grin on her lips as the Labrador came up to her and she rubbed behind his ear. A wave lazily lapped the shore, the sun reflecting off the ocean in bright gold, and she knew this was how she would always remember this moment.

ACKNOWLEDGMENTS

Thank you to my wonderful publishers, Thomas & Mercer; my editor, Megha Parekh; my agent, Amy Tannenbaum; and all my readers who have stuck with me through the years. I'm more grateful than you can ever know.

ABOUT THE AUTHOR

At the age of thirteen, when his best friend was interrogated by the police for over eight hours and confessed to a crime he didn't commit, Victor Methos knew he would one day become a lawyer.

After graduating from law school at the University of Utah, Methos sharpened his teeth as a prosecutor for Salt Lake City before founding what would become the most successful criminal defense firm in Utah.

In ten years Methos conducted more than one hundred trials. One particular case stuck with him, and it eventually became the basis for his first major bestseller, *The Neon Lawyer*. Since that time, Methos has focused his work on legal thrillers and mysteries, earning a Harper Lee Prize nomination for *The Hallows* and an Edgar nomination for Best Novel for his title *A Gambler's Jury*. He currently splits his time between southern Utah and Las Vegas.